RAINY DAYS FOR THE HARPERS' GIRLS

IT'S WAR BOYS!

ROSIE CLARKE

Boldwood

First published in Great Britain in 2020 by Boldwood Books Ltd.

A CIP catalogue record for this book is available from the British Library.

Paperback ISBN 978-1-83889-154-1

Large Print ISBN 978-1-83889-752-9

Ebook ISBN 978-1-83889-156-5

Kindle ISBN 978-1-83889-155-8

Audio CD ISBN 978-1-83889-241-8

MP3 CD ISBN 978-1-83889-749-9

Digital audio download ISBN 978-1-83889-153-4

Boldwood Books Ltd
23 Bowerdean Street
London SW6 3TN
www.boldwoodbooks.com

1

Could it really be almost two years since Harpers Oxford Street Store came into existence? Ben Harper opened one eye and watched as the wife he adored eased herself up from the sitting position she'd assumed on the floor. Sally had taken up a form of yoga to calm herself and bring health to her and her unborn child, due sometime in the first weeks of June that year, and, at first amused, Ben now enjoyed watching her as she breathed deeply and performed the gentle exercise routine she'd set for herself. She was so beautiful, the line of her arms serene and elegant as she went through the positions she'd taught herself from her library book. His wonderful Sally, the wife he'd never thought could be his, and now his reason for being.

Married the previous September, it was early March 1914 now and they'd been man and wife for nearly six months. She'd fallen for their first child soon after their wedding and was blossoming with every day that passed. Ben knew that he was fortunate to have her and, although the thought of being a father scared him, it also thrilled him. He would have his own son or daughter to follow on and inherit the store one day. Ben was filled with a desire to make Harpers the most magnificent emporium in London's wonderful Oxford Street. Life was so good it terrified him, because he couldn't believe his luck would last.

Sally had reminded him three weeks ago that the second anniversary of the store's opening was coming up that month. Not that Ben had forgotten, but he'd let her think it, because he knew she had so many plans and he'd wanted to hear them. She and Marco, their talented and brilliant window dresser, had been planning the windows in secret for weeks.

A slight frown creased his brow, because he wasn't sure his artistic friend had yet recovered from the loss of his young lover and companion, Julien. Theirs had been a deep and close relationship and Julien's death was a tragedy. The more so because it was caused by a father whose pride wouldn't let him understand that his son was different – and that was all it was really, Ben thought. Julien's father had let his old-school morals and fear of scandal overrule his love for his son and now bitterly regretted it, though he blamed Marco. Ben wanted to shake the man and make him see sense, make him forget his stiff-necked pride, but he supposed that the family reputation would not allow it. If Julien's father admitted the truth, then he must take responsibility for his son's death.

Yet why had his prejudice caused him to ruin both his son's and Marco's lives? Ben pondered the question. People were not the same to look at, so why should they feel the same when it came to falling in love? Attitudes were changing and many would no longer condemn such a love, no longer see it as black and white. Ben did not understand why Marco had loved a young man rather than a girl, but he knew that love was real – as real as his own was for Sally. To lose Sally would leave Ben feeling empty and devastated and he knew Marco had suffered terrible agony and remorse over Julien's death, blaming himself, though it was not his fault but another's. Ben respected Marco both as a professional and as a person and he'd done his best to help his friend in every way he could since the tragedy that had devastated his life. Marco was quietly carrying on, living with dignity, his deep grief hidden from the world but there to see when you looked into his eyes.

Sally was standing now and looking down at him in the bed, her dark hair slightly longer than usual, with the morning light highlighting the hints of red as it waved on to her shoulders. Ben's gaze dwelled on the curve of her stomach and he felt a surge of love and pride. It was his child she was carrying – a boy, Sally said, though she had no way of knowing, but for Ben, Sally was usually right. Her advice concerning the store was always good and, so far, she hadn't put a foot wrong. Her own departments were the most successful, but trade was steady throughout the store and Ben had been busy with his own plans of late, secrets he hadn't yet told his wife, because he needed to be sure and he wanted them to be a surprise. When he'd first heard that the tobacconist next door to Harpers Emporium, was to be sold he'd taken the first opportunity to view it. Although not a large property in itself, its relatively cheap price meant that he could just afford to buy it and expand the departments. Sally thought they needed bigger shoe and lingerie departments and Ben wanted a toy department as well as a confectionary hall and a florist. He'd already had meetings with the district council about the change of purpose for the flat above the tobacconist's shop and it was there he would put the confectionary, next to the florists. The toy shop would be in the old shop, once it had been opened out, with as little disruption as he could manage. Sally could take the middle floor for whatever she wanted, when all the building work had finished. She was keen to build up her cosmetics department by importing some of the wonderful perfumes, creams and other toiletries that were becoming all the rage in New York.

Would she be pleased with her surprise or annoyed that he

hadn't told her of his plans? Ben hoped it would be the first and felt slightly guilty that he hadn't shared earlier. He held out his hand and she took it, sitting on the edge of the bed and bending down to kiss him. She smelled gorgeous, of some soft flowery perfume she said she wanted to stock in the shop. Made by Yardley, now of Bond Street, London, the toilet water was an English product and well established. Sally had tried the whole range and approved it before ordering: soaps, talcum powder, bath salts and a light cologne for the store. Ben liked it too, thought it was very Sally and encouraged her to buy everything. He wasn't sure how well it was selling yet, but he'd seen the discreet and pretty display on the ground floor, together with some special creams his sister Jenni had sent over from Elizabeth Arden's store.

'What are you thinking?' Sally asked suddenly. He realised she was looking at him intently, a hint of mischief in her face. 'You're hiding something – I know it. Is it to do with the anniversary of the store?'

'In a way,' he said and laughed up at her. 'You read me just like a book, don't you?'

'No, but I know when you want to tell me something and can't...'

Ben laughed and caught her, bringing her down to him for a lingering kiss. 'We opened two years ago in March 1912 and now it's March 1914 – and today I sign for the premises next door to Harpers, which will give us over two thousand extra square feet of selling space...'

'You got it!' Sally gave a squeal of pleasure and flung herself on him, hugging and kissing him. 'I was sure you were trying for it, but you didn't even tell Mr Marco or Mr Stockbridge...'

'I wanted it to be a surprise for you,' he said and grinned as he sat up and brought his long bare brown legs from the bed. As he stood, he towered over his wife by a head and shoulders, strong, confident and full of life. 'I know you want bigger lingerie and shoe departments. I've planned for a confectionary hall and a florist upstairs and a toy shop on the ground floor – you can use the middle bit as you like...'

Sally nodded. 'Lovely! I think florists and confectionary yes, and I knew you wanted the toy department – but I think that should be on the top floor.'

Ben's eyebrows rose but he didn't contest her statement, waiting for the explanation he knew would come.

'Because mothers and fathers will take the lift up for their children's gifts but flowers and sweets are often impromptu purchases and should be within easy reach.' She looked at him thoughtfully. 'Belgian and Swiss, of course, but I think we should try to find sources nearer to home, too – someone that is selling something different and special, and needs more exposure and would be glad to get a large order from Harpers...'

'And I suppose you already have an idea about that?'

Sally nodded, eyes sparkling. 'I just might...'

'What would I do without you?' he asked and nodded. 'As usual, you're right, Sally. I was thinking of the children eager to dive in to the toy shop – but you're the sensible one. Mothers and fathers who can afford it will spend the earth on their children and taking the lift to the top floor is nothing.'

Sally nodded and rubbed her swollen belly gently. 'You'll do anything for your children,' she said lovingly. 'Sweets are often for a loved one, but sometimes just because you want to treat yourself and no one will bother with the lift then, even if they are delicious – you do mean them to be extra special, I hope?'

'I certainly do,' Ben grinned. 'Belgian chocolates, handmade and packed in paper cases and fancy boxes. That's the way to sell the finest chocolates, I believe, do you agree, my love? Beautiful chocolate cakes and fluffy meringues too – and some of the children's favourites, like burnt toffee pieces, coconut ice and pear drops... big jars of them that the children can purchase two ounces of if they want.'

'It all sounds wonderful,' Sally said. 'It makes my mouth water just to think of it. I'm so glad you managed to get the extra space, Ben...'

He watched as she moved away to take off her silky dressing robe, which she'd worn to do her exercises, and replace it with her delicate lingerie and a smart black dress with a white lace collar and a loose jacket that discreetly covered her bump.

'Are you going into work today?' he asked. 'I thought we might go somewhere special for lunch to celebrate?'

'Yes, we could easily do that,' Sally agreed. 'I have two appointments early this morning and then I've finished for the day. We might try that new restaurant of Mick's...' She glanced over her shoulder at him and smiled. 'He sent us an invitation for the opening... I think I put it on your desk somewhere.'

'Yes, I saw it,' Ben said and nodded complacently. He'd been jealous of her Irish friend, Mr Michael O'Sullivan, at one time, but he now needed no convincing that Sally loved him and only him. 'All right, we'll go there if you like...'

'It's just a suggestion,' she said and her eyes teased him. 'Are you going to stay there all day and watch me?'

'I was enjoying the view,' he said. 'My appointment with the solicitor is at eleven this morning. I'll pick you up at twelve thirty at the store and you can tell me where to go.'

'I'd better book to be on the safe side, because Mick's restaurants usually get busy...'

Ben nodded, making for the bathroom as his wife finished dressing. Mick was becoming quite the businessman. He owned a half share in three restaurants now and they had all been reviewed in various newspapers and magazines as being good food at sensible prices and he was about to open a fourth. Mick was clearly bent on becoming successful in his own way.

However, he'd sent flowers and chocolates to both of them at Christmas and Ben had sent him an invitation to the event he was holding at Harpers on its second anniversary. They were both of them businessmen and it couldn't hurt to keep in touch. It was always better to make friends in business rather than enemies. Sally had told him how Mick had helped her when her friend Sylvia had been in trouble; it hadn't completely erased Ben's jealousy but it had subdued it.

Selecting a pale blue shirt and a deep blue tie to match with the navy pinstripe suit he'd chosen, Ben smoothed back his dark hair, straightened his tie and then picked up his wallet and keys. He actually had two appointments that morning, not one – and the second was one he had no intention of telling his wife about just yet...

* * *

Sally spoke to the two representatives one after the other. Both were exactly on time and she gave each of them sizeable orders for leather handbags and a variety of silk scarves.

Glancing at her watch, she saw that she had an hour before Ben was due to pick her up and decided to make a tour of the various departments, starting with the men's before coming down to the ladies' fashions and then her favourite: hats, bags, gloves, scarves and jewellery.

Sally reflected that she'd always thought fashions were her favourite area, but since she'd been the buyer for Harpers, she'd discovered a love of beautiful jewellery and quality bags. Also, it was where she'd begun her career at Harpers and where her friends worked; at least, Beth and Maggie still worked there. Rachel was now the official floor walker – which meant she toured each floor of the store in turn, watching out for anything out of place or needing attention. If any of the staff had a problem, they could consult Rachel and she would either sort it or take it to Mr Stockbridge, the store's general manager – though Rachel often brought little things to Sally, because she would solve it quickly and without fuss.

'Poor Mr Stockbridge always seems to be up to his eyes in advertising accounts, staff requests and stock lists,' Rachel had confided in Sally once. 'He probably needs his own secretary, but Miss Summers does yours and Mr Harper's work as well as his...'

Sally had taken her hint and interviewed a few girls from the agency, picking a young woman to help her and promoting Miss Summers to be Mr Stockbridge's assistant, which meant grateful smiles all round.

Sally thought Ben had been catapulted into running the store before he was really ready. When his Uncle Gerald had died a few weeks before Harpers was due to open and bequeathed partial ownership to Ben and his sister, it had cast them into a crisis of funding. It was left to Ben to finish setting it up as best he could and perhaps a few corners had been cut, resulting in the staffing being less than adequate. Then, before Ben could get things moving, tragedy had struck and he'd been forced to return to America to sort out the personal grief of his sick wife. No one had known that he'd been supporting her for years in a hospital, where she was kept alive only by the excellent nursing he'd paid for until her death, which had in the end been a relief for her.

During his absence, Sally, Mr Stockbridge, Mr Marco and the various department heads had somehow managed to keep the store afloat and make a small profit. Ben's sister Jenni had contributed to this success with her experience and encouragement, but it had been a difficult time and could have resulted in the store's collapse.

Ben had returned to London once he'd cleared his affairs in New York and his presence had made a huge difference, not just to Sally, though his whirlwind courtship had swept her off her feet, but to the store. Since then, more girls had been taken on, and Fred Burrows had two younger men working under him in the basement. Stanley Kirk was in his thirties, strong and energetic, able to heft the heaviest of boxes with ease, and young Luke Redding was sixteen, willing to learn and a bit on the cheeky side. Even so, there were times when they were rushed to keep up with restocking all the departments. Goodness knows how Fred had managed alone! If Ben's new departments were to work, Harpers would need more staff, in the basement as well as on the floors.

The wage bill was already huge – together with lighting, heating, stock, insurance and taxes, it took a small fortune to keep the store solvent. Sally knew they were very fortunate that they didn't have to pay rent and owned the building – but would Ben need to borrow to fund the new space?

She shrugged off the slight worry. Finance was Ben's department. Sally didn't ask and she didn't interfere. Although she believed that he didn't have a great deal of cash to spare, he was always generous to her, buying her small gifts and taking her out for meals. As yet they hadn't been away for one of the foreign holidays Ben had promised her, but that was due to her being busy and carrying their first child. Sally had kept remarkably well, apart from a small amount of sickness in the first weeks, but the doctor had advised her not to go on long journeys either by car or train. She was just over six months into her pregnancy now and expected the birth in late May or early June.

'Your ankles have swollen slightly,' the doctor had told her when she last visited his practice. 'Nothing to worry about – and much better to keep active than to sit about. Go for walks rather than sit at your desk, Mrs Harper...'

'Yes, I shall,' Sally had said and she'd walked to the library and taken out the book on yoga, which she did regularly each morning now when she rose. The exercise helped to ease any aches in her back and it made her feel calm; the swelling had not got any worse.

Walking into the hat department that morning, she saw that someone had done a beautiful display of the new styles she'd bought for the spring and summer: pinks and blues and a deep maroon looked wonderful together.

'That looks lovely,' she said to the young woman who was just adjusting a stand. 'I think that maroon straw is priced at thirty-five shillings – quite a lot, I know, but it is rather special... so it's good you've made a feature of it.'

'Yes, it is, Mrs Harper,' Janice Browning agreed, an odd expression in her eyes. 'Just right if you can afford it and you're going to a garden party or a wedding...'

'Mrs Harper...' Beth Burrows said, coming up to her. 'Lovely to see you – you look very well...'

'I feel it,' Sally said. 'I think the yoga exercises are making all the difference...' Her gaze moved over her friend anxiously. Beth had lost her first baby the previous year, just before Christmas, and it had upset her terribly. Sally herself was feeling so lucky. She had to pinch herself sometimes to make sure it wasn't all a dream – a girl from a convent school, abandoned by her mother as a baby and forced to find her own living from the age of sixteen and now happily married to the man she loved and carrying their first baby. Was it possible she could really be this happy? 'How are you, love?'

'Oh, much better,' Beth replied and smiled. 'No, really, I'm over my disappointment now.'

Beth was making light of what had happened, Sally felt. She'd been attacked by the man who had first married and then caused her aunt's death and consequently lost her own baby. Sally had read in the paper a report that said Gerald Makepeace's trial was coming up soon. He was being charged with one count of murder, three of embezzlement and one of grievous bodily harm. It was likely the man would hang, and if ever a rogue deserved it, it was surely the man who had deceived and then beaten and killed Beth's aunt for the insurance money and the shares she'd secretly left to her niece, which had become so valuable now and enabled Beth to set aside money for her and her husband's future. Beth hadn't expected anything and she'd been stunned by the value of the shares, doubled because her mother had also owned shares they'd all believed worthless. Because of the bequest, Beth's husband, Jack, had been able to buy a controlling interest in the hotel he'd always wanted and was doing well, making it into a profitable business.

Sally wondered how the news of Gerald's trial was affecting Beth. Did she feel satisfaction that Gerald was going to pay for his crimes or was she still too upset over it to even read the reports in the newspapers?

Clearly, she didn't want to talk about it, so Sally smiled and said, 'Is Jack pleased with the way the hotel is going?'

'Yes, I think so,' Beth said and then saw a customer making her way towards her counter. 'Excuse me, Mrs Harper, I should serve that lady. I know just what she's come for...'

Sally nodded and moved away, watching as Beth smoothly served the woman with a beautiful silver locket and chain and a leather bag. They were good friends but at work called each other by their surnames, as was the practice at Harpers.

Sally had been buying in extra stock since Christmas where she could. Some things were seasonal and she couldn't lay in extra because fashions change, but wherever she could, she'd bought more than they would normally need so that while she was confined with the birth, the various departments she was in charge of buying for would survive her absence without suffering.

Wandering over to the counter selling scarves, Sally spoke to the junior who was wrapping one gentleman's purchase of a pair of ladies red leather gloves, while Maggie Gibbs served a young woman with a pretty pink and blue silk scarf. Marion Kaye, the junior salesgirl, blushed, clearly overwhelmed to be noticed by the boss's wife, but went on with her task without faltering.

Sally spoke with all of the staff before moving on and taking the lift to the ground floor. There were sufficient customers for her to feel that all was well as she moved from counter to counter, noting stock levels. The exquisite French overlaid glass vases that Jenni Harper had ordered and sent over were sticking a little; Sally had thought them expensive at the start and an idea came to her as she took the lift back to the top floor. She would suggest it to Ben over lunch...

For a moment as she stepped out of the lift her head seemed to spin and she clutched at the wall. She felt slightly nauseous and stood for a moment to steady herself.

'Are you unwell, Mrs Harper?' Ruth Canning, the girl she'd employed as her personal secretary looked at her anxiously as she entered her office. 'May I get you a drink of water – or a cup of tea?'

Sally drew herself upright. She wasn't going to give into a silly little dizzy spell. 'I should like a cup of tea when you're ready,' she said, glancing at a sheaf of papers in Ruth's hand. 'Is that the stock list I requested from the men's department?'

'Yes, Mrs Harper,' Ruth said. 'I was just going to check one of the figures with Mr Simpson. It didn't look right to me...'

'I'll deal with it,' Sally said and took the sheaf of papers. Ruth was an excellent helper and if she said there was a mistake there would be one, but any challenge must come from her, Ben or Mr Stockbridge. She could just imagine the reaction of the head of the men's department if her secretary challenged him. Ruth was eager and bright but apt to charge in too quickly.

'Yes, Mrs Harper. I just thought he might like to correct it himself before it came to your attention...'

'He probably would,' Sally said, 'but that won't do, Miss

Canning. You must leave these things to my discretion...' the reprimand was mild, hidden by a smile, but it was there. The staff had a hierarchy all its own and any breach of etiquette was frowned on by the supervisors. However, Sally knew that she'd done much the same when she was just a new buyer and not the wife of the Store's owner. So, she didn't want to scold Ruth for what she knew was a good intention. 'Thank you for pointing it out to me... your sharp eyes are such a help...'

Ruth beamed with pleasure and Sally reflected that it did far more good to praise than to scold. 'Now, I could just murder that pot of tea...'

Sitting in her comfortable office chair, Sally realised that the brief moment of dizziness had passed, just as it had twice before. There was nothing wrong. It was all part of carrying a baby, but if she told Ben, he would wrap her in cotton wool for the last months of her pregnancy and that was the last thing she wanted...

2

Marion Kaye left work at the same time as Miss Gibbs. Miss Gibbs had told her she could call her Maggie outside working hours, but as her junior, she didn't feel that she ought, even though Miss Gibbs was very friendly towards her.

'What are you doing this evening?' Miss Gibbs said, smiling at her. 'I'm going to my first-aid classes and I wondered if you would like to join? It's for a good cause...'

Marion looked at her uncertainly. 'I'm not sure... how much does it cost? Only, I give Ma all but a shilling of my wage and I couldn't afford to pay more than tuppence...'

'It is absolutely free,' Maggie told her, her eyes bright with warmth. 'If you want something to eat, you have to pay, but the classes are given free – it's because the organisers think if ever there is a war, we ladies ought to know how to bandage someone properly and lots of other useful things...'

'It sounds really interesting and I'd love to come...' Marion said, a note of longing in her voice. She loved working at Harpers and being one of the girls and would like to go out with friends in the evening, but her mother needed her help at home. 'I can't manage it this week – but I'll ask Ma. She might let me come next time...'

'You tell her it is all very proper and safe,' Maggie said. 'We're taught by trained nurses and a respectable doctor lectures us once a month. I would see you got on the right bus home...'

'Thank you, Miss Gibbs...' Marion said with a little blush. 'You're so kind to me...'

'I told you, call me Maggie outside working hours,' Maggie said and impulsively squeezed her arm. 'I know what it feels like when you have to get home, because you're needed. My father was ill for months before he died and I needed to help look after him...' She sighed. 'I still miss him...'

'Do you miss your mother?' Marion dared to ask.

'Sometimes, but not the way I miss Poppa.' Maggie's smiled wobbled. 'He loved me so much and he was so disappointed when his accident prevented me from training to be a teacher – but I'm happy at work...'

'You live with Mrs Craven and Miss Minnie from the dress alterations...' Marion blushed. 'I'm sorry. She told me to call her that...'

'Yes, I know,' Maggie said reassuringly. 'Miss Lumley hates her surname and asked to be known as Miss Minnie instead, which is what everyone has called her for years. Her sister Mildred was Miss Lumley and I think she's still grieving for her, so we always call her Miss Minnie.' Maggie smiled. 'She didn't really have a proper interview. Rachel spoke to Mrs Harper and she invited her for coffee, took one look at her work and gave her the job. She is a wonderful seamstress...'

'Yes, I know. I'd love to have something made by her, but it's so expensive...'

'Oh, very,' Maggie agreed and sighed. 'Beautiful to see though...'

'I'd better go,' Marion said regretfully, 'or I shall miss the bus and Ma will worry if I'm late...' She would have loved to stop and talk to Maggie, but if she did, she would be late home and everyone would be waiting for their tea.

Marion ran to her stop and clambered on the bus as it pulled to a halt. She climbed the winding stairs to the top level and found a seat. Several passengers were sitting there, but it wasn't as crowded as downstairs, because some people didn't like riding in the open air, especially if it was wet or cold. That evening it was chilly but dry and Marion rather liked the feel of the wind in her face. She'd got her plain grey felt hat well pinned down on her short dark hair. Her sister Kathy had cut it for her at Marion's request, because it had just been too much trouble when left long. Short, it curled into the nape of her neck and about her face; long it frizzed everywhere and she had to drag it back and secure it with hairpins, which never stayed put, so because she had no time to spend putting it up, she'd let Kathy chop it off. The result had brought a few tears, but at work the girls had liked it and Mrs Burrows had told her it suited her – it saved twenty minutes or more in the mornings, making it possible for her to do all she needed to and still get to work on time.

Rush Terrace, in which Marion lived with her mother, sisters and younger brothers, was a row of tall, narrow houses, all of which had long back gardens, which made them lucky, because everyone grew vegetables and some kept a few chickens. Marion knew that in other similar streets some of the back-to-back houses only had a tiny back yard, but her home had a good garden that her brothers dug and tended so they always had plenty of vegetables in season. She had two brothers at home still, her elder brother Dan having gone off more than three years previously after a violent row with his father over his treatment of their mother, and two sisters younger than herself. Their father worked on the ships and was seldom home, something they all felt relieved about, despite the shortage of money his absence caused. Dan had fought him and suffered a painful injury, but he'd gone because if he'd stayed, he might have done something he would regret. Sometimes in the past year, Maggie's leek and potato soup had been all they had for supper, but now that she was earning, things were a little better.

Opening the back door and walking into the kitchen of her home, Marion's heart sank. It had been one of Ma's bad days. On her better days, she made a little effort to tidy up, do washing or ironing or make their tea, but from the look of things, she'd done nothing.

'Where is Ma?' Marion asked of her sister. Kathy was still at school but helped as much as she could before and after school hours. Marion could see that she'd given the younger ones a bit of bread and dripping for their tea. 'I thought we had some sausages?'

'Ma left them on the table while she went out to hang a towel on the line,' Kathy said. 'She only left the door open a moment and next door's dog swiped the lot...'

'That damned dog,' her younger brother said and wiped his snotty nose on the back of his sleeve. 'I'm hungry, our Marion, and I don't like dripping...'

'Nor don't I...' chimed in five-year-old Milly.

'Well, you will bloody well have to put up with it,' Robbie said and glared at no one in particular. 'I bought them sausages wiv me last shillin' and I was lookin' forward to havin' one fer me tea wiv a bit of mash...'

'I bought a tin of corned beef in my lunch break,' Marion said, sensing a row brewing. It had been meant for the following day, but she would have to find something else for that if she could scrape up enough from Ma's change pot. 'Kathy, help me do the spuds and, Robbie, you and Dickon can cut the corned beef – thin slices and no pinching a bit or there won't be enough to go round...'

'Cor, I love corned beef,' her elder brother grinned at her. Robbie was a good lad. His work down the wood yard on the docks brought in nine and sixpence a week, which was an excellent wage for a lad not quite sixteen years old. He spent every penny of it on food for the family, leaving Marion to cover everything else their father's meagre wage did not supply. Mr Kaye worked away on the ships and came home for a couple of nights every few weeks. He gave his wife a third of whatever he'd earned to keep his family while he was gone and spent the rest on drink and fancy women. At least that was what Ma had told her eldest daughter.

'That devil ruined me health and me life,' she'd once told the then fifteen-year-old Marion when feeling so ill she thought herself about to die some two years previously. 'I'm no use to you kids, so you'll have to be mother, lass – but don't let that devil near yer or you will end up like me…'

Even at that tender age, Marion hadn't needed to be told what her mother meant. In a house with walls so thin that every sound could be heard, she'd listened to her mother's cries for some peace when her father was at home.

'Sure, you're an unfeelin' woman, Kathleen,' Bill Kaye had accused his wife. 'I wonder why I married yer – but the red hair had me fooled. I thought there was some fire in yer, but yer a milksop. If yer won't do yer duty, yer can't blame me if I go astray…'

Bill Kaye had at that time worked on the docks as a ship's carpenter, but he'd signed on to sail with a merchant ship that traded at various ports in Europe and in Britain and his work now kept him away from his home and his wife's bed. He took out his anger on all of them by giving his wife a clout whenever he felt like it, and his children stayed clear or caught his fist on the side of the ear if they got in his way.

Marion's eldest brother Dan had joined the merchant navy as

soon as he was sixteen, lying about his age because he looked older. He'd been home only twice since and both times given his family presents and ten pounds, which he'd pushed into Marion's hand.

'You're the only one in this family with any sense,' Dan had told her. 'Take care of them, Marion, and I'll help yer as much as I can...'

'You're a good brother, Dan,' Marion had replied. She would have hugged him but knew Dan couldn't stand to be touched. She wasn't sure why then, except that her father had gone after one of the other dockers once and hammered him with his fists until the man couldn't stand. After Dan left home, Marion's mother had hinted that one of the dockers had physically abused him in a way that was shameful. He'd come home crying as a lad of ten years and his father had stormed off in a rage to deliver punishment to the man that had abused him. Bill Kaye had been arrested by the police but let off with a warning after they discovered what his victim had done to the young boy. One of the police officers said he didn't blame him and he'd have done the same in his shoes. Dan had said it was the only time his father had ever done anything for him, adding that it still didn't make him a decent father. Marion hadn't understood as a child, but she did now and she felt sympathy for her brother's hurt and humiliation.

'I wish you'd come home, Dan,' Marion had told him when he'd given her money from his wages. 'It would be easier if you were here with us...'

'Nah, I'd knock Pa's 'ead orf or bleedin' try,' Dan said angrily. 'I can't stand the way he treats our ma, Marion. It makes me savage because she just lets him walk all over her as if she's a doormat...'

'If she stands up to him, he hits her,' Marion said and saw the nerve flick at Dan's temple. 'She doesn't have a choice, because if he left her, she couldn't feed us or keep a roof over our heads.

We'd have to go in the old poor house what the Sally Army run nowadays – or live on the streets...' Bill Kaye was the head of his family and his wife had few rights. If she'd left him, he wouldn't have paid her a penny, even for the children, so she had no choice but to stay and take whatever punishment he handed out. None of the other children were strong enough to stand up to him, even though Marion had tried to reason with him when he was sober. They all knew that they had to stay clear when he'd been drinking because he didn't care who he clouted then. Marion sometimes wished he'd stay away and never return, because the few pounds he brought home were not worth the pain he inflicted on his family.

'I'll never marry unless I can give a woman a decent home and enough money to feed and clothe her and the kids properly...' Dan had vowed furiously, his eyes sweeping round the damp walls that crumbled if you hit them too hard and the dirty cobbled floor that was never clean even after Marion scrubbed it until her hands were raw. The one tap over a shallow sink only had cold water; water for washing and cleaning had to be heated in the copper in the scullery. It made the work twice as hard for their mother, whose health had steadily been deteriorating since the birth of her last child, who, poor mite, had not even drawn breath.

Marion cooked some cabbage and the potatoes, then mashed them with a scraping of marge, some salt and pepper and served her brothers and sisters first before sitting down to her own portion.

'Has anyone been up to see Ma?' she asked as she ate her meal.

'I went up as soon as I got home,' Robbie said. 'She told me to go away. I asked if she wanted a cup of tea and a bit of toast. She said she wasn't hungry and to leave her alone.'

'I'll go up in a minute,' Marion said. She looked at Dickon.

'You can help Kathy do the washing-up – Robbie will you bring in some wood and coke for me please? I've got some washing to do and I'll scrub the kitchen floor if I can manage it after you've all gone up...'

'I already lit the fire under the copper fer yer,' Robbie said. 'I knew yer would wash the clothes since Ma hasn't...'

Marion finished her meal and got up, taking her plate to the sink. There was never any wasted food in her house, everything was cleared from the plates and she knew the lads could have done with more. She could offer them bread and jam and Robbie would probably help himself if he was hungry. As long as he left her a slice for her lunch the next day, she didn't mind. They all knew that food was precious. You didn't waste it and you ate only your share or someone else went hungry.

Leaving her siblings to wash the dishes and saucepan, Marion went up to her mother's bedroom. She could smell the sourness of vomit and her stomach curdled, but she braced herself. It wasn't Ma's fault she was so ill. Marion didn't know if it was her father's either, though six children were a lot for any woman to bear and she knew of at least three miscarriages. These bouts of sickness and pain had started to happen after the last stillborn child and Marion wondered if something inside Ma hadn't healed properly, but she wouldn't have the doctor and, in truth, they would find it hard to pay him if he visited.

'Is that you, Marion love?' her mother asked weakly. 'I'm sorry about the sausages. I only went out for a moment and the door didn't shut...'

'It's the latch,' Marion said. 'It needs fixing...' If her father were here, he could do it easily, but he wouldn't bother unless his wife put herself out and that meant another row.

'You should get someone...' her mother's weak voice said. 'The sausages cost more than the price of a new lock...'

'Not unless Dad does it himself,' Marion said. Sometimes, she thought her mother had no grasp of what things cost these days. 'I reckon half a crown at least.'

'Not if you ask Mr Jackson...' Mrs Kaye insisted. 'Tell him what his dog did and he might do it for free...'

'If Dan was here, he'd do it, but he'd make the neighbour pay for it,' Marion said. 'I'll go around and speak to him if I get time.... there's the washing and the floor...'

'Leave the things to soak and I'll try to rinse them in the mornin',' her mother offered.

'I'll see...' Marion replied. She hesitated, then, 'Will you have something to eat, Ma – or a cup of tea?'

'Kathy got me a drink. I don't want anything else – get on with whatever you need to, love...'

Marion sighed as she went down the stairs. If she left the clothes soaking, they would be there when she got home the next day. She would put them in for a while and pop round next door, see what Mr Jackson had to say, but she hoped the dog was shut up, because it was always jumping up at people and Marion was afraid it might bite.

She negotiated the back path to their neighbour's kitchen door, avoiding a bicycle that had been parked against the washing prop but fallen down, taking the wooden prop with it, and then stepped over three pairs of working men's boots that looked as if they needed a good clean. Mrs Jackson had a husband and three hulking great sons at work in the building trade, four daughters, two employed at the laundry, one married, and one – the pride of her mother's life – training to be a nurse.

It was Paula Jackson, or Nurse Jackson, who opened the door to her, and Marion breathed a sigh of relief. Paula was friendly and often stopped to say hello if they met in the corner shop.

'Marion, lovely to see you – will you come in?' Paula invited. 'If you can squeeze in for my monsters...' She called her brothers names all the time but they only grinned. 'What can I do for you?

Mum said yours didn't look so good when she saw her in the yard. They had quite a chat about that suffragette, Mary Richardson, what damaged a painting at the National Gallery, I believe...'

So, Ma had lied about only being gone a moment. Marion drew a deep breath. 'I'm sorry to trouble you, Paula, but do you think your dad would fix the lock on our back door please? Ma left it open this morning and a dog got in and pinched the sausages we were supposed to have for tea...'

'That will be where the varmint got them from then,' Mrs Jackson said, coming to stand behind her daughter. She smiled at Marion. 'I saw it scoffing them but was too late to rescue anything. I'd take my stick to it, but these daft lumps would cry buckets...' She jerked her head in the direction of her sons, who were eating their tea of lamb stew and mash. 'I'll see my husband comes round this evenin' and does it for yer, love...'

'Thanks, Mrs Jackson...' Marion said and then blushed as Reggie Jackson loomed up behind his mother. He towered over them all, a tall, broad-shouldered man with nearly black hair and blue eyes.

'I'll do it now, Ma,' he said and grinned at Marion. 'It's my dog so my fault – and I'll be round right away, Miss Kaye...'

Marion mumbled something and bolted. If anything terrified her more than the Jackson's dog, it was Reggie. The way he looked at her made her want to hide herself, because there was such laughter in those eyes. Ma said Reggie Jackson was too good-looking for his own sake and the plague of all decent girls and if they weren't careful, they'd be left with the trouble and he'd be off to some fancy foreign place without a care. Ma was prone to saying such things. She was always warning both Marion and Kathy to be careful of men, but Milly was too young to understand yet. Marion and Kathy did, despite Kathy being only days off her thirteenth birthday. They knew and they'd taken the warning to heart, because neither wanted to end up like Ma.

'Mr Jackson is coming,' Marion mumbled as she entered the kitchen. She loaded the rush basket with more dirty clothes and took them into the scullery, dumping them into the hot water in the copper, and started to rinse those she'd already soaked in the sink, as she heard the voices in the kitchen. The lads were laughing and talking to Reggie. They liked him and he sometimes played football with them in the street, something their father had never done.

Marion delayed her return to the kitchen until good manners drove her back. The least she could do was offer a cup of tea and, of course, payment.

The lock was finished and Kathy had already made the tea when Marion returned. Her sister was smiling, clearly enjoying Reggie's company, as were the boys.

'Thank you so much, Mr Jackson,' Marion said. 'How much do I owe you please?'

'Nothing at all, Miss Kaye,' he replied, his grin making her stomach clench. He had no right to be so good-looking and nice and a decent girl had better be on her guard. 'Any little jobs you need doin' are free to you and your family – and I still owe you for the sausages.'

'No, that is quite fair; you've repaired the lock,' Marion said.

'I bought the sausages,' Robbie chimed in. 'They cost me a bob...'

Reggie laughed and looked at her. 'I dare not give you the shillin', Robbie – but I'll take yer to the footie on Saturday if yer like?'

'Thanks, Reggie!' Robbie looked at him adoringly. 'I don't care if yer dog did eat me sausages if I get ter go to the footie...'

'Right yer are then,' Reggie said. 'Shall we take the young'un an' all?' He jerked his head at Dickon and Robbie frowned but then relented.

'Yeah, all right, he can come too...'

Marion went to the door to look at the brand-new lock. It must have cost him far more than the sausages. 'You had no need to do that...' she whispered, 'but thank you...'

'You're welcome, Miss Kaye,' he said and smiled at her and something in his eyes made her heart stand still before racing on. 'Anytime, anywhere – I'm always at your service, Miss Marion...' The twinkle in his eyes scared her to death and she took a step back. 'Me dog likes yer – and if he thinks yer OK, yer must be...'

The cheek of him! She caught her breath as he walked away, standing to watch despite herself. At his gate, Reggie turned and winked and then he was through and walking up to his back door.

Marion returned to her work. She wanted to get all the clothes rinsed and hanging up to dry in the scullery before she went to bed – and it didn't look as if she would have time to do the floor...

3

'Will you be working late again this evening?' Beth Burrows asked her husband Jack as she reached for her warm coat and pulled it on that morning in mid-March. The wind still had a bite in it even though Mr Marco had dressed Harpers' windows with spring clothes, daffodils and Easter bunnies. They were a colourful sight and had already brought customers in looking for the new hats, but she wasn't ready to give up her winter coat just yet.

'I should think so,' Jack said and kissed her briefly, looking distracted. As part owner and manager of a hotel, he was always working extra hours to make it profitable and she knew things had improved since he'd made lots of changes to the way things were done and improved the décor. It was now producing a reasonable profit, though not enough to make anyone rich. Beth sometimes wondered if he'd jumped in too soon, but he seemed pleased with what he was doing, so she didn't say much, even though she regretted her husband's long hours. 'Don't wait supper for me, love. I can grab something at the hotel...'

'Yes, I know...' She smothered a sigh because this wasn't how she'd imagined it would be. Jack had spoken of running a hotel that they could live in and manage together. Now Beth spent most of her evenings at home with Jack's father Fred Burrows and saw her husband for a few hours at the weekend. 'I might go to a meeting with Rachel Craven...'

'Those women's suffrage things...' Jack frowned at her. 'I would never deny you anything, Beth, you know that – but all that marching and demanding equal rights for women... well, it isn't going to happen. It would be better if you stayed away. I don't want the police throwing you in prison...'

Beth moved towards him, half curious, half annoyed. He'd known she was a member before they married and she wasn't going to let him get away with that remark. Other husbands might forbid their wives to be members or take part, but Jack should know better and respect her views. 'Would you disown me if it happened?'

'No! You know I wouldn't,' Jack said genuinely horrified. Yet it was happening in homes all over Britain. Working men were some of the worst and they bullied their wives to try and stop them joining the suffrage movement, but since the death of Emily Davidson, more and more women of all classes had joined, and quite a few men too. The way the suffragettes were being treated, force-fed in prison and beaten when arrested, was terrible, and Beth knew Jack was only concerned for her, even though pride had driven her to ask. Jack looked down at her and smiled. 'You know I love you, Beth, and I agree that women should have the vote if they want it – why not? I can't see things ever being equal in the workplace, the men just won't stand for it, but you should all be paid a fair wage and treated decently.'

'So that's why I married you,' Beth teased and kissed him again, relieved that he wasn't going to start laying down the law the way many husbands did. 'You don't mind if I go then?'

'Of course, not – but get a taxi home, love. We can afford it and I don't want you running the risk of being set on by louts...' He smiled and reached out to touch her cheek. 'I'm only concerned for your safety...'

'I'll probably walk to the bus stop with my friends, but if there's no bus, I'll take a cab,' Beth promised.

She understood why Jack worried, because feelings against the Women's Movement were running high. The militants had angered many, both in government and out, and a lot of men simply did not see why their wives, daughters and sisters were shaming them by speaking out in support of such disgusting behaviour. Men with money took care of their womenfolk, some even went so far as to grant them an allowance that made them almost independent, but they still considered that the feminine mind and body was too weak to be considered as an equal to men. Only very special men understood that women could be as strong and determined as they were themselves, that they didn't want to be petted and treated as fragile beings but as intelligent humans with minds of their own.

Beth smiled as she followed her father-in-law out to the bus stop. Fred Burrows had once been the headmaster of a boy's school. He'd fallen out with the governors because he refused to use the cane in his school and because of that he'd been asked to resign and had ended up working at Harpers as the goods manager, seeing that all the stock reached the department it was intended for. Beth was happy that he'd resigned rather than give into bullying for two reasons: one, because it showed the kind of man he was and, two, because she'd met her husband through him.

'Feeling a bit down in the dumps, love?' Fred asked, glancing at her face. 'You should put your foot down, Beth; tell Jack you want to go somewhere nice – to the theatre or the pictures...'

'He took me dancing for my birthday,' Beth said, smothering a sigh. 'Jack wants a better future for us, Dad, so how can I complain?' She smiled at him with affection, because he was a lovely man and she was so fond of him.

'Most wives would,' Fred replied and grinned at her. 'Don't let the fun go out of your lives. Make sure he takes you somewhere at the weekend...'

'Yes, I shall,' she said and touched his arm in gratitude as their bus arrived and they jumped on. Fred was the first to get his money out and paid for both their tickets. 'I shan't be home for supper this evening...'

'I'll buy a pie and a pint, mebbe see Harold down the pub. He likes a chat and a game of darts now and then...'

'Yes, that would be nice – give him my regards,' Beth said, grateful to the ex-Scotland-yard detective who had solved the mystery surrounding her aunt's so-called accident, when she'd been pushed down the stairs and died in hospital of her injuries. She looked at him curiously. 'Have you ever thought about getting married again, Fred?'

'No, never,' he said and sadness passed across his face. 'I was happy in my marriage and I could never replace my wife... Besides, I've got you, Jack and Tim... and your friend Miss Gibbs comes to tea sometimes. I'm happy to work overtime at the store when I'm needed and I've a few friends I see when I want...'

Beth nodded. 'You didn't mind my asking?'

'I know you're wondering if I'll be lonely when Jack finally finds you somewhere to live nearer the hotel...'

'Yes, I was,' Beth confessed. 'I suppose that's silly really. You lived alone for much of the time before I moved in...'

'The lads were at school during term time and then working, Jack on the ships and Tim now in the Royal Flying Corps – but I served my time in the army as a youngster and I think you learn to be independent there...'

'Yes, I expect so...' She hesitated, then, 'Is it because you served as a soldier that you think there will be a war?'

'No, it's what I read in the newspapers,' Fred said seriously. 'It might be just a skirmish and over in a few weeks, but it's been brewing for a while out there in the Balkans. It will only take one spark to set the whole thing off...'

Beth was silent. Fred was very fond of reading *The Times*, which had just announced it was going to cut its price in half, to one penny. She sometimes picked up the papers her father-in-law abandoned and she'd read about the troubles in Ireland, with Ulster teetering on the brink of civil war only last month as the British government dragged their feet over the Home Rule Bill. Even though she looked mainly for news of the suffragettes, one of whom had slashed a famous painting in the National Gallery in January that year, which Beth thought foolish and unnecessary, she had noticed all the reports of unrest in various parts of Europe. One paper insisted that the arms race was becoming dangerous and lambasted the British government for sitting on its hands while Wilhelm II, Kaiser and Emperor of Prussia, prepared for war. Most people scoffed at such reports, believing it was warmongering and foolish, but she knew that Fred took it seriously. Mr Churchill certainly did, demanding a larger budget for the navy than ever before, which brought accusations from the opposition that he was risking national security by angering neighbours across the Channel.

It seemed to Beth that the German ruler was a hard man with no feelings. He'd gone so far as to ban a dance called the tango for his troops, because it was said to be too intimate. He'd even called on people to shun those who continued to perform what was a popular dance. What kind of a man would do that? Beth loved to dance. Jack had taken her a few times, though they mostly stuck to the waltz or the two-step, but she would have loved to do the more daring tango if she'd known how.

'If war did come,' she said slowly, looking at Fred, 'would Jack have to go – and Tim?'

'Jack wouldn't be the first to be called on as he's married,' Fred said, 'but Tim certainly will be in the thick of it. He's already been flying over German factories and shipyards, helping to take pictures. My son is excited to be flying and nothing would keep him out...'

'Maybe it won't happen,' Beth said hopefully as the bus slowed to a halt and they descended into the rush and noise of Oxford Street. A small crowd was gathering round Harpers and pointing at the windows. It was one of the new displays for the second anniversary of opening day, and there was a display of glass and china, some of which was advertised as being a free gift to the first six customers to spend thirty pounds in the china and glass department. 'Oh, look what Sally has done...' She frowned thoughtfully, 'Do you think anyone has that much to spend all at once?'

'A rich uncle or father perhaps,' Fred said. 'It's a good sales ploy, Beth, and it has certainly drawn an audience...'

The free vases were just one of the special offers; men's suits were offered with a free shirt and collar; ties were given free with a spend of more than twenty pounds.

'Gosh...' Beth drew a wondering breath. 'I think we must be the only department that doesn't have any special offers...'

'It's because you're always busy anyway,' Fred said. 'Besides, we've got a week of these special windows, so yours may be another day...'

Beth nodded and smiled as she noticed that a small queue had formed at the front of the shop. Free offers and special reductions had brought a surge of extra custom, but would it tail off as soon as the offers were over?

* * *

It was a quarter past nine when Beth realised that Marion Kaye probably wasn't coming in that day, because she was very late and, normally, she was no more than a minute or so, if that, and she tried hard not to be late these days. As soon as Mrs Craven made her tour of the floor, Beth asked her if she'd heard from her junior salesgirl.

'No, not as yet,' Rachel Craven replied with a frown. 'It would not be easy for her to let us know if she was going to be late – but usually a relative can either telephone or call from a box if someone is sick...'

'I know she has difficulty at home,' Beth said. 'We haven't been rushed off our feet this morning, so we shall manage quite well – but if we did have a surge of customers, it would make things difficult at break time.'

'The ground floor and the men's department are where all the customers are this morning,' Rachel told her with a smile. 'I even gave the girls on the china and glass department a hand with wrapping a large gift. A gentleman has purchased a set of crystal wine, sherry, whisky, port, brandy, liqueur and water glasses, three crystal decanters, also a leaded crystal fruit bowl and a set of desert dishes and triumphantly carried off his two matching vases for spending sixty pounds.'

'Goodness me!' Beth cried astonished. 'He must be wealthy to spend so much on glassware...'

'He said it was a wedding present for his daughter – and he particularly wanted the vases for himself. He has been debating whether or not to buy a pair before this and he couldn't believe his luck that he got them for nothing...'

'I suppose it is worth it to turn so much stock over,' Beth said, 'but it seems extravagant to give so much away...'

'Apparently, Mrs Harper thought it would bring customers in and Mr Harper said it is often done in America...'

'Yes, she mentioned something of the kind to me,' Beth said. 'But more than fifteen pounds is a lot of money to give away...'

'I suppose they didn't cost that much and they were not selling...' Rachel shrugged. The vases would have cost half that much wholesale and it still left Harpers a small profit on the glassware sold. 'I must get on, Mrs Burrows. I understand the men's department is rather busy just now...'

Beth watched her leave and then a few customers came in and started looking round. One of them asked what was reduced and Beth told her that they had no reductions at the moment. She made a face of disgust and left, as if she considered she'd been cheated, but a gentleman asked to see a selection of leather bags. He bought two, one for his wife and another one for his sister. Beth took his money and gift-wrapped the bags for him. It was only her second sale of the morning and again she wondered at the wisdom of these bargains, though, of course, Mr Harper had wanted to make a bit of a splash for the second anniversary of their opening – and it wasn't Beth's place to decide.

* * *

Sally came down to the department later in the day. She asked how trade was going and Beth told her it had been slower than usual.

'I suppose that was to be expected because of the increased trade elsewhere,' Sally said, frowning. She rubbed at her forehead and sighed. 'Perhaps it wasn't such a good idea, but it did shift those vases and I've already replaced the crystal and china we sold, at least I've reordered. I thought a free gift was better than a reduction...'

'Mrs Craven said it worked very well on the ground floor,' Beth said and looked at her anxiously as Sally put a hand to her back. 'Are you well, Mrs Harper?'

'Yes, just a little backache,' Sally said and smiled. 'I'll just have to put up with it – and my doctor says I shouldn't sit about...'

'Oh, they tell you all sorts of things these days,' Beth said. 'Women were told to relax and rest for weeks before birth once. I think some of them turned into invalids... some of them still do...'

'Well, I have no intention of fading into the wallpaper and I shall work until I'm forced to give up,' Sally said and laughed. 'Ben is taking me to the theatre this evening. I've been wanting to see *Pygmalion* for ages...'

'Oh, lovely. I hear Mrs Patrick Campbell is wonderful...'

'The critics are calling it a triumph, though I understand some of the language is a little bit salty...'

Beth laughed. The paper had reported one of Eliza Doolittle's remarks as stars and an exclamation mark, but everyone knew what it meant, and the word was making the rounds of smart society with a lot of winks and nods.

'You should get Jack to take you,' Sally suggested. 'You'll need to queue for tickets, unless you book ahead, but I'm sure it will be worth it...'

Beth smiled and agreed, but she didn't have time to queue up for tickets, and even if she had, she would most likely end up going with Fred or a girlfriend, because Jack didn't have time to take her to the theatre. Besides, on his rare nights off they liked to go dancing or to a good meal out. Beth considered herself lucky, because many of the girls she'd known at school were married to men who went no further than their local pub. At least Jack took her somewhere nice when he did have a night off.

4

Marion was woken before it was light by Kathy shaking her; she grumbled as she struggled to open her eyes and ask what was wrong.

'Milly's awful bad,' Kathy told her as she sat up and looked at her. 'She has been sick three times and I can't wake Ma...'

Marion was out of bed in a trice and hurried into the room next door where Kathy and six-year-old Milly slept. The two boys were still sleeping in their room and she was glad because Robbie would have to leave for work soon after six-thirty and Dickon had exams at school that day. Dickon was the bright one of the family and Marion hoped he would stay on at school and be something more than a manual worker one day. She would do what little she could to make sure it happened.

Milly was grizzling and feeling very sorry for herself. Marion frowned as she questioned whether her sister had pain in her tummy or her head, but she simply shook her head and knuckled her eyes.

'Feel bad,' she complained and was promptly sick again on the floor.

Behind Marion, Kathy gave a wail of despair. 'I've cleared up after her twice,' she said. 'I've got cookery class today, Marion, and they're going to show us how to make sweet pickle. I really want to learn how to do it...'

'Mum should look after her, so you can go...' Marion said without turning round. She was feeling Milly's forehead, which felt warm and moist. 'Can you get me some cool water and a cloth, love? I think she has a fever...'

Moaning about the unfairness of life, Kathy went off and soon returned with a small bowl of cool water and a cloth. Marion bent over her sister, smoothing her face and hands with the cool water. Milly sighed and looked at her miserably, but she'd stopped whimpering.

'Try and sleep now, love,' Marion said. 'You'll feel better in a bit – and I'd better see how Ma is...'

Going through to her mother's room, she found that she had also been sick in the night. Mrs Kaye was sweating and feverish, lying motionless so that Marion's heart stood still and for a moment she thought she might be dead. However, when she touched her, Ma moaned slightly and moved her hand away, as if in denial.

'Leave me in peace...' she muttered. 'For God's sake leave me be...'

'It's all right, Ma, it's only Marion,' she said. 'You're not well – you and Milly both have it.' Only Ma was even worse than her little sister. Marion couldn't wake her properly or get her to answer even though she tried a little shake but that only brought pitiful cries that made her hesitate. Ma obviously thought she was being attacked.

Feeling angry with her absent father, Marion hurried to fetch fresh water and a cloth. She bathed her mother's face and hands, smoothing the cooling cloth up her thin arms and round her neck. She was perspiring and hot, the sweat soaked into her dark hair.

Tears stung Marion's eyes as she looked down at the woman lying there with a mixture of pity, love and exasperation. Why didn't Ma try to help herself more? She wasn't the only woman in these streets that had a bullying husband, and Pa wasn't too bad if you didn't get on his wrong side. Robbie knew how to handle him, standing up to him with determination but a hint of humour. Dan would have come to blows, because his temper was as hot as Pa's, but Robbie had a way with him. He was a bit like Reggie from next door...

Marion felt a hot flush as she recalled Reggie's wink. He'd called her Miss Marion and something in his eyes had told her he liked to tease. Robbie could be that way too – and he was her favourite brother...

Shaking her head, Marion forced her mind back to the crisis in hand. What did she do about her mother and little sister? They were both quite ill, but did they need a doctor? If it was just a little tummy upset, Ma would be annoyed if they spent money they needed for other things on a visit from the doctor – and yet they could be really ill...

At the back of her mind, the thought that she was letting Mrs Burrows down and might lose her job at Harpers kept pricking at her – but what could she do? Kathy wasn't truly old enough to have the burden of her family's sickness thrust on her and so Marion had no choice but to stay. It was no use thinking about her job at Harpers. Her duty was here!

Ma was settling down a little now, just as Milly had earlier. Marion decided to go down and make up the range and put the kettle on. She would have a cup of tea and then see how they were in an hour or so.

Kathy crept down the stairs after her. 'I'm sorry I had to wake you,' she said. 'I know you need your sleep...'

'You did the right thing,' she said and smiled at the younger girl. Kathy already had too much responsibility for a girl of her age. 'Don't worry, love, you'll go to school in the morning – I want you to get on and do something better, be a secretary or something when you leave...'

'I want to get married and cook lovely things for my family,' Kathy said. 'I'm going to marry a man with money – someone who will put his wages on the table every weekend and not spend it all down the pub...'

'Good for you,' Marion said. She didn't think she would ever marry. Men were so unpredictable. Of the ones she knew in her own street, only three of them spent less time in the pub than they did at home. Mr Jackson was a good provider and gave his wife her share regular as clockwork, even though he liked a drink once a week. All his sons gave their mother money for their keep, which was why Mrs Jackson had a new winter coat most years and no one in that house ever went short of anything. Most of the other women complained of having to raid their husbands' pockets for pennies when they were drunk just to put food on the table – and Marion would never live like that!

At six o'clock, Robbie came down to the kitchen dressed for work. He looked at his sisters, who were eating toast at the table. 'Milly is cryin' again,' he said. 'I looked in on her and I think she might 'ave been sick...'

'Again!' Kathy stood up with a sigh. 'I'll go to her, Marion...'

Marion looked at her brother. 'I'm sorry if I woke you, Robbie...'

'Nah, it was time for me to get up anyway,' he said. 'I could do wiv a bit of that toast and a cuppa if there's any goin...'

'Of course, there is,' Marion said. 'I'll make a fresh pot – and you can have marmalade or drippin' on your toast.'

'I'll have dripping – but cheese in my sandwiches for docky, if there's any left?'

'I've already made them, cheese and sweet piccalilli,' Marion said. 'It's the last of what Ma made...'

'Thanks, Marion.' Robbie grinned at her. 'You know I'm partial to Ma's piccalilli. Pity she hasn't made any more...'

'Kathy wants to learn and she has a lesson today – so perhaps she'll make a batch for us this weekend...'

'You could do it if you ever had time,' Robbie said. His expression became serious. 'It isn't fair, Ma expecting you to do everythin'...'

'I don't mind,' Marion said. 'Really, I don't – but I want to go out with a friend next week...' If she still had a job to go to. If she was sacked, Miss Gibbs would think she'd let them down and wouldn't want to know her.

'Let me know when and I'll stay around so you can go...'

'If Ma lets me...' Marion began when Kathy burst into the kitchen, white-faced.

'It's Ma... she's on the floor and I can't get her to respond to me. She's been sick and she's messed herself...'

'I'd better get the doctor,' Marion said. 'I thought I'd wait until a bit later, but if Ma's that bad I'd better ring him now.'

'I'll do that,' Robbie said and swallowed his last bite of toast. 'Do you need me to help yer get Ma on the bed first?'

'I think you'd better...' Marion said. She went quickly upstairs to the bedroom and saw the sight that had met Kathy's eyes. Ma was whimpering, her eyes closed. The room stank of Ma's vomit and Marion motioned to her sister to open the window a little as she and Robbie lifted their mother on to her bed. Robbie was very strong and took most of the weight. He was frowning as he looked down at her.

'She's very sick, Marion. Do you want me to stick around?'

'No, you need your wages,' Marion said and shook her head. He earned more than she did at Harpers. 'I can manage here and we can't afford to lose two lots of money. I may not be able to get in today and I'm sure to be fined...' She didn't say that she might lose her job but knew it was a possibility because she'd been warned twice about being late.

Kathy fetched hot water as Robbie went off to ring the doctor before going into his work. Marion stripped off her mother's soiled nightgown and washed her all over before putting on a new one. Fortunately, she'd managed to get out of bed before the vomit and mess came out of her and so the sheets didn't need to be changed.

Gathering up the soiled things, the two girls looked in on Milly. She'd been sick too and had soiled her bed. Between them, they washed and changed her and the bedclothes. Marion took them down to the scullery and put them in cold water in the copper to soak.

'Wash your hands well,' she said to Kathy. 'We've got to try and keep ourselves healthy, love...'

Kathy looked at her, then, reluctantly, 'I could look after them...'

'No, you get ready for school,' Marion told her. 'I'll see what the doctor says when he gets here, but I know I might not get in to work at all...'

The doctor didn't arrive until nine-thirty. He followed Marion upstairs to the patients. Milly was looking a little better by then, sitting up, pale and wan, dried tears on her cheeks, but she hadn't been sick again.

'I think this one is on the mend,' Doctor Phillips said as he examined her tummy. 'Bad as it was, I think it was just a nasty tummy and sickness. I'll give you a bottle of medicine for her, which you can fetch from my surgery – and now I'll take a look at your mother...'

Marion followed him into her mother's room. Ma was lying with her eyes shut, her skin cold and clammy to the touch as if she were just too weary to open her eyes. The fever had passed, but she hadn't come out of it as Milly had.

Doctor Phillips took her pulse and then stuck his stethoscope to her chest and back. He shook his head and frowned. 'How long has she been like this?'

'She was sick and had the runs earlier,' Marion said. 'It was watery and it looked like there was some blood in it...'

'I suppose you just cleared everything up.' He nodded, because it wasn't a question, it was what she would do. 'I think Mrs Kaye might be a little more serious than your sister, Miss Kaye; she's lost a lot of weight. I'm going to recommend that you watch over her and keep her cool – but if there is more dysentery, then keep some of it for me to see please...'

'Yes, sir...' Marion felt cold all over. 'I'm due at work... in fact I'm late...'

'Your younger sister or brother should have stayed home... or perhaps you did the right thing.' He frowned at her. 'Your mother may take a turn for the worse, Miss Kaye. I shall call again later today, but if you're worried, ring me – ask a neighbour to do it or to come in while you do. Your mother must not be left alone or she might die...'

'She won't die – she can't...' Marion stared at him in horror.

'If she is no better when I return, I shall arrange for her to be taken into the infirmary,' he replied and wrote something on his pad. 'Now, I'll give this to one of your neighbours. Is anyone your particular friend?'

'Mrs Jackson might go to the chemist if she has time...'

'Well, you can't, because I need you to watch these patients,' he told her. 'You will light a fire in your mother's room, make sure she doesn't get too cold, and as soon as she is able, she needs some hot tea or soup inside her... just a thin soup if you have it or milk and a drop of sugar or honey and lemons, of course; they always help if the throat is sore...' He looked at her sternly. 'Your mother must not be left alone while she is so ill – please understand that, Miss Kaye.'

'Yes, I understand,' Marion said. 'I don't have any lemons, but we do have sugar and milk.' Honey was a treat and wouldn't last more than a day in this house and she only made soup when she had time. 'I could make some soup with carrots and onions or potatoes...'

'Yes, when Mrs Kaye is able to take food, a nice thin vegetable broth will be the very thing... no meat or anything heavy...'

Marion nodded; her heart squeezing as she looked at her mother's pale face. Ma hadn't moved, even the flicker of a finger or an eyelid.

'You are quite clear about my instructions?' Doctor Phillips asked as they went downstairs. 'Now, I need to wash my hands please...' His gaze moved around the room. 'If you have carbolic, you should scrub as much as you can manage of this room, the bathroom and the kitchen. Mrs Kaye could not fight an infection in her weakened state...'

He was making her feel the house was dirty, when she cleaned and scrubbed as often as she had time. The unfairness of it stung. How was she expected to do everything? Houses like this were impossible to keep clean, whatever you did!

Marion hurriedly supplied soap, warm water from the kettle and a clean towel. The doctor washed his hands, smiled at her and then walked to the door, turning to look at her.

'Now, a fire in Mrs Kaye's room, warmed milk for your sister, just a little to settle her tummy – and, above all, watch your mother and get help if she takes a turn for the worse. I shall return later...'

Marion nodded and hurried to collect what she needed, taking the coal bucket, wood and paper up to her mother's room. It didn't seem that cold to her, but the doctor knew what he was talking about, so she lit the fire and put the guard up. She went down to the kitchen then and boiled a kettle and heated a little milk in the pan, adding some sugar to it.

Milly was still looking sorry for herself, but clearly better. She was able to take her milk and drank it slowly and carefully, then smiled sleepily at her sister, snuggled down in bed and promptly fell asleep. Marion stroked her head, smiling at her innocence, and then went next door to her mother.

She touched her mother's hands and found they were warmer, a little moist now. Was that what the doctor had wanted, to warm her up, make her sweat out the infection, whatever it was? However, she still wasn't moving and she didn't answer when Marion spoke to her.

It was eleven o'clock when the back door opened and Mrs Jackson called out to her. Marion left her mother and ran down to the kitchen. Mrs Jackson had brought the medicine bottles and also a loaf of fresh bread, some oranges, a home-baked seed cake and a dish containing a casserole of something that smelled delicious.

'I thought you might not have time to shop, so I cooked a little more for you,' she said kindly. 'Now, is there anythin' more I can do for you, Marion?'

'You're very kind, thank you. Could you keep an eye on Ma while I nip down to the shop and ask Mr Rosen to let me use his phone to ring Harpers and tell them I shan't be in, please?'

'Yes, of course, love,' her neighbour said. 'I'll go upstairs and look in on them both while you nip out...'

Marion snatched up her purse and raced down to the corner shop. Mr Rosen was serving a customer, but as soon as he heard about her mother, he told her to go through to his parlour and use the phone. She rang the office at Harpers and explained that her mother and sister were ill and that she hoped to be in the next day with fingers crossed. The girl who took the message was friendly enough, but Marion worried what her supervisor would think – and yet she had no choice. She couldn't leave her mother.

She then returned to the shop to pay Mr Rosen for her call and purchase a jar of honey and six eggs, but he didn't have any lemons in his shop.

It took her about fifteen minutes to get there, make the call and return home and when she burst into the kitchen, she discovered Mrs Jackson making a pot of tea.

'Your ma has just woken up and asked for a cup of tea,' she said. 'She seems very poorly, Marion. I hadn't noticed how thin she was gettin' – arms almost like sticks.' Her eyes held sympathy as she looked at Marion. 'I'm mostly next door, Marion, and if you ever need anything, just ask. My boys are good lads and I never go short of anythin' – there's always a bit goin' spare...'

Marion flushed, because she knew Mrs Jackson was being kind, but Ma hated charity and she wouldn't even have asked for help if she'd been consulted.

'Thank you for what you did,' Marion said. 'We can manage most times. Robbie always brings his wages home; I don't earn much yet, but it helps – and Dan gives us a bit when he comes home... so does Pa...' A few bob if there was any left after he'd been to the pub.

Mrs Jackson shook her head, her expression betraying what she thought of Marion's father. 'Well, I shan't press you – but my Reggie likes you, young Marion, and he would want me to offer... so we're always there...'

Marion felt hot all over. She thanked her neighbour but was glad when she left. She carried a tray with two cups of tea up to her mother's room and found Ma lying back against her pillows with her eyes closed.

'You shouldn't have troubled Mrs Jackson...' Ma said weakly. 'It was kind of her to come but...'

'It was the doctor insisted...' Marion said and Ma's eyes opened.

'Marion, you didn't call him out!'

'You were ill and so was Milly. I had to... I thought one of you might die...'

'Oh, if Milly was bad...' Ma's eyes closed and she leaned back weakly against the pillows. 'For her sake... it doesn't matter about me...'

'How would I go to work if you were gone?' Marion asked and brought her a cup of hot sweet tea. It wasn't what the doctor had recommended, but it was what Ma wanted.

'You could let Kathy stay home,' her mother said. 'Milly will be at school in another year – and then Kathy can watch her... I shan't be missed then.'

'Ma, don't!' Marion said, feeling hollow inside. 'We all love you – think of us...'

'I've hung on until you're old enough to cope,' Ma said and sipped her tea. 'He's broken me, Marion. I've got nothing to go on for...'

Marion turned away angrily. Her mother was ill; she didn't know what she was sayin'. Once she felt better, she would regret it.

'You'll be all right,' she said, struggling to hide her feelings. 'You've got to be, Ma. Milly still needs you.'

'I suppose she does...' Ma sighed, pushing away the hardly touched tea. 'For a bit longer – but I count too, Marion, and I've had enough...'

Marion's tears trickled down her cheeks as she left the room and went to see if her little sister was all right. Milly was sleeping but her temperature was normal. She'd taken her mother's illness lightly – but Marion knew the doctor was right, something more, something fundamental, was wrong with her mother. She didn't know if it was a physical illness, but, whatever, it was dragging her down, sucking her will to live.

When Doctor Phillips returned, she would tell him what was worrying her. Perhaps if he sent her mother to the infirmary, they could make her better... but did her mother really want to be well again? Did she use her illness as an excuse to keep her husband from her bed?

5

'That is beautiful work...'

The man's voice made Minnie's spine tingle and she caught her breath, hardly daring to turn around. It couldn't be him and yet she'd heard the name of their manager and wondered, but somehow it was still a big shock to see him standing there in her room.

'I was away when Mrs Harper took you on, so I wanted to welcome you to the staff...'

'Mr Stockbridge...' the word was strange on her lips, because he'd always been Jonathan to her.

For a moment, her hands lingered on the exquisite gown she'd been embroidering. Minnie made herself breathe slowly, but she knew him, the feeling of intimacy so awkward after all these years but still there. He had changed little, a bit wider round the middle perhaps, but still that same grave face and open grey eyes that seemed to see into her soul. She wasn't sure if he remembered her – but why should he? He'd had so much more in his life than she'd ever experienced... and they hadn't met for over twenty years, when she'd told him she could never marry him. Yet, as she stared at him, it was if it were only yesterday.

'Miss Minnie...' he said and the sudden shock in his eyes told her that he'd just realised who she was and was stunned. 'I saw the name, but it didn't occur to me that it could be you...'

'Mr Stockbridge,' she replied her cheeks on fire. 'I didn't realise you were the manager here, well, not at first. No one told me until after I started working in the department...' It had been too late to draw back then; besides, she'd been curious as to what he would look like after all these years.

'How are you – and Miss Lumley?' he asked, frowning as he recovered from his shock at seeing her.

'Mildred passed away last year,' she said, a catch of sadness in her voice. 'It meant I couldn't afford to go on living in the boarding house. Mrs Craven offered me a home and she spoke to Mrs Harper about a position for me. Mrs Harper was very kind and said she'd never seen such exquisite work...'

I'm sorry to hear about your sister...'

'It was such a shock...' Minnie said in a choked voice.

'Yes, of course, it would be. I hope you're feeling better now?'

'Yes, thank you...' Minnie offered a small smile.

'Well you're here now.'

Yes, I was very lucky to get the position.'

'I was interested when I saw the invoices for your work,' he told her, explaining why he'd come down to visit. 'We've done alterations before this, but the embroidery is new...' He was struggling against shock or emotion, she wasn't sure which, and she gave him time to recover.

'It can make such a difference to a plain gown,' Minnie said, enthusiasm coming to her rescue and banishing the crippling shyness. Her love for her work overcame the embarrassment at seeing him for the first time in years and she spoke of what was in her heart. 'How is your wife? I heard you married...' And Mrs

Harper had told her he had a daughter named Becky, who was seventeen years old, but she'd been too reticent to ask more questions.

'My wife died soon after our daughter was born,' he said soberly. 'I live alone with Becky and a woman comes in to do the housework and cooks a meal for us sometimes. I often make do with a light supper and Becky has her lunch at school when she goes but she is capable of making her own these days... quite the young lady now...' He smiled at the thought. 'A lovely girl...'

'Oh...' Minnie wasn't sure what to say, but then she realised he was talking too much because, like her, he wasn't sure what to say. This meeting was just as awkward for him. 'I am so sorry you lost your wife. It must have been hard bringing up your daughter alone...'

'My mother was alive then, if you remember?'

Minnie nodded. She remembered his mother very well. Mrs Stockbridge had not particularly liked Minnie and she'd often wondered if that was why he'd accepted her refusal of his proposal so easily.

'She helped and I employed a nurse until Becky went to school. It was difficult, but I had a little money from my father's will...'

Minnie sympathised with his predicament. She knew only too well how hard it could be living on a legacy from a parent and a small wage. Of course, as Harpers' manager, he would now be earning far more than she ever had from her sewing.

'Is your daughter well?'

'Yes, very – she is the light of my life...' He coughed nervously and then recovered his composure, assuming his role as manager. 'Well, I shall leave you to get on with your work, Miss Minnie – and welcome to Harpers. We like our staff to be happy...' He hesitated, then looked back at her and for a moment she saw the old

Jonathan, the man she'd loved so very much. 'It's wonderful to see you again, Minnie...'

'Thank you, sir,' she said and emotion rose in her throat, making her incapable of further speech. She thought she saw a flicker of something like regret in his eyes as he moved away.

After he'd gone, Minnie discovered she was shaking. She'd never expected to see Jonathan Stockbridge again, hadn't imagined he would bother to visit her room. After all, he was the general manager and she was just a seamstress; she wasn't sure she would have taken this job if she'd known he was the manager here before she'd applied for the position and then she hadn't been able to turn it down because she'd needed it so badly. However, now that awkward first meeting was over and it would never be as bad again. He would probably avoid her department and she would do nothing to attract his attention. His embarrassment had been painful, she'd seen that at once – and she was sorry. He'd married a few months after she'd told him she could never leave Mildred and that showed he hadn't felt the deep love that had stayed alive in her heart all these years. A love that she must never disclose to him or anyone!

Tears were hovering, but she blinked them away as someone entered the workroom and came towards her. Thank goodness! It was only Miss Gibbs – dear little Maggie who shared her home with her. She made an effort to paint on a smile and greet her.

'Mrs Burrows sent me with these so you can check the colour for the embroidery you're doing for Mrs Smythe-Jamieson, Miss Minnie.' Maggie showed her the hats she was carrying in her large box. 'You wanted to make sure the blue matched exactly your thread...'

'Oh yes, of course I did,' Minnie said and went to her box to take out the two threads she'd selected earlier. 'I'd forgotten for a moment...'

'Are you all right, Miss Minnie?' Maggie asked, a flicker of concern in her eyes.

'Yes, perfectly, my dear,' she replied, though it was taking all her courage not to burst into tears. 'There we are – now look... yes, I think this one matches perfectly. And the pink is just right for hat number two...'

'Mrs Smythe-Jamieson was so particular,' Maggie said. 'I'm glad we checked, because she would have been cross if they hadn't matched.'

'I'm sure you're right,' Minnie said and smiled. 'The customer must have what she wants, Maggie dear – oh, forgive me, I should call you Miss Gibbs...'

'No one else is listening,' Maggie said, smiling at her. 'The hats are paid for, so I shall leave them with you and then Mrs Smythe-Jamieson can try her dresses and hats together and she will see how well they look...'

'You are such a thoughtful girl, my dear.'

Maggie admired Minnie's latest work; an evening gown, which was hanging from a stand nearby. 'You embroider so beautifully, Miss Minnie – one day I'd like you to do something for me.'

'Of course, I will,' Minnie said. Her hurt was easing now and it was all due to this young girl who was so kind and friendly. 'I'll make your wedding dress one day...'

'I would love that,' Maggie said and laughed. 'All I need is someone to ask me to marry him...'

'You have a very nice young man...'

'Yes, Tim Burrows is lovely, but he's more interested in the Royal Flying Corps at the moment. He's learning to be a pilot and all his energy goes into that. When I do see him, we have tea and talk, but it's mostly about his work and the men he flies with...'

'Gentlemen are often that way,' Minnie said gently. 'One day he will surprise you by saying something lovely and then you'll fall in love and marry him, you'll see...'

'Miss Minnie, I do love you,' Maggie cried with a laugh. 'I am so glad that Mrs Craven brought you to live with us.'

'And it was my lucky day,' Minnie said. 'I was so alone after my sister died, but now I have you and Rachel – and Mrs Burrows too.'

'We're all friends here at Harpers,' Maggie replied with a naughty smile. 'Mrs Harper calls us Harpers' girls and says we're all her family... and I love her too.'

'Yes, she is very kind,' Minnie said. 'She told me to call her Sally, but, of course, I don't – one must not take advantage of another's kindness. She is my employer's wife and I shall never forget that she gave me this wonderful job...'

'You more than repay her kindness with work like this,' Maggie said. 'I must go or Mrs Burrows will think I've got lost. I shall see you this evening.'

Minnie smiled as she left. Maggie's arrival had saved her from making a fool of herself! The tears had been so close, but there was no point in giving way to them. So stupid of her to let the past affect her in that way. She had been shocked to see Jonathan, but she should not have let it affect her like that – it was so many years ago and she'd made her choice. She'd chosen Mildred, because her sister could not have managed without her, but she'd never stopped thinking of the man she'd given up. Even when she'd seen the report of his wedding in the paper, she'd continued to hold his memory dear. Strange that she hadn't known he was a widower. Perhaps she hadn't seen the announcement in the paper. Mildred had not always purchased one, of course, because she said it was an unnecessary luxury.

It was so foolish, because he clearly had not felt the same about Minnie, because he would not have married so soon had he loved her. Now it was time for her to put the past behind her and get on with her life. Jonathan had his own life and a daughter; he was no longer interested in the woman that had turned him down. She had new friends and a new life, to regret what she'd lost so long ago was a waste of her feelings and something she refused to indulge in.

6

'You're so lucky to have a boyfriend,' Becky Stockbridge told Maggie when they met for tea at her home that Sunday afternoon. 'I never meet any interesting young men – and I don't think Papa would let me go courting if I did...'

'Of course, he will one day,' Maggie said and smiled. 'You're only seventeen...' She hesitated, then, 'Besides, Tim is really just a friend – I'm not sure we're courting. We just have tea together sometimes...' Maggie was thoughtful for a moment, because she wasn't sure how she felt about Tim or he about her.

'Seventeen and a few months,' Becky reminded her. 'I think you had a boyfriend when you were my age or younger.'

'Yes, I did, but it was a mistake,' Maggie admitted. 'I don't think it would have happened if my father hadn't been so ill and then...' She shook her head, because his death still hurt after all this time. 'Ralf seemed charming, but he took his mother's side when I needed him and after that I couldn't trust him...'

'I should think not!' Becky said and slipped an arm about her waist. 'I'm so lucky you decided to be my friend, Maggie. I've finished school now my final year exams are over – and I'd love to find a job somewhere…'

'Why don't you come to Harpers?' Maggie suggested. 'It would be fun, because we'd see each other more…'

'I asked Papa if I could, but he said no…' Becky pulled a face. 'He says I can't work behind a counter – but if I pass my exams for shorthand and typing at night school, I can apply for a job in the accounts office…'

'That would be just as good,' Maggie said. 'Do you think you will pass?'

'The typing is easy; I have excellent speeds – but it is the shorthand.' Becky pulled a wry face. 'It's hard and my tutor said she couldn't make out my squiggles without squinting…'

'Well, I can't make out shorthand at all,' Maggie said and laughed at her friend's solemn face. 'Don't worry, you'll do it – and your father only wants the best for you. I think you'll earn another five shillings in the office at least…'

Five shillings a week extra made a big difference and was worth the effort, but Becky clearly wanted the freedom and excitement of being at work with other young girls.

'I asked my father and he said I could come to the first-aid classes with you, Maggie – but he put his foot down over the Women's Movement. He says I may not attend the meetings or the marches…' Becky pulled a rueful face. 'I would defy him and go anyway – but he's so lovely to me, so kind and trusting that I can't…'

'Mr Stockbridge is very nice,' Maggie said. He'd been kind to her even before she became Becky's friend and she couldn't encourage his daughter to break her father's trust and attend the meetings. 'The classes are interesting and can be fun. I asked Marion Kaye to come and I think she will if she can – but she was off work one day this week. Her mother and sister were ill and she called in after eleven to let us know. Mrs Burrows was very understanding but if she does it too often...' Becky's father was pleasant, but he was also strict and if staff were late too often, they were warned three times and then dismissed. Marion had been warned twice already. Some supervisors would have dismissed her instantly.

'Well, I shall come with you both,' Becky said. 'Papa says there is safety in numbers – he just doesn't like me going out alone at night.'

'Well, you can understand it,' Maggie said. 'We always walk in twos and threes to the bus stop; no one walks alone unless they're older and want to.'

'That will be all right then,' Becky said. 'Let's finish this lovely cake Mrs Meadows baked for us. It is really delicious – and Papa prefers his fruit cake. She made one for him all to himself...'

'Are your mother and sister better now?' Maggie asked Marion when they were taking their coats off at work on Monday morning. Marion had returned to work after taking a day off to care for her sick mother.

'Milly is fine, up and running about,' Marion said. 'My mother comes down during the day again now but goes back to bed before I get home... the doctor says she should go to the clinic to be checked over, but she won't...'

'Is there something seriously wrong with her?' Maggie asked.

'Doctor Phillips thinks so... she's got so thin...' Marion caught back a sob. 'I think it's just because she's so unhappy. She said she didn't care if she died...' Marion faltered. 'If that happened, I'd have to stay at home and look after my sister – they might even take Milly and put her in a home. None of us is considered old enough to live without Ma's supervision and my father wouldn't come back on a permanent basis...' Without her mother, everything would fall on Marion's shoulders and sometimes she wondered how she would cope. Yet someone had to keep a roof over their heads and she was the eldest, apart from Dan, who hadn't been home for months now.

'Oh no! That's terrible.' Maggie looked at her in horror. 'When my father died and my mother... went away... I could have lived with my uncle, but I went to stay with Rachel and Beth...' She bit her lip, because even if Rachel would take Marion in, she couldn't be responsible for her brothers and sisters. 'Isn't there any way you could persuade her to go to the clinic and see what is wrong?'

Marion shook her head. 'I think she wants to die,' she said and then stopped as Mrs Burrows walked in and began to take off her coat. Blushing, Marion gave a little squeak and hurried into the department, beginning to uncover the hats, as if she feared that she would be reprimanded for talking, though there were ten minutes to go before they needed to be on the floor.

'Is Marion all right?' Beth asked and Maggie hesitated.

'Yes, she's fine,' she said, 'but her mother is unwell all the time. The doctor has asked her to go to the clinic at the infirmary for a proper check over, but she won't...'

'Perhaps she cannot afford the fees,' Beth said, because many women would hesitate before spending money they needed for other things on a health check.

'Marion's doctor says the clinic is free to her if she goes in on a Friday when he's there – he didn't charge them a penny for visiting twice when Marion's brother rang him.'

'Generous,' Beth said with a little nod. Most doctors charged their patients, even if they were sometimes paid with a few eggs or some garden produce if money was short. 'Perhaps it is pride then... she feels it is charity...'

'Marion is worried about her. She says if her mother dies, the council might take them all into care – because she's the eldest at home and her father works away, as does her elder brother... and she's afraid she might lose her job if she stays away too often...'

'That is something to face if it happens,' Beth said but looked serious. 'I can't do much unless she asks for my help, Maggie – but I would help in any way I could. The rules are strict here, but I'll do what I can – though if her mother dies it will be out of my hands...'

'Yes, I know...' Maggie looked at the little watch she wore on her dress. 'It's time I got to my counter, Mrs Burrows.'

Beth nodded approvingly. The formality began once they were in working hours and Maggie never forgot it, even though Beth was one of her closest friends. It wouldn't do to take advantage and she wouldn't dream of doing it either – but she did hope that Beth could help Marion, because it would be too dreadful if her mother died and some of the family were taken into care.

* * *

Maggie left work that evening, pausing to read the boards outside a cinema on her way home; they were proudly announcing the showing of the first feature film in Britain in full colour: *The World, the Flesh and the Devil*. It would be nice to go to the pictures, but Rachel wasn't much interested in the cinema and Maggie hated going alone. She had no plans that evening, because Becky was going to the theatre with her father and Tim Burrows was away at the Royal Flying Corps base where he was stationed. She thought that Rachel and Minnie were going to visit some mutual friends, which would leave her alone. She would probably spend the evening washing her hair, even though she'd done it recently.

'Miss Gibbs – may I ask you to stop and talk for a moment...'

Maggie's heart caught as she heard Ralf's voice and she spun round to see the man she'd once been briefly engaged to standing just behind her. 'Ralf!' she cried. 'You made me jump...'

'I'm sorry. I never meant to scare you...'

'Oh, I wasn't frightened, just surprised. How are you? I haven't seen you for ages...' she said, recovering quickly.

'No – I've been down on the Sussex coast for the past six months or more,' he said. 'We've been flying missions over the sea and training...' Like Tim Burrows, Ralf was also in the Royal Flying Corps.

Maggie felt a chill at her nape. 'Please don't mention that word war...' she said passionately. 'Mr Burrows is convinced there will be one and his son Tim seems to relish the idea...'

'I suppose it's what we flying chaps expect and live for,' Ralf said ruefully. 'I promise not to mention it again – if you will let me take you for tea...'

Maggie hesitated. Ralf had asked her out several times after she'd left his mother's house more than fourteen months ago and she'd refused. Then he'd disappeared and she hadn't seen him again until that evening.

'I suppose there is no harm in it, as long as you understand that we can never be more than friends,' she said firmly. 'How is your mother and your sister?'

Ralf frowned, as if her statement had displeased him but answered politely. 'My sister is married and very happy... my mother went to live with a spinster friend of hers in Hastings. I see her very occasionally, but I write to her once a week...'

'I see... I'm sorry if that was my fault...'

'How could it be?' Ralf asked. 'Once I'd joined the Royal Flying Corps, I could no longer live at home and my sister's wedding was already arranged for last spring. It was my mother's choice to leave London and I have no opinion about it – I simply wished her well.'

'But you have no home...' Maggie said, feeling vaguely guilty.

'I have my work and my friends. Besides, my home would need you in it to be worthwhile...' The longing in Ralf's eyes then made Maggie's heart catch and for a moment she wanted to cry. She'd thought herself so much in love with him once, but it had ended when he let her down, showing no sympathy over her mother's illness and subsequent death.

'That's silly,' she said, but she knew he meant every word, because it was in his eyes. 'I'm sorry, Ralf. I never intended to hurt you...'

'It was my mother's fault and mine,' he admitted and smiled at her. 'I had no idea what a treasure I had, Maggie. It wasn't until you gave me back the ring that I understood what a damned fool I'd been...'

'Oh, Ralf...' She caught back a sob. 'I don't know what to say...' She felt sad that he'd been hurt, but her feelings had moved on and she could not give him what he wanted from her.

He reached out and took her elbow, guiding her into a pleasant little tearoom and towards an empty table. 'You don't have to say anything,' he told her. 'I just want to spend a little time with you – perhaps we could meet occasionally when I'm in London. It won't be that often...'

Maggie nodded but the waitress had approached and she waited until their order was given and they were once more alone.

'I'm not sure...' Maggie said, flustered and embarrassed to refuse, even though she'd told herself she would never forgive him for not supporting her when her mother lay dying. 'But only as friends – if you expect more, then perhaps we should not...'

'And that is your final word?' Ralf asked.

'Yes,' she managed. 'We could be friends but no more...'

Ralf was silent as the waitress returned with their tea and a plate of cakes. She sipped her tea but found that she wasn't hungry and declined the cream cakes, though Ralf tucked into one with evident enjoyment. Afterwards, he looked at her and her eyes were drawn to a little smear of cream on his mouth.

'I enjoyed that,' he said and his eyes were intent on her face. 'You won't change your mind?'

Maggie shook her head and she saw the acceptance in his eyes.

'Then I think you are right. Thank you for today, but I shall not trouble you again...'

Maggie found it impossible to speak as he summoned the waitress, paid for their tea and then left. She felt sorry that what had begun so brightly had ended this way and yet she knew it was right.

As she got up to leave the little café, Maggie knew the only man she wanted to meet for tea in future was Tim.

* * *

'Did you have a good evening?' Maggie asked when Minnie and Rachel returned from their visiting.

'Yes, not too bad,' Rachel said. 'We visited our old landlady and old friends at the boarding house and then called on my mother-in-law, because she wants Minnie to make her a new dress...'

'Oh, that's rather nice...'

'Yes, I suppose,' Rachel agreed. 'It helps Minnie supplement her income and she likes embroidering, so she was happy.' Rachel sighed. 'What about you? What did you do? I felt a bit mean for leaving you alone...'

'I went out to tea with a friend,' Maggie replied, not meeting her eyes, because she didn't want to tell her who she'd had tea with; Rachel would think her a fool to meet Ralf again.

'Oh, well, that's all right then... Minnie wants to take us both out to lunch on Sunday – unless you're going to visit Becky Stockbridge?'

'No, her father is taking her to visit her maternal grandmother in Henley,' Maggie said. 'I can have lunch, but I shall be meeting Tim Burrows for tea on Sunday.' He'd written to tell her he would be home and she was looking forward to it. Suddenly, she was looking forward to seeing Tim again very much.

7

Rachel was thoughtful as she brushed her hair that evening. Was she imagining it or were both Minnie and Maggie hiding something from her? She'd noticed Minnie fidgeting a couple of times when they were speaking to Rachel's mother-in-law that afternoon and there was a look of sadness in her eyes that hadn't been there until the past day or so. She sighed and shook her head, putting it down to Minnie's loss of her sister. Rachel had hoped she was settling in well with them and in her new job, but it seemed she was still grieving. However, there was little she could do except be kind, gentle and give her time.

Maggie was a different matter. She had recovered from the death of her parents and the look in her eyes hadn't been sadness; it was more as if she'd done something, she was uneasy about and didn't want Rachel to know. Yet she was an honest girl and Rachel knew it couldn't be very much. Again, she could do little unless Maggie confided in her...

Mind you, Rachel had her own secrets. She'd told no one that she'd been out to lunch the previous Sunday with William Bailey, the gentleman she'd met at Harpers and been out with a few times to tea and lunch until he let her down. Her friends would think she was mad, because of the way he'd betrayed her with that awful article he'd put his name to in the papers condemning the Women's Movement, which meant so much to her and to her friends.

For a long time after she'd discovered his betrayal, Rachel had tried to keep William at arms' length, but in the end, she'd allowed him to talk to her and then to take her out sometimes for tea or lunch – but she hadn't told her friends she was meeting him again. She wasn't sure why, except that she was certain they would think her foolish to trust him after he'd betrayed her so badly. However, he had explained that he hadn't written the offending article but merely allowed his name to be attached to it, and he had admitted he was wrong.

'I wish I'd spoken to you in the first place – or just refused to have anything to do with the article,' he'd told Rachel when he'd taken her to tea that first time. 'I wouldn't have hurt you for the world – please believe me. I certainly do not consider you a fool. I was advised it was a good angle to get me a seat in parliament but had I realised that it would alienate you, I would have told them to keep their seat.' He'd smiled at her remorsefully. 'In fact, I did – I'm standing for a different constituency and they happen to be pro-suffragette...' His eyes had twinkled at her in the way she'd always liked. 'Can you find it in your heart to forgive me please?'

Rachel had found she was laughing. William had a sense of humour she liked, as well as being kind and generous, and she just hadn't been able to stay angry with him for long. In fact, the more she knew of him, of his good works amongst the poor and his sympathy for the miners, the more she liked him. Besides, there had been a spate of rather foolish attacks on famous paintings and the pier at Great Yarmouth, which she thought foolish and detrimental to the cause.

Sighing, Rachel thrust thoughts of William to one side. She

had other problems that needed her attention. Her mother-in-law wasn't looking as well as she had and seemed to complain almost the whole time, she and Minnie were with her. Rachel didn't mind for herself, but she thought her mother-in-law might have made an effort because Minnie was visiting – but she had always been a selfish woman.

Why didn't she just leave her to get on with it? Rachel sometimes thought she was a fool to continue to visit her late husband's mother. She'd begun it after Paul's death, because she was grieving and it was her last link with the husband she'd lost, but there was nothing between them now – nothing but her sense of duty...

And then there was that little problem at work. Rachel had been told by two of the department heads that small items had disappeared from stock quite recently.

'A little compact was missing from the cosmetic counter,' Mrs Rowes had told Rachel when she'd asked her why she was doing a stock take midweek. 'It had rouge in it and cost three shillings and ninepence. I know it isn't much, Mrs Craven – but we've never lost anything from this department before...'

The same thing had been reported by Mr Brown, head of the men's department. 'A silk tie, Mrs Craven. Worth four shillings and sixpence. Not a huge amount – but still, one does not like petty theft. I would swear that it wasn't one of my staff...'

'A customer?' Rachel had asked and he'd frowned.

'My staff are vigilant and I keep an eye on the counters myself – but it may have happened when I was on my break...'

'I suppose these things happen,' Rachel had told him, 'but report it to Mrs Harper and do your best to see it doesn't happen again...'

'One thing...' Mr Brown had hesitated. 'I hate to cast aspersions when I've no proof – but I saw a girl from one of the other departments in here the day the tie went missing. She was near the silk ties, but I didn't see her take anything...'

'One of the girls – do you know her name?'

'I've seen her in the store. I think she may work in your old department, but I couldn't swear to it...'

Mr Brown had described the girl as having reddish-brown hair. Rachel knew that one girl in her old department had that colour hair, but without proof she could do nothing – except keep an extra sharp eye out for pilfering.

Work problems should stay at work!

Rachel got into bed and closed her eyes. She had her room to herself again now, because they had decided she should and the others didn't mind sharing. It was nice having her own room, but she hadn't minded Maggie sleeping in the other single bed.

Once again, her thoughts returned to William Bailey. Rachel enjoyed meeting him for tea and lunch – but if he wanted more than friendship – and she sensed he did, could she really trust him?

Rachel had thought her marriage to Paul happy, but at the last he'd turned bitter, almost as if he blamed her for his debilitating illness, as if he resented that she would go on living after he was gone. At the end, he'd told her he still loved her and begged her forgiveness. She'd kissed him and told him she loved him, but the hurt had gone deep. It made her grief harder and for a long time she'd felt as if she could never trust or love again, but gradually the hurt had faded and she'd been able to remember the good times, the happy days when Paul had been so generous and kind, even though they'd never had much money to spare.

Life with William would be very different. He had a private income, inherited from his family, and a well-paid if precarious job as a Member of Parliament. Yet she knew that he didn't have to earn a wage and if she became his wife, she would be secure for life

– but she would not marry him for that reason. Her job and friendships at Harpers meant too much to her to be given up lightly. Of course, she didn't know for sure if he would ask her to be his wife.

Smiling at her own foolishness, Rachel went to sleep. He would ask when he was ready, and she was quite content in her job at Harpers. She wasn't sure that she was prepared to give up her independence to be a wife. Paul had always insisted that she must stay at home to take care of him, but she rather liked working and perhaps she would prefer to remain at Harpers rather than disappear into the background like so many wives.

* * *

Rachel checked her watch after she hung her jacket up in the cloakroom and placed her bag in her personal locker. It was a good system at Harpers and ensured that there was no pilfering of personal items; Sally had introduced it after a couple of girls had had a few shillings taken from their purses. No one had been caught and it was felt too awkward to question the staff over small thefts, though she'd been told to keep her eyes open for any unusual activity.

Leaving to start her first tour of the store, Rachel began with the ground floor, her sharp eyes moving over the counters, checking that everything was in place and nothing left on the floor or out on the counters. The cleaner was usually reliable, but on two mornings she'd picked up litter from the previous day. It was strange how ladies who looked very smart would carelessly drop a bus ticket or a receipt on the floor.

She was aware that the premises next door was in the process of being made ready to become a part of Harpers but wasn't sure whether any work had yet been done as no one had said anything about it to her, and Mrs Harper was not in as much as she had been because of her pregnancy and so Rachel didn't see her as often as she had once.

Everything on the ground floor was perfect and she stopped to watch as Mr Marco moved the blinds to gain access to his latest window display. He was so clever and he insisted on keeping everything secret until the last moment so that the staff was as surprised as the crowds that gathered to see the windows revealed whenever they were changed.

He turned and saw her, winked and then disappeared behind the blind. Rachel smiled to herself. Everyone liked Mr Marco, who always had a smile or a word for them – but she sometimes sensed he hid a secret sorrow from the world, though he'd never spoken of it and she would never dream of asking.

Seeing a girl scurrying towards the lifts, Rachel frowned. Janice Browning was cutting it fine; another minute and she would be late. Rachel wondered if Beth was strict enough over timekeeping. When she was the supervisor for the bag, hat and scarf department, she'd jumped on anyone arriving late, because once you let it go, the girls took advantage – or some of them did.

Frowning, Rachel took the lift up to the next floor and was in time to hear Beth telling Janice that she was only just on time. Maggie was already at her counter and Marion was rearranging the hat stands, which was supposed to be Janice Browning's job. She'd thought they looked particularly nice recently and now knew why. Janice wasn't the artistic one; it was Marion's work.

'Good-morning, Mrs Burrows,' she said and smiled. 'The department looks very nice. I congratulate you – and you, Miss Kaye. That colour combination is excellent...'

She noticed Janice Browning shoot a look of dislike at Marion and realised she may have made a mistake. By noticing and praising Marion's work, she might have upset the older girl. Rachel knew that jealousy could sometimes cause trouble between the girls and decided not to mention that Miss Browning had been a little late. After all, it was no longer her job and Beth must manage it herself.

'I shall get on,' she said. 'I will speak to you later, Mrs Burrows...'

With a nod of her head, she left them and continued her tour of the shop. Only if Beth came to her with a complaint about a member of staff could she do anything to help.

8

'When will you get the keys for the new property?' Sally asked her husband as they were dressing for work that morning in early April.

'I expect today,' Ben said, grinning at her like a small boy with a huge ice cream cornet. His eyes were sparkling, the excitement barely hidden. 'I've made an appointment with a builder at four this afternoon and I hope to get the ball rolling.'

'At last it's ours,' Sally nodded her approval. 'Lawyers always seem to drag their feet – I can't wait to see it...' Her hand went surreptitiously to the small of her back.

'Impatient one,' Ben said and moved towards her, concern replacing the glee. 'Does your back hurt again?'

'A bit,' she admitted, 'but I'm all right, so don't fuss...'

'I know you won't stop working until the last minute,' Ben said, 'but don't neglect yourself, Sally. You're very important to me – and to Harpers...'

'I know.' She smiled up at him. 'I'm not an invalid, Ben. I'm just having a baby.' And it wasn't that long to go now, only a month to six weeks according to her doctor's opinion.

'But it's my baby and you're my wife,' he murmured as he took a tie from the selection hanging on the back of his wardrobe door. 'Is this one right with this suit?' He held it against him.

'It's all right – but this is better,' she said and took one slightly darker from the selection. 'This tones well...'

'See, I can't even dress myself without you,' he said and laughed as she shook her head and disappeared through the bedroom door, across the wide hall to their kitchen.

Sally hadn't been able to eat much first thing in the early weeks of her pregnancy but now she was hungry all the time and she started on her favourite iced biscuits as she waited for the toast to brown.

* * *

Mr Marco was waiting for Sally when she arrived at her office. He looked as if he was about to burst with news, so she put a finger to her lips, because the new window displays were a secret. Once inside and the door firmly shut, she said, 'Well, did you get her?'

'Yes, she has agreed to do it,' he said, his eyes lighting with triumph. 'I told her we were both in love with Eliza Doolittle and adored her performance and that we're devoting a whole window to her and the show – and she said she didn't normally agree to do publicity for stores, but she would for us.'

'That's wonderful,' Sally said. 'I'm thrilled. I loved *Pygmalion* when Ben took me to see it on the opening night at His Majesty's Theatre and Mrs Patrick Campbell was brilliant as Eliza. I'm so pleased she agreed.'

'She is coming into Harpers the morning we unveil the window and she will sign autographs if anyone wants – and they will. I wouldn't mind betting we'll be swamped.'

'Yes, I'm sure we shall,' Sally agreed. 'Congratulations, Mr

Marco. You've pulled off a coup by persuading her to come – how did you manage it?'

'Well, I've met her at theatrical parties with a friend, who just happens to be a friend of a friend of hers...'

Sally nodded. She knew that Mr Marco was moving in artistic circles these days. He had – at least on the surface – got over the tragic loss of his lover and seemed to be out most evenings, either at the theatre or a party given by someone in that world.

Sally's secretary brought in coffee after he'd departed, together with a plate of pink-iced biscuits. Sally ate them all while she drank a cup of coffee. When her appointment arrived, she ordered more coffee for him and invited the representative to sit down.

'I hope you've brought something nice for me to see, Mr Charles?'

'I think you will like our new lines,' he said and placed a smart jeweller's case on the desk. It was made of maroon Morocco leather with brass clasps and when opened revealed three layers lined with sheepskin. On each layer were several pieces of jewellery. The top two layers had silver jewellery, much of it similar to stock she'd bought before, but when he showed her the bottom layer, a little gasp of pleasure left her lips.

'Beautiful...'

'It's lapis lazuli, Mrs Harper. I thought you would appreciate it...'

'I do, very much – but what sort of price can you give me?'

The representative smiled confidently as she picked up the beautiful pieces one by one to admire them, her fingers moving over the deep shine of the stone with reverence.

'You know I always give you a special price, Mrs Harper – and as this line is very new, I can do quite a good deal for you...'

* * *

When the representative left nearly an hour later, he had an order for three hundred pounds and Sally had six beautiful pieces of lapis lazuli jewellery on her desk. She'd ordered quite a few of the silver pieces, some of which she'd bought before, and several more pieces of lapis lazuli, some set in silver and some in 9 carat gold. Mr Charles had allowed her to pick six pieces from his stock and the rest would be delivered the next week.

It was more expensive jewellery than they'd stocked before, perhaps too expensive for the ordinary woman to purchase for herself as a treat, because it started at two guineas for a simple brooch and went up to five for a more elaborate piece. However, husbands, brothers and doting grandfathers often spent as much or more on gifts for loved ones and they would be the buyers of these wonderful Art Nouveau pieces.

Ben had actually bought Sally a wonderful lapis lazuli pendent set in 18 carat gold and given it to her over dinner the evening he'd secured the purchase of the shop. It had taken her breath away and she'd scolded him for spending so much money on her.

'I wanted you to have it,' he'd told her with a smile. 'You're worth it – and one day it will be diamonds from head to foot, Sally.'

'You spoil me,' she'd said. 'I love it – and no diamonds could ever be as good...'

Lapis lazuli was a special stone, not just because of its wonderful deep blue colour but because it was mystical and Sally knew there were myths and stories surrounding such stones. It was said to be the stone of royalty, honour, gods and power and to help its wearer to wisdom and truth. As she priced up the items she had, Sally decided she would visit the library and research it more. If Beth and the girls knew the stories and could tell the customers, it would help to sell the jewellery and they would need to push them because these pieces were so expensive.

Mr Marco would feature them in the window when she had more stock, make a display around these special pieces in some way. If she could find a suitable myth, he might design a window about the story and make it as magical as she felt the stones deserved. He was such a talented designer that she knew he would do it justice.

Leaving the office, Sally went down to her favourite department. Beth was serving a customer with jewellery; Marion Kaye was wrapping silk scarves for a customer, while Maggie served another with leather gloves. Janice Browning was putting two of the new spring hats into the fancy boxes.

Sally felt pleased to see the store so busy. The free gifts and special window display, together with the champagne and chocolates offered to customers on the ground floor, had brought the crowds for their anniversary back in March. However, the profit margins had been small that week and she was uncertain whether her gamble had paid off. The trick was to sell more at the right price so that they made a healthy mark-up and turned over the stock at a good rate. Fortunately, Mr Marco's windows seemed to attract crowds every week. It was because they kept the blinds up until they were finished and he was so clever that people often stood and stared for ages, taking in all the little things he'd done to amuse and titillate the senses.

Janice Browning came up to her when her customer had gone and Sally congratulated her on her sale.

'Oh, I like to serve my customers, Mrs Harper,' she gushed. 'I think it's because I give them such good advice that they buy more...'

'Well, done, Miss Browning,' Sally said with a crisp nod. Something about the girl grated on her nerves, though she was an excellent salesgirl. 'Excuse me now; I must speak to Mrs Burrows...'

Beth had finished serving her customer and Sally went up to her, showing her the lovely pieces of lapis lazuli jewellery.

'It looks expensive,' Beth said as she touched it reverently. 'Is it just these few pieces?'

'For now, but I've ordered more. Mr Charles let me have these from his stock. He only does that for special customers... at least that's what he said,' Sally said, smiling, because she knew the little tricks the representatives used to flatter her and persuade her to buy. It didn't always work, because Sally knew exactly what she wanted the minute she saw it but always held out for the best price.

'Well, they are expensive, but I've sold three bracelets at thirty-five shillings this morning, all as birthday presents, so they should sell as gifts...'

'Yes, that is what I'm hoping for,' Sally said. 'We've done well with that particular representative's stock before, so fingers crossed...' She frowned, placing a hand to her back and giving a little sigh. 'Do you know, I think I shall have to...?' She was going to say sit down, but before she could finish, her head went fuzzy and she started to sway.

Beth rushed to catch her before she could fall and Marion brought a chair. Together, they lowered her on to it and Beth supported her as Maggie brought a glass of water.

In another moment, Sally's head had cleared. She sat up straighter and apologised. 'I'm so sorry,' she said. 'That was foolish of me...'

'You need to rest,' Beth said. 'Shall I help you to the office – or order you a taxi?'

'No, I'll be fine,' Sally said firmly. 'It was just a little faintness. I dare say I need my lunch. Ben will be here soon.' She looked round at the girls. 'You will oblige me by not mentioning this to anyone.'

'Of course, Mrs Harper,' Marion, Maggie and Beth said instantly.

Janice Browning went to serve a customer who had just entered the department.

'Do you want me to come up with you?' Beth asked.

'No, I'll be fine now,' Sally said, smiled and walked out of the department. Her head had cleared and she was annoyed. What a nuisance that she'd turned faint like that. She hoped none of the customers had noticed, because if they had, Ben would learn about it very soon and then he would probably insist that she stopped coming into work, and she really wasn't ready to that just yet.

* * *

Ben arrived with flowers and the keys to the building next door. Sally had ordered sandwiches and a salad for them, which they ate together in the office. Ben drank a glass of wine to celebrate, but Sally had orange juice. She was feeling fine again and looking forward to viewing the new premises.

'We can have a walk round before your builder turns up,' she suggested. 'I'd like to see what I think before you two get to work on it.'

'Of course, you would,' Ben laughed. 'No doubt you will turn all my plans upside down – but it will be for the better...'

Sally smiled. She'd already had her say, but she was too excited to delay her visit until four and couldn't wait to grab her jacket and follow Ben into the street and then into the empty property.

It smelled of tobacco and something she thought was aniseed but the shop was spacious and there was a huge storeroom behind it which could be opened out for better use. It had stairs up to the flat above and Ben had previously mentioned putting in a lift to make it easier for their customers.

Upstairs, it was divided into living rooms, a kitchen, hall and, on the top floor, four bedrooms and a bathroom, but all the internal walls could come down to open up for the various departments they had in mind. It would take steel lintels and special beams in the ceilings, Ben explained, to make it safe, but the potential was there.

'It's wonderful,' Sally said and hugged him excitedly. 'I'm so glad you managed to finance it. I think the extra departments are just what we need.'

'Yes, I know. My uncle always had his eye on this building, but the owner wouldn't sell to him then.'

'Well, you did what he couldn't.' Sally leaned in to kiss him. 'I'm so happy, Ben...' she murmured and then her head started to spin. She fell against him and Ben caught her and held her to him, his strong arms saving her from a fall. 'Oh dear... I feel a bit odd...'

'You fainted,' he said and bent to sweep her up in his arms, holding her safe against his chest. 'I'm putting you in a taxi and taking you home, Mrs Harper – and then I'm calling the doctor. If my information is right, that is the second time you've swooned today.'

'Traitors...' Sally muttered, but she was feeling too weak to argue and it was rather nice having Ben look after her. She would let him call the doctor, but she had no intention of retiring to her bed until the birth...

* * *

News of Sally's illness, brought a visit from Mick, bearing a huge bunch of spring flowers and a large box of special cakes that his chef had made specially for her. He came on the following Sunday and Ben welcomed him in, inviting him to stay for lunch.

'I'm cooking steak, jacket potatoes and salad, but you're welcome to stay.'

'Thank you, I should have enjoyed that, but I have a business lunch...'

'Don't you ever sit still?' Sally challenged and he grinned at her.

'Pot calling the kettle black?' he said. 'Sure, I might go back to Ireland for a few days in the summer to visit me cousins, but ask Ben – business comes first...'

Ben laughed and shook his head. 'I'm keeping out of it,' he said.

However, the two had sat and talked business. Sally made coffee and they all ate Mick's delicious offerings and it was nearly twelve before he decided he had to dash.

'Now, don't you be overdoing it, Sally Harper,' he warned before he left. 'We don't want to lose you...'

Sally frowned and looked at Ben. 'He's nearly as bad as you...'

Ben smiled oddly. 'Mick thinks a lot of you – but I know he's just a friend and I'm not jealous, but he is right. You should take notice of your friends, Sally. We all need you and you've got to rest more.'

Sally made a rude face at him. Ben laughed and went off to prepare their lunch, leaving her to browse the latest fashion catalogues that Ben had brought home. She could see several lines for the autumn she rather liked and she pulled her pad towards her, beginning to make notes about the new sleeves and necklines that had caught her eye. A little dizziness wasn't going to stop Sally doing her job if she could help it...

'How is Mrs Harper now?' Rachel Craven asked Ben when he arrived at work the next Monday morning. 'I hope she isn't too cross with me for telling you, but when Miss Browning told me she'd fainted in the department, I thought it best to let you know. I'm very fond of Sally, but she tends to carry on even if she isn't feeling too good.'

'Thankfully, the doctor says it's just a passing phase,' Ben told her, showing his relief. 'When she passed out on me the other day, I was terrified, but her doctor thinks it quite often happens at this stage. He says she's as healthy as a mule – and as stubborn – and the best thing is to let her carry on. He advised that she should work mornings and then have a little rest at home in the afternoons and, eventually, Sally agreed.' He grinned. 'Her friend Mick called round and told her not to overdo it and I think that finally got through to her – I hope!'

'Well, that is good news,' Rachel said and looked genuinely happy.

Ben thanked her. He knew she was one of Sally's best friends and he wouldn't dream of telling his wife who had passed on the news of her first faint. Rachel Craven had done it because she cared about Sally, but it would still annoy her, so the identity of the tell-tale would never pass his lips.

Smiling to himself, he walked into the office he shared with Sally. She was having the morning off, not to rest, but to have her hair done. Ben had arranged for the stylist to come to the flat, making sure that his wife followed doctor's orders and had at least a day at home before returning to work, albeit just in the mornings.

'Good morning, sir,' Sally's secretary greeted him. 'How is Mrs Harper this morning, sir?'

'Frustrated,' he replied with a grin. 'She wanted to come to work – but I'll be taking her appointments today.'

'Yes, sir, of course,' Ruth Canning replied. 'Mrs Harper was seeing the rep for leather bags at ten-thirty and Brown's Clothing – ladies' suits and coats for autumn – at eleven-fifteen...'

'Ah...' Ben wrinkled his brow. 'I shall see the rep for leather bags, Miss Canning, but I think it may be best if you ask the clothing rep to send his catalogues over so I can take them home for Mrs Harper and reschedule his appointment for one morning next week.'

'Yes, sir, that's a very good idea. He can send the catalogues over with a lad – or leave them for you to take home. It will give Mrs Harper something to do rather than twizzling her thumbs.'

'You know my wife very well,' Ben said and laughed. 'Do you think you could rustle up some coffee please – and I'll have some biscuits, chocolate if you have them...?'

'Yes, sir, of course.'

Ben sat down behind the desk. It felt wrong to be here without Sally and he felt a cold chill down his spine. If anything happened to her... but it wouldn't! He'd lost a girl he'd loved once, but that had been a young man's calf love and his feelings for Sally were so much stronger, so deep and fundamental that sometimes they frightened him.

'Mr Harper...' Ruth Canning popped her head back round the door. 'Someone is here... He asked to see Mrs Harper, but when I said she wasn't here, he asked if you would see him...'

'Does he have an appointment?'

'No – but he says he's a friend of Mrs Harper's...'

Ben frowned. 'What is his name?'

'Mr Michael O'Sullivan.' She made a face. 'He's Irish.'

'You mean Mick!' Ben was on his feet immediately. 'Ask him to come in and bring another cup.' Ben walked round the desk as Mick entered and offered his hand. 'I'm afraid Sally isn't here today, Mick. The doctor said rest today and then just mornings at the office. You know my wife; nothing will make her give up entirely.'

'It wouldn't be Sally Harper if she did,' Mick replied with his easy grin. 'I shall come straight to the point, Ben. I was going to offer you both a chance to come in with me on a new hotel I've been told about. I intended to mention it yesterday, but somehow the time just flew and I had to dash.'

'A hotel this time?' Ben's brows shot up. 'Sally has told me that your chain of restaurants started with a horse your uncle left you?'

'Yes,' Mick laughed. 'It won an important race and I sold it for a small fortune, so I did – and invested the proceeds wisely. All four restaurants are busy and earning money and I was offered this hotel, but I don't have the funds to buy it alone, so I thought of you and Sally...'

'Unfortunately, I've just sold my soul to the bank to extend Harpers,' Ben said, feeling disappointed. Mick seemed to have hitched his fortunes to a star and he would have enjoyed being his business partner. 'I'm sorry, but at the moment I can't help you.'

'That's a shame,' Mick replied. 'I've no doubt I can find funding, but I should have liked to have you and Sally on board. Your wife has some very good ideas, Ben.'

'That I know...' Ben hesitated, then, 'She'll have a little time on her hands while she waits for the birth of our child – I am sure she would be only too delighted to view the place with you and give you the benefit of her opinion.'

'And you wouldn't mind?' Mick's eyes sought his inquiringly.

'Providing you take good care of her and return her all in one piece,' Ben said easily. He had no need to be jealous and Mick was a decent bloke when you got to know him.

'Then I shall ask for Sally's advice.'

'Why don't you come over for dinner one evening?'

'I should enjoy that – if it won't cause your wife too much trouble?' Mick said. 'And I hope you know that I'd like to return the hospitality at my latest restaurant when you have the time?'

'We'll do that when she's feeling better. As for dinner at ours, I'll order a meal in,' Ben assured him. 'We shall look forward to seeing you – say on Thursday?'

Mick hesitated and then nodded, 'Thursday it is.' Mick's strong fingers closed around Ben's outstretched hand. 'Thank you for seeing me, Ben. I appreciate it,' he said, nodded and went to the door. There he looked back and said, 'Take care of your wife, Ben. She's very precious...'

'That you can bet on...'

Ben sat down after the other man left. He smiled in triumph. The foolish jealousy he'd still been harbouring against Michael O'Sullivan had truly gone. Mick was a man to watch as regards business, because he was clearly going to be successful, and Ben would certainly consider the idea of going into partnership with him in the future when the funds were available.

* * *

Sally ate the salad and home-cooked ham that the restaurant had sent up with little new potatoes. It was delicious and the piquant dressing suited her taste because it was a little sweet and at the moment Sally craved sweet things. The doctor had told her that she ought to eat less of the iced biscuits and more fruit and salad, hence the meal she'd chosen, followed by fresh fruit salad and cream.

She drank the orange juice with her meal, relishing its coldness as it slipped down. It was nice having a refrigerator of their own, something Sally had never had until she moved into Ben's flat. It was a lovely big one, the professional size similar to those a restaurant would have, because Ben said he was used to a large cold box in the States. He didn't often talk about America, except to celebrate the special holidays, like Independence Day on the fourth of July and Thanksgiving, but whenever he did mention his country, it was usually to comment how they did things bigger or better. Sally had thrown a cushion at him once and told him to stop bragging, but it wasn't that – it was just the way things were. His sister Jenni had told her the same when she was over on a visit.

'I love England, it's so small and quaint,' she'd said and she'd been so sincere. 'I love London's old buildings – and that funny bridge and the Houses of Parliament and the little cobbled lanes and how fresh and green it all is... but, oh, Sally, the drains can be awful when it's hot and the plumbing is ancient...'

Jenni had thought the plumbing terribly antiquated, even in the expensive hotel she liked to use. She complained it sometimes woke her in the night, gurgling and banging, and she said the average refrigerator was impossible.

'How can you find room to keep things in that tiny little box,' she'd complained when Ben first moved into his apartment, so he'd bought a huge commercial one, and Sally had to admit it was wonderful, because it kept fruit from spoiling too quickly.

Finishing her lunch, she heard the doorbell ring and went to look through the spyhole at who was there. At first, she wasn't sure who it was and then, as the woman turned towards her, she saw her face and gave a cry of surprise and pleasure. It was one of Mick's business partners and the part-owner of a lovely old pub and restaurant.

'Marlene!' she cried as she opened the door. 'Please come in – what on earth are you doing here? I'm glad you came but...' She laughed at the lovely surprise of seeing her visitor.

Marlene smiled at her and presented her with a small parcel wrapped in white tissue. 'You look wonderful,' she told Sally and kissed her cheek. 'Mick sent me to see how you were. I made some baby things for you – and he practically forced me to come. I thought he might bring them, but he said I should...'

'For me – how lovely!' Sally exclaimed and took the soft parcel. She opened it carefully and saw the lacy shawl, little coat and bonnet and bootees all made in beautiful two-ply white wool. 'These are gorgeous... did you really make them?'

'I like to crochet,' Marlene said, surprising Sally. 'I never had my own children, though I had a stepson for a while... until his father ran off with a younger woman...'

'Oh, Marlene, that is sad. I'm so sorry,' Sally sympathised, because she could see it had hurt her friend.

'I was devastated at the time, more for the loss of that kid than anything – but it was about then that I met Mick...' Marlene smiled fondly. 'He was kind to me when I needed a friend, Sally – and I never forgot it. I think he became all the sons I never had wrapped up in one and I'm very fond of him.'

'Mick is a good friend,' Sally agreed.

Marlene smiled in agreement, but then her smile disappeared. 'Speaking of Mick reminds me – that little tart Sylvia had the cheek to come and ask for her job back the other day. I said no, of course.'

Sally nodded her understanding. Her one-time friend Sylvia had taken advantage and then let her down – there was something sly about her. A little cog clicked in Sally's brain. She'd seen that kind of look in Janice Browning's eyes when Sally had been unwell in the department and realised now that it was slyness. The thought made her frown as she understood why she'd instinctively felt distrust towards the girl, though at the time she'd had no reason for it. Something about Janice did not ring true.

'You're not feeling faint again?' Marlene asked anxiously. 'Your husband told Mick you'd been unwell...'

'No, I'm fine,' Sally promised her. 'I was just remembering something... to do with Sylvia, but don't let us think about her. How is the restaurant going?'

'We're always busy,' Marlene told her. 'Mick has an opportunity to invest in another place – a hotel this time. I just hope he doesn't stretch himself too far. He needs extra funds and sometimes he can be reckless.'

'Mick is confident in his own ability,' Sally said. 'If I had a thousand pounds in the bank, I would invest it in whatever he wants to do, but I don't.'

'I have some savings,' Marlene said. 'Mick doesn't know, but my aunt died and left me five hundred pounds. I don't know whether to hang on to it or invest it for when I retire.'

'Mick will double it for you,' Sally said and Marlene nodded.

'Yes, I know that in my heart, but I've always been careful...'

'Live for the moment,' Sally said blithely. 'No, actually, don't do that – if you're not comfortable, invest a part of it and keep the rest for a rainy day...'

Marlene laughed. 'That is my dilemma. I want to put the lot in so Mick can get what he needs, but supposing it all went wrong?'

'Ben is putting all he has into Harpers,' Sally told her. 'He has even borrowed to take on the new premises – but you have to believe in the future. I would put all I had in, but you must make up your own mind...'

'I think I'll probably be brave,' Marlene said. 'I know that five hundred pounds would mean the world to Mick right now.'

Sally nodded. 'I think you've made up your mind – so shall we have a cup of tea and a slice of fresh cream sponge I have in the cold box?' She thought for a moment, then, 'I've saved fifty pounds from my wages since I've been working at Harpers – would you put it with yours and give the five hundred to Mick, please?'

'I'll invest the fifty pounds for you,' Marlene agreed, looking pleased. 'I can keep a little nest egg back for myself then and still give him the five hundred he needs.'

'Don't tell him,' Sally said. 'It's just between you and me.'

Marlene smiled. 'No wonder Mick thinks the world of you – you're a lovely girl, Sally Harper. I shan't forget what you've done.'

The two women smiled at each other and their talk progressed to other things like fashions, Marlene's friends and Sally's pregnancy as they drank tea and ate slices of cake. The time flew and Marlene glanced at the clock on the mantle and laughed.

'I have to go, Sally. I have a pub to open and masses to do...'

'Of course. Thank you for coming. I'm always pleased to see you...'

As Marlene got up to leave, the front door bell rang. Sally answered it and smiled as she saw who was standing outside her flat.

'Mr Marco,' she said as he thrust an enormous basket of flowers and fruit at her. 'How lovely – and I'm so pleased to see you...' She kissed Marlene's cheek. 'Come and see me whenever you have time,' she said and Marlene promised she would. Sally closed the door behind her and beamed at Mr Marco. 'Have you brought me the ideas for the new windows as you promised?'

He nodded his eyes bright with amusement. 'Ben thinks I just brought the flowers, but I smuggled them out so you have something to amuse yourself with and don't get bored.'

Sally laughed. 'Thank goodness! I can't sit here and twiddle my thumbs all day. Now I can look at your sketches and feel that I'm still part of Harpers.'

10

Rachel Craven dressed for her dinner date that evening with care. She wore a slim-fitting midnight-blue gown of soft velvet and a little white silk evening cape edged with ribbon, her shoes were silver, as was the little bag she clutched. It was an outfit she'd bought when Paul took her out for their fifth wedding anniversary and she hadn't worn it since. Paul's illness had shown itself just a few weeks after that evening and for a long time Rachel couldn't even look at the dress, but it suited her and was as good as new. She'd debated for a long while before deciding to wear it, but it really was time to put the past behind her. The greys and blacks she habitually wore were fine for work and shopping, but for an occasion like this it would be wrong to be dressed in half-mourning. She needed to keep her engagement with an open mind and an open heart.

Glancing at her reflection in the long cheval mirror, Rachel asked herself the question that had hovered at the back of her mind for weeks now – what was she going to say when William Bailey asked her to be his wife? Rachel was certain now that it was a matter of when rather than if; he had hovered on the brink more than once and she knew that if she'd pushed it just a little, he would have spoken.

He'd talked about his home in the country, about his work and his need for companionship. 'I don't want my wife to be just in the background like a shadow,' he'd assured her the last time they'd been out for a meal. 'There will be some entertaining, especially if I become a minister – but I want to know that on cold winter evenings and Sunday mornings, I shan't be alone in my old age...' He'd given her that special look then. 'Don't you feel the need for companionship, Rachel?'

She'd answered him vaguely, even though she'd known what his questions were leading up to, telling him about how much she enjoyed sharing the flat with the girls from Harpers and her job. He'd looked thoughtful and then changed the subject to the play they were going to see later.

Rachel hadn't been ready for a proposal then, but she'd decided that she was now. William was right. Beth had already moved on and Maggie would do so one day. Minnie might struggle to find another home, but Rachel knew that she wanted more than just friends. There was no relationship like that of marriage, especially if it was good. Her marriage to Paul had been good before his illness and she knew enough of William now to believe it might be even better being his wife. She thought she was ready to try...

Well, he would speak this evening or walk out of her life for good. Rachel knew that the dress she was wearing would open the way for his proposal and it would be her answer that determined the future.

'That's the doorbell,' Minnie said, popping her head round the door. 'I'll answer while you finish getting ready, Rachel dear – and, if I say so myself, the embroidery on the front panel makes your dress look even better.'

'Yes, it does,' Rachel said with a smile, because it was Minnie's work that had made it a little different.

She dabbed a drop of her special perfume behind her ears and on her wrists and then picked up her long white evening gloves. Dinner and the theatre; it was so long since she'd been spoiled like this and she was going to enjoy every second and, yes, she believed she knew what her answer would be.

* * *

Minnie sat looking blankly at the wall after Rachel had gone out with her gentleman friend. She'd looked so lovely, much younger than she normally did, and Minnie knew that she would come back with a ring sparkling on the third finger of her left hand. Rachel hadn't said anything, but Minnie knew in her heart. She deserved it, of course she did! Minnie wished her well and wanted her dear friend to be happy, but the thought of returning to a boarding house like the one she'd lived in with her sister for years filled her with dread. She'd been so happy here with dear Rachel and that sweet little Maggie. How could she face the future without seeing their faces every morning?

Minnie angrily wiped away a tear of self-pity. She would not give into these selfish thoughts! Her friends must not sacrifice their happiness for her as she had years ago for Mildred. After their father died and they were both left with so little to live on, Minnie had known that she could never leave her sister. Without her, Mildred's existence would have been even more deprived and miserable – and so she had told her dearest Jonathan that she could never marry. He hadn't believed her at first and begged her to be his wife, but she'd been steadfast. Minnie had been torn in two, hurt by seeing his pain at her rejection and yet she'd known she had no choice, even though it had broken her heart. Mildred could never have lived as his dependent; she thought Jonathan a soft fool – and so Minnie had given him up.

She'd only regretted it now and then during the years she'd spent supplying the embroidery that made Mildred's plain sewing so popular, because she sincerely loved her sister and was content to work with her. The pretty day dresses and evening gowns they made for others all showed evidence of Minnie's talent somewhere, even if it was just an edging to a sleeve or a tiny motif on a pocket. Besides, Jonathan had soon married and that had shown her that he hadn't truly loved her...

No, she'd made the right decision and she wasn't going to brood on it now, even though her heart raced every time Mr Stockbridge came up to the department and now and then she wondered what might have been. In hindsight, she knew marriage to him could have been wonderful.

She never used Mr Stockbridge's first name, because he was the manager and it wouldn't be right, even though he could never be anything else but Jonathan to her. Now, she made herself remember the good times with her sister. Mildred had thanked her as she lay on her deathbed.

'I know what you did for me,' Mildred had said, gripping her hands. 'It's your time now, Minnie – find love, success and be happy, I beg you...'

It was so easy for Mildred to say, but Minnie was no longer a young girl in the first flush of beauty; she was nearly forty and a spinster. What man would look at her and want her for his wife?

Shaking her head, Minnie knew she had lost her chance for love and happiness. Rachel still had a chance and Minnie would not deny her for the world – but what would she do without her?

The door of the apartment opened and Minnie looked up in expectation of Rachel's arrival, but it was Maggie. She came in looking pink-cheeked and full of life and it made Minnie smile.

'Did you have a good evening, Maggie dear?'

'Yes, I enjoyed it – and, do you know, Marion Kaye turned up at the classes this evening!'

'You weren't sure if she would come, were you?'

'She thought it might not be possible, but she came – and she was so good at everything. Mrs James said she is a born nurse.' Maggie went through to the kitchen to put the kettle on. 'Becky Stockbridge came as well. Marion and I made sure she got her bus home safely. Becky couldn't do the chest compression properly, but she soon got the hang of bandaging...' her voice drifted away as she went into the bedroom, returning just as Minnie was wiping away a foolish tear. 'Is something wrong, Minnie dearest?'

'Oh no, nothing at all, dear,' Minnie lied, though the mention of Jonathan's daughter had made her want to cry – that girl might have been hers! Maggie's excited chatter had made the emotion well up in her and that was so foolish! 'Just a bit of a headache that's all. I'm so glad you all enjoyed yourselves...'

'Why don't you come next week?' Maggie said suddenly. 'To the first-aid classes – we all ought to learn, just in case. You could come to the women's meeting too, if you'd like. Beth can't get away much these days and if Rachel is busy, I'd like company walking home – that's if you'd like to...?'

'What a lovely girl you are,' Minnie said, cheering up instantly. 'Yes, I should like it very much. Rachel did say I should join, but Mildred would not have approved...'

'We don't join the more militant groups,' Maggie said and smiled. 'We march wearing our sashes and carry banners, but we don't smash windows or blow things up.'

'I don't think I could,' Minnie said faintly, but the girl's enthusiasm made her smile and then the door opened and Rachel walked in. She looked happy but bemused and Minnie knew even before she took her gloves off that she had important news.

'Oh Rachel,' Maggie cried as she spotted the gorgeous sapphire and diamond cluster ring. She hugged her, whirling her round in a circle. 'That is fabulous – and it matches your dress so well.'

'It is a beautiful ring, dearest, Rachel,' Minnie said. 'I'm so happy for you, and you look beautiful.'

'William says I should wear blue more often,' Rachel smiled, still looking as if she wasn't quite sure what she'd done. 'He says I've made him the happiest of men.'

'I hope that he deserves you,' Minnie said and went to kiss her cheek and admire the ring in more detail. It was expensive and looked gorgeous on Rachel's hand. 'When shall you be married, Rachel dear?'

'William would like it to be soon,' she replied. 'I told him I need at least three months.' She smiled at Minnie and Maggie. 'I have no intention of leaving you two in the lurch. I shall ask around and find someone to share the flat with you.'

'I think Janice Browning would share with me if I want,' Maggie said. 'I don't know if there's anyone you could bear to share with, Minnie?'

'I haven't thought of it' Minnie swallowed hard. 'I could pay a little extra to keep my own room perhaps; I do have a few savings...'

'I'll ask around before we decide,' Rachel said decisively. 'Don't say anything to Miss Browning yet, Maggie. I might find someone more suitable.'

'I'd rather have someone like you,' Maggie said, 'but I don't grudge you your happiness, Rachel dearest. I'm so very pleased for you both.'

'Yes, well, I feel very lucky,' Rachel said. 'William says he doesn't mind if I stay on at Harpers for a while, but eventually he will buy a house in his constituency and I shall play the part of a politician's wife, but not before he is promoted to be a minister, and, of course, we'll keep his flat in London because we shall be here often.'

'So, we shan't lose touch...' Minnie said, hoping her voice didn't give her longing away. It wouldn't do to make Rachel feel guilty, because she'd been so very good to her.

Rachel turned and beamed at her. 'I don't intend to lose touch with any of my friends at Harpers – you all mean far too much to me.'

Minnie's eyes filled with tears but she blinked hard. What a silly billy she was for fretting! Rachel was her true friend and she would never be alone while she had friends like Rachel and Maggie.

11

'Ah, Miss Gibbs,' Mr Stockbridge said as he approached Maggie that Friday morning. 'I wondered if you would like to come to lunch with Becky and myself on Sunday. I have to leave afterwards to visit someone I've been neglecting and I don't want my Becky brooding on her own...'

'I should love to, sir,' Maggie said, 'but I had promised Minnie that I would have lunch with her...' She hesitated, then, 'I expect you've heard that Mrs Craven is engaged to be married?' He nodded. 'She is going out with her fiancé and that would leave Minnie alone...'

'Then you must bring her too,' he said and smiled as if it were settled. 'I know Miss Minnie. She does excellent work in our dress repairs and alterations – and I've been meaning to ask her about making a special dress for Becky.' He put a finger to his lips. 'I'm giving a party for my daughter later this summer when she is eighteen and I want her to have a very special gown...'

'Minnie would love to do it for her – and I can get her measurements easily,' Maggie said, feeling excited for her friend. 'Becky is very lucky to have you as her father, sir.'

'I'm the lucky one,' he said and gave her a look of sympathy. 'You must miss your own family, Miss Gibbs.'

'I do, sir...' She caught back the sigh. 'Especially my father – he spoiled me just like you do Becky.'

'I dare say he believed you worth it.' Mr Stockbridge checked his watch. 'Now, don't forget to ask Miss Minnie. We shall expect you at twelve-thirty prompt.'

Maggie hid her smile as she walked away. Mr Stockbridge was kind and generous, especially to his daughter, but he did expect his orders to be carried out. It was not so much an invitation to lunch as an order, but Maggie didn't mind. Mr Stockbridge's house was a bit like Beth's aunt's had been before her unfortunate marriage, with spacious rooms and electricity and a bathroom, even though it was an end of terrace. It had a small garden, which was mainly flagstones interspersed with flower beds, many self-seeded and roses. Mr Stockbridge wasn't a brilliant gardener, but he tended his roses and they flowered well into the autumn, though, to give him his due, he didn't have much time. His life was divided between Harpers and the daughter he adored and he had little time for anything more.

It was busy in the department all day. Maggie sold six silk scarves and five pairs of leather gloves, all to different customers. She noticed that her supervisor had sold several pieces of jewellery and when there was a quiet moment, she went to look at the display case.

'I love those lapis lazuli pieces,' she said. 'Becky likes jewellery and I know she would adore that pendent, but I couldn't afford it even if I save from now until her birthday...'

'They are rather expensive,' Mrs Burrows said and smiled.

'You need to get someone to share with you... perhaps her father...'

Maggie shook her head. 'He is getting her something special, but it is a secret. I can't tell anyone.'

'Becky would not expect you to buy her anything like that,' Mrs Burrows said. 'Unless you combined a birthday and Christmas present...'

'Yes, perhaps I could.' Maggie looked thoughtful. 'Mr Stockbridge invited me and Minnie to lunch on Sunday. He doesn't want Becky to be on her own, because he has to visit someone later.'

'Well, that will be nice for you both – I'm sure Minnie will enjoy it. You told me the house is very nice...'

'A bit like your aunt's was...' Maggie said and then blushed. 'Sorry, I shouldn't have mentioned her.' She was anxious in case she'd upset her friend because of the terrible tragedy of Aunt Helen's death, but Mrs Burrows shook her head.

'Yes, you should. Aunt Helen ought to be remembered. She should never have married that rogue,' Mrs Burrows looked sad. 'Who could have known what a trickster he was?'

Maggie hesitated, then, 'Will you go to his trial – that awful man's...?'

'No, I shan't attend Gerald's trial,' Mrs Burrows told her, her eyes dark with remembered grief. 'Both Fred and Jack said it was a bad idea – but Fred is going to pop into court and listen to him being charged and he'll go back for the verdict – but Harold says he'll hang...'

Both girls shivered at the awful thought, then Maggie nodded. 'He deserves it. He is an evil man and the law is right, he should be punished harshly.'

'Yes...' Maggie saw sadness replace the repulsion in her friend's eyes.

However, Mrs Burrows saw some customers entering the

department then and it was back to business. 'Return to your counter, Miss Gibbs – Miss Kaye won't cope alone,' Mrs Burrows said, becoming the efficient supervisor once more.

Maggie went back to the scarves and gloves. Marion Kaye had started to serve a gentleman with a pair of grey leather gloves for his girlfriend, but Maggie was soon showing silk scarves of all hues to a fussy lady who didn't know what she wanted. When she at last decided on the first scarf Maggie had shown her, paid and departed, it was time for her break.

'You and Miss Kaye can go together today,' Mrs Burrows said. 'Miss Browning and I will hold the fort until you return.'

Maggie frowned because it wasn't often they were allowed to take a break together.

'I think Mrs Burrows is going to give Miss Browning a telling-off,' Marion said. 'She was rude to a customer who couldn't make up her mind over a hat this morning. I know Mrs Burrows heard what she said, but I don't think Janice knows...'

'What did she say?' Maggie was shocked, because you were never rude to your customer no matter what.

'She said she had other customers to attend to and it was plain to see that the only hat that suited the customer was the black one. She went off and didn't buy anything...'

'No!' Now Maggie was horrified. 'How could Janice? No one ever speaks like that to a customer.' She didn't truly like Janice Browning, though she tried not to let it show, but there was something about her that seemed a little secretive, a look in her eyes as if she were laughing at them all.

'She did – I think she's in a bad mood, something to do with her family,' Marion said. 'She lives with her grandmother, because her mother went off with a man three years ago and her father is on the ships.'

'Did she tell you that? She never speaks of her family to me.'

'It was after I was away and she sympathised with me for

having to look after my sister, said she'd had a rotten home life too...'

Maggie nodded, feeling sympathy for Janice. Living with her grandmother, who was probably old-fashioned, couldn't be much fun – especially as her mother had run off with a man who wasn't her husband. 'That's rotten luck for her – but she can't take her distress out on the customers.'

'No, she can't and that is what Mrs Burrows will tell her,' Marion said and sighed. 'It isn't easy when things are wrong at home, Maggie – but once you're at work you're a Harpers' girl and you can't let the side down.'

'You're so right,' Maggie said. 'I wish you could come and stay with us, Marion, be my flatmate when Mrs Craven leaves, but I know you can't.'

'I wish...' Marion looked wistful. 'I'll never be able to do that – not until Milly is grown up and all the boys are at work. Kathy could stay home once she's finished school, but it wouldn't be fair to her.'

'Is your mother not getting better?'

Marion shook her head. 'Sometimes, I think the problem is in her mind, Maggie. She isn't coughing now and the fever cleared up a couple of weeks ago, but she's no better in herself. If she comes down, she does hardly anything and then goes back to bed...'

'I'm really sorry. Is there nothing anyone can do to help?'

'In some ways, it would be better if Dad came home for good and took charge of things – but I know he would say I had to stay home to care for her and Milly. At least this way I get some time here and a bit of money of my own.' And, Marion knew, her father's temper made life unhappy for them all. They needed his wages but perhaps it was better that he stayed away.

Maggie knew that her friend's small wage mostly went on food for her family, but she got a shilling or two to spend when there was a bonus. Because the more valuable items attracted more bonuses, Mrs Burrows had decreed that if anyone on the department earned a bonus it was split between all the girls equally. It made the system fairer, because, otherwise, those selling small-value items would not stand a chance of earning extra. Janice had pulled a face over that, declaring it unfair, but she'd taken her share when Maggie had earned the five shillings on three occasions and she hadn't said no when Mrs Burrows had shared her own bonus. It was usually the jewellery counter that earned the most bonuses and that was why Mrs Burrows had decided on the share system.

'It wouldn't be fair to the rest of you if I took it all,' she'd said. 'So, we are going to share it out once a month. I shall take charge of the bonuses and then it will be split equally between the four of us.'

Janice had looked sulky, but as yet she hadn't earned a bonus herself and so she'd stopped calling it unfair. Maggie had wondered why the hat department wasn't selling as much as it had when Beth had been on that counter, but now she thought she knew. Janice tucked a wisp of reddish-brown hair behind her ear, giving Maggie an odd look. She had a sulky way with her and Maggie thought she might be a little sly. She made up to Mrs Harper whenever she entered the department, making sure that she looked busy, but Mrs Burrows had told Marion to rearrange the displays of hats on more than one occasion because Janice had neglected to match the colours properly. She just grabbed whatever came next instead of picking them thoughtfully.

* * *

When they returned to the department after their lunch, Janice was serving a customer with scarves. She sold one, packed it and took the money and then glared at Maggie as she returned to her counter.

'She came back for that green one with the tassels,' she said grudgingly. 'I haven't crossed it out – because you're back so you can do it.'

Maggie nodded and went to her receipts book as Janice left for her break. She noticed that Janice had sold two other scarves but neither of them had been crossed off in the stock list. Frowning, she drew a neat line through them.

'Is something wrong, Miss Gibbs?' Mrs Burrows asked.

'No, it's all right,' Maggie said. 'I'm just checking on what has been sold...'

'Yes, I see.' Mrs Burrows nodded. 'I know three scarves were sold – even though I was busy on my own counter.'

Maggie bit her lip. 'Is – is Miss Browning in trouble?'

Mrs Burrows hesitated, then, 'She has been warned, Miss Gibbs. I dare say you know why and I have nothing more to say.'

'Yes, Mrs Burrows.'

Maggie decided to check through her sales book and her stock. Nothing else was missing, but she would keep an eye on Janice Browning in future. If she hadn't spotted the discrepancy, she could have been blamed for stock going astray. Had Janice done that deliberately, hoping to get her into trouble? The girl could be friendly when she chose, but she was sulky and sly and Maggie didn't quite trust her. She wondered whether she should speak to Marion or Mrs Burrows, but didn't like telling tales about her colleagues. However, in Maggie's opinion she wasn't to be trusted...

* * *

Minnie returned to her room after taking half an hour for lunch. She had a special order she wanted to get on with so had returned earlier than she needed. As she entered the sewing room, the smell of flowers made her look for the source and she was surprised to see a tiny bunch of lily of the valley and violets in a little glass vase on her table.

'Oh, how lovely,' she said involuntarily and went to pick it up and smell the delicate perfume. Her favourite flowers were roses, of course, but as yet they were only in tight buds, but next to them, she loved these lily of the valley and violets.

Who could have brought her such a gift? Minnie tried to think but couldn't imagine who would do such a thing. Rachel was a good friend, but it wasn't the sort of thing she would do, though she would mention them to her friend that evening just to make sure – but if it wasn't her, who else could it be? It was a lovely surprise and romantic in a way… but Minnie didn't think she had any admirers. Unless… A flush swept up her cheeks. Surely it couldn't be? And yet Jonathan Stockbridge was possibly the only person in the world who knew about her love of these flowers…

12

Ma hadn't touched a thing all day, though she'd been down to make herself a cup of tea and it looked like the last piece of cake Marion had made the previous Sunday had gone, but the loaf and nutritious cheese were untouched. It was almost as if her mother was willing herself to die...

Sighing, Marion washed all the dishes that her brothers had left that morning after she'd departed for her work at Harpers and then started peeling potatoes, carrots and slicing onions. She'd bought two shillings' worth of sausages and Mr Barlow had slipped an extra one on for her after removing them from the scales, giving her a wink behind his employer's back. It meant that Robbie and Dickon could have two, while she, Kathy and Milly had one – because Marion knew that if she gave one to her mother, it would be wasted.

Another treat would be the sweet piccalilli that Kathy had made at cookery classes at school. It was absolutely delicious and the jar was already half eaten, but now that Kathy knew how to make it, she would do so as often as they could afford the ingredients.

Once the vegetables were gently boiling on the range, Marion went upstairs to see if her mother needed anything. She was lying back with her eyes shut and didn't speak until Marion asked if she wanted some tea and toast.

'I have some honey – or an egg I could poach or scramble...'

'Toast and a little honey please,' Mrs Kaye mumbled. 'I'm not really hungry, but I suppose I must....'

'Only one slice, Ma?' Marion said, looking at her anxiously, because some days she seemed as if she'd lost the will to live. 'You're not sick, are you?'

'Just sick of life...' came the answer.

'Oh, Ma, won't you at least try – for Milly's sake?'

Her mother sighed. 'Mrs Jackson took her for a walk and I think she's still there...'

'Yes, I know,' Marion said. 'She waved to me from their garden when I came home – she's playing football with one of the lads.'

Milly was playing with Reggie. He sometimes got home earlier than Marion, because she had to shop after she left Harpers and he'd obviously decided to play with Milly until Kathy and the boys came home. Dickon was with them and they would all be in for their tea soon enough.

'Sorry, I'm late,' Kathy said, bursting into the kitchen as Marion was spreading honey on her mother's toast. 'Mrs Bright asked me to have tea with Jilly as it was her birthday and she showed me her presents – and gave me a huge slice of cake. There's enough for all of us...' She pulled a face. 'Jilly's mother made her a new dress and her elder brother bought her a silver locket and chain.'

'She is a lucky girl,' Marion said. 'Don't envy her, Kathy. I'll make you a new dress as soon as I can manage it.' Her wage at Harpers was small, but she had her share of the bonus and she might earn more soon if she did well at work.

'I know – and I don't mind. I only went because Jilly asked me to tea and it makes more for the others if I've had mine...' she said generously, as thoughtful as always.

'That was kind of Mrs Bright,' Marion said. 'Did you have a nice tea?'

'We had salmon and cucumber sandwiches with the crusts cut off, sausage rolls, strawberry jelly with tinned peaches and birthday cake.'

'Goodness me!' Marion said. 'You were treated. I didn't realise it was such a splendid tea.'

'Jilly's birthday was on Sunday, but her mother said she could bring her best friend to tea today and she chose me...'

'Lucky you,' Marion said. 'You won't want any sausages then this evening?'

'I'm full up.'

'I'll have Kathy's share,' Dickon offered, coming in with Milly in his wake. 'I'm starving...'

'You always are – you can share it with Robbie or take it cold in a sandwich tomorrow.'

'Shall I take Ma's toast up?' Kathy said as Marion went to put the sausages in the frying pan.

'Yes, please,' Marion replied over her shoulder. 'I've got the kettle on, but you can set the table when you get back...'

Marion concentrated on frying the sausages, which were brown and sizzling when Robbie came in and hung his jacket and rucksack on the back of the door. As he opened the back door, Reggie's dog poked his nose in, wagging his tail excitedly.

'Watch out he doesn't grab the sausages!' Marion yelled and Robbie shooed the dog away. It looked reproachfully at Marion, as if she'd somehow let it down, but she wasn't tempted to feed it. Reggie fed the dog himself and it was just drawn by the tempting smell.

'That smells good, Sis, no wonder that dog was wagging its tail,' he said and grinned at her. 'I've just seen Reggie next door – you do know he's crackers about yer, don't yer?' Robbie looked pleased with life. 'Reggie has got two tickets for the footie this weekend – Chelsea is playing and he's taking me with him. I reckon he thinks it's the way to yer 'eart – spoilin' me to get to you...'

'Robbie, don't talk daft!' Marion felt her cheeks burning. 'He isn't – he's just friendly with us all.'

'Oh yeah, well that's why he gets that soppy look on his face when he talks about you,' Robbie said. 'He asked me if I thought you would go to the church social with him on Saturday night...'

'No, of course not,' Marion said hastily. 'I never heard anything so silly... besides, I shall take Kathy and Dickon, and Milly can come too if Ma isn't well enough to look after her.'

The social at St Peter's was a family occasion. Mothers, fathers, grandmothers, brothers, sisters and young children were all welcome and the entertainment was a mixture of dancing to a quartet hired for the occasion, tombola draws, whist drives and lots of people just sitting about eating rolls of cheese or salad and drinking tea or range squash. Invariably, the older men disappeared during the evening and popped into the nearest pub for a beer, before returning in time to escort their family home. Only the young men who were courting stayed all evening to dance with the girl of their choice.

'What about me?' Robbie asked. 'Why am I left out?'

'I didn't think you wanted to come,' Marion challenged. 'Last time, you said it was for sissies and wouldn't go with us...'

'Well, this time I shall – and I'll help pay for the tickets.' His grin grew broader. 'I got a pay rise this week, an extra five bob! What do yer think of that then?'

'Oh, Robbie, that's wonderful,' Marion said. 'You must keep it for whatever you want. You already give me two thirds of what you earn – more when it's rent day.'

'I'll keep an extra three bob fer meself and give yer the two,' Robbie offered. 'I know how hard yer work, Marion, and they don't pay yer much.'

'I'll get a rise in the summer,' Marion said and smiled at him. 'Mrs Burrows says we'll all get five shillings each bonus at the end of this month – unless we earn more.'

'You should buy yerself somethin',' Robbie said. 'Get a bit of material from the market and ask Mrs Jackson to help yer make a new dress – she's got a sewing machine that works...'

Their mother's machine had jammed years ago and no one had repaired it. Mr Kaye claimed he had no time and it would be too expensive to take it to a shop, so any mending or making had to be done by hand.

'She might let me borrow hers,' Marion said. 'I don't need many clothes, because I wear my uniform for work – but I should like a new dress for Sunday best.'

'You ask her,' Robbie said and winked. 'I'll bet she'll offer to help you out.'

'Well, I might,' Marion said, feeling pleased, because Robbie's pay rise would make a big difference. She could save the extra two shillings he gave her to use for emergencies. It would be there to help with the rent or any unforeseen bill they had to meet.

* * *

Marion popped next door after she'd finished ironing her brothers' shirts and sorting the dirty washing to soak in the copper. Mrs Jackson opened the door herself with a big smile. Reggie's dog had decided to forgive her for not giving him a sausage and came bounding over, rubbing himself round her legs.

'Come in, love,' Mrs Jackson said. 'That stupid hound of

Reggie's seems to have taken to you. I've just made some cocoa; do you fancy a cup?'

'I'll be making ours when I get back,' Marion said but followed her into the kitchen, where Paula and Reggie were seated at the table, playing a game of cards and laughing at each other.

'Here, Daftie,' Reggie said and his dog settled at his side. 'I hope he didn't bother you, Marion?'

'No, of course not.' She blushed as he grinned at her, recalling her brother's remarks.

'Sit down then, Marion,' her friendly neighbour said and pushed a plate of biscuits in front of her. 'I made those ginger ones especially for Reggie, they're his favourite.'

Marion took one and bit a small piece. It was crumbly and delicious and she ate it all. 'You are a very good cook, Mrs Jackson.'

'I've got all day to do it,' she said cheerfully. 'My men see I don't have to go out to work.'

Marion nodded, because Mrs Jackson was lucky. All four of the Jackson men worked hard and none of them wasted their wages in the pub; a couple of drinks on a Friday night and they were home to tip their money up on the table.

'I wanted to make myself a new dress for Sundays,' Marion said. 'If I bought some material on the market, would you let me make it on your machine please?'

'Of course, I will.' Mrs Jackson beamed at her. 'You bring it round and I'll help you cut the pattern and pin it on you to fit and then you can use the machine to sew it.'

'It's ever so good of you,' Marion said shyly. 'Ma has a treadle machine, but it doesn't work.'

'Reggie...' Mrs Jackson was about to say something, but a flash of the eyes from her son stopped her. 'Fetch me some wood in, there's a good lad.'

Reggie got up obediently and went to fetch wood for the fire. 'One of my lot could probably fix your mother's machine,' Mrs Jackson said after he'd gone, 'but you bring your material round and I'll help you to make your frock look good. I worked up the dress factory for a couple of years before I married. I've done quite a few jobs in my time, afore we were better off like.' She smiled at her. 'You've got a lovely job, Marion love. I've looked in the ground floor, but it's all too expensive for me...'

'And me,' Marion sighed. 'It's nice touching the things though, but I couldn't buy anything.'

'You don't need to – a bit of material and the right knowledge and you'll have a dress as smart as they sell.'

'Someone told me you had some experience of dressmaking,' Marion said. 'I made Kathy a dress for her birthday, but it took me ages to get it right – if you helped, I could probably make her another one as well as mine.'

Reggie returned with a load of wood, which he placed next to a bucket already filled with kindling. He went to the sink to wash his hands, and then, without turning his head, 'I was wondering if you were goin' to the social, Miss Marion?'

'Yes, I'm taking them all,' Marion said but didn't look at him. 'Ma won't come, but we'll all go – it is a good night out for everyone and it helps the church funds...'

'I wondered if you might come with me,' Reggie said and turned to face her.

Marion's breath caught in her throat and she hesitated, but then something in his look made her smile.

'I won't come with you, Mr Jackson, because I'll be looking after my younger sisters – but if you ask me to dance, I should like that...' She blushed furiously, surprised at her own boldness, but his grin told her that he liked it.

'Right then,' he said. 'It's a promise – you heard her, Ma,

Paula, she's promised to dance with me.' His eyes teased her. 'It's a solemn promise, you can't go back on it on pain of death.'

'Stop teasing her, Reggie,' his mother said. 'You can walk Marion to her door; make sure she gets back safe.'

Marion stopped herself protesting that she didn't need an escort to get next door. It wasn't even dark out and she knew her neighbours too well to fear an attack, but his mother had sent him to give him a chance to talk to her.

Her skin felt hot and prickly as Reggie followed her out of the door. She swallowed because her throat was dry and she didn't know what to say to him. He didn't seem to have much to say either, but when she reached her door, he touched her arm.

'I'd like to take you out without your family sometimes, Marion,' he said. 'I know you've got things to do in the house – but we could go for a walk and tea somewhere on a Sunday afternoon...'

'Yes, we could,' Marion smiled, feeling a spurt of excitement. He looked so nervous and that quelled her fear. Reggie was so big and strong and yet there was gentleness in him. She'd seen that when he was playing football with her little sister. 'I think I should like that, Mr Jackson – but you know my family comes first. I have to look after them.'

'Aye, I know,' he said and smiled. His gaze seemed to caress her. 'But who looks after you, Marion? One day you will need someone to love and care for you.'

He winked at her and walked away, leaving Marion's heart pounding. She went into the kitchen, ignoring the expectant looks from Robbie.

'Well,' he said as she poured the cocoa into mugs minutes later. 'Did he ask you?'

'Yes, but I told him I was going with my family. Milly and Kathy are looking forward to it.'

'And?' Robbie persisted. 'We saw him walk you back, Marion.'

'I told him I would dance with him if he asked...' she said, nursing the secret of her Sunday walks to herself for the moment. It was a little too precious to share with her teasing brother just yet. 'Drink your cocoa, Robbie. I'm going to take Ma's up and then I need to get ready for the morning. I mustn't be late or I could lose my job.' Working at Harpers meant so much to her, but her mother wouldn't understand that – all she thought was that Marion might get more working in a factory, but that would be like being in hell after the glory that was Harpers' Emporium.

13

Minnie looked at herself in the mirror that Sunday morning, checking that her hair was neat and her dress looked clean and smart. Going to lunch with Jonathan and his daughter was a big thing for her and she'd almost said no, but then something had made her change her mind. After all, what harm could it do? She was going as Maggie's friend and she desperately wanted to meet Becky, Jonathan's daughter.

'Are you ready, Minnie?' Maggie asked and she turned for inspection. 'Oh, you do look lovely – blue suits you well…'

It was the first time Minnie had worn her favourite bluebell-coloured dress since Mildred died. Strictly speaking, she ought still to be in mourning for her sister, but Mildred had told her to be happy and she wore black at work all the time; it felt good to be wearing a pretty dress again.

Rachel looked at her as they went into the sitting room and smiled. 'That dress suits you, Minnie. You should hurry, both of you, you don't want to be late – and don't worry about me. I shall be with William all day.'

The two companions kissed her and told her to have a lovely

time with her fiancé and then went out of the house together, clutching the fruit cake they'd made between them as a gift for their hosts. Chattering and laughing, they caught the bus that would take them to Jonathan's house. His home was out towards Clerkenwell, but in a nicer area, just before the wholesale jewellery centre with all its little workshops, so they got off and walked to the row of terraced houses. Several trees were growing in a green space opposite and Minnie thought what a pleasant street it was, very similar to the one she and Mildred had grown up in before her father moved into the big house. It was after the move that Papa had started speculating and investing in shares and it was the shares that had lost him much of his money, leaving his daughters struggling to manage on their income after his death.

'Welcome to our home,' Jonathan was at the door with his daughter, a huge smile of welcome on his face. It made Minnie's heart catch and she felt she was back when they'd first met and fell in love and he'd smiled at her then in just that way. 'We've been looking forward to you coming – and this is my daughter Becky. Becky, my love, I've told you about Miss Minnie – she works in the alterations department at Harpers...'

'A little offering,' Minnie presented the cake. 'We made it together.'

'Minnie made it, I just put it in the oven,' Maggie said and laughed as Minnie blushed.

'Lunch won't be long,' Becky said and offered her hand. Impulsively, Minnie leaned forward and kissed her cheek. Becky smiled, looking surprised but pleased. 'Do come in both of you and take off your coats and hats. The food is almost ready.' She looked at her father. 'I've got something I want to show Maggie – why don't you take Miss Minnie into the garden and show her the roses? Papa is very fond of his roses, Miss Minnie.'

'Oh yes, I love them too...' Minnie blushed as she remembered. He'd proposed to her as they admired her father's roses, just before the illness that killed poor Papa...

'Yes, do come and see them,' he said and smiled at her in the way she remembered from all those years ago. 'These young things have secrets – and we have a few minutes before dinner is served. I have some lovely red roses, still in tight bud at the moment, but gorgeous in May and June. I seem to recall your favourite was always the damask roses.'

Minnie's heart caught as he looked at her. Did he truly remember after all these years that it was the really old-fashioned roses that she loved more than anything?

'Oh yes,' she said and blushed. 'Papa had a beautiful pale pink one and it smelled wonderful. Not all roses smell as good as those did.'

'Mine are all perfumed,' he said. 'I remember you telling me that to be perfect roses should smell sweet...'

He'd remembered that too! Minnie's heart pounded as she followed him into the small garden. There were stocks and other sweet-smelling flowers in the borders, but the roses were growing well and would be a riot of colour and perfume soon and almost all of them were damask roses. It was almost as if he made his garden for her... She felt tears sting her eyes, but she blinked them away quickly. It was foolish to let her imagination run away with her, but when she allowed herself to look at him, she could see that he was remembering too.

'Do you remember, Minnie?' he said and her throat swelled with emotion. 'Do you recall where we were when I asked you to marry me and you said yes?'

Minnie nodded wordlessly, because they were standing by the very rose; she knew it would be a full-blown pink rose that smelled wonderful once the tight bud had opened. 'Yes, of course I do, Jonathan...'

'You promised to wed me and then changed your mind...' He looked at her sadly. 'You broke my heart the day you told me you couldn't ever marry me...'

'You knew why,' she said and her voice broke. 'You understood that Mildred couldn't manage without me...'

'Yes, I understood. I knew you were too sweet and generous, too loyal to desert your sister, and she didn't like me enough to live with us, but I never stopped loving you, Minnie. I married because I was lonely and Becky's mother was a nice girl – but I always loved you, and, if I'm honest with myself, I believe I still do...'

'Oh, Jonathan...' she whispered. 'How could you? After all this time?' How could he still love her as she was now? She'd been a young girl when they parted, in the first flush of her beauty, and the years had stolen her prettiness, replacing it with an older, sadder face and a fuller, less ethereal figure.

'Yet I do...' His smile swept her back, through the years of regret and selfless devotion to her sister to a sunlit day and a young man who had poured out his heart to her. Now, here he was, just the same to her as he had been on that fateful morning and she felt giddy with an emotion she could hardly credit but must be happiness.

'I don't know what to say...'

'Is it too late?' he asked, the croak of emotion in his voice. 'Mildred isn't there between us now – but perhaps you've forgotten me?'

'No, how could I?' Minnie whispered faintly. 'I never stopped loving you...'

'Minnie...' His hand was reaching for hers when a voice from the door behind them stopped him.

'Poppa – lunch is ready...'

'Later...' he said urgently to Minnie. 'I have to go out after lunch, but I'll be back for tea – and I'll walk you home, if you will let me. The girls may want to go off by themselves for a while.'

'Yes,' Minnie said and blinked hard. 'We'll talk later, but only if it doesn't upset your dear little girl...'

Jonathan smiled and gestured for her to go in and she did so, greeted by Becky, who took her hand and led her through to the dining room. She was chattering away with Maggie and telling her what a nice lunch they were going to have, which gave Minnie time to recover herself.

Jonathan had never stopped loving her, but she wasn't sure what that meant. He had a grown-up daughter and Becky might object to her father courting a woman he'd known before her mother. Minnie smiled at her nervously. She could never take her own happiness at the expense of someone else's, yet she knew that it was meant to be. Fate had decreed they should meet again and when they walked home later, she would tell Jonathan how much she wanted to be his wife – providing Becky was happy with the idea.

'I can't tell you how much it means to me to have found you again,' Jonathan said as he walked her home that evening. 'I know you will think it is far too soon to think of anything more than friendship – but I am going to say this, my dearest Minnie. I lost you once and I couldn't live with myself if I just let you drift away from me. I want us to be together for the rest of our lives...'

'Jonathan...' Minnie gasped, not quite sure what he was saying to her. 'Do you mean...?'

'I asked you to marry me years ago and I lost you. I understand that you felt you needed to support your sister, dearest, but I want you to know that my love never died and, as far as I am concerned, you are still the lady I wish to have as my wife.'

'So many years...' Minnie said, feeling as if a wind had swept her off her feet. 'I don't know... I'm not the same as I was and you have a daughter to consider.'

'I love Becky very much, but I do not see her as an obstacle – unless you do?'

'Oh no...' Minnie felt almost giddy with excitement, nerves and a feeling that she must be dreaming. 'I know we've only just met but already I love her as if she were my own.'

'I know she will love you, too so there is nothing to stop us marrying. If we hesitate now, we could spend the rest of our lives regretting it, dearest. I know it seems too soon, but I don't want to waste another moment of our lives...' Jonathan took her hand and kissed it. 'You are as beautiful now as the day I first met you, Minnie Lumley, and I know my heart – but I shall give you a little time to know yours...'

Minnie smiled at him shyly. She believed she knew her heart and it was telling her to seize this chance with both hands and never let go. 'I think I might like to be your wife one day,' she said shyly. 'But I do need a little time to catch my breath, Jonathan. It has all been rather sudden...'

'You must have known who left the flowers in your sewing room at Harpers?'

'Well, I did think...' She blushed as she recalled holding the vase of Lily of the Valley in her hands and inhaling its fragrance. 'I couldn't believe it was happening to me, Jonathan. I had given up all hope of love, you see.'

His smile lit up his face, which was as dear to her as it had always been. 'Know that you are much loved, Minnie, and always will be, whatever your answer.'

'Oh, Jonathan, my very dear friend...' Minnie smiled tremulously. In her heart, she knew he was right to speak out now, even though so many years had passed. They had wasted half their lives; they could not afford to waste any more. 'I shall give you my answer very soon, I promise...'

'Then I am content,' he said, pressing a kiss on her hand.

She sighed with content because he was so old-fashioned and courteous and it was exactly what she liked and needed.

14

Rachel noticed that Minnie was quiet and thoughtful that evening. She'd returned home from her lunch at Mr Stockbridge's home with a large bunch of wonderful flowers picked from his garden. The scent of narcissus permeated the apartment and lasted for the next few days, as did Minnie's odd mood. She listened to what the others were saying, complimented Maggie on a new dress and asked Rachel about her new home and what she planned to do, and yet, whenever they were occupied elsewhere, the thoughtful, slightly sad look came back to her eyes.

Was she worrying about what would happen when Rachel married? Rachel had racked her brains to think who might share the flat with Maggie and Minnie when she left, but none of the girls looking for a room seemed right. It made her feel guilty that she would be letting her friends down, but she really wouldn't recommend that they ask Miss Browning.

She couldn't help thinking about what the head of the men's department had told her. He seemed to think Janice Browning had been in his department when the silk tie went missing, but he hadn't seen her take it – and Rachel did not feel justified in going to Sally Harper unless she had proof. No one else had reported anything missing to her, so perhaps it was just an isolated incident and a coincidence that Janice happened to be in the department... and yet there was something about that girl...

Perhaps Rachel was being unfair, but she didn't quite trust Janice. She felt instinctively that the girl wasn't quite what she pretended to be. Beth had told her that when Sally fainted, she'd particularly requested they keep her secret and neither Beth, nor Maggie, nor Marion had mentioned it. Although Rachel had felt she ought to tell Sally's husband for her own good, she didn't approve of Janice running behind Sally's back to her. There was something sly about it somehow and Sally would have hated it that the girl had discussed her personal business with anyone.

Rachel didn't like to see her friend unhappy, though Minnie didn't seem to be unhappy, just thoughtful and a little wistful. It was obvious that she had secrets and unless she chose to confide them, Rachel did not feel able to ask what was wrong. No doubt it was just a little unease about what would happen after Rachel married.

She put all thoughts of her friends from her mind and wondered about the visit to William's apartment, which she'd arranged for the following week. It would be their home once they were married and William was concerned that she should change anything she needed to her own taste. It would be nice having her own home again, though she thought she would miss her friends sometimes and she didn't really know William well yet.

* * *

Minnie saw the hot house roses in her room when she arrived at work on Monday morning and knew immediately that Jonathan had placed them there in a little cut-glass vase for her. There were only three perfect blooms, but they must have been so expensive, because his own roses were not yet in bloom! She picked them up, smelling their sweet fragrance. Beneath the vase was a small white envelope and inside was an invitation to the theatre and dinner the following evening. His thoughtfulness touched her heart and she smiled, because Jonathan was determined to court her.

What a lovely gesture it was and she felt thrilled to know that her life was just beginning all over again. The years of lonely nights and evenings spent working just to keep a roof over Mildred and her own head were behind her and the future opened out, glorious and exciting, because suddenly she was loved and she loved. She could have a home of her own and a husband to love her, as well as a lovely daughter to make a fuss of and take out to buy clothes and to parties and tea at her favourite places.

'Oh Mildred,' she sighed. 'I do wish you'd known happiness like this, my dear. You just never understood there was so much more to life.'

* * *

'I'm meeting William for lunch today,' Rachel said to Minnie Sunday morning at breakfast. 'We're going to look at his apartment first – I hate to leave you alone all day, because I know Maggie is going out...'

'Oh no, Rachel, you mustn't worry about me,' Minnie said and smiled a little mysteriously. 'I'm going to church with a friend. We like the early morning service, so I shall leave straight after breakfast and I'm not sure when I'll be home...'

'Oh, good,' Rachel said, surprised but relieved. 'Well, have a good day, Minnie, and I'll see you this evening.'

'Thank you, my dear – and I hope you have a nice time with William.'

'I shall.'

Rachel noticed that Minnie was wearing a pretty dress and hat, but she hadn't stopped to gossip before she left the apartment and Rachel had no time to spare as William was calling for her at ten o'clock that morning.

He was at the door before Maggie had departed and she called goodbye to the girl as she went straight out so as not to keep him waiting.

'You look lovely,' he told her. 'Is that a new hat? I like it very much, Rachel.'

She smiled and nodded, because it was nice that William noticed she'd gone to some trouble to look her best for him.

'Are we going straight to your apartment now?'

'Yes...' He looked at her hesitantly. 'I hope you will like it – and you can change anything – but if you hate it, I can sell and buy something else...'

'I'm sure it will be lovely.'

Some fifteen minutes later, Rachel looked round the spacious apartment, which overlooked a garden square. It was twice the size of the one she shared with her friends at the moment and had beautiful friezes round the walls and long sash windows. At the moment, the colours were a little sombre, but all she needed to do was change the wallpaper for something lighter and less majestic and hang new curtains in a toning shade. The furniture was Sheraton, pale walnut and satinwood and beautiful.

'It is lovely,' she breathed. 'Oh, William, I had no idea it would be like this...'

'You're sure you like it? I want you to be happy, my dearest Rachel. I may not have told you how very happy you've made me?'

'Only a hundred times,' she said, teasing him.

'So, you can be happy here?'

'I only want to change some colours,' she told William, smiling up at him. 'The furniture is lovely, where did you get it?'

'It belonged to my mother and she left it to me,' he said. 'I think her mother bought it new when she was a bride because it is Regency and was no doubt expensive at the time. If you would prefer something more modern, Rachel dearest...'

She placed a finger to his lips. 'No, thank you, William, I love your apartment and I only want to change the wallpaper in our bedroom and the curtains in some rooms.'

'Then do whatever you wish,' he said and produced a key. 'I'm putting the apartment in your name, Rachel. If anything happens to me, it will save you a lot of bother...'

'Nothing will happen,' she said and lifted her head for his kiss. 'We shall be married and live happily ever after.'

'In fairy tales,' William said but laughed. 'I know you had a hard time after your first husband died, Rachel, and I don't want that for you again. I'm going to protect you and spoil you, because I'm lucky to have found you, my darling.'

'We've both known unhappiness,' she said and smiled into his eyes. 'Now we have the rest of our lives to be content and care for each other...' She hesitated, then, 'Minnie asked me if I wanted children the other day. I told her yes if it happened – and I know you said it won't matter if I can't, but...'

'Dearest one...' William touched a finger to her lips. 'It's you I love, Rachel. If God gave us a child, I should love that child, but I shall not regret marrying you if it doesn't happen. Until you came into my life, I felt so alone – and now I sing in the bath...' His eyes danced with mischief. 'I may not be able to hold a tune, but it makes me happy and I only sing when I am happy.'

'Good.' Rachel smiled and turned to survey the room. 'I think blues and greens in here instead of these muddy fawns – and damask pink in the bedroom...'

'It's time these colours were changed,' William agreed. 'Father bought the place from a retired colonel and he hadn't decorated for years. They were both ill and then he had a heart attack and Mother died suddenly. I meant to do it, but I couldn't bring myself to ...' He frowned for a moment. 'My sister wanted me to change everything after my wife died, but Mary doesn't really care much for anything but appearances and she thought this place old-fashioned.'

Rachel shook her head. William didn't talk about his family much, but his sister was Lady Martin and moved in circles way above Rachel's experience. She supposed it was the reason he hadn't asked her to meet his family before this and steeled herself for what came next.

'My sister, aunts, uncles... they can all be a bit forbidding,' William told her. 'However, there's no getting out of it, I'm afraid – we have been bidden to lunch next week.' He reached out to touch her cheek and then kissed the tip of her nose. 'I'll protect you, my love, but they keep asking to meet you and if I don't take you, it looks as if I'm ashamed of you.'

'Are you?' she asked, realising for the first time that there was a vast gap between her world and his.

'You know I'm not,' he said. 'I'm as proud as a dog with two tails – but I know how spiteful Mary and Lady Honoria can be – she's my father's sister. My mother's family were much nicer, but they're all gone.'

'I'm sorry.'

'Yes,' he said, 'so was I – but Mama and Aunt Jane both died of a lung fever, within a few months of each other, though at the time we had no idea. It was just so sudden. I thought it was the shock of my father's death – but she'd been ill for years and told no one.' His eyes darkened with pain. 'I lost my wife a few months later...'

'That was a terrible time for you...'

'Yes, it got a bit dark for a while,' William said. 'But then I visited Harpers to buy some gloves and the whole world changed for me...'

'I do love you,' Rachel said and lifted her face for his kiss. 'I shall enjoy making this into our home.'

'One day we'll get a nice house in the country,' William promised, 'but this apartment will always be yours so you can come to town and visit friends whenever you wish.'

Rachel nodded and smiled, because it was a nice thought and meant she didn't have to say goodbye to her friends when she left Harpers. In the meantime, there was the visit to William's family and that made her slightly nervous, because she knew she wouldn't be the kind of woman they would expect him to marry...

15

_____

'Isn't it beautiful here?' Minnie whispered as she and Jonathan sat together in the ancient church, attending the rector's service. It was a sixteenth-century church and the precious stained-glass windows sent a myriad of colours over the worn stone flags. In her white-gloved hands, she held the little prayer book Papa had given her for her fifteenth birthday, which she'd used every Sunday with Mildred for years, and two beautiful red roses, the very first to bloom from his garden and he'd given them to her. 'I always feel so at peace in church, don't you?'

Jonathan Stockbridge nodded and for a moment he placed his hand over hers. Then they were on their feet and singing the last hymn of the early morning service before following the small congregation outside to the April sunshine.

'Shall we walk in the park for a while?' he asked and Minnie smiled.

'Oh yes, please, just for a while. I know you have friends for lunch and dear Becky will be expecting you.'

'Why don't you come back with me?' he suggested, but she shook her head regretfully. 'I'm sure Becky would be delighted...'

'Not yet, my dearest Jonathan, not without an invitation from Becky. You must talk to her and tell her about me – ask her if she would be hurt if we were to become more than friends...'

'I'm damned if I'll lose you again,' he said. 'It broke my heart when you sent me away, Minnie. I couldn't go through that again...'

'You will not lose me,' she said and squeezed his arm gently. 'However, I should hate to make Becky feel as if I were pushing her out or trying to take her mother's place.'

'I'm sure she already loves you,' he said and his eyes shone with tears. 'How could she not? You are the most gentle, sweet and loving woman I have ever known, Minnie, and I know my daughter will want to make me happy... and it will make me happy to have you in my life permanently.'

'Then speak to her and I'll come to tea with Maggie a few times so that she gets used to me. I'll always be your friend, even if she cannot bear me to be your wife, but I will not hurt her...'

'You always think of others,' he said and kissed her hand. 'Perhaps it is why I adore you, Minnie Lumley, but whatever anyone says, you will marry me one day, because I don't think I could bear it if you didn't.'

* * *

After Jonathan had left her to keep his appointment with his daughter and the friends she'd invited to lunch, Minnie went to visit her friends at the boarding house where she'd lived for so many years with Mildred.

Her old landlady welcomed her and invited her for a cup of tea and a ham sandwich, which she accepted graciously and spent a pleasant hour reminiscing. As she left the boarding house afterwards, Minnie felt sure that she had made up her mind – and she had a quiet, warm feeling inside, as if Mildred's spirit had approved her decision. She'd felt very close to her sister in their old home and, in her mind, she'd spoken to her.

'Am I doing right, Mildred?' she'd whispered.

'Of course, you are, Minnie. You wasted enough years on me; take your happiness while you can – don't waste your life the way I did...'

Tears wetted Minnie's cheeks. Mildred had been a confirmed spinster, but perhaps there had been a lost love in her life too – one that she'd had to give up for their father, a love she had never confided to her sister. Minnie wondered if that was what had made her so bitter against men in general.

She would never know the truth now, but she felt that her sister was urging her on, telling her not to waste another moment of her life, and she knew that she would tell Jonathan very soon that she would be his wife. She had to trust and believe that Jonathan's daughter would be happy with the idea...

* * *

Rachel and Maggie had returned from their own activities when Minnie got back from her visit to her old lodging house. They were full of what they had seen and done and Minnie let them talk. She wasn't ready to tell them her news – and until she had Becky's blessing, she wouldn't be sure it was really going to happen, even though Jonathan vowed it would.

He was so impatient for her to say yes, and that made Minnie a little afraid. For so many years, he'd been just a dream to her and she'd shed so many tears in the darkness when Mildred was sleeping – but now he was there, large, masculine and very passionate. She'd been brought up to be a proper young lady and though in her dreams she'd succumbed to her lover's feverish kisses, her dreams stopped there, because she had no idea what happened in the marriage bed. No one had ever told her anything. Her mother had died when she was still a child; Papa wouldn't have dreamed of mentioning any such thing; and Mildred had never spoken of the intimacy of marriage, except once.

'Ladies do not enjoy that kind of thing,' she'd said when Minnie had asked her what she ought to expect from her husband. 'It is necessary for children, but once you have them – it is preferable if your husband finds his carnal pleasures elsewhere...'

Why had her sister said such a thing to her? Had she hoped to put her off marriage because she wanted her to remain a spinster? From hindsight, and with the maturity of years, Minnie thought it might have been the case. She'd also begun to suspect that more lay behind Mildred's bitterness than she'd ever guessed and wished they might have talked more while her sister lived.

However, Minnie had been young and careless then and the touch of Jonathan's hand had sent shivers of pleasure down her spine. She'd dreamed of her wedding night, because she loved and trusted him, but the years since had planted doubts in her mind. She'd seen unhappy marriages, where the wives were beaten and badly treated, and Mildred had complimented her on her lucky escape.

'Now you can see what I have saved you from,' she'd told her sister on more than one occasion, and despite Minnie's instinctive rejection of her claim, the memory still lingered.

Would she enjoy being a wife? Sometimes she wondered. Yet her heart still raced whenever Jonathan was near and she still liked the smell of his soap and the trace of hair pomade. He always looked and smelled clean – good enough to eat, someone had once said to her with a wink.

Minnie smiled at the memory. She did not think that particular lady shrank from the physical side of marriage.

'You look very thoughtful,' Rachel said, bringing Minnie's thoughts back to the present abruptly. 'Is something the matter?'

'Oh no, nothing at all,' Minnie said. 'Did you enjoy your day, Rachel?'

'Very much,' Rachel said. 'William's apartment is lovely. He says I can change anything I want – décor, furniture, curtains but most of it is beautiful...'

'He is generous and kind,' Minnie said. 'Is that why you decided to marry him?'

'Partly,' Rachel agreed and looked thoughtful. 'I believe I can trust him, Minnie, and that is a big thing for me. The physical attraction was there right from the start – it is something that either happens or it doesn't. I know that William will make me happy and the rest is just a bonus.'

'He must love you very much,' Minnie said and smiled. 'I'm so pleased for you, Rachel.'

'I shall make certain you and Maggie have somewhere to live,' Rachel told her. 'You mustn't worry about the future, Minnie.'

'Oh, I'm not,' Minnie assured her. 'If you will excuse me, dearest Rachel, I have some work to do – for Becky's dress. I'm doing it in my own time, so I need to work when I can.'

Minnie smiled and went to her own room to take up her sewing. Rachel was worried about her, but she couldn't tell her the news that would reassure her. No, she must make certain that Becky was happy first – and also, she did not wish to overshadow Rachel's wedding. At the moment, the whole of Harpers was buzzing over it and Minnie's own news must wait.

16

'So, when do you think the wedding will be?' Sally asked when Rachel went up to her office to tell her about her plans.

'We are thinking sometime in July or August,' Rachel said. 'I want to redecorate and buy new curtains – but I shall not be leaving Harpers for a while. William's work is in London for the time being and so we'll live in the apartment. If we have a family, then I expect we shall move to the country...'

'Yes, that is a good option if you can afford it.'

'William says it is good for his political image to have a working wife – shows he's a modern man and he's right behind the Women's Movement now, Sally. I've converted him and he intends to speak in parliament for us – but he doesn't agree with the militant wing blowing things up, and I feel the same.'

'We always did disapprove,' Sally said and smiled at her. 'Ben feels the same – and it makes sense. People listen if you repeat your message often enough, but militant action only makes them angry.'

Rachel nodded. 'Well, I must get on, Mrs Harper. I noticed

that the umbrellas and walking sticks are a little depleted. Perhaps you should mention it to Mr Stockbridge. He seems a little absent-minded at the moment. I told him that men's suits needed more stock and I don't think he heard me; he certainly didn't answer...'

'In that case, I'll take a look myself. Mr Brown does most of the ordering for the men's department and I'll check with him – but I'll speak to Mr Stockbridge about the walking sticks.'

Rachel hesitated, wondering if she should mention her suspicions about Janice Browning, but Sally started talking about some new stock and the opportunity was lost. After all, she couldn't be sure the girl was a thief and it would be awful to cast aspersions if Mr Brown had made a mistake – he hadn't even been sure of the girl's name, just that she worked in the hat and bag department.

Deciding to leave it until she had more to go on, Rachel smiled and took her leave. She saw Mr Marco leaving the lift and smiled at him.

'Good morning, Mr Marco...'

'Mrs Craven,' he said and smiled at her. 'You are looking very beautiful, if I may say so, and may I congratulate you on your engagement, though I should wish you happy and congratulate the lucky man.'

'Thank you...' She hesitated, smiled because he was not the first to congratulate her that morning, then, 'Have you finished the latest window?'

'Not until tomorrow,' he said. 'I'm working on an idea with Mrs Harper.' He smiled secretively. 'It's going to be a bit special.'

'I shall look forward to seeing it,' she said and moved on.

Leaving the lift at the next floor down, Rachel headed for the dress department, catching sight of Mr Stockbridge as he left the alterations room. He was smiling and looked a bit bemused, as if he was lost in thought. She hesitated, wondering if she should have a word about the walking sticks, but he seemed distracted, so she decided to wait and speak to him in his office later.

* * *

'It's a secret,' Marco told his employer a few minutes later when he saw him on the second floor. 'Sorry, Mr Harper, I can't tell even you – Mrs Harper would have my tongue cut out if the secret got out before we're ready.'

Ben Harper laughed. 'All right, I shan't push you, Marco, because Sally would never forgive me.' He hesitated for a moment. 'Perhaps I shouldn't ask – but is everything all right with you now?'

Marco felt the ice at his nape and for a moment he felt the bleakness of loss sweep over him. He would never forget the moment he'd learned that Julien had hung himself out of shame – the shame of loving another man instead of the girl he was expected to marry. Julien's father had scorned their love, called it vile names and made his son feel unworthy and, torn between the two, Julien had taken his life in despair. The man had destroyed his own son – how could he live with that guilt? Surely it would hang like a dark shadow over his life forever?

How did anyone get over something like that? For a time, Marco had wanted to die too. Perhaps he should have done – it might have been better than carrying this load of guilt and pain, and yet something inside him was determined to live. He wouldn't let that bastard win. Julien's father had destroyed him, but he wouldn't destroy what they had while Marco lived, because it had been good and pure and true. He would cherish his memories of Julien and not allow his father's prejudice to tarnish them through narrow-mindedness.

'I live,' he told Ben now, because he was his friend and he couldn't lie to him. 'One day I may love again, but not yet. To lose the one you love as I loved Julien shatters your heart into a thousand pieces. It doesn't go away – imagine losing your Sally and you'll know how I feel...' He drew a deep breath. 'But thank you for asking, I'm told time will heal the pain. I can only hope so.'

'I can't even contemplate losing Sally,' Ben said. 'Sorry doesn't help – but if there is anything ever...' Their eyes met for a moment, sharing their understanding and friendship and then Marco raised his head, his strength reasserting itself.

'Much appreciated.' Marco's mouth smiled even though his eyes still held the bleakness. 'I'll let you know. I don't think I could have got through without Harpers. The windows are my life and all my real friends are here, Ben. The crowd I hang out with at night are just that – it's you and your wife and Fred in the basement amongst others. They are the ones I would give my life for.'

'Don't speak of dying. I need you alive.' Ben looked at him intently. 'Sally needs you. We both love you – come and have supper with us soon, please.'

'Thank you, I shall,' Marco said and smiled properly. 'I know you are my friends, you and Sally – but I was thinking of the country...'

Ben frowned, 'You think a war is coming, too? Fred Burrows is certain of it.'

'There may be a war if the trouble in the Balkans keeps flaring up,' Marco said, grimacing. 'If it happens, I'll fight, Ben – because good friends are worth dying for if you have to...'

'And at the moment, you don't much care if you do?' Ben asked, touching the heart of it.

Marco nodded grimly. 'Let's hope it doesn't happen,' he said and then his smile returned. 'You tell Sally I refused to tell you her surprise. See you later, my friend.'

Marco walked away, knowing that Ben Harper, friend and employer, was watching him, concerned for him and anxious. Perhaps he should've kept it all inside, but you didn't lie to friends, and it was good to talk to someone who understood and didn't condemn.

17

'Look at that!' Beth said to her father-in-law as she showed him the paper she'd bought on the way to the bus stop that evening in mid-May. The newspaper boy's insistent cry had aroused her curiosity and she scanned the headlines, reading aloud, 'The police arrested fifty-seven protestors as they attempted to reach Buckingham Palace. All they wanted to do was present a "Votes for Women" petition to the King and they arrested them... it's just not fair!'

Fred nodded his agreement. 'I got an early edition, Beth. They've grabbed Emmeline Pankhurst again and she looks frail and ill – they ought to leave her alone, poor woman.'

'They say the demonstration was a thousand strong and some of them used weapons to try and break through the police cordon.' Beth felt tears sting her eyes. 'Why couldn't they just let them deliver the document? What harm could it do?'

'None, as far as I can see.' Her father-in-law patted her arm, 'I'm glad you weren't there, Beth.'

'I couldn't take time off,' Beth said. 'Sometimes I think I'm not a very good member. I only go to the meetings when it suits me and I haven't been on a march for ages...'

'Those who do run the risk of arrest and the treatment in prison is so harsh,' Fred said. 'I call it barbaric – and I wouldn't want a member of my family being treated like that.'

Beth sighed. 'I know, but I do admire the women who risk everything for the cause. I know some of them have little to lose, because they come from terrible homes and some have brutal husbands.' She frowned, because many other women had joined the cause and they were educated women from respectable backgrounds. 'I'm so lucky that I don't want to risk my job and all we have, though sometimes I feel guilty when I think of those that do.'

'You're with them in spirit,' Fred said, looking sad. 'I'm all for peaceful protests – but the militants make it worse for the rest of you.'

Beth didn't answer, feeling thoughtful. The bus had arrived and they boarded together. She tended to agree with Fred, though her heart went out to the women who had been arrested. They would be subjected to all manner of rough treatment, forced to wear prison clothes, offered foul food and when they refused to eat, force-fed with a tube up their nose. Beth understood why women who had been treated that way became hard and more determined, because it was a wicked way to treat anyone who just wanted equal rights.

Fred frowned over the paper Beth had given him. 'Have you seen this article about the new super tax the government brought in earlier this month? They've reduced the threshold from five thousand a year to three. Ten pence halfpenny on an income of a thousand and one shilling and four pence on two and a half thousand pounds – and this new super tax is up to five pence in the pound if you earn more than seven thousand pounds.'

'I don't need to worry yet then,' Beth joked. 'I'm nowhere near the minimum.'

'But Jack might be if he makes the hotel pay,' Fred said. 'Once he has that running properly, he could easily earn five thousand a year or more.'

'So, he will have to pay super tax.' Beth pulled a face. 'It doesn't seem fair, does it? He's struggling to make a profit and when he does...'

Fred shrugged. 'Could be worse, love – if those damned Serbians keep stirring up trouble, we'll have more to worry about than a bit of income tax...'

'Oh, Fred, don't,' Beth said. Her father-in-law had been muttering about a war for years and nothing had come of it. 'I'm sure the government is too worried about other things, like the Irish Home Rule bill, to want a war.'

'They may not have a choice,' Fred said darkly. 'Here's our stop, Beth. You go home and I'll nip down the pie shop and fetch us some supper to save you cooking tonight.'

'Thank you,' she said gratefully. 'It's been a busy day – and one of the girls got in a muddle with her stocktaking and I had to help her sort it out. She'd been taking hats from the reserves without marking them up in her book and it took me an hour to get it straight.'

'You should speak to the manager or Mrs Craven,' Fred said. 'If she is careless or defiant, she needs a warning...'

'I've given her two warnings myself,' Beth told him with a frown. 'She said it was the junior's fault – that she'd told Miss Kaye to put them in the stock book. Marion denied it and I tend to believe her – but if I report one, I have to report both to be fair, because one of them should have made sure the hats were recorded in the stock book as well as the sales book. It is Miss Browning's counter, but Miss Kaye often fetches new stock for her...'

'If the junior fetched new stock for you, what would you do?'

'I'd write it down myself,' Beth said firmly and nodded as her father-in-law got off the bus and gave her his hand to help her down. 'Yes, I see what you mean – it is Miss Browning's responsibility, not Marion's. I'll have to think about it...'

'Time to forget about work,' Fred said. 'You tell that son of mine to get home on time this weekend and take you somewhere nice – dancing and dinner – and he'll hear from me if he doesn't.'

Fred departed to fetch their supper as Jack would once again be working all hours, and Beth let herself into the kitchen, smiling over his last remark. The range had died down and she made it up so that they could boil a kettle for their tea. As she busied herself with setting the table, Beth's thoughts cleared. It was Janice Browning's fault and perhaps it might do her good if Mr Stockbridge gave her an official warning. Beth might speak to him when she got the chance. It could bring Janice to her senses before things went too far – and Fred was right, it was time she and Jack went out for some fun again; she shouldn't be thinking about work in her own time.

* * *

'I wanted to select some of your lapis lazuli jewellery for my special window,' Mr Marco said when he came up to the department on Tuesday morning and spoke to Beth. 'Mrs Harper has come up with a wonderful idea – and I believe you have all your stock in now?'

'Yes, I do,' Beth replied, smiling at him. Mr Marco was a favourite with many of the staff and everyone loved it when a new window was unveiled.

'I'll show you some that has just come in. Mrs Harper priced it, but I haven't put it in my stock book yet.'

She brought out a box which was filled with tissue-wrapped

items and began to reveal the lovely pendants, bracelets, broches and earrings. Most were silver, but a few were 9 carat gold. Beth spread fifty items on the velvet pad for him to see and watched as he unerringly picked the most attractive pieces. By the time he'd finished, he'd selected twenty-five of the most outstanding jewels.

'I need to list these as taken for the window,' she said and beckoned to Marion. 'Can you help me, Miss Kaye? I want you to list the stock number, description and price of each piece that Mr Marco takes with him, please. They must be listed on a paper for Mr Marco to take with him and I need a copy for my book.'

'Yes, of course, Mrs Burrows.' Marion smiled at the window dresser. 'These are lovely. I shall look forward to seeing the window, sir.'

Beth placed the pieces that were not chosen back in their box and returned them to her safe in the office. She locked it and put the key in her desk and then returned to the counter. Mr Marco had gone, taking the stock he'd chosen with him. Marion was serving a customer.

She sold a leather bag, wrapped it and dealt with the customer's change and then turned to Beth. 'Mr Marco says he will make a copy of the list and keep it in his files for reference, Mrs Burrows. I put our copy in the top drawer with the receipt book.'

'Good, well done, Miss Kaye,' Beth said. 'Could you rearrange that design of hats in the corner please? It looks a little jaded – perhaps a few styles that haven't been out, but make sure to list them if you bring them through.'

'You want me to list them?' Marion questioned. 'Miss Browning told me it was her job…'

'Yes, it should be, but in future, if you bring them out, please list them yourself.'

'Very well, Mrs Burrows.' Marion went off with a little frown.

Beth wondered if she'd done right, but she didn't want a repeat of what had happened before.

Three customers entered the department at that moment and two of them headed to Beth's counter. Maggie served the other with scarves and Beth sold a leather bag, one piece of the lapis lazuli jewellery and a silver bangle with amethysts. The gentleman had bought one item of jewellery for his daughter and one for his wife.

Beth was tidying her stock away when she heard raised voices and saw that Miss Browning was verbally attacking Miss Kaye. The department was momentarily free of customers, but she could not have a quarrel between staff on the floor and went quickly to stop it.

'What is going on here?' she asked Miss Browning.

'She wrote up my stock book,' Janice Browning said accusingly. 'It is my job and if she's done it wrong, I'll get the blame...'

'Show me.' Beth held out her hand for the book. She looked at the list of hats used, mentally checked them off with those displayed and nodded. 'These are perfectly correct, Miss Browning. Miss Kaye has done what I asked, because I did not want a repeat of what happened the other day.'

'You always take her side,' Janice said sulkily. 'It's not fair...'

'I beg your pardon?' Beth said, looking at her sternly. 'You said Miss Kaye should have done it because you were busy last time and, since you were serving, I asked Miss Kaye to make sure nothing was mislaid. I believe you owe her and me an apology.'

'I don't see why,' the girl glared at her. 'Oh, all right, I apologise – but it isn't right...'

'Perhaps you should take your break now, Miss Browning...'

Janice Browning glared at her and walked off without another word.

Beth nodded to Miss Kaye and walked back to her counter as a customer entered the department. She hoped she'd done the right thing, but Janice Browning couldn't be allowed to question her authority.

* * *

It was when she returned from taking her own lunch break that Beth looked for the list of jewellery Mr Marco had requested for his window display. Marion Kaye had told her she'd placed it in the top drawer with the stock and sales book and Beth wanted to copy it into her book before it got lost. She looked in the drawer, lifting up the sales book and then the stock book and then ran her hand along the back of the drawer in case it had got stuck, but there was no list. Marion was standing watching Miss Browning serve and Beth beckoned her over.

'Yes, Mrs Burrows, what may I do for you?'

'Where did you put the stock list for the things Mr Marco took?'

'In your top drawer with the sales book and stock book.' Marion's eyes went to the drawer. 'Where is it?' She lifted the books out and ran her hand round just as Beth had done, then went to the front of the cabinet to see if it had somehow fallen down, but it hadn't. 'I did put it there, Mrs Burrows. I know I did...'

Beth frowned. 'Who served on this counter while I took my lunch?'

Marion hesitated, her eyes flicking to Janice Browning, but she didn't answer.

'Yes, I see – well, we must hope Mr Marco took a copy as he said he would,' she said with a frown.

'Oh, I copied it into your stock book too,' Marion said. 'Mr Marco suggested it and he wrote out the list while I entered it in your book.'

'That was thoughtful of him and very sensible of you, Marion.

Thank you – and I'm glad you did it, because I know I can trust you to look after things properly.'

Marion smiled and returned to her place in time to pack the hats for Janice Browning. She did it so beautifully and that was the only reason that Beth allowed her to remain as Miss Browning's assistant most of the time. The list had disappeared and Beth knew that only one person could have taken it and there was but one reason she would have done it – to cause trouble for Marion, perhaps to see her dismissed and just because Beth had asked her to make sure the stock was written up properly. What sort of a chip had she on her shoulder that she would try to get Marion reported to the manager? Mr Stockbridge could very well have decided to sack her and Beth knew how important this job was to her.

What kind of a girl would deliberately try to get another sacked? Beth frowned over it. She'd been uneasy over Janice Browning for a while now and if she'd been spiteful herself would have had her sacked instantly, but everyone deserved a second chance. However, she would keep an eye on Miss Browning and if she saw any signs of malice towards either Maggie or Marion, she would speak to Mrs Craven and ask her advice. In fact, she might talk to her that evening and see how she would treat an incident of this nature.

* * *

'I'm glad you told me,' Rachel said as they had a cup of coffee across the street from Harpers, in Bessie's café, and talked about Beth's problem. 'It is probably because you're not much older than she is and she knows you haven't long been promoted, she thinks she can get away with things.'

'So, should I tell her I know? Should I force her to explain? She already thinks I favour Miss Kaye.'

'I imagine that list will turn up somewhere in the next day or so, probably in Miss Kaye's bag or jacket pocket.'

'You think Miss Kaye lied?'

'No, but Miss Browning will know her trick didn't work, so she will try something else – and you have no proof she took it. Maggie could have taken it and so could Marion Kaye – in fact, Mr Marco could have taken it with him...'

'He didn't,' Beth said. 'But you're right; I have no proof, which is why I didn't accuse her immediately.'

'I should watch her closely and if you have any reason to suspect her of dishonesty report her to me or Mr Stockbridge – but if it is just spite against another member of staff, then perhaps we could move her to another department.'

'I wish I could arrange for her to be moved.' Beth shook her head. 'No, I'm being weak. I have to make her respect me and behave decently.'

'Sometimes it just isn't possible to do that with sly girls,' Rachel said. 'Try not to worry about it, Beth, but be careful not to judge. You have to be fair to all your staff and give Miss Browning the benefit of the doubt until you catch her in a lie.'

'Yes, thank you, I see that now,' Beth said and felt relieved. 'I wondered if you and Maggie would like to come to tea on Sunday – Miss Minnie too, of course.'

'I should be delighted,' Rachel said, 'but Minnie and Maggie are both having lunch and tea with Miss Stockbridge. Maggie took Minnie there a few weeks back and she got on so well that she's been invited back three times since...'

'Oh, I am pleased. I spoke to her in the alterations department the other day, just popped in to ask about a suit I've seen I should like to buy. I tried it on, but it is too big on the waist. Miss Minnie told me it would be no trouble to alter it – and said she would be happy to do it for me in her own time for nothing, but I insisted on paying something.'

Rachel nodded. 'Your aunt used to make your clothes or alter them for you, of course. Minnie is very good – better than most seamstresses I've met.'

'Yes, I've seen some of her work and it is lovely. I'd love to have her make me a dress for evenings – something to go dancing in.' Beth sighed. 'The gowns Harpers stock are too smart and too expensive for me. I want a simple design with some embroidery to make it special.'

'Yes, I feel the same,' Rachel said. 'I've been meaning to ask Minnie to make me a new evening gown. I dare say she could set up in business for herself if she chose, but she likes working at Harpers.'

Beth nodded thoughtfully. 'We should speak to Sally,' she said. 'Why doesn't Harpers have a bespoke facility for women who would like to have an evening gown designed just for them? Minnie could be in charge and do the embroidery herself.'

'That is a brilliant idea, Beth,' Rachel said. 'Now that she has more room in the new building, they could take what was the lingerie department for the bespoke gowns.' She smiled at her. 'Shall I suggest it, or shall you?'

'Why don't we take Sally out for a meal one evening?' Beth said. 'You, Maggie and me – the original Harpers Girls – and I've made her some baby things...' She hesitated. 'We're well into May now and her baby is due the second week of June, she thinks, so it should be fine if we do it soon.'

'Yes, let's ask her,' Rachel said. 'We can give her the gifts we have and tell her our idea together.'

18

'It won,' Ben said, looking triumphant as he entered the sitting room of their apartment, where Sally was sitting sipping orange juice, a pile of the new autumn and winter catalogues on the little onyx and gilt wood coffee table beside her. 'Durbar ii won the Derby at Epsom and I'm a hundred pounds richer.'

'Clever you,' Sally said, looking up for his kiss. She could smell the whisky on his breath and smiled. He'd obviously been celebrating with a couple of drinks and might have been just a little tipsy. 'What will you do with your fortune?'

'Spend it on my beautiful wife,' Ben responded promptly, savouring the kiss. 'You smell delicious – good enough to eat...'

Sally's eyes sparkled with mischief. 'That is the prawn, salmon and cod pie Mrs Hills popped in the oven for our supper. She has done some green beans and shredded cabbage ready, so I only have to turn the cooker on.'

'I'd planned on taking you out somewhere...'

'Tomorrow perhaps,' Sally said and looked surprised as he handed her what looked like a card. 'What is this?'

'Rachel Craven gave it to me,' Ben said. 'I think your friends are planning a little surprise for you, Sally.'

Sally opened the cream envelope and looked at the pretty card inside. 'Oh, Rachel, Beth and Maggie want to take me to dinner on Friday evening...'

'Yes, I thought it was something like that,' Ben said and placed an affectionate hand on her swollen belly as she stood up. 'I expect it will be a little party with presents for the baby.'

'That is so lovely...' For a moment, Sally's eyes watered, because she was so lucky. Before she'd started to work at Harpers, she'd been lonely, but now she had friends, a wonderful husband and she was carrying their child: a child that would belong to her and Ben, theirs to love and cherish always. Sally would never abandon her baby to the unforgiving care of nuns, as she'd been by the mother she couldn't remember. She felt so full of emotion that the tears hovered and she dashed them away.

'You shouldn't cry,' Ben said softly and his arms surrounded her. 'I love you so much, Sally Harper.'

'I know – I love you, too,' she said and turned to kiss him. 'I'm glad we're staying in tonight.' Her eyes sparkled as she looked up at him. 'I wouldn't mind an early night...'

'You're a wanton woman, Sally Harper,' he said and smiled as she laughed and went through to the kitchen to check on their meal, because she was a little too far advanced in her pregnancy for passionate lovemaking. 'Is Mrs Hills working out all right then?'

Sally had been reluctant to let anyone into their home, but Ben had insisted she had help to clean and cook, to make sure she ate properly on the days when he wasn't with her at lunch. She was still going in to Harpers some mornings, but with the birth of their baby imminent, he didn't want her left alone too long.

'She's a treasure,' Sally admitted. 'You were right, Ben. I

couldn't manage to look after things – I can't even bend down to cut my toenails at the moment.'

'I'll do them for you,' he offered instantly, 'Whatever you want, my darling. I'm here for you.'

'I know,' she said and then gasped. 'Oh, he kicked me, that's the fourth time today. I'll be black and blue inside before he's done.'

'He is impatient to join us,' Ben said and smiled as she placed a hand tenderly on her large bump. Sally glowed from head to toe, her pregnancy suiting her more as the months passed and she neared her time, though she now suffered a lot of backache. 'Did the doctor say when he could be born?'

'It might be tomorrow or two weeks,' Sally said. 'Babies tend to do it their way and come when they're ready, especially the first.'

Ben nodded. Sally was healthy and carrying their baby as well as she did everything else, but he would be happier when the birth was over and he knew she was safe.

* * *

'That is so beautiful,' Sally said as she unwrapped the delicate shawl that Rachel had made for her. It was made of white woven wool and edged with fine lace and completely different to the one Marlene had made for her. 'I shall use it for his christening.'

'So sure it will be a boy?' Maggie teased.

'It couldn't be anything else – he kicks so much, he's going to be a footballer,' Sally said. She smiled round at her friends. 'You've all given me lovely things and I'm so grateful, because you made them and that takes love and time, so I shall treasure every one.'

Beth had made a coat, bonnet, bootees and mittens in white. Maggie had knitted a pleated dress in white two-ply wool in a very lacy pattern that must have taken hours of work. Sally's eyes filled with tears of happiness, because she'd never expected that she would ever have such friends.

'I like knitting,' Maggie told her, 'especially if it is a difficult pattern – it's fun and I don't go out every night.' Maggie went to her first-aid classes, meetings of the Women's Movement once a month and on Sundays she met either Tim Burrows or had tea with Becky Stockbridge. On only rare occasions did she go to a theatre with Rachel and sometimes Minnie.

'I like to knit when I get time,' Beth said. 'Fred goes to the pub twice a week and I usually settle with a book and some knitting. I just do plain and pearl stitches; Maggie has done all sorts.'

'Where is Minnie this evening?' Sally asked. 'Didn't you ask her to come too?'

'Well, we wondered if we should,' Rachel said, 'but she told us she was going out with a friend, to dinner I think...'

'Really?' Sally was surprised. 'I didn't know Minnie had friends who would invite her to dinner...'

'No, she doesn't – or didn't, as far as I knew,' Rachel said and smiled. 'I have a feeling it is a man, but she didn't say and I didn't like to ask.'

'No!' Sally laughed. 'How lovely – do you know who?'

'I have no idea...' Rachel said. 'I think there may have been someone years ago, but I don't know anything about him.'

'I think she met this friend again quite recently,' Maggie said, making them all look at her attentively. She looked mysterious and shook her head. 'No, I shouldn't tell you, because it isn't my place – Minnie will tell you when she is ready.'

'Yes, but how do you know?' Rachel asked, frowning.

'Because a little bird told me,' Maggie said and laughed. 'No, I really can't tell you, it isn't my secret. I know because someone whispered in my ear and she ought not to have done...'

Rachel and Beth stared at her. 'You mean Becky Stockbridge, don't you?'

'My lips are sealed,' Maggie said, but the laughter was in her eyes. 'Don't you dare tell Minnie I said anything.'

'Well, I never...' Rachel looked thoughtful. 'I saw her talking to Mr Stockbridge at the store the other day and she was laughing. I thought how much younger she looked, but I didn't guess.'

'Well, he told me to bring her to tea. He wanted a gown made for Becky's eighteenth birthday in October and asked me to get her measurements without telling her why. He intends to have a little party for her... but I think it was partly an excuse to talk to Minnie...'

'Goodness!' Rachel said, genuinely astonished.

'Becky is a lucky girl,' Beth said. 'You're lucky too, Maggie, having a friend like Becky.' She shook her head in wonder. 'If you're right about Minnie and Mr Stockbridge that is lovely, because Minnie will be happy again.'

'I think she is,' Rachel said and smiled. 'So that's where all the flowers came from.' She looked at Maggie. 'So, what other secrets did your friend tell you?' she asked curiously. 'What do you two get up to?' Her eyes gently teased Maggie.

'Becky and I get on so well,' Maggie said. 'Becky is learning shorthand so that she can become a secretary but she would make a wonderful nurse. She is so good at first aid, but she says her father would never allow it. He loves her, but he can be quite strict.'

'He is lenient compared to many fathers,' Rachel assured her and looked up as the waiter hovered. 'Now, are we all having a pudding...?'

'Yes, please,' Maggie said, perusing the menu.

Beth was looking at Sally, who had suddenly clutched at herself. 'What's wrong, love – are you in pain?'

'I've had a persistent backache all day,' Sally said, frowning.

'I'm sorry, but I think I have to go home. You should stay and finish your meal...' She rose a little unsteadily to her feet and then gave a little cry. 'Oh! I think something's happening. I think my waters have broken. I don't think I have time to get home and summon the midwife we'd booked; can you get me a taxi please? I need to get to the hospital...'

* * *

Rachel had sent a waiter for a taxi, paid the bill and told Beth and Maggie to stop and finish their meal, but they both refused and so they all piled into the taxi with Sally, Maggie sitting on the little pulldown seat that faced the others as the car rushed them to the London Hospital. Ben had booked a first-class midwife and a special doctor to attend the birth of their child, which she'd chosen to have at home. However, it was happening at least a week sooner than they'd expected and the nearest hospital was a better option for a baby in a hurry to be born.

For Sally it was a blur of pain mixed with laughter and the reassuring smiles and touches of her friends' hands as they helped her in and out of the taxi, her pains getting closer and closer together. Somehow Rachel made a wheelchair appear and Sally was pushed into the labour ward with her friends clustering round her. There, Rachel took charge and Beth and Maggie were banished to the waiting area with instructions to telephone Ben and tell him he was about to be a father.

Then the pain took over and Sally suddenly found herself screaming as her body fought to push the new life into the world. She was conscious of Rachel there by her side, holding her hand, smiling and encouraging her, and then, briefly Ben. The nursing sister, outraged by his appearance in her maternity ward, banished him as soon as she entered the room, telling him he should go home and wait until he was summoned. He went reluctantly, because she was a formidable woman and reminded him of her strict rules of no men in the ward during the birth, but Rachel refused to budge. She urged Ben to leave, telling him they would ring him as soon as it was over and he went with a last reluctant look over his shoulder and an angry glare from the midwife. It was Rachel who sat by Sally's side as her ordeal intensified, her hand that Sally crushed when the pain became too bad and she who whispered into Sally's ear and made her laugh and then cry as the pain twisted and turned until she almost felt she couldn't bear it; then, with a whoosh of blood and fluid, a scream from Sally and a cry of joy and triumph from Rachel, her child was born in the early hours of the morning.

'You've got a beautiful little girl,' Rachel said. 'Oh, Sally, she is lovely – and absolutely perfect. All her fingers and toes are there.'

Suddenly, they were both crying with relief and the sheer joy of seeing the beautiful child, alive and well.

'Thank you,' Sally gasped to the nurses and to Rachel. She gripped her friend's arm. 'Tell Ben – tell him we have a lovely little girl.'

* * *

Sally slept then, worn out by her ordeal. When she awoke, it was morning and the sun was shining in at the window. She'd been moved to a small private room and she was alone. The door opened and a young nurse entered.

'Ah, Mrs Harper,' she said. 'I'm glad you're awake. Baby is waiting for a feed and then your husband wants to see you.'

'Ben is here?' Sally smiled. She was still a little weary but happy. Tears were on her cheeks as a nurse put the child into her arms and told her what to do. Watching with tender pride as the baby took her feed. She looked at the nurse shyly. 'Will you ask my husband to come in please? He should see this.'

The young nurse glanced over her shoulder. 'Sister will have my guts for garters if she knows,' she said with a conspiratorial whisper. 'She doesn't know he's here, but he turned up and I didn't have the heart to send him away – just for a few minutes then...'

'We won't tell her you let him in,' Sally said and the nurse giggled and went off to send Ben into the small room.

'Sally darling,' Ben said, placing a huge bunch of roses beside her bed on the little table. 'What a clever girl you are.' He was smiling, relieved, looking at her with love and pride and, as the baby finished feeding, Sally let him take the baby and nurse her, treasuring the look in his eyes as something she would hold inside for the rest of her life. 'She is so wonderful... look at her little hands and those eyes...'

'Shall we call her Jenny, after your sister, but spelled with a y?' she asked and Ben nodded. 'Jenny Beatrice Harper...'

'Lovely idea, darling. She is beautiful like her mother,' Ben whispered emotion making his voice husky. 'My little Jenny...'

Jenny Beatrice Harper had been born. They had a daughter to carry on the store after them, but perhaps next time she would give Ben the son she knew every man wanted.

'I'm sorry it all happened so suddenly. It wasn't as we'd planned – me at home with the private midwife and doctor, Mrs Hills and you...'

'Perhaps it's just as well,' he said and looked at her with love and pride. 'We've got her all the sooner – and the midwife says she will come for a few days when you come home, Sally.'

Sally's eyelids felt heavy. She was almost falling asleep as sister came bustling into the ward and took the child from Ben's arms, ordering him from the room.

'You will leave now, Mr Harper. Our mother needs to rest – you may return this evening – during visiting hours.'

Sally saw Ben wink at her as he was almost thrust from the

room. Sister was bustling about and spoke sharply to the young nurse when she returned to take charge of the baby. Sally wanted to protest that it was their fault not the nurse's, but the weariness stole over her and she fell asleep, a smile curving her lips.

* * *

Ben Harper had fallen in love for the third time in his life as he looked into the brilliant blue eyes of his child. Sally had been so sure it was a boy, but as far as Ben was concerned nothing could be more wonderful than the exquisite creature that looked up at him from her gossamer shawl. Her hair was fine and dark but already curling over her ears and her face was pink and perfect, none of the awful redness that some newborn babies were reputed to have. Ben hadn't actually ever seen a newborn before, but he was certain no child had ever been this perfect. Her eyes had been so knowing as they looked up at him, as if she knew that she already had him curled around her little finger – and such tiny little fingers they were, but all there and everything as it should be.

How could he ever have doubted it? Sally always took everything in her stride, so why would she give birth to a less than perfect child? Ben grinned as he moved about his apartment that afternoon. How empty it seemed without Sally! She'd turned all their careful plans upside down by giving birth early. It was so like her to go swanning off to dinner with her friends and end up presenting him with his first child at four o'clock in the morning. A nice relaxed home birth would have been so much better for her and he'd arranged for her to have the best care.

He'd poured himself a large brandy as soon as he got back to the flat and drunk it straight down. God; that was nerve-wracking, even though he hadn't been in the hospital during the birth. The taxi ride to the hospital after Maggie's phone call had him on thorns and then that dragon of a nurse had thrown him out before he could tell Sally how much he loved her. God, she had a face like a wet week in November! If Sally hadn't looked so tired, he might have argued with her, told her how ridiculous it was that he couldn't be with his wife when she needed him, but he'd let her throw him out to save his wife any stress. The rule that men were not allowed at a birth seemed ridiculous to Ben. He'd wanted to be there, to help Sally through the pain, but there was no arguing with the dragon sister!

It hadn't stopped him returning later that morning, though – and that young nurse had been a sport, letting him into the little private room he'd paid for while Sally was feeding their baby. He knew she'd be in trouble for that and he made a mental note to make sure she hadn't lost her job over it. If, by chance, the demon sister had got her dismissed, Ben decided he would take her on at Harpers. He'd thought once or twice they ought to have a medical presence in case of illness. It was an idea to consider...

He wasn't sure he could go through the agony of not knowing what was happening to Sally again; he'd been terrified she might die or would lose the baby and be devastated by her loss. No, he didn't think he could stand the agony of imagining her in pain and stress, even to get the son and heir most men wanted to carry on their empire – but Jenny Beatrice would be perfectly capable of doing that, of course she would, because look at her parents and aunt.

He downed his brandy and lit the cigar he'd been saving for the occasion. He didn't really care for them, preferring his Passing Clouds cigarettes, but it was what men did when a child was born, so he smoked half of it before stubbing it out. Ben just couldn't stop smiling as he paced the floor, unable to relax.

He was a father. Sally was his wife and Harpers was doing well. What more could any man want? Ben couldn't think of a thing. A feeling of unease crept over him suddenly – when things were so good, something had to go wrong. It was Sod's law and Ben knew how swiftly tragedy could strike.

He wished that his sister Jenni was here to talk sense to him. She would tell him to grab hold of his happiness and not let the doubts in, but that niggle at the back of his neck would not let go. Jumping up, he telephoned the hospital. A rather grumpy-sounding nurse answered.

'Yes, maternity ward, how may I help you?'

'I just wanted to know – are my wife and daughter all right?'

'Who is speaking?'

'Ben Harper...'

'Just one moment, Mr Harper...'

The seconds seemed like hours until she returned, sounding even more grumpy.

'Sister says they are both fine. Mrs Harper is asleep and baby has taken her second feed.'

'Oh, that's good, thank you.' Ben replaced the telephone receiver and laughed out loud. What a fool he was, doubting because everything was too perfect. He would stop worrying and send his sister Jenni a telegram telling her the news.

19

Ben stared at the man in disbelief as he delivered his ultimatum. The builders had agreed their price and stripped out all the walls and knocked the rooms into one big space and now, a couple of days later, they were demanding more money.

'What do you mean you want an extra three thousand or you walk off the job?' he asked. 'We agreed a price for the whole job and I'm not prepared to pay more.'

'Then yer can finish it yerself,' Dick Mitchell said rudely. 'Come on, Bingo, Jed, Charlie, we're goin'...'

'You can't just walk off like that,' Ben protested. 'What am I supposed to do now you've torn it apart?'

The man shrugged. 'Buggered if I care,' he replied. 'If yer don't get them lintels in sharpish, the whole bloody lot will fall down – but that's yer problem, mate. Call me when yer ready ter talk – but the longer yer leave it, the more it will cost...'

Ben stared after the men as they walked out. He'd heard of people being held to ransom like this, but he hadn't expected it to happen to him, though he knew back home bribes were often paid to firms to keep the men on site. This was England, damn it!

He'd expected them to behave like gentlemen and stick to their bargain...

What the hell did he do now? Ben puzzled over it. He'd had difficulty in finding builders with the right expertise in the first place, because quite a few had told him they didn't want to work for an American. He'd been quoted ridiculous figures and thought he was getting it done for a reasonable price, but if he paid their demands now, he would go way over budget and he already owed the bank as much as they would lend him.

Ben knew everyone thought he was rolling in money because he was American. Unfortunately, being born the other side of the Atlantic didn't make him a millionaire. He owned a medium-sized store that made a small profit but could easily tip into the red if things went wrong and he just couldn't afford to be black-mailed like this.

Leaving the property, Ben locked up and pocketed the keys. He hated having to go home and tell Sally that he'd failed, but he could see only one way out – and that could cost him a fortune. It might even lose him Harpers and he was damned if he was going to give into a blackmailer.

Frowning, Ben didn't see the man coming towards him until he almost walked into him. 'Hey!' a voice he recognised said. 'What did I do...?'

'Mick...' Ben blinked at him. 'Sorry, I wasn't looking where I was going.'

Mick grinned at him. 'I expect being a father does that to you – sleepless nights and all that. Congratulations on having a lovely girl, by the way. I got a peek at her when I visited Sally two days ago – but I wasn't allowed to stay more than ten minutes. A fire-breathing nurse almost threw me out...'

'I've met her,' Ben laughed. 'Sally only came home yesterday and she would still be there if I hadn't engaged my own nurse to look after her at home. They wanted to keep her another week, but you know my wife – she'd had a week in the hospital and she wasn't prepared to stay another day. The dragon sister wanted to keep her in, but I went over her head and brought Sally home in a private ambulance.'

'Good for you,' Mick said. 'So, if it's not sleepless nights – what is the problem?'

Ben swore softly. 'I don't suppose you know a good builder who won't try to cheat me and walk off the job, do you?'

'Ah, I see.' Mick nodded. 'I might know someone who could help – why don't we have a drink to celebrate the birth and talk about it?'

'Really? You might know someone?' Ben's brow cleared. 'I'll take you up on that – Mitchell has me over a barrel.'

'Ah, you didn't use Dick Mitchell, did you?' Mick frowned. 'He's a lying, cheating devil and you're well rid of him. If you give into his blackmail, he'd bleed you dry, Ben. I can give you a few names – but there's a good chap I know and he owes me a few favours.'

'Thanks,' Ben said and grinned. 'I don't mind admitting that this could break me, and with the situation the way it is…'

'Yeah, things are a bit dicey one way and another,' Mick said. 'It's nearly lunchtime. Why don't we go to a pub I know and talk about it?'

* * *

Ben felt relieved he'd bumped into Mick as they parted later. He already had a new builder who was starting on site in the morning and his price was less than that rogue Mitchell's in the first place. It seemed that Michael O'Sullivan was a good man to know. He had contacts all over London and Ben was convinced that he would do well to join forces with Mick at some time in the future. Mick had somehow raised funds to go ahead with his latest project and was already moving in a new manager and staff.

'I'm going to make that the last one for the moment,' he'd told Ben, 'and if I were you, I'd hang on to any cash you have goin' spare. I think the situation in Europe looks unstable – the Kaiser is spoiling for a fight, if you ask me, building up his forces. He doesn't do that for the fun of it and I've got friends who think there's trouble brewing out there.'

'Yes, I agree,' Ben had replied. 'I keep thinking it may just blow over – some riots and violence over there but contained…'

'It's what we all hope for,' Mick had said and shook his head. He'd sipped his pint of dark bitter beer. 'Now, let's forget war and talk about how your daughter and wife are getting on. How does it feel to be a father?'

'Wonderful,' Ben had said and smiled, letting go his inner tension. 'As soon as she's feeling better, you must come and have a meal with us. Tell us all about your new hotel.'

'How's my best girl then?' Reggie was waiting at the end of the lane for Marion as she got off the bus that evening. 'Are you coming for a walk with me on Sunday afternoon?'

'It depends if Ma is all right,' Marion said but smiled at him. 'I want to, Reggie, I like being with you – but you know my family comes first...'

'I know,' he said and smiled. 'You wouldn't be my Marion if they didn't, but I'd like to court yer properly, ask yer ma and make it official...'

'Now, don't talk daft,' Marion said, even though he made her want to smile. 'Just because you danced with me at the social doesn't make me your girl, Reggie Jackson.'

'I danced three times with yer and walked yer home,' he said and his eyes met hers steadily. 'Everyone knows that means we're courtin' – everyone but you.' His eyes teased her.

She laughed and shook her head. 'You will have to try a lot harder than that,' she challenged. 'We're friends, but we're not courtin' yet – and I have to get in and get the tea on...' She thought of something and nodded. 'Thank you for those lovely new potatoes. They're earlier than Robbie's and they were lovely for supper last night.'

'You're welcome. I'll have some peas soon.' He looked at her longingly. 'I could take yer down the pub later; buy yer a port and lemon...'

'The day I let you buy me a port and lemon down the pub, you might as well put a ring on me finger,' she stated and saw his eyes light up.

'I'll be looking forward to that,' he said. 'I'll get yer ter admit yer me girl one of these days, Marion Kaye, you see if I don't...'

'We'll see,' she said and ran the last few steps to her kitchen door. There she turned to look and saw him watching her. Pleased, she waved and went inside.

Kathy was at the sink, washing a cup and saucer. 'I made Ma some Bovril in a cup and she drank it all,' she said, 'but she wouldn't have any toast.'

'Well, the Bovril will do her good,' Marion said and smiled. 'I've got a tin of corned beef or sausages for supper – which do you want?'

'I should like the corned beef,' Kathy said. 'Reggie's mum gave me some beetroot out of their garden and I've cooked it. I like red beet with corned beef and mash.'

'Yeah, it's lovely,' Marion said. 'It was nice of Reggie's mum to give us some of the beetroot from her garden.'

'Reggie told her to – he would give you anythin' he had,' Kathy said, looking at her a little enviously. 'I wish it was me he wanted, Marion – I'd take him like a shot...'

'You're not yet fourteen,' Marion reminded her. 'Far too young to get married, Kathy.'

'I know, but I want someone like him when I do. You're lucky, Marion. Yer don't want ter throw yer chances away, Reggie Jackson is one of the best. All the girls round here are after him, but he only has eyes for you.'

'Well, I like him,' Marion conceded, because she wasn't ready to admit her feelings might be a lot more, even to herself. 'But I've got tea to cook and then there's the washing and Ma to think of...' Her mother didn't seem to be getting any better, though she was no worse. Perhaps that was because Pa hadn't been home recently and they all knew that the longer he stayed away, the better for all of them. 'And I like my job at Harpers. If I'm lucky, I might get promoted soon...'

For most young women, marriage meant the end of going to work and having fun with their friends. Marion wasn't ready for that yet, even though she did like Reggie a lot.

* * *

Marion was early for work the next day. She hadn't been able to sleep for a while and she was awake early, which was unusual for her. She didn't know if it was because of what Kathy had said about being careful not to lose Reggie. Her thoughts occupied her as she walked briskly to work, enjoying the warmth of the day and the fresh air.

Shrugging off her troubling thoughts, Marion went into Harpers, inhaling the smells and taking in the lovely things all round her. It was so nice working here and she felt a spurt of happiness just being one of Harpers' girls; she walked through the ground-floor counters to the lift, and up to her department. There, she hung her coat in the cloakroom and started removing the covers from the hats and brushing them gently to make sure they had no dust on them.

'Currying favour again, I see...' Janice Browning's sarcastic voice made Marion jump. 'You're always playing up to Mrs Burrows – teacher's pet, that's what you are.'

'Don't be daft,' Marion said, refusing to be cowed by her. 'I'm just doing my job, as you should – and if you don't like it, hard luck.'

'You snotty little bitch,' Janice said, squaring up to her. 'I'll get you back one of these days, you see if I don't, getting me into trouble...'

Marion thought she was about to hit her but then heard the voices of Mrs Burrows and Miss Gibbs as they entered the department.

Janice moved away, her eyes narrowed menacingly as she mouthed a silent warning at her.

Turning away, Marion ignored the other girl. Janice was mean and spiteful and very jealous. She hadn't started tidying up to gain favour with Mrs Burrows but just because she enjoyed her job. Janice worked for a wage and didn't care about Harpers or the people that worked with her, but Marion loved the store and the colleagues she worked with; it was like paradise coming into this lovely place with all the beautiful things around her. She felt it was a privilege and never stopped feeling grateful that she'd been given the job.

'Ah, Marion, I see you got started early,' Mrs Burrows said. 'That is excellent. I have a feeling we're going to be busy today. Mr Marco has a lovely new window and people always come to see them on the first day.'

Marion nodded, feeling excited. When she had her break, she would pop down and look at the window from outside the shop. She was as curious as the people who crowded there to see the blinds come down – and she liked Mr Marco. He was always so kind to her, smiling and winking in that cheeky way of his.

She sighed with content, because life was good right now. Her job made her feel happy and she was lucky to be courted by a gentle man she trusted and was beginning to have feelings for. If things went well, she would soon earn a few more shillings and that would make all the difference to her family.

Feeling the malevolent gaze of Janice Browning on her back, she turned and felt chilled. Why did the other girl hate her so much?

'Come along, Marion, take your place,' Mrs Burrows said. 'I have a feeling it will be a good day for us all.' She stopped by one of the hat stands and frowned, looking at a pale blue straw. 'What happened to this – Janice, Marion?'

'What is wrong?' Janice asked. 'I haven't seen that before – did you put it out, Marion?'

'No, I don't think so.' Marion went to look at the hat, which was priced at thirty-five shillings. The ribbon had been ripped away from the straw and was hanging loose. Gasping, Marion looked at Janice and caught the glimpse of malice in her eyes. 'I brushed the hats as usual, Mrs Burrows – but I don't recall this being here...'

Mrs Burrows picked it up and looked at it. 'It almost looks deliberate,' she said. 'Fetch another hat, Miss Kaye – and then you can take this to Miss Minnie in the sewing room and ask her if she can repair it.'

'Yes, Mrs Burrows.' Marion hardly dared to look at her. 'If I did it, I'm very sorry...'

'I think Miss Minnie will be able to repair it and no harm done,' Mrs Burrows said but frowned at both of them. 'I hardly need to remind either of you that these hats are expensive. Damage like this would normally have to be paid for – but fortunately I do think Miss Minnie will be able to disguise what has happened.' Her gaze narrowed. 'Just make sure it doesn't happen again...'

'Creep,' Janice hissed at her as she passed her. 'Next time you may not be so lucky...'

Marion looked at Janice. She couldn't mistake the look of triumph in her eyes now. She'd done it herself hoping to get Marion into trouble, but there was no way she could prove it and

Mrs Burrows could quite easily have stopped the money out of her wages...

Marion turned away. She'd known for a while that Janice didn't like her, but now she knew that the girl was dangerous and decided to keep away from her as much as she could.

21

'I know it isn't your birthday,' Tim said as he handed Maggie a box of chocolates and a small posy of flowers when they met that weekend. 'I just wanted to give you a present...'

'Oh, Tim, you spoil me,' Maggie said and smiled at him. They were on their way to have tea at his father's house and he'd also bought chocolates and flowers for Beth. 'It is a lovely surprise, thank you.' She smelled the little posy of roses and lily of the valley, inhaling the wonderful perfume. 'I love lily of the valley and you seldom see it, except in expensive shops.'

'I know – Beth told me she bought you some perfume last Christmas.' Tim grinned. 'I'm off to the coast for a few weeks, Maggie – training, flying over the sea, they said...'

'Oh... I shall miss seeing you,' she said and felt a pang of loss which she quickly dismissed. 'I do enjoy our outings together.'

'We don't leave until next weekend,' he said. 'I managed to get tickets for *Pygmalion* on Tuesday – I thought you might like to see it?'

'Oh yes, I should love to, but they're like gold dust,' Maggie said. 'How did you manage to get them? Beth said there was a queue when she tried, so she gave up.' She smiled reminiscently. 'Mr Marco persuaded Mrs Patrick to come into the shop when he did that wonderful display featuring the show... it was a huge success for Harpers. People queued to see her and she was wonderful. I got her autograph myself...'

'Then you will enjoy the show. A friend of mine had them and, well, I won them from him in a card game,' Tim said and laughed. 'He said it was them or wait for pay day to settle what he owed, so I grabbed these because I thought you would like them.'

Maggie frowned at him. 'I should like to go, but I'm not sure I approve of gambling...'

Tim nodded and looked half ashamed. 'Dad would kill me if he knew – but it helps to pass the time, Maggie. Sometimes, when we're not training, it gets boring, so the chaps like to gamble. It's only for a few bob...'

'Even so, it is a bad habit,' Maggie said. 'I shan't tell your father, but it's not a good idea, Tim.'

'I know, but I'm not addicted. Some of the chaps are, but I only do it when I'm bored.'

'I thought you loved flying?'

'Yes, I do – and I've passed all my exams, but...' He shook his head. 'I can't explain, Maggie. But I promise I'll stop if it upsets you.'

'Don't promise if you can't keep your word.'

'I can and I will,' he said. 'It was never more than a way to pass the time. Some of the chaps drink a bit too much, some gamble and some smoke... well, stuff that isn't good for them. I think that's stupid, but I'll stick to a flutter on the horses in future.'

Maggie looked at him. 'You don't have to do what I say, Tim – but I care about you. My father always said gambling was a fool's game, but if it's just for fun...'

'I'll stay clear of it from now on,' he promised. 'You know I'd do anything for you, Maggie love...'

Maggie shook her head at him. Their bus had arrived at its stop and they got down, Tim giving her his hand to help her jump the last bit. They were laughing as they walked round the back and into the kitchen, where Beth was making ham sandwiches.

Tim presented her with the flowers and chocolates and she thanked him. Fred smiled and told Maggie to sit down and he took her coat to hang it up for her. Everyone started talking and laughing and they were soon eating their tea and enjoying themselves.

Maggie forgot about the gambling. Tim had promised he wouldn't let it become a habit and she trusted him. She smiled at him across the table and he winked at her. Maggie saw Beth smile and knew she'd seen the look pass between them.

* * *

Maggie was serving a customer when Mr Stockbridge entered the department that Monday morning. He seldom visited the departments, leaving that to Rachel and Mrs Harper, when she was back at work, but he was looking pleased with himself.

'Becky asked me to let you know she would be coming to the first-aid classes with you again and...' He paused thoughtfully, 'If I allowed her to attend the meeting at the Women's Movement, could you assure me that she would not be caught up in anything violent or illegal?'

'I don't belong to the militant branch of the movement,' Maggie assured him, wondering what had changed his mind. He was normally so strict about where his daughter could and could not go. 'Sometimes we are heckled at our peaceful meetings, but we do nothing to arouse hostility...'

He nodded, looking serious. 'Good, then I shall give it some thought and let Becky know my decision.'

Mrs Burrows came over to her counter after he left, looking anxious. 'Are you in trouble, Miss Gibbs?'

'Oh no, Mrs Burrows,' Maggie said and smiled. 'Mr Stockbridge was giving me a message from Becky.'

'Oh, I see...' Mrs Burrows looked very surprised. She obviously wanted to know more, but several customers entered the department all together and she was forced to return to her counter.

Maggie served six customers on the trot and sold scarves to all of them. She was busy writing the sales up and crossing off the stock list when Mrs Harper came in. It was the end of June now and she'd recovered quickly from the birth of her daughter but only came into the store occasionally, when she had something special to do, because she needed to be at home to nurse her baby. She'd told Maggie that Ben didn't want her to come in for weeks yet, but she'd compromised by popping in for short visits. Mr Marco was with her on this occasion and gallantly carrying a pile of boxes, which he placed on Maggie's counter.

'These have just arrived,' Mrs Harper said. 'I'm trying a new supplier and I wanted to show you them myself – I want you to take particular note of customers' remarks and how many of these you sell. Your information helps me to know whether I'm buying the right stock...'

'Yes, of course, Mrs Harper,' Maggie said and smiled.

'Oh, Mrs Harper...' Janice Browning sidled up to them, leaving Marion to cope with a difficult customer alone. 'I wanted to ask if you would be buying any more of those straw boaters... We've sold six of them.' She shot a malicious glance at Marion. 'Including the one Marion damaged and Miss Minnie repaired...'

In fact, Marion had sold four out of the six, but Janice allowed Mrs Harper to think that she had sold them. Maggie frowned.

She'd once considered asking Janice to share a room with her, but she'd changed her mind. If she had to go into a boarding house, it would be better than sharing with a girl she now very much disliked. Janice had deliberately drawn Mrs Harper's attention to the fact that a hat had had to be repaired by Miss Minnie, but instead of asking questions Mrs Harper ignored her and Maggie felt pleased. Janice had been trying to make trouble, she was sure of it. Maggie liked Marion and if Janice was trying to get her sacked, perhaps she ought to warn her, just a few words to be extra careful when checking her stock...

22

'Trouble brewing after Habsburg heir assassinated in Balkans!' The newsboys were shouting all over London. 'Tension is mounting between Serbia and the Prussians since the terrible murders earlier this month. Buy me paper, sir, read all about it!'

Ben stopped to purchase the *Standard* on his way home that July evening. He sat in the back of the taxicab moments later and read the lurid account of the double murder and the mounting tension it was causing in Europe.

'Terrible goings-on, ain't it, sir?' the friendly cabby remarked.

'Yes, perhaps worse than we yet realise,' Ben replied.

The Archduke Franz Ferdinand and his morganatic wife, the Duchess, had been shot while on a visit to Sarajevo, the capital of Bosnia. As the heir apparent to the Austria-Hungarian Empire, this was dire news and had set the Balkans alight with anger and outrage. The incident had occurred the previous Sunday, when someone had thrown a bomb at them and the Archduke had thrown it back into the road, accidentally injuring someone in the following car. Then, as the royal car was forced to go slowly through the crowds, the assassin had darted out and shot the

Archduke in the neck; his wife flung herself across him to try to save him from further injury and received a fatal wound to her stomach. She died quickly, her husband following a short time later. The papers had been full of it for days.

After the brief retelling of the tragedy came speculation by the journalist as to whether the murders had been a Serbian plot. The culprit had told the police he wanted revenge for the oppression of the people of Serbia and was rumoured to be part of a secret group of army officers calling themselves the Black Hand. The newspaper reporter had written that, if this proved to be the case, Austria would take strong action against the murderers. More details concerning the atrocity were coming out day by day.

Ben frowned as he read that no soldiers had lined the route and there had been no change after the first attempt. Surely someone should have taken more care of royal visitors, rushed more protection to the royal party? The assassination had all the hallmarks of a conspiracy in his opinion.

He tucked the paper into his leather case, where a sheaf of new catalogues from various firms had been placed. Sally had not yet returned to work, even though she was becoming restless and sometimes popped into the store just for an hour to see people and talk shop. However, there was no prospect of her returning to work for a while yet.

Jenny wasn't feeding as well as she ought and so although they'd discussed taking on a nanny, Sally had decided to take at least another month or two off to ease her baby through the first few weeks of her life, and then she would only do a few hours in the mornings until the baby was weaned. They were both devoted to the little person who had taken over their lives and Ben had paced the floor several nights in a row with a crying baby in his arms to give Sally a rest, but the previous night, Jenny had settled and woken only for her feeds, which meant they could both get some rest.

He frowned as he paid his driver and went into the apartment building. Sally liked to read the papers, but he was reluctant to show her the latest headlines, which were prophesising war soon. Ben wasn't a warmonger by any means and he hoped nothing terrible would come from this latest outrage, but for how long would Austria put up with these kinds of attacks and insults? It was likely that, before long, this nasty business could escalate into a full-blown war.

* * *

'She smiled at me today,' Sally said when Ben laid down his case and took off his jacket.

He walked towards her and accepted the sweet-smelling bundle from Sally's arms. As yet they hadn't needed a nursemaid, because Mrs Hills was so good. She was only employed to cook and clean, but Sally had soon discovered she was a fount of knowledge where babies were concerned and small worries were soon smoothed over by Mrs Hill's experience of four children.

'It was wind,' Ben said, looking at his daughter. 'You know the hospital midwife told you they don't really smile for ages yet.'

'I don't care what that pompous nurse said,' Sally retorted with a laugh. 'I swear she smiled – and Mrs Hills thought so too.'

'Oh well, if Mrs Hills thought so...' Ben grinned, willing to accept whatever Sally said. 'I brought you those catalogues you wanted – and I've got half a dozen parcels for you in my case...' He could have bit his tongue off as Sally went immediately to the case and opened it. She took out the parcels and catalogues and then the newspaper.

'That is awful,' Sally said, glancing at the headlines. 'I was talking to Mrs Hills about it earlier – Sidney told her what they were saying about the likelihood of war when she came in. I don't know where he gets his information from, but he always seems to know the news before the papers.' Sidney was their porter and often related bits of news they hadn't yet heard when he brought up post, flowers or early morning newspapers. 'I think he has a pigeon post from Downing Street.'

Ben smiled ruefully. Had he really thought he should keep it from Sally? He might have known she would be aware of the news as soon as he was.

'Do you think there will be a war now?' Sally asked. 'Fred Burrows has been saying it will come for ages – this couldn't be it, could it?'

'Well, it might,' Ben admitted and took his sleeping child to her cot, tenderly kissing her brow before laying her down. 'I don't think we need to worry, though, Sally. I know Britain might get drawn in, but it won't be a big war. I'm sure it will all blow over in a few weeks. It is so volatile out there – they are forever having a go at each other...'

'Yes, but this is more serious, isn't it?' Sally persisted. 'If Russia and Austria and others go to war... well, we've signed treaties that say we have to help.'

'Yes, sure, I know,' Ben agreed and tried to turn the subject because he didn't want his wife upset. 'Dinner smells good – what is it?'

'Beef bourguignon with new peas, carrots and potatoes,' she said. 'Mrs Hills said we might as well make the most of good food while we can...'

'Oh, it will never get that bad,' Ben said cheerfully, 'but she can make me special meals as much as she likes. I'm starving.'

'Me too,' Sally said. 'I shall have to be careful. She spoils me so much that unless I get back to work more often and watch my diet, I shall never get my figure back...'

'Nothing wrong with your figure – more for me to cuddle up to.' He smiled and kissed her. 'And you don't need to be back at work for a while, love – you can do a little buying from home if you need to, but if you tell me what you want, I'll see to things for you...'

'And nothing fits me,' Sally grumbled, ignoring his offer. He knew she was torn between wanting to care for her baby herself and getting back to her desk, but she was just going to have to be patient for a while. 'I'm going to get a bicycle and ride into work, Ben. I don't mind being a size thirty-six, but I know I'm not going to settle for a thirty-eight.'

'Women and clothes,' he said and grinned at her. 'Look at those catalogues and buy yourself a new wardrobe.'

'I might buy something floaty to get me through the summer,' Sally agreed, 'but I want to be back to my normal size by Christmas.' She smiled at him. 'By the way, there's a letter from Jenni on the table. She says she's happy and hopes she will get to see us soon and she has sent some things for the baby...' She hesitated, then, 'Perhaps we could have the christening when she's here. She said she would like to be a godmother...'

'That's just like Jenni. And maybe we should ask Mick to be Jenny's godfather?' Ben said and smiled, putting an arm about Sally's waist.

'He'd like that – yes, why not?' Sally agreed. 'I'll have to diet I suppose but that might not be good for Jenny...'

'Why bother? You're not fat, just cuddly...'

'But I prefer me slimmer. I had an eighteen-inch waist,' Sally said and pouted, but then a cry from the bedroom distracted her. 'I'd better see to Jenny. Get the casserole out while I see if she is all right.'

Ben smiled as she hurried away to see to the baby. He nodded to himself as he lifted the delicious casserole from the oven. If Sally was worrying over getting her figure back, she wouldn't be fretting about a war and with any luck the politicians would be able to sort things out and everything would settle down again. He hadn't said anything to Sally, but with some of their stock coming from America and much of the raw materials English manufacturers used in their products also sourced abroad, it could make things difficult for a while if war did break out. In the morning he would speak to Stockbridge about ordering in as much stock as they could hold, even if they kept it in the basement for months. He reflected that it was lucky Mick had given him the name of a good builder. If war was coming, the men would flock to join up and he didn't want to be left in the lurch again.

War would make a difference to all their lives, especially if it escalated the way it looked as if it might. He was an American and, as his wife, Sally was entitled to an American passport for her and the child – and yet Ben wasn't the kind to cut and run. Even if things got difficult here, he wouldn't desert the country that had become home to him. Only in the very worst circumstances would he consider sending his wife and child away to safety.

* * *

'There – I told you it was coming,' Fred said as he showed Beth the same article Ben and Sally were reading, had he known it. 'It was planned – that wasn't a random madman havin' a go, it's part of a Serbian plot and war is inevitable, it has to happen now!'

'Fred, please don't,' Beth said. 'I know it looks bad but...' She looked up as her husband walked in the kitchen door, her face lighting with pleasure. 'Jack – you're home early!' He was so busy at the hotel that he seldom got home before nine or ten in the evening.

'Yes, I decided to make an effort and I've left my assistant in charge of seeing the new guests in this evening. I thought we'd go out somewhere – if you haven't eaten?'

'I was going to cook lamb chops,' Beth said. 'They will keep for tomorrow – but what about you, Fred?'

'I'll have a pie down the pub,' Fred said. 'You two go out and enjoy yourselves while you can...'

Jack frowned at him. 'You could come with us, Dad – make it a celebration...'

'No, you take Beth and have a good night,' Fred told them. 'I'll meet my friends and have a good natter. You young ones should enjoy yourselves. You don't get much time to yourselves.'

'We'll go somewhere nice,' Jack said. 'Somewhere they have a band and we can dance between courses.'

Beth jumped up with excitement and hurried upstairs to have a wash and put on a pretty blue dress with a skirt that flirted in a frill just above her ankles. She sprayed some of the perfume he'd given her for her last birthday behind her ears and on her wrists. Jack had changed his shirt and suit at the hotel; he kept some of his clothes there to save coming home and she thought how smart he looked. When the taxi arrived and he gave the driver the name of a prestigious hotel, she looked at him in surprise.

'The Ritz is expensive, Jack – are you sure you want to spend so much money?'

'Why not? We don't do it often enough, Beth. I've been trying to build the business up, make a good future for us – but now I wonder if I've been a fool...'

'What do you mean?' Beth asked, but he shook his head.

'It doesn't matter – let's enjoy this evening.'

'It's because of what happened, isn't it?' Beth asked, feeling a cold shiver at her nape. 'You think there will be a war, like Fred says...'

'Yes.' Jack looked at her in the dimness of the back seat of the taxi. 'I'm merchant navy, Beth, at least I was. If there is a war, I'll have to go back...'

'You were on cruise ships not merchant vessels,' Beth

protested as the chill crept down her spine, but she'd known this in her heart already.

'They will need men with experience of the sea. I know ships and the men who sail them need men like me to feed them and keep things running. I'll have to go if I'm needed, Beth – and I'll be in it from the start because they won't have enough trained men...'

'Perhaps if you're on a merchant vessel it won't be so bad,' Beth whispered, but she could see by Jack's face that he didn't agree and she knew why he'd come home early to take her out. If war came, her husband would be at sea, perhaps for months on end, and sometimes ships sank, especially when at war...

Beth's throat tightened and for a moment the tears threatened, but she choked them back. Jack's first thought had been for her, which showed how much he loved her and she would be a fool to spoil their evening. Never in her life would she ever have expected to be taken to a place like the Ritz. Life had improved so much for her since her marriage and the inheritance that had enabled Jack to buy his hotel. She wasn't going to ruin her special treat, so she would worry about the war when it came.

23

Sally searched the papers for news every morning as soon as it was delivered. The papers were still rumbling on about the Irish Home Rule Bill and the way the King had appeared to side with the Ulster Unionists, making what she considered extremely rude remarks about His Majesty. Although, of course, kings normally remained impartial when it came to politics, so perhaps, he'd drawn the sarcasm on himself? At Wimbledon, Dorothea Chambers had beaten Ethel Larcombe for the ladies' singles title in the tennis championships and Kaiser Wilhelm II had reaffirmed his country's support of Austria. She saw an article about the Royal Naval Air Service being established and realised it was all a part of the build-up to war.

It was time she thought about returning to work for at least a few hours each day and not just popping in when she felt like it, Sally decided, as the month of July moved inexorably on. Jenny was now nearly seven weeks old and blooming, and the lazy days of being spoiled by Ben and Mrs Hills had been all too few. With a war looming, her buying expertise would be needed more than ever. She knew that young men were already talking about joining the armed forces if, as seemed increasingly likely, war happened, and, although she might have wished to spend longer at home learning to know her baby and just enjoying being a mother, Sally didn't need Ben to tell her that buying in stock was even more important now.

Besides, he had his hands full with the new extension, which had proved more problematic than he'd imagined, even though Mick had recommended a good builder. So, Sally must make an effort to spend at least an hour or two each day at the store, choosing the hours when her darling daughter was sleeping. Much of the ordering could be managed from home on the telephone, of course, but she needed to talk to some suppliers and that could only be done at Harpers or their workshops. Should Britain be forced to join a war, it would become more difficult to source all they needed from overseas, therefore she ought to order in as much as she could now.

Jenni's cable didn't surprise her in the least when it arrived.

Sending large consignment of goods by next shipment. Hope to visit soon. Long to see my namesake! Love, concerned Jenni.

Sally cabled her back immediately:

Adore to see you. Need glass, china, textiles and cosmetics. Love as always, busy mum Sally xxx

Jenni was busy buying as much as she could, but Sally wondered if they had sufficient funds to cover it all. She would have to ask Ben, because one of them might have to speak to the bank manager about a small loan to tide them over – and yet he already had so much on his mind that she hated to bother him. It made it all the more important that she did her job, either here at home, where she would prefer to be with her little darling, or, when necessary, in the office.

Ben had already spoken vaguely of employing a nanny. He'd asked her what she thought of the idea. Sally came from working-class stock and nursery maids were something only the rich did in her estimation, but although Mrs Hills would be happy to care for Jenny when Sally was forced to leave her, Ben felt a part-time nanny would be a huge help to them. Sally had wrestled with the idea, torn between wanting to care for her child herself and the need to look after their business. Harpers was doing well now, but she knew it would only take a few mistakes in the buying for them to slip into the red in their accounts and she couldn't let Ben down, even though he kept telling her she should stay home and rest. She was perfectly well now – and country women gave birth to their children and were back in the fields working within days – only the aristocracy considered it necessary to rest for months after a birth. Most working women had to be up and caring for their family within a couple of days despite being told to rest for three weeks. They simply could not afford to do it. Sally was lucky enough to be able to employ people to help her.

Her mind made up, Sally rang the employment office that morning and asked for a sensible, capable nurse with plenty of experience. The agency sent her ten applicants to interview and after talking with six starchy, prim-faced women who frightened the life out of her and had Mrs Hills shaking her head in the background, she gave the job to Pearl Baxley.

'You're twenty-three and you had a year training as a children's nurse,' Sally read from her references. 'What happened – why didn't you continue your career?'

'My mother was very ill and I had to go home and take care of her and my sisters and brothers – Mum has five children under twelve.' It was a large family but many working women had ten or twelve children and struggled to support them. Their husbands refused to consider birth control and woe betide any wife who tried to practise it herself, for she would probably be accused of being wanton and having a secret lover.

'Good grief! How does she manage?' Sally asked, because one tiny baby was all she could contemplate caring for at the moment. 'Can she spare you?'

Pearl laughed. 'She is much better now, Mrs Harper. The last birth pulled her right down and she had three months in bed, but now she's well again – and my eldest sister Sapphire is nearly twelve. She helps Mum when she gets home from school – and my brother Ron helps with chores. Dad works on the construction sites all over the country, so he's not home much...'

Sally hid her smile, because Pearl's father obviously made the most of his home time with so many children. 'Don't you want to return to nursing now that your mother is better?'

'The agency told me about you, Mrs Harper, and the wage is twice what I would earn while I train – and Mum can do with the money...'

'Well, you seem a sensible girl and you must know how to take care of a young baby.' Mrs Hills was beaming and nodding her head. 'I think I should like you to start immediately if you can...'

'I'll start now,' Pearl said and smiled at her. 'Dad will be home soon and he'll get paid this trip – he was out of work for a while after he broke his shoulder in a fall. One day I might finish my training, but I'd love to work for you...' Pearl's smile lit up her face. 'I came into Harpers when it was first opened and you showed me a lovely silver bracelet. I couldn't quite afford it, but I saved up until I could and someone else sold it to me... she said you'd been promoted...'

'Yes, I was,' Sally nodded. 'I thought I'd seen you before. Well, Pearl, I'm so glad you answered my call. Some of the nurses the agency sent scared me to death. I want someone who will love looking after my little Jenny, not treat her as if she is something to be hidden away.'

'Oh, I shall,' Pearl told her. 'Palladium – that's my brother – we call him Pal...' Pearl's eyes twinkled. 'Mum called us all after precious stones or rare metals. My second eldest brother is called Silver – Mum says because his hair is like silver...'

'Poor lad,' Sally sympathised. 'What do you call him?'

'He begged us to call him Fred, but my sister Ruby calls him Ver and he answers to it.' Pearl laughed. 'Your little girl is lucky – Jenny is a lovely name.'

'Yes, it's after my sister-in-law, but she spells her name with an i at the end.' Sally smiled as she placed Jenny in Pearl's arms and saw the way the girl's face creased in a smile. 'Would you like to wear a uniform?'

'Yes, please,' Pearl said. 'People know who you are then – I have some tunics at home until you decide what you want.'

'I've picked it out and it will be here tomorrow,' Sally said. 'I'll give you two for a start, but you can ask if you need more.' She remembered it being a struggle to buy uniforms when she'd started at Harpers.

'Ah, I think Jenny needs changing...' Pearl said. 'Can you show me where her bedroom is please?'

'I'll do that, Pearl; you can get used to things before you start,' Mrs Hills said and glanced at Sally. 'Shall I tell the other applicants that you've chosen your nurse, Mrs Harper?'

'I'll do that on my way down,' Sally said, picking up her bag and a light jacket. She set her hat on her head and went out, leaving Mrs Hills and Pearl to become acquainted. A little pang of loss struck her as she closed the door at leaving her baby so soon, but she shut it away. She would only be gone a few hours and then she would be back with her little darling. The walk into Oxford Street would do her good, help her shed the few pounds she needed to so that she could get into her clothes, and it was time she got back to her job, even if it was only part-time for a while.

* * *

Everyone looked surprised as Sally walked into the store alone and up the stairs; she'd been popping in with Ben for a flying visit and given advice about various orders before, but now they recognised she was back to work properly. Most of the staff smiled and nodded, those close enough congratulated her and a few were brave enough to ask if she was feeling better and if the baby was well.

Mr Marco followed her into the lift and smiled at her. 'Your husband owes me a pound,' he said and winked at her. 'I bet him you would be back at work before the end of the week and he said it would be at least two weeks yet...'

'I've just engaged a nurse to look after her for a few hours a day and Mrs Hills is with her so I know she is quite safe. Ben hasn't met Pearl yet,' Sally said and smiled in response to his remark. 'I'll be in for just an hour or two a day for a start, preferably when Jenny's been fed and is down for a nice long sleep.'

'Of course, the baby comes first,' Mr Marco said. 'I'm glad you're in, I wanted to ask you about my new ideas. I'm sure you knew the *Pygmalion* window had crowds ten deep and the police had to move them on; the lapis lazuli window had huge crowds for a week – the idea of a magical grotto all done in shades of green and blue with silver gave us the illusion of an undersea grotto just as we'd hoped. Everyone wanted to know about the legend of the Greek hero who went in search of a magical stone to heal his lover and dived deep beneath the sea to find it for her.'

'Did the leaflets all go?' Sally asked, smiling because they'd come up with the myth between them and she'd written a little fairy tale and he'd decorated the page with images.

'Yes, every last one,' he said. 'I think Ben told your secretary to reorder everything because there was a run on the lapis lazuli jewellery...'

'Just as we'd hoped,' Sally said. She hesitated as the lift stopped at the top floor. 'Do you have anything special to discuss?'

'I'm thinking about something; I thought we might have a fairground in miniature, because they always cheer people up,' he said and then frowned. 'I think we should do as many summery and happy windows as we can before it all goes dark...'

'You mean this business in Sarajevo?' Sally sighed. 'It's why I came back sooner than I'd hoped. Ben will have enough worries without trying to do my job as well as his own. He has all the new building to sort out and it seems there is always a new problem. Everything is simple when you look at the plans, but there's always a hitch.'

Mr Marco nodded sympathetically. 'I know – and the need to keep it all under wraps and not hinder the customers is paramount.'

'Well, I have several phone calls to make,' Sally said decisively. 'I know what I want from the brochures, but they always have some bargains for the personal shopper, so I'm going to visit as many as I can before everyone starts warmongering and people get into a panic and buy more than they need and it all goes mad.' Sally knew that they would need to stock the basement with surplus stock, because when people panicked, shelves could be emptied in hours and it might become difficult to replace all they needed. They might even have to regulate what customers were allowed to buy – and she would need to consult Ben about that, but Marco was talking and she brought her wandering thoughts back to the present.

'And I shall make a tour of the departments and see what I can steal away for my strawberries and cream window.' He smiled at her. 'Wimbledon may be over for the year, but the rest of us still want strawberries and cream and cucumber sandwiches, don't we?'

'Long lazy days on the beach or by the river,' Sally said, nodding her agreement. 'Give us something quintessentially English, Mr Marco, something to make us proud – something worth fighting to preserve...'

'I knew you would understand,' he said, giving her a look of warm affection. 'Others may already be full of jingoistic nonsense and it's only a matter of time before we shall have to show our support for the troops – but until then let us celebrate all that is good and beautiful in our country.'

Sally smiled as he walked away. Mr Marco might have once been Italian or partially French, but he was completely British now and she shared his desire to give their customers a happy summer before the darkness of war descended on them all.

* * *

'Did you hear that Sally is back at work today?' Maggie asked Beth when she returned from her lunch break. 'I spoke to Mr Marco on my way back up here and he said they'd had a fruitful discussion about the windows. I told him how much we all loved the sea grotto and he said it was mostly Sally's idea.'

'It certainly pleased the customers. I saw women and children staring at it for ages and the little ones loved the mermaid and all the beautiful seashells.' She shook her head. 'It must take Mr Marco ages to source everything he needs for a window like that, he's so clever.'

'Yes, he is,' Beth agreed. 'Back to your counter, Miss Gibbs – we have customers.'

There was a stream of customers shopping. At least three told Maggie that they'd come in for the scarf they wanted now, because if war came, they might not get it in a few months. Beth had similar remarks and Marion said that the customers she'd served with hats had said the same.

Janice Browning had reported in sick that morning. Beth had told her that she was being transferred to the ground-floor department the following week and would be serving on the glassware counter. She'd pulled a sulky face but said nothing more. However, the next morning she'd called in sick, saying she had a sore throat, and although she'd come in the next day, she was off again today. Beth suspected that she was taking days off to apply for jobs elsewhere, but it was no longer a concern to her. Marion had taken over her job and, although she hadn't been told, Beth had recommended her to move up to salesgirl and asked for a new junior to take her place.

'I feel juniors I can train are so much more respectful and they learn quickly. Janice had experience elsewhere and resented my telling her that I wanted things done a certain way – so if it could be arranged...'

'I shall speak to Mr Stockbridge,' Rachel promised. 'I'm fairly certain he will agree, but it isn't for me to say.'

Beth didn't press her, because she was right. Mr Stockbridge would make the decision. She hoped Marion would be promoted permanently, because it would mean a rise in wages for her and she knew how much extra money was needed in that home. Besides, the girl was helpful, obliging and honest and that should go a long way. However, she hadn't mentioned it, because it wouldn't do to raise Marion's hopes and then nothing came of it. So, she would wait until Rachel had spoken to the manager and see what happened.

24

Marion sensed something the moment she opened the door and walked in and then she smelled the pipe smoke and knew that her father was home on one of his flying visits. She felt a shiver of anxiety, because Ma was always worse when he paid one of his infrequent visits.

'Home then at last, girl,' her father boomed at her as he came down the stairs. 'Maybe I'll get something to eat before I starve. That lazy slut upstairs refused to get up and make me some food.'

'Ma hasn't been well,' Marion said defensively. 'I bought some sausages, Pa – and I'll put some mash and cabbage and onions on for you in a minute.' Her heart sank, because it meant most of what she'd bought for their supper would go on her father's plate.

He looked at her hard and then nodded. 'I've heard how hard you've worked to keep this family goin', Marion. This is fer you, lass – spend it wisely because there's no tellin' when I'll have more fer yer.' He plonked a handful of notes and coins on the table. She stared at it, half afraid to reach for it in case he slapped her hand away. 'There's ten pounds there, girl,' he muttered. 'That lazy cow upstairs doesn't deserve a penny of it, but it's up ter you what yer do with it. I'll be away fer months and there's no guarantee that I'll be back…'

'What do you mean – are you leavin' us?' She was torn between relief and fear that they wouldn't manage, though his contributions were seldom more than a couple of pounds when he was home.

'Don't be daft, Marion,' her father grunted. 'Yer know I'm on the ships – and yer must know a war is comin'?' Marion nodded slowly. It was all people talked about on the buses now. 'Well, I'm one of the poor buggers as will be bringin' food back fer the rest of yer – and I'll likely go down with me ship one of these days. So, you and Robbie will have to take care of the family.' He frowned a her. 'Well, don't stand there like an idiot – get me bloody tea on, girl!'

'Yes, Pa.' Marion scooped the money up before he could change his mind and put it in her apron pocket. She would hide it away with the rest of her savings, because if anything happened to him, these handouts would be finished. They had never amounted to more than a few pounds, but put aside it was the rent for six weeks or so and that was a big help.

The door opened just as she was serving her father's meal and Robbie entered, together with Dickon and Milly, who had been playing next door.

'I bought some chips and a box of eggs…' Robbie said and stopped as he saw his father tucking into a plate of four sausages, mash, fried onions and cabbage. 'You're home then, Pa.'

'Yeah,' his father nodded at him, his mouth filled with perfectly fried sausage. 'Well, yer sister can cook – sit down and have yer chips and no doubt she'll get yer a bit of something else.'

'Milly, would you like an egg for your tea?' Marion asked. Her little sister shook her head and beckoned. She bent down and the child whispered in her ear that she'd had bread and jam and cake next door. 'I see – then just a glass of milk for you.'

'Robbie, Dickon, I've got sausage and a bit of fried bread if you fancy it with your chips. We'll save the eggs for breakfast – or you can have them hard-boiled with your docky bag...'

'I'll have the sausage and fried bread,' Robbie said and Dickon nodded his assent.

Marion served them all and then went upstairs to her mother with a cup of tea and a piece of bread and butter and a big ripe tomato sliced thin and sprinkled with salt and a drop of vinegar.

'I'm not hungry,' Mrs Kaye whined. 'Take it away.'

'You have to eat something,' Marion coaxed. 'The tomato smells lovely, Ma, and I bought it especially for you.'

'You eat it...'

'No, it is for you – and the tea is hot and sweet as you like it. Pa is eating his tea; he won't bother you.'

'Give it here then,' Mrs Kaye said and bit into a slice of fresh crusty bread. She smelled the tomato and then put a slice in her mouth, unable to stop it curving with pleasure. 'That is lovely.'

'Eat it all up. Pa will probably go down the pub with Mr Jackson later. You'll be all right, Ma – he knows you've been ill.'

Her mother nodded, but the tears were not far away. 'It's never stopped him in the past.'

'I know – but he's not in a bad mood, perhaps he'll leave you alone...'

Mrs Kaye nodded. She was quiet as she ate the meal Marion had lovingly prepared for her, then, 'You're a good girl, Marion. I just hope you make the right decision when you marry.'

Marion was thoughtful as she went back downstairs. She hadn't even considered getting married, even though Reggie Jackson had made it clear he was courting her. Since the church social, where he'd danced with her three times, bought her two glasses of orange juice and a chicken sandwich, and given Milly a big bag of home-made fudge he'd bought from one of the stalls, he'd been round several times. He'd invited her to Sunday tea, taken her for a walk on a nice Saturday night. Marion had worn the new dress she'd made with his mother's help and they'd stopped for a drink at the pub, sitting outside in the garden. He'd had a pint of pale ale and Marion had an orange juice; he'd offered a gin and orange or a port and lemon, but she'd stuck to her orange drink.

Since then, Reggie had presented her with a quarter-pound box of Fry's chocolates, a fruit cake his mother had made, bunches of flowers from his garden and a big bag of fresh peas he'd grown himself. He couldn't have made his intentions clearer and he'd told her he would take her to a dance on her birthday.

'I'd take yer out more,' he'd told her after their last walk together, 'but I know yer busy, Marion – and if I take yer to the music hall and dancing folk will think we're engaged.'

'Perhaps you shouldn't take me out on my birthday...' she suggested shyly. She would be seventeen then and around here that was considered old enough to be courting proper – married and with a baby on the way in many cases. The girls mainly worked in factories or canteens and often married young to escape the drudgery of their lives. Marion thought herself fortunate to have landed a wonderful job at Harpers and often had to pinch herself to make sure it was true.

'It's all right, Paula and her lad are comin' too, so we're goin' together,' Reggie had replied. 'It was Paula who suggested it – Ma wouldn't let her and Keith go on their own, so I said I'd buy tickets for us. I knew it was your birthday and I thought...' He'd looked at her hopefully then.

'I'd love to go,' Marion had told him. 'It's kind of you – and Paula – to think of me.'

'I'd like to think of you more,' Reggie had said, taking her hand for a moment and caressing it with his fingers. 'You're only young, Marion, and I'm twenty. Ma says it's too early for us to marry yet, because I need to save a bit, so I can't ask – and you have to look after Milly and the others...'

'We hardly know each other,' Marion had said because sometimes the look in his eyes made her tremble inside. She wasn't ready for marriage yet and she was glad Mrs Jackson had told him it was too soon. 'I do like you, Reggie – and I'm glad you come round for me sometimes...' It was as much as she could say to him. They were neighbours and friends and Marion felt proud that he'd singled her out, because there were lots of young girls around here who would have jumped at the chance to walk out with Reggie Jackson.

'I like you a lot,' he'd told her with a smile that made her tingle right down to her toes. 'One day I'll say more, Marion, but not yet...'

'Thank you,' she'd said, because she didn't know what else to say. Marriage was a big commitment and Marion was enjoying her life. Working at Harpers was fun now she was getting used to it and if she fell for a child it would all end. Besides, Pa would never allow it – and Ma needed her at home. Even if Reggie moved in so that she could carry on looking after her family, she wasn't ready to say yes. Marion had seen that there was more to life than the existence her mother had in these lanes. Perhaps if she worked hard, she might get on and make something more of her life, maybe even become a senior sales girl at Harpers...

* * *

'So, the news is excellent,' Beth told Marion the next morning when she called her over. 'Mrs Craven spoke to Mr Stockbridge and he is going to find us a new junior, which means that you will be promoted to salesgirl, because you're nearly seventeen now – and your wage will be sixteen shillings from next week.'

It was more than twice what she'd earned so far! Marion felt a surge of joy, lifting the dark cloud that had hung over her since the previous evening when her father had returned home drunk from his outing to the pub. He'd lurched into the kitchen, knocking into the table and spilling cocoa from the mugs she'd been going to take upstairs.

'Be careful, Pa!' she'd dared to object and his fist had swung out, catching her on the side of the head and knocking her back against the sink.

'Don't tell me what to do, girl,' he'd said and sworn at her, a filthy nasty word she'd never heard from him before.

Marion had shrunk back as he'd lurched towards the stairs.

A few minutes later and she'd heard her mother's cries, begging him to stop hurting her, screaming and weeping desperately. Marion had started towards the stairs, but Robbie caught her arm, holding her back.

'He's hurting her,' she'd cried tears on her cheeks. 'I have to stop him...'

'You can't,' Robbie told her. 'Dan tried and he knocked him down the stairs, broke his wrist and half killed him. Why do you think he cleared off and left us? I know there's no sense in trying. I'll fetch the doctor to her when he's sleeping it off.'

'Oh, Robbie...' Marion had said despairingly. 'Are all men this brutal to their wives?' To know that her mother was suffering such pain and they couldn't help her just tore her apart. Wild thoughts of asking Reggie to interfere went through her mind, but that was a last resort. Neighbours and friends did not interfere between husband and wife, even when they were aware of brutality in the home. Only a few men would actually be able to stand up to Marion's father, and though Reggie would have a go, she couldn't ask him.

'The ones that get mindlessly drunk often are,' her brother had answered her question and anger was in his eyes. 'The law should stop them, Marion, but unless he actually kills her, they will do nothing. Dan tried everything – police, lawyers, the lot; they all told him they couldn't do anything except warn Dad and he just swore at the one that tried – so Dan cleared off.'

'So, shall you go too?' Marion had asked then.

Robbie had shaken his head. 'No, because you and the others need me – but I won't help her until he's asleep. I can't...' He'd looked uncomfortable. 'I'm not a coward, Marion, but if he half kills me, I can't work and I'd lose my job – and you couldn't manage without my wage.'

Mrs Burrows was talking to her again, bringing her mind back sharply. 'Did you hear what I said, Marion?'

Marion blinked away her tears. 'Yes, Mrs Burrows, I was just shocked – it is wonderful news, thank you. It was so good of you to recommend me.'

'Well, I thought you deserved it,' her supervisor said. 'Don't let me down, Miss Kaye. I've spoken out for you – so no more being late.'

'No, Mrs Burrows, I shan't be late.'

Kathy had stayed home that morning to look after Ma. Their mother had a black eye and there were bruises all over her. Robbie had gone for the doctor, but he'd refused to come until the morning, so Kathy had offered to let him in. Milly had been sent next door to stay out of the way. Pa had slept until about seven in the morning and then got up and walked out without washing or asking for something to eat. Marion hoped he wouldn't be there when she got home that evening.

Marion had been told she could take over the hats. Maggie liked being on the scarves and gloves and had asked if she could keep her counter, but Marion was delighted with her promotion once it sunk in. She set about rearranging the displays every chance she got and when Mr Marco came in later that morning, he complimented her on the changes she had made.

'You could have a future in window dressing,' he told her and nodded as he walked round each display. 'I might ask for your help another day – if Mrs Burrows could spare you.'

'I need my staff,' Mrs Burrows said, coming up to them. 'She's made a difference already, hasn't she – so what can we do for you?'

'I want six beautiful hats,' Mr Marco said. 'The kind you would choose if you were invited to a special wedding or a garden party.'

'I think we should let Miss Kaye choose them for you,' Mrs Burrows replied. 'She has a good eye and she knows what she has in the stockroom.' Her gaze moved to Marion for a moment. 'I know I don't need to tell you – but make sure to list the hats as for window dressing.'

'Yes, Mrs Burrows,' Marion and Mr Marco answered together and he winked at Marion.

She hid her smile, went into the stockroom and came back with eight hatboxes. I think these will be just what you need.' She put them on the counter for Mr Marco to choose which he wanted and then turned away to serve a lady who had decided she wanted to purchase a white straw hat with pink roses on the brim.

Mr Marco chose six of the hats and wrote down the stock numbers and description for her. He departed, leaving the two he hadn't needed on the counter. Marion checked the list and the hats – everything was correct. She returned the hats to the stockroom and then went back to her counter, serving three customers before she was told to take her break.

As she went downstairs, intending to pop into the basement and speak to Fred Burrows, she saw Janice coming in the front door. She had clearly been shopping in her lunch break and was carrying several bags. Her eyes met Marion's and the look she gave her spoke volumes; if looks could kill, Marion would be stone dead!

* * *

Janice saw the expression in Marion's eyes and grinned inwardly. Good, the smug little bitch was afraid of her! If she wasn't now, she would be by the time Janice had finished – the other snooty bitch too, and Mrs High and Mighty Burrows. She hated them all, looking down on her as if she were something the cat had dragged in.

She knew they talked about her behind her back. She was sure that Maggie and Marion Kaye had plotted together to get her demoted to the ground floor. Well, damn them all! She would get even before she left. She'd already helped herself to as much stuff from Harpers as she could get her hands on. It was amazing how careless some of the staff were, turning their backs on her to serve a customer because they thought she was to be trusted. She'd doubled her wages most weeks since she'd been here and now she was ready to move on. Not that she'd found another job in London this time – they all wanted references and she hadn't been able to sneak into the manager's office to steal a piece of headed paper, as she'd done at her previous jobs.

A sneer touched her mouth. That stupid old Stockbridge had sent for references from the address she'd given him, and when Janice sent the reply herself, he'd been completely taken in. Because she knew exactly what time the post was delivered each day, Janice had excused herself for a bathroom break and looked for the genuine letter from her last employer. She'd known they would stamp it with their logo and it had been easy enough to remove the genuine letter from the porter's rack in the basement and destroy it, replacing it with the glowing report she'd written herself.

That Fred Burrows had looked at her oddly a couple of times, but he was always too busy to take too much notice and once, when he'd inquired what she wanted, she'd fooled him by asking if she could be of any help by taking the post up to the department. He'd thanked her and refused her offer, but he hadn't been there when she filched the letter that would have exposed her – and the young lad was too busy reading his comic to bother.

Janice found that in most places she worked the staff were careless, making it easy for her to take what she wanted from stock or sometimes cash, if they left the tea money lying about. However, things weren't going her way this time. No employer would give her a job without a reference and she'd found it impossible to get one here. Mrs Craven had told her she hadn't worked for Harpers long enough to have deserved a reference from them yet and Janice had her own reasons for not approaching the manager. She wasn't ready to hand in her notice yet, and when she did leave, it would be in a hurry, straight after she collected her wages from the office at lunchtime, as usual on a Friday. Why should she work out her notice and risk getting caught? No, she would have to move on quickly once she'd finished what she had planned for Harpers, perhaps out of London.

An unpleasant smile touched her mouth. She'd been on a farewell tour of the shops she knew were easy to rob, filling her bags with stolen goods. In Selfridges that morning, an alert floor walker had been eyeing her for a while and she'd had to leave without taking anything there, but most other shops just accepted she was a busy shopper and she'd got a good haul to sell to her fence before she went off to Birmingham or Manchester, another big town anyway.

Janice would have a nice little nest egg to see her through until she'd reinvented herself; it was easy to fool some folk and half of them didn't check references. However, she wasn't finished with Harpers yet – or those mean bitches in the bag and jewellery department. She intended to have something of theirs, even though they checked everything so carefully. It was a matter of thieves' honour that she got something from the ones she hated most, just to cause them a problem, if nothing more...

* * *

Marion was asked to cover for Maggie while she went to lunch. She served a gentleman with a scarf and some gloves and then hovered between the two counters. Three women came in and made for the hat counter and Marion went to serve them. She was busy but caught sight of a black dress from the corner of her eye and was just in time to see someone take a scarf from Maggie's counter and stuff it in her bodice.

Unable to leave her customers, Maggie signalled frantically at her supervisor. Mrs Burrows had her back turned, because she too was busy serving and before Marion could do anything to stop her, the girl in the black dress had walked out of the department.

'Excuse me, Madam, one moment...' Marion said and went hurriedly to Mrs Burrows, whispering in her ear. She looked at her startled, nodded and told her to return to her customer. 'I'm so sorry, it was important...' Marion apologised and the customer smiled and said it was perfectly all right.

It was at least ten minutes before Marion was free to speak openly to her supervisor. 'I'm sorry, Mrs Burrows. I caught sight of her as she went to the counter from the corner of my eye. By the time I realised what she had done, she was gone. I couldn't call out or stop her, but perhaps I should have done. I didn't want to cause a fuss when we had so many customers...'

'You are quite sure it was Miss Browning?'

'Yes, it was,' Marion said and tears were in her eyes. 'I saw her come into the store earlier with bags of stuff and the look she gave me – she must have guessed we'd be just the two of us now, because Maggie was at lunch, and she took a chance we'd be too busy to stop her...'

'We will ask Maggie to check her stock when she gets back.'

'It was a light green silk,' Marion said. 'I'm so sorry. I should have shouted stop or something...'

'You didn't want to cause a fuss in front of customers,' Mrs Burrows said and nodded. 'You did the right thing, Marion – yet it seems so rash and impertinent to do it right under our noses.'

'I could hardly believe she dare do it...'

'No, nor I,' Mrs Burrows agreed. 'She obviously hoped to put the blame on you or Miss Gibbs.' Janice had taken a chance she wouldn't be noticed in the lunch-hour rush, because she knew the girls took it in turns to fetch their wages and have their break – or perhaps she no longer cared if she was seen?

When Maggie returned, she confirmed that a silk scarf in green and priced at thirty-five shillings had gone. 'If you hadn't caught sight of her, either you or I would have been blamed,' Maggie said, frowning. 'That is just what she wanted – but what a risk to take while customers were in the department...'

'She counted on us being too busy to notice,' Marion said, 'and I only just saw her from the corner of my eye, because I had three customers and Mrs Burrows had two herself...'

'She chose her moment cleverly,' Maggie said. 'Where is Mrs Burrows going?' Their supervisor had waited for her return to leave the department.

'She is going to report the incident to Mrs Craven,' Marion said. 'How did Janice dare to do it? I can't understand her.' She shook her head. 'If they find it in her things, she could be arrested...'

'She will be sacked immediately,' Maggie agreed.

They both had customers then and all speculation was at an end. Maggie served on the bags, while Marion sold two hats. When Mrs Burrows returned, they were all busy for half an hour and it was only then that they learned the truth. Janice Browning had given in her notice, been paid her wages and left Harpers at lunchtime, immediately afterwards without serving her notice. As a last act of defiance and rebellion, she had taken her chance to steal the scarf in the hope of causing trouble for the other girls in the department.

'What will Mr Stockbridge do about it?' Maggie asked, looking shocked.

'I don't know,' Mrs Burrows said. 'Mrs Craven thinks she will have got rid of the scarf and anything else she may have taken before the police could search her lodgings. She was looking for another job and she might even have moved. I'm not sure that the management will think it worthwhile to pursue her now that she has moved on.' She frowned in annoyance. 'And that was another lie she told us all – there was no sick grandmother. She is living in lodgings somewhere, so the police think...'

'So, she will just get away with it...' Maggie said in disgust.

'If an employer asks Harpers for a reference, mention may be made – but perhaps not. After all, we cannot prove that she stole it, only that she left without serving her notice – which is bad enough. Marion saw her, but I fear it is only Marion's word against hers as it stands...'

'I should have shouted and made her stop,' Marion said regretfully. 'It could have been me, that's what they'll think...' She lifted her head. 'Will you search my things, Mrs Burrows?'

'It isn't necessary.'

'Please,' Marion's eyes filled with tears. 'I want you to be sure I didn't take it and try to blame her...'

'If you search Marion's things, you should search mine too,' Maggie said instantly.

'I have no intention of searching either of you,' their supervisor said. 'We know who took the scarf and why – the police may need proof, but we don't. Please do not let the incident upset either of you and now back to your counters.'

The girls obeyed and the department had customers throughout the afternoon. Trade was brisk and they all sold something, though the flurry of customers they'd had earlier was not repeated.

25

'That girl must have hung about waiting her chance,' Beth told Fred when he met her that evening after work and they caught the bus home together. 'She knew how we work and was brazen enough to walk right in and steal from under our noses...'

'Some people have no shame,' Fred said and shook his head. 'I saw her hanging about the basement a few times and wondered what she was up to, but she seemed a helpful girl and I didn't suspect her of wrongdoing. She obviously felt so bitter about being moved that she wanted to pay you back and was willing to take a huge risk.'

'Marion should have called out to me, but she didn't know what to do and I can't blame her,' Beth said and frowned. To have cried thief would have caused a fuss and upset customers, so perhaps Marion had done the wiser thing.

'Would you have gone after her and stopped her – with all those customers about?'

Beth thought about it and then shook her head. 'I had jewellery on the counter. I could have lost more than a thirty-five-shilling scarf.'

'You need another assistant or a junior,' Fred said. 'In a busy department like yours, three of you just isn't enough at times.'

'Yes, we must have our junior,' Beth agreed. 'Mrs Craven said a new girl will start next week.' She nodded. 'Of course, that is why Janice Browning took her chance today. She was leaving anyway and she'd been paid her holiday money. Maggie said she'd seen her entering the store with bags, not from Harpers but somewhere else she'd been shopping. No one would notice a scarf in with all the other stuff. I wonder if she took anything else...'

'I wouldn't mind betting they will find a few things missing from other departments when they start looking. If she had the cheek to steal from your department, she quite possibly took something from others.'

'That would make it more serious,' Beth said. 'I think I shall pop up and see if Sally has time to speak to me in the morning. If anyone knows if stock is missing, it will be her.'

* * *

Sally smiled as Beth was sent through to her and immediately asked Ruth to fetch coffee and biscuits. 'I know you're busy,' she said, 'but Rachel told me she would pop into the department and keep an eye on things while you came to see me. Miss Browning would be foolish to try it again, because we're all on the lookout for her now, but she might not know what's good for her.'

'So, you agree with me that she might have stolen from other departments?' Beth asked anxiously.

'Yes, unfortunately, I have proof,' Sally said. 'There are several items missing from the lingerie department – so easy to stuff in a pocket or inside your dress – and a new tweed skirt. The junior says she remembers Janice taking three items into the changing rooms, but when she went in to fetch them after she left without buying, only two remained. She reported it to her supervisor at once, who alerted Mrs Craven just ten minutes after you told her about the scarf. So far, we believe an expensive fountain pen, a silver milk jug and a man's silk tie have all been taken – and all these things in the space of the last couple of days...' Sally sighed. 'There is always a certain amount of pilfering in a shop like this, but most of it started when she came here. Ruth and I checked the records and, until Janice came, we had lost only two items from the ground floor, but after she started, at least one stock item was lost each week until yesterday, when there seems to have been a flurry of thefts.'

'It was her revenge for being demoted, as she saw it.' Beth sighed. 'I thought I was avoiding trouble, but it seems I've cost you dear...'

'You had nothing to do with it,' Sally said. 'The girl was bad and should never have been employed here. I have spoken to the police and given them a description; they think she is probably a habitual shoplifter and gave false references when applying for the job, though we can't work out yet how she managed to get false references through to us. It is a great shame and Mr Stockbridge is very upset at being taken in. He says that he wrote to her reference and received a very good answer from her former employer. She was supposed to be a model employee...'

'She probably stole the headed paper the letter was written on,' Beth suggested and Sally inclined her head but still looked puzzled. 'Fred saw her hanging around his department...' She gave a cry of understanding. 'Of course! She watched for the letter to appear in the post rack – perhaps it had the name of her previous employer stamped on the envelope, as many do – and swapped it for her own reference.'

'You could be right.' Sally stared at her incredulously for a moment. 'I fear she may have done – but how can one tell with a girl who can look you in the eye the way she did and make out butter wouldn't melt in her mouth?'

'Some of the girls could have lost their jobs over missing stock,' Beth said, feeling upset. 'It is very unfortunate – one bad apple...'

'Thankfully, she doesn't seem to have started stealing a large amount from us until she was moved from your department,' Sally replied. 'I dare say she has been taking stuff elsewhere and eventually the police will catch her.'

'Yes.' Beth shook her head. 'Don't you think it's sad?'

'Sad and foolish,' Sally agreed. 'We've both had hard times, Beth, but neither of us would have thought of stealing. I can't feel too sorry for her when I think of all the hard-working men and women who labour all week for the price of one of the items, she took.'

'I'm not excusing her,' Beth said, 'but she could have made something of herself. I was thinking she might take over a department one day...'

'That is for honest people like you, dear Beth,' Sally said and smiled at her. 'Now, let us think of something nicer – Ben was wondering if you and Jack would come to dinner at the flat one evening...'

'We should love to,' Beth said. 'When were you thinking?'

'Ben said this weekend.' Sally's smile dimmed. 'He thinks the situation in the Balkans is worsening. The Russians are mobilising and the Kaiser is making threatening noises...'

Beth had a sinking feeling inside as she thought of what was happening abroad. 'Jack says he'll be needed if war breaks out...'

'Yes, I know, it's horrid,' Sally said. 'Ben being American, won't be called on...' A little shudder went through her. 'I wouldn't put it past him to join if we declare war...'

'I asked Jack what would happen to the hotel. He says his

partner will manage – he's too old to volunteer – and his father can keep an eye on things.'

'Fred won't leave us, will he?'

'He says he's too old for the army, but he'll volunteer for home defence or whatever is required.' Beth blinked hard. 'I can't believe he'll be accepted for anything like that. War won't come here, surely...'

'I shouldn't think so, not for a minute,' Sally agreed. 'Ben says it will be a storm in a teacup, but he thinks a lot of young men will join up just for the fun of it...'

'Fun!' Beth looked at her in horror. 'Surely there's no fun in men getting shot at?'

'You know what men are like when it comes to war and adventure,' Sally said and shrugged. 'No one thinks it will be much fun, but the youngsters will join up in flocks. Some will think it's easier work than they have now and patriotic too; they want to do their bit for King and Country'

Beth finished her coffee. She hadn't eaten one of the chocolate biscuits, because she felt suddenly sick and shivery. 'Well, I wish the foreigners would all go away and fight their own wars. Why should our men get involved?'

'I agree, but we're women,' Sally said and laughed. 'Cheer up, Beth – the navy will probably get their gunboats out, fire a few rounds and then the enemy will run home.'

Beth laughed as her friend intended. 'You're wicked, Sally Harper. How is that little darling of yours?'

'Adorable,' Sally said, 'and quite happy with her worshippers at home. Pearl and Mrs Hills have combined to spoil her and I'm with her for most of her feeds. I think she only has to open her mouth and one of them has her out of the cot and on their laps.'

'You'll never do anything with her if they pick her up all the time,' Beth said. 'My mother always said babies should be left to cry because it spoils them if you pick them up every time they do.'

'Try telling that to Pearl and Mrs Hills,' Sally said and made a face. When we get home, Ben is just as bad, always picking her up and telling her how beautiful she is – she will be vain, of course.'

'No, she won't, because she's your daughter,' Beth said and glanced at her watch. 'I'd better get back or Rachel will kill me.'

'Has she given you a date for her wedding?' Sally asked, standing up and smoothing biscuit crumbs from her elegant dress. 'I think it's soon now, early next month. She mentioned an invitation on its way only this morning...'

'Yes, it's all arranged for the 15th August,' Beth replied. 'She said it was sooner than she'd anticipated, but William had persuaded her to bring it forward just in case. She is a bit worried about what Miss Minnie and Maggie will do when she moves out...'

'You mean about renting the apartment?'

Beth nodded. 'I think Fred would agree that we could offer Maggie a room for a while and I suppose she could share with Miss Minnie, if they wished...' Her father-in-law was so easy going that she knew she didn't even have to ask if he minded her friends staying in his house.

'I know Maggie will be all right with you, but Miss Minnie... well. She was Rachel's particular friend and she might not feel comfortable...'

'Well, the offer is there,' Beth said and, at Sally's invitation, kissed her on the cheek. 'I'll tell Rachel on my way back to the department.'

* * *

'That is so kind of you to offer,' Rachel said. 'I'd planned to give them until September to find somewhere, but William begged me to bring the wedding forward. He is very worried about the situation and says he will not wait to be called if it happens – his grandfather was a cavalry officer and so was his father. He went into politics instead, but if it's war...'

'Sally says a lot of men will rush to join up,' Beth said and shuddered. 'Jack says he'll be needed, but I keep hoping it won't really happen.'

'I think it has been inevitable that Russia and Germany would go to war since the assassination,' Rachel said. 'It's just a matter of time...'

'Oh hell!' Beth muttered and then flushed. 'I beg your pardon, but you know how I feel.'

'Of course, I do, Beth; we all feel the same,' Rachel said. 'Thank you for the offer – I shall speak to both Minnie and Maggie this evening and hear what they have to say...'

'Good.' Beth smiled and watched as her friend left the department. She'd been surprised when Rachel first said she would marry again so soon, but now she was pleased for her friend. Everyone should grab their happiness while they could.

* * *

Beth spoke to Fred about the room that evening when they got home. She'd mentioned it before and he'd told her to go ahead and offer it to her friends. He nodded his approval.

'I doubt Miss Minnie would want to stop here long, but it's somewhere for her to come if she's stuck,' he said thoughtfully. 'However, that young Maggie – well, I dare say she'll be glad to be here with you.' He smiled. 'It will be a bit of company for you at night, Beth. If Jack is away and I'm on fire watch...'

'Fire watch?' Beth looked at him in surprise. 'Is that what you expect to be doing?'

'I've already joined the volunteer unit,' Fred said. 'We'll be needed to help with fires and the like at night – the enemy may have spies here and they will try to sabotage our factories, so they'll need volunteers to keep a watch at night, and some of the regular firemen will be joining up to fight...'

'Surely they are needed here?'

'Aye, they are, and most will see it as their duty to stay and keep London safe, but some of the younger ones will be off as soon as the call comes.'

'It hasn't happened yet – and it's a holiday this Monday. Bank holiday and everyone is looking to have fun – a day at the sea with the kids...' Beth frowned. 'I don't see why we should fight at all, Fred. Our government offered to mediate and they turned them down, said we were presumptuous...'

'British insolence they called it,' Fred said and nodded his agreement. 'We ought to tell them all to go to hell, Beth, but there's only one way to do that.'

Beth sighed. Fred read every single line of every report on the situation and he was convinced Britain would have to fight despite all the voices raised against it. She supposed a lot of the men at Harpers felt the same way and wondered just how many of their staff would have to fight, if it came to it.

* * *

Marco looked at himself in the dressing mirror of his bedroom. He had a smart flat not far from Harpers, which he had furnished exquisitely and his flair had made it a perfect example of Art Deco decadence – at least, that was what Julien had told him, teasing him as they spent precious hours here. It seemed so lonely without him.

He was due to attend a private party that evening. Given by an actor well known for his flamboyant ways and his sexual tastes, Marco was an honoured guest and he knew there would be good food, the best wines, cigars and witty company. He was welcome at all the theatrical parties, because his talent was recognised and no one cared that he had loved a young man rather than a girl – many of his friends had the same tastes. All of them were considered outsiders by mainstream society, except by the enlightened few such as Fred Burrows and the Harpers.

Fred was very worried about the coming war, Marco knew. He had two sons, both of whom could be called upon to give their lives for their country. Marco had spent an hour talking to him in the basement earlier that day, discussing the coming war as he sourced bits and pieces he needed for his latest window. Marco liked the man who had come to Harpers because he'd refused to be a bully and cane the boys in his school – Fred was a man of principle.

'I'd fight if they'd have me,' he'd told Marco over a cup of hot sweet tea. 'It's the duty of any man that can – but I fear for my sons. If I could go for them I would…'

'Yes, I believe you would.' Marco had smiled, because he respected Fred and all he stood for. Also, he knew that Julien would have joined up already.

Marco smiled oddly as he switched out the light and prepared to leave for the evening. He would go to his party because he had nothing else to do – but he already knew where his duty lay and he wouldn't shirk it. Men of his age would be needed; he was only forty after all and could still fight or march if need be, though it was likely he would be used in other ways. Perhaps in the stores or the canteen. When the call came, he would answer.

26

Dinner with Sally and Ben was lovely and they all talked and laughed over the meal, enjoying the chance to relax and share their thoughts, hopes and dreams for the future. Ben and Jack went into a huddle when Sally took Beth off to see her daughter and the ominous words, conflict, war and mobilise, were heard as the women left the room.

'It won't all be war talk,' Sally reassured Beth as she took her into the child's bedroom, which was pink and white, with lots of lace, soft fluffy rugs and toys, and reassuringly calm. 'Ben wanted to have a chat with your husband about the hotel. He won't be joining up, at least for a while, and he says he'll offer to cast an eye over things for Jack. He has some idea of them going into partnership in a restaurant at some point ...' Sally made a wry face. 'At the moment, every penny we have is tied up in Harpers' new premises, but Ben would like to diversify in the future and I'm sure that's what they will be talking about.'

'Oh, I see, that would be wonderful, Sally.'

Beth looked down at the face of the child; soft and flushed with sleep, she was beautiful and a pang of regret went through her because, so far, she had failed to conceive another child after losing her first.

'You're so lucky to have her, Sally...'

'Yes, I know – even when she wakes us every hour through the night,' Sally said and laughed. 'Although she isn't as bad now. I give her a feed at night and she settles, but Paula feeds her with a bottle during the day and that makes it easier for me. The midwife at the hospital would not approve, but my doctor said that it was better for me to do it that way if I wanted to work – and I do.'

'You're so brave,' Beth said. 'A lot of women wouldn't dare to go against the midwife.'

'In rich families, the child is often breastfed by a wet nurse, of course. Luckily, Jenny has taken to the bottle, which is good because it means I don't need to be here all the time.'

Beth nodded, because Sally was always so modern and full of new ideas. She would never adhere to the old rules that a woman must stay at home and nurse her baby herself. Perhaps that rule only applied to the ordinary woman and women from the aristocracy had never nursed their own babies. Yet Beth felt that perhaps Sally was missing out on that special bond between mother and child. Was it possible that she could have a good marriage, loving husband, beautiful child and a job that a lot of men would love to have? Was she pushing her luck too far?

'You'll have a child one day,' Sally said gently. 'It will happen, Beth, you just have to be patient.'

'I know – but this war...' Beth couldn't voice the fear inside her. If Jack volunteered for the merchant navy and his ship was sunk... She shook her head. It was wrong and foolish to think like that and she had to be strong for him, because he was the one who would be leaving all he'd strived for to serve his country.

'We'd better go back,' Sally said as the baby continued to sleep, undisturbed by thoughts of war. 'I thought she might wake so you could hold her, but she's so peaceful I don't like to wake her.'

'Oh, no, please don't,' Beth said and looked at the baby again. 'She is so perfect...'

'Yes, she is,' Sally agreed.

They returned to the sitting room and found the men drinking brandy in Ben's treasured old glasses that he'd found in a London antique shop; they were Georgian glass and very precious, a sign that he valued his visitors. He saluted his wife with a loving smile and inclined his head to Beth.

'Your husband is going to be my partner in a new high-class restaurant in Oxford Street when we find the right premises,' he announced enthusiastically. 'It won't be for a while, perhaps a few years, but we'll call it Harpers to tie it in with the store, but Jack will be a partner and, in the meantime, I'm going to look after his interests at the hotel while he's away...'

Beth looked at Jack and saw he looked pleased, if a little stunned. He didn't know Ben Harper as well as she did and hadn't realised what a powerful force he could be when he was enthusiastic about something. Jack looked as if he'd been picked up by a strong wind and carried further than he could yet comprehend. It was probably all talk brought on by the fine brandy, but the idea of diversifying might be something for the future – if Jack ever got the hotel to the stage where his manager could take it over and he didn't need to be there all hours. However, she wouldn't count her chickens just yet. Men tended to get big ideas over their after-dinner drinks.

'We need that little café next door to us to sell up and we could keep it all together,' Sally said and saw a gleam in her husband's eye. Both men had clearly been enjoying the brandy and Ben was already thinking about the adjoining properties and lining them up in his mind. 'But not just yet please, we mustn't run before we can walk.'

'No need to remind me,' Ben said. 'Jack knows I'm not ready to move on it yet, but we've agreed a way forward for the future.' He beamed at them all. 'It's something to strive for – something to survive for... for our families.'

'I'll agree with that,' Jack said hoarsely and then grinned. He lifted his glass. 'To the future of Harpers – all our futures.'

'All our futures!' Everyone sipped their drinks and Beth and Sally smiled at each other in amusement.

More drinks were produced and they all had a nightcap before Beth and Jack left in a taxicab.

'It's just as well I didn't bring the car,' Jack said as they were driven home. 'I'm not sure I could have made it; I might have had one too many...'

'It was that twenty-five-year-old brandy,' Beth said and smiled as he lolled against her. Her husband wasn't used to fine wines and brandies and it had gone to his head a little. 'Ben is very generous – perhaps too much so.'

'He has a good head for business,' Jack said. 'Good man to have on your side, Beth – even if he is an American...'

'Jack! He's Sally's husband and my boss.'

'Well, I said he's a good bloke,' Jack said and laughed a bit too loudly. 'I don't usually care for American's, but he's all right.'

'Yes, he is,' Beth agreed. Some of the staff at Harpers hadn't been sure when he'd first announced he was taking over the store after his uncle's death, but he'd proved to be a good boss and by marrying Sally he'd surely put down roots in London that he wouldn't want to pull up? 'Everyone likes him at Harpers.'

'Of course, they do,' Jack agreed and nuzzled her neck. 'Are you tired, Beth? I'm not. A bit carried away, but happy and a little bit amorous...'

Beth laughed up at him, her arms sliding about his body as she went to him without reserve. She'd drunk enough of Ben's brandy to let all her inhibitions fly away and as Jack laughed, kissed her passionately and then carried her up the stairs to their room, she was conscious of feeling happy. At that moment, the war and all it entailed was far from her thoughts.

Jack made love to her that night with a passion and hunger that took her breath and made her cry out his name. She had never felt as good as she did when they touched and loved, reaching a far place that she hadn't known existed until that night. Yes, she'd gradually come to pleasure in her husband's arms, though it had taken her a while to let herself feel it, but this time she was swept away and afterwards lay with tears on her cheeks and her body tingling with love and yet a feeling of utter content.

'Oh, Beth, my darling, I do love you so much,' Jack said and promptly fell asleep with his head on her naked breasts.

Beth stroked his hair gently, her tears trickling into her mouth so that she could taste the salt. He was so precious to her. She hadn't realised quite how much she loved him until these past few days, when the possibility of the war had raised his ugly head.

27

'Oh, that is so kind of Beth, inviting us to stay with her for a while,' Minnie said when Rachel told her what had been suggested. 'I can see how helpful that would be...' She seemed to hesitate, then, 'I am not quite sure, though it might be a good idea for a time.'

'I'm sure Beth doesn't expect you to stay there for ever. Maggie is looking forward to it, but, of course, she knows the whole family...'

'Yes, of course...' Minnie looked pensive. 'Beth is always so kind and I love dear Maggie and I should be quite comfortable sharing with her – it's just that my circumstances may alter soon...'

Rachel waited, but Minnie didn't enlarge, just looked vague and either excited or uneasy. She wasn't sure which but felt it wasn't her place to push. The suggestion had been made because neither she nor Maggie had had much luck looking for a room they liked. They couldn't afford to keep the flat on and Rachel had given notice, which meant they would have to leave a few days after her wedding. She'd felt very guilty over it for a while, because it seemed so unkind to turn them out – especially Minnie, who she'd invited to share. It might have been better to leave her at the boarding house, but the flat was nearer her new job at Harpers and Minnie had seemed so much happier once she'd settled into the job. Especially after she'd started going to tea with Becky Stockbridge every weekend. She seemed to have a new spring in her step and her eyes were bright, her mouth always turning up in a smile. Sometimes, Rachel could hardly recognise her as the timid sister of Mildred and wondered what had given her this new energy and confidence.

She spoke to Maggie on Sunday morning after Minnie had gone out for a little walk. 'You are happy about moving into Beth's after my wedding, aren't you?'

'Yes, very much so,' Maggie told her. 'You know I stayed with Beth at her aunt's and I like Fred and of course there's Tim. He goes home as often as he can. Jack is like a big brother to me. I shall miss seeing you every evening, Rachel – but I shall see you at Harpers. You won't be giving up your job?'

'No, not for the present,' Rachel agreed. 'William is going to make inquiries about joining the Army in some capacity as soon as we've had our honeymoon. His family would expect it, because they've always had military connections and, in the event of a war, he feels it is the right thing to do – though he may not be front line, of course. We thought it best if I continue to work until it all blows over, because he might be away a lot. Everyone thinks this conflict will not be much, Maggie. William is confident that it will be settled by Christmas. If they had only listened to our government, there need not have been any of this trouble at all, but he says we shall have to send a few gunboats and rap them over the knuckles a bit; he thinks it inevitable.'

'Tim says he thinks they may get a bit of action in the Royal Flying Corps and he thinks it is great fun,' Maggie said with a frown. 'I can't see how it can be – after all, they use guns and things and that means men get hurt, doesn't it?'

'Yes, I think it is inescapable that some will be hurt – even killed – but hopefully they will pull back on the brink and we may still avoid it.'

'Fred Burrows doesn't think so...' Maggie bit her lip. 'The men seem to be so excited over it – but I think it's horrible. I wish they would all stop talking about it. Why does it have to happen?'

'It's all a matter of treaties and alliances,' Rachel said. 'William explained it all to me, but I can't remember half of what he said – but apparently we have to support France and Russia, and Germany and their allies are the aggressors. It all seems nonsense to me and I just keep hoping they will all see sense and talk it over rather than fighting.'

'Yes...' Maggie let out a sigh and decided to change the subject. 'Minnie and I are going to lunch with Becky and Mr Stockbridge again this week. Tim has to work, so I said I would, because Minnie was keen, though I should've liked to go to a meeting of the Women's Movement. Some of the members are saying that the militants should scale down their activities in the event of a war. They won't like it because they still haven't achieved what we want and some of them have been treated so badly – but to do otherwise would make us traitors. Just because we don't like the way the government treats Mrs Pankhurst doesn't mean we can betray our country by causing problems...'

'Oh, I do agree,' Rachel said instantly. 'I've never really liked the idea of using violence – and those bombs could have hurt a lot more than just property. I do not hold with murder, even if it is in a good cause.'

'I feel the same as you and so does Beth,' Maggie said. 'I want the vote for women as much as anyone, but I don't want to kill anyone to get my way.'

'I'm going to miss having you about all the time,' Rachel said, smiling at her fondly, 'but we shall meet at work – and you will have to come and have tea with me sometimes. You can always ask Becky to come with you – or Tim if you wish...'

'Yes, I shall, thank you,' Maggie said and kissed her cheek. 'You've been such a good friend to me since my father died. I don't know what I should have done without you and Beth, Sally, too, of course, but she seems above me these days, even though she doesn't mean to.'

Rachel nodded. 'Sally is very busy, Maggie, and she has Harpers to look after. Mr Harper relies on her for so much – and, of course, she has that beautiful little girl.'

'She is gorgeous,' Maggie said. 'Sally brought her in to the office the other day and then took her on a tour of all the departments. I thought she was beautiful.'

'Yes, I saw little Jenny, and I think she will grow up to be as charming as her mother,' Rachel said. 'Well, I must get ready. William is calling for me shortly. We're going to his house and taking some of my things...' She paused and laughed. 'It was so funny when he took me to meet his family. They were trying to be polite, but they didn't know what to say to me, because they'd never heard of a woman working as a supervisor and they seemed to be confused as to whether to welcome me to the family or dismiss me to the servants' quarters.'

'Oh, Rachel, how could they be so unkind?'

She smiled and shook her head. 'No, really, I didn't mind. William warned me they were funny old things – and why should I mind? He loves me and they won't do anything to offend him.' She shook her head at the memory. 'Shall you be back for tea, Maggie?'

'I think we'll probably stay for tea and come home at about seven...'

'I'll be back by then too so we'll catch up this evening.'

* * *

On Monday morning, the newspapers reported that the United Kingdom's Royal Navy had been mobilised. The Kaiser had already declared war on the Czar of Russia and tension was heightened. Everyone was waiting for the news that would plunge Britain into war. The newsboys all over London were shouting the news that the British government had warned Germany that they would stand by the treaty of 1839 and protect the French coastline.

It was a bank holiday and for Rachel the day seemed to drag. Minnie had gone out first thing in the morning wearing her best summer frock and hat and Maggie had gone to meet Tim, who had a day off from his unit. William had told her he would be at meetings all day and she spent the morning packing bits and pieces and pacing the flat that suddenly seemed too small.

After eating a solitary lunch, she packed some home-made cakes and caught the bus to see her former mother-in-law. Mrs Hazel Craven greeted her with a smile that didn't reach her eyes.

'I suppose this is the last time I shall see you,' she said sourly, looking at the beautiful diamond ring on Rachel's left hand. 'You won't bother with me when you're married to that man.'

'I see no reason why I shouldn't visit now and then, as I always have,' Rachel said. 'I thought we were friends, Hazel – the fact that Paul died and I'm going to remarry should make no difference to that.'

To her consternation, Hazel burst into tears, sobbing into her lavender-scented handkerchief. 'I thought you would forget me now...'

'Of course, I shan't,' Rachel said and suddenly realised how lonely Hazel must be. Paul had been her only child and unlike Rachel she had not found work or made lots of new friends. 'I shall never forget Paul and I shall never forget you. I hope that when I am settled in my new home you will come and have lunch or tea with me sometimes, and I shall still visit.'

She wiped her tears. 'What a foolish woman I am, Rachel. You seem so busy and happy with that job – and now you've found a new love...'

'Yes, I am very lucky,' Rachel told her. 'But if this awful war starts, my William will join up and that means I'll be spending a lot of time alone, I shall certainly need all my friends and that includes you, Hazel.'

'Thank you,' she said and then gestured to the kitchen. 'I'll just go and put the kettle on.'

* * *

Rachel stayed until gone seven, talking and sharing tea and cakes. Hazel showed her the dress and coat she intended wearing to the wedding and a hat she'd bought especially, in Harpers.

'Very smart,' Rachel said. 'I'm so glad you're coming to the wedding, Hazel. I don't have any family other than you and I really appreciate it.'

Hazel had pressed a soft parcel into her hands. 'It's good linen I had when I was first married,' she told Rachel. 'I don't use it now and I'd like you to have it.'

'Thank you, I should love it,' Rachel said and kissed her cheek. 'William's family have accepted me; I was made welcome at their home for lunch, but I know they don't really approve – and you really are my only family apart from William.'

She left Hazel Craven happier than when she'd arrived, making up her mind to encourage her to take up some kind of charity work when she next saw her. Her former mother-in-law would never look for paid work, because she hadn't been brought up to think of it. Hazel did not have Minnie's talents with a needle, so wouldn't be able to find genteel work she could manage, so lived on the income from the money her late husband had invested for her. It was sufficient for her to live decently and she didn't have to go without anything, though she didn't have a great deal to throw away either and she must have thought long and hard before buying a new hat for Rachel's wedding.

Rachel had known what it was like to have to count the pennies after Paul died, but she'd found work and now she was to marry a man who she knew to be comfortably off, if not rich. He had already told her that he would be setting aside a sum of money for her that would be hers to do with as she wished.

Some of his personal fortune was in shares and he was concerned because the stock exchange had announced it was closing its doors and would not reopen until things were more settled.

'I've put money aside for us both in case there should be a crash,' he'd told her. 'But, as I was unable to liquidise my holdings, I could take a hit – so it's just as well I put some away for you.'

William wanted her to be independent of his family, because although they'd been polite while she was in their home, they hadn't seen her as being of their class and she would never wish to ask them for anything.

Afterwards, William had told her his thoughts. 'If anything should happen – and I'm not thinking it will – but if it should, you will be independent for life, Rachel. I don't want you to sink into genteel poverty as many widows do, so that money is yours.' He'd smiled as she'd tried to protest. 'No, my dearest one, I am adamant. You will continue to work for a while, as it is your pleasure, but I shall make you secure. I'm not a very wealthy man, but I am very comfortably placed, which I know you do not care for one jot, but you will oblige me by accepting my gift.'

Rachel had simply kissed him. What else could she say. She'd never told William how difficult things had been for her after

Paul died, but he knew and he was making sure it could not happen again. She was grateful and it just made her even more certain that he was the man she loved and she was doing the right thing by becoming his wife.

When she got back to the flat that evening, Rachel discovered that both Maggie and Minnie were there, sitting drinking a glass of wine, which was unusual, as their usual bedtime drink was a cup of milky cocoa.

Minnie blushed as Rachel looked at them. 'What is the celebration?'

'Go on, tell her,' Maggie said and the excitement was bubbling out of her. 'Show her your hand, Minnie.'

Minnie slowly raised her left hand to show the pretty ruby and pearl five-stone ring. 'Will you congratulate me, Rachel? Mr Stockbridge – Jonathan and I – we are to be married.'

'Goodness gracious!' Rachel was astounded and sat down on a chair before her legs went from under her. 'I had no idea – neither of you breathed a word. Did you know, Maggie?'

Maggie giggled but shook her head. 'Becky told me she thought her father was sweet on Miss Minnie and I knew he smiled all the time when she was around. They went to look at his roses a lot and I understand there were walks in the park...' Her eyes teased Minnie. 'Tell Rachel all of it, Minnie.'

Minnie's cheeks were on fire. 'I had no idea he was the manager when you encouraged me to work for Harpers,' she said. 'I was just so pleased to be here with you and dear Maggie – and Mrs Harper gave me the job without my going through the usual channels. And then... I saw Jonathan after I'd begun work. He came to the department and we knew each other at once. We talked and he asked me to make a dress for Becky and, well... you see, he was the man I gave up for my sister when Papa died...'

'Minnie!' Rachel stared at her. 'I'm flabbergasted; I had no idea. You never said one word...'

'Well, what could I say? I knew that I had never stopped loving him, but I had no idea that he might still remember and think of me. He cared for his wife, but he told me that he has always loved me...' Her face lit in a smile of wonder and delight. 'I feel as if I'm dreaming, Rachel.'

'That is wonderful,' Rachel said and went to embrace her. 'I couldn't be happier, Minnie. I'm so glad you've found happiness.'

'I never expected it at my time of life,' Minnie said and glanced at her ring in disbelief. 'I knew Jonathan had married, but I had no idea that his wife had died, leaving him with a young daughter to bring up alone.'

'Well, that is wonderful,' Rachel repeated herself because she was still in shock. Minnie had hinted earlier that she might have plans of her own, but it had never occurred to her that she might marry. 'Do you know when?'

'In September we thought,' Minnie said. 'You will be married and Maggie will be living with Beth. I shall also take advantage of Beth's kind offer, just for a few weeks. I need to make my dress, but Jonathan will take all my things to his home when I move, apart from a few personal bits.'

Rachel looked at Maggie, feeling like laughing. 'You haven't got any surprise announcements, have you?'

'No, not yet,' Maggie said but looked thoughtful. 'Tim and I are in no hurry to do anything – but I might have other plans...' She laughed and shook her head as Rachel questioned with her eyes. 'No, I'm not certain yet, Rachel.'

'Well, I think I need a glass of that wine,' Rachel said as Minnie set hers down hardly touched.

'I was just about to make some cocoa,' Minnie said. 'I had a sip or two, Maggie dear, but I couldn't manage any more.'

'I'll have yours,' Rachel said. 'I've had quite a few surprises this evening and I could do with a nightcap...'

28

Marion felt the excitement as she walked into the department on the Tuesday morning after the bank holiday and started to uncover the hats, removing the silk squares that protected the expensive items from dust overnight and readjusting some of the stands. Mrs Craven was talking to Beth and Maggie and, after a moment, she went to join them.

'Ah, Marion,' her supervisor said. 'As we all know, this is a momentous day for us all. So, today, we speak as friends, but, of course, formality returns once the floor is open. The country is now on the brink of war, which will affect all our lives. However, there is something of a different nature I wish to talk about first – Mrs Craven has been telling us that Miss Minnie is to marry Mr Stockbridge and quite soon. Obviously, the circumstances brought about by the military situation makes everyone uneasy and so they are not going to wait for a long engagement.'

Marion had to think for a moment and then her brow cleared. 'Miss Minnie works in the alterations department.' She'd thought the woman was a confirmed spinster and felt surprised, but struggled not to show it. 'I didn't know they were courting...'

'Nor did anyone else...' Mrs Craven said and laughed. 'It was quite a surprise, but a very nice one. I am delighted and she is very happy.'

'Did you know about it, Maggie?' Marion asked.

'I knew they liked each other a lot, but I had no idea they were so advanced. It's because they knew each other years ago. They were in love, but Minnie's father died and her sister couldn't manage alone, so she gave up her chance of happiness to be with Mildred.'

Mrs Burrows nodded and looked sad. 'Yes, of course, she would. Together they could survive, but her sister would not have managed alone.'

'Could she not have lived with them?'

'She would have been their dependant and I dare say she would not have agreed,' Mrs Burrows said. She knew exactly the reasoning for Miss Minnie's sacrifice for it had happened to her too, but it was her mother who had refused to let her marry Mark, whereas Miss Minnie had done it voluntarily for her sister.

'It's very romantic, isn't it?' Maggie said and laughed. 'Becky is thrilled over it, because she doesn't remember her mother and she has grown to love Minnie – so she will be happy to have her move in with them.'

'Will Minnie give up her work with Harpers?' Marion asked.

'I expect she will work from home, just come in once or twice a week and pick up orders. She is so good at her work that I'm sure she will want to continue, but she won't come into work every day. I think Harpers will need another seamstress, because the alterations have taken on a lot of work since she's been there – whoever they choose will have to be good to replace her,' Mrs Craven said. 'But Harpers brought them together – as it has all of us – and it is important in all our lives I know.' Everyone nodded, because it was more than a place of employment, Harpers was a feeling of being part of something, of belonging.

'Excuse me for asking,' Marion said, 'but have you seen the headlines this morning? Germany has invaded France and that means it will definitely be war, doesn't it?'

'Yes, I think we've all seen the news, but it's not official yet. We have to wait for the King's announcement, but it is sure to come,' Mrs Craven said and looked grave. 'It is worrying, but there's nothing any of us can do, Marion, and Harpers will carry on as usual and we'll all come in to work each day and support each other and the store...' She paused, then, 'It is terrible news, but I don't think we should let it overshadow Minnie's wedding news.'

Marion heard Maggie's indrawn breath as though she would deny that statement, but she didn't say anything so Marion didn't either. Mrs Craven departed then and told them she would let them know of any developments later in the day. Mrs Burrows told them to get to their counters and the department door was officially opened. Within five minutes, the first customer arrived. She came to Marion's counter and asked to try on some hats. Marion noticed that several more customers arrived soon after and both Mrs Burrows and Miss Gibbs were soon busy. Marion's customer selected three hats and brought them to the counter.

'I can't make up my mind and I'm going to buy them all,' the woman said. 'After all, we don't know what will happen now, do we? If things go badly for us, we might not be able to buy a new hat...'

Marion was puzzled and then she realised what the customer was thinking; if there was a war, it might cut back on supplies and the shops wouldn't have as much stock to show.

The rush lasted until lunchtime and then, just as Marion was about to leave for her break, Mrs Craven entered the department.

'Mr Harper has called a meeting for this afternoon when we close,' she said. 'We shall close the doors half an hour early so that none of you will miss your bus home.'

'What is it about?' Marion asked fearfully, though she already knew because the anticipation of war was in everyone's minds.

'Have any of your customers mentioned what's going on?' Mrs Craven asked, but Marion shook her head. 'Apparently, there are cheering crowds in Downing Street... people singing the national anthem and they're gathering outside the palace, calling for the King and Queen.'

'Someone told me about that,' Mrs Burrows said. 'I think she also said they are going to open recruiting offices all over London – the whole country. Men will be joining up...'

'Yes, that is exactly what will happen,' Mrs Craven agreed. 'William is going to wait until after the wedding. We'll have a couple of days away and then he'll join a cavalry regiment. He was born on a country estate and has good riding and shooting skills so I'm sure he will be accepted.'

'Jack will go back to sea,' Mrs Burrows said and Marion saw tears in her eyes.

'What will happen to Harpers if all the men go rushing off to war?' she asked timidly.

'I expect that is what Mr Harper wants to talk about,' Mrs Craven said. 'Some of our staff are too old to join the army, others too young – and we have quite a few women, so I dare say we shall manage.'

Marion was told to have her lunch. She went out and found a seat on a bench in the nearest square and sat down to eat her sandwiches and an apple. It was sweet and crispy and she enjoyed the luxury of having fresh fruit. She thought there were a lot of men about and a definite air of anticipation and excitement. The newspaper stands were busy as people rushed to buy the latest editions and the word war echoed on the vendors' lips.

Marion ate her apple thoughtfully. Reggie had bought a bag of ripe English apples for her and the others and, after sharing them out, Marion had saved one for her own lunch.

Reggie was so generous to her. Every week there were a few sweets for Milly, a small bottle of mild beer for her brother and a ticket for the football when in season. He often brought some fruit or a small bar of chocolate for Marion and she knew that in his own way he was courting her. He hadn't taken her out often, just a walk in the park and the dances they shared at the church social, but he had taken her to one dance at the Methodist Hall on her birthday, where a quartet had played romantic music all evening, and she'd felt as if she were in heaven as he taught her to waltz and do various other fancy steps. Previously, Marion had only been able to do the barn dances they did at the church socials, but Reggie had taught her the tango as well as the waltz, which was very daring, and yet he made her feel special as he held her as gently as if she were made of precious china.

Would Reggie have to fight? Surely, he wouldn't sign up? He had a good job on the docks and his work was necessary, he didn't need to go rushing off to war. There were regular soldiers for that, weren't there?

She shook her head because the idea that Reggie might have to go to be a soldier upset her. Suddenly realising the time, Marion began to run. She had just five minutes to get back and if she was late, Mrs Burrows would be cross – she could lose her job.

She must have been a couple of minutes late back, but Mrs Burrows was serving a customer and didn't seem to notice. Marion hastened to stand behind her counter and was soon serving a customer. The first rush seemed to have tailed off, but sales were still brisk. More than one customer hinted that she was buying now in case she couldn't get what she wanted later in the year.

It was a short afternoon because of the early closing and then everyone went up to the café on the top floor to hear what Mr

Harper had to say. Everyone was chattering, but when their employer appeared, it all went suddenly quiet.

'Thank you for coming, ladies and gentleman,' Mr Harper said and Marion thought you could have heard a pin drop. 'You will all have heard the dreadful news today and I know that some of you will be wondering what to do – well, I have this to say: any man who signs up to fight for this wonderful country has my admiration and my promise that his job will still be his when he comes back after it is all over. We shall take on youngsters and older men and ladies too – and, as I hope to expand Harpers, there will still be a place for anyone who has worked here but went to do his duty...' A few cheers broke out and Mr Harper held up his hand. 'I am not a coward and if it becomes necessary, I shall join up myself, but for the moment I'm staying on here to make sure we all have jobs to return to...'

More cheers and then a voice from the back said, 'You're American, sir, you don't have to fight...'

'I choose to live here and if Britain were invaded, I'd be out on the streets with a gun like the rest of you,' Mr Harper said. 'You have my word that I shall be doing my bit for Britain as well as Harpers and I already have a large ship packed as full as it can get on its way here. I'm doing my best to make sure we have stock to carry us through any conflict.'

'Those bloody Germans won't dare fire on an American ship,' someone cried angrily.

'I am hoping our flag will keep us safe, but I don't know how long that neutrality will last – war is war, gentlemen, and I think it won't be long before they think we're fair game if we're heading for Britain with food and ammunition, which I think you can count on. As for our ladies – we're going to rely on you and perhaps recruit more of your sisters and daughters so we can carry on...'

'They'll wish they hadn't if they do,' a woman's voice said and Mr Harper smiled.

'Thank you for the vote of confidence, ma'am, I agree with you – and I hope this nonsense is all over by Christmas, if not before.'

There was a chorus of agreement and anger too, because war was unsettling and though many of the younger men were keen to do their bit, women and older men felt more cautious and uneasy about the prospect of such a war.

Mr Harper went on to tell his staff that any men wishing to leave should let the office know and they would be paid to the day they left and any holiday pay due to them.

'Once again, I want to reassure you that no one will be penalised for doing their duty and we shall honour your sacrifice and be happy to greet you when you come home to us...'

A few cheers met his last words and some questions, then the meeting broke up and everyone drifted away. Marion collected her jacket from the cloakroom and went down to the staff entrance, where Fred was overseeing the exodus. She smiled at him and asked how he was.

'I'm very well, miss,' he said, looking at her kindly. 'If you're worried about something you can always ask me. I'll still be here whatever happens and I'll do what I can.'

'No, no, I'm all right,' Marion assured him and went out into the street. She heard the newsboy's cry, which was echoing all over the country. She hesitated and then purchased a paper, scanning it before catching the bus home. The headlines screamed at her, making her shiver.

Special edition! It's War Boys! Germany ignores ultimatum and invades Belgium. Britain is officially at war! Time for patriots to show their mettle and sign up for King and Country...

Marion shivered, feeling a sudden chill even though it had been a warm day. She hated all this excitement, as if it was a party instead of men getting ready to shoot at each other. The streets seemed to be filled with young men all of a sudden, dashing here and there, laughing and shouting, jesting, almost as if it were Christmas and something to celebrate. In contrast, young women were looking anxious and seemed in a hurry to get home.

She was approaching her bus stop when someone came up behind her and took her arm. Shocked, she swung round and found herself looking at Reggie Jackson.

'Reggie! What are you doing here?'

'I've been to sign up for the Army,' he told her and grinned. 'I thought I'd wait for you and we could have a cup of coffee – or just travel back together...'

'Oh, Reggie, why did you do it?' Marion asked, distressed. 'Your job is important – I don't think they would have thought ill of you if you hadn't joined...'

'The gaffer told us to go and sign on if we wanted – said he'd take us back when we came home but we should do our duty.' Reggie's eyes were bright with excitement. 'Everyone wanted to join, but some of them were too old, others too young. The sergeant was weeding them out, sending the young lads of fourteen and fifteen home, but all the bosses on the docks have told the men to fight if they want.' He looked serious for a moment. 'That Sir Edward Grey, the Foreign Secretary, said, "The Lamps are going out all over Europe and we shall not see them lit in our lifetimes"– but I reckon the British Tommy will soon put that right...'

'Mr Harper told our men that their jobs will be safe, too,' Marion said and shook her head. 'Shop assistants can be replaced by women but you can't, Reggie. Surely you needn't volunteer?'

'I'm not a coward, Marion,' Reggie said. 'If the lads need to fight, then I can fight as well as any of them.'

'Of course, you can,' she said suddenly cross. 'But I shall hate you if you go and get yourself killed...'

'Oh, Marion, it would almost be worth it just for that,' Reggie said and grinned. He looked delighted. 'It's the first time you've given me any sign that you care.'

'Well, of course I do, you daft...' she cried but got no further, because right there in the street, in the full view of everyone, Reggie grabbed her and kissed her on the lips. As Marion stared at him in shock, he laughed in delight.

'I've been working up to that for weeks,' he said. 'I thought you might hit me if I tried.'

Marion gave him a half-hearted punch in the shoulder. 'You're horrible, Reggie Jackson, and I like you a lot – and you're not to go and get killed. Do you hear me?'

'I won't,' Reggie said. 'I'll be comin' back fer yer, Marion Kaye. Yer can bet yer sweet life on it. When I do, we'll be married. It might be next year or the year after, and I don't know where we'll live or how we'll manage, but you're my girl now and that's the end of it.'

29

'She has been fretting,' Sally announced as she entered their sitting room where Ben was working on some papers. He looked up with a frown. 'Pearl said she's been unsettled all day. It couldn't be a tooth yet, could it?'

'It's too soon for her to be teething surely?' Ben said. 'If you're worried, Sally, give the doctor a ring...'

'No, I think she might have a little tummy upset, but it's nothing much.' She walked to glance over his shoulder. 'Are you looking at Jenni's telegram? She is on her way over. I didn't think she would come now, but she says she's coming anyway.'

'Good, I'll be glad to see her; there's something I need to talk to her about. I just hope she'll be all right, though the American flag should safeguard the ship.' Ben frowned and took some papers from his briefcase. 'I wanted to check our balance at the bank, but they're closed. I hope it won't be for long.'

She nodded, understanding his concern. 'I doubt they will close many days – we all need access to our money.'

'I'm glad I don't have shares to worry about.' He placed his papers on the table and she looked over his shoulder.

'Are they the final drawings for the fittings for the extension?'

'Yes, they've turned out rather well,' Ben said, 'but it almost seems wrong to be thinking about this now, Sally. I know everyone is saying this war thing will be over in months, but it still means young men will die and I felt pretty rotten sending them all off when I'll be safe at home...'

'Ben, don't,' Sally said sharply. 'We agreed that it would be foolish for you to rush off and join up. They will have thousands of volunteers, many of whom will probably never see the outside of a training camp if it all fizzles out in a few weeks.'

'But will it?' Ben said. 'I was talking to a man I know; he's a friend of Jenni's husband and over here on some diplomatic mission – he's a senior General in the American army and he told me in confidence that he believes the German army to be stronger than we in Britain believed possible. It might mean that things don't go our way quite as swiftly as we think...'

'What about the French army and the Russians?' Sally said. 'The papers have been saying that the French are the elite cavalry and very efficient fighters. Surely, they won't just roll over and let the Germans push them aside. We shan't be on our own.'

Ben nodded, but the worried look didn't leave his eyes. 'I spoke to a few of the men personally, the first to let us know they were leaving – and that's why I called the meeting, because I knew they would want to go and would worry about what happens afterwards. I reassured them their jobs will be waiting – I just hope they come back for them...'

Sally shivered because his words chilled her. The papers were so confident it would be easy and yet Ben's friend was hinting that it might be much worse than anyone imagined. She cocked her head to one side as she heard her baby start to cry again.

'She sounds really upset, Ben. Do you think the doctor will think I'm a silly mother fussing for nothing if I ring him?'

'If you don't, I shall,' Ben said. 'She's our little princess, Sally. I don't want her suffering even from a tummy upset if some medicine can help.' He went through to Jenny as he spoke. She didn't stop crying as soon as he picked her up, which was unusual and made Sally even more anxious.

'I'll ring him now.' Sally went out into the hall and took the earpiece, speaking into the telephone as the operator came on. She gave the number she needed and was told to hold on while she was connected. Several rings later, the phone was answered.

'Doctor Mendelson…'

'It's Sally Harper, doctor – Jenny is unwell and has been all day. She won't settle and I think she has a tummy upset, but we've given her gripe water and it doesn't help…'

'I'll come straight away, Mrs Harper. There is a nasty bug doing the rounds at the moment and it can be dangerous to very young children. I'm very glad you called me; some mothers leave it too late…'

Sally thanked him and went back to Ben. She told him what the doctor had said as he tried to comfort the baby. Jenny looked flushed and just kept on whimpering.

'She's very hot, Sally. I just hope we haven't left it too late…'

'But Mrs Hills said…' Sally stopped because Ben was glaring at her.

'Mrs Hills is here to clean,' he said and he was angry. 'She isn't the child's mother, you are. You should have called the doctor as soon as you realised she was unwell.'

Sally bit her lip. She'd thought that the combination of Pearl and Mrs Hills was enough to protect her darling girl, but now she was terrified that her baby might be really ill, and if she was, Ben would never forgive her.

* * *

'Give her this medicine every three hours,' Doctor Mendelson said after he'd examined the child. 'I'm pretty sure that in Jenny's case we have an unpleasant tummy upset and nothing more – for which we can think ourselves lucky. We've lost three young babies in the last twenty-four hours and we've no idea why, just that it is a very nasty infection that nothing seems to help.'

'You're certain she doesn't have this other infection?' Ben asked sharply. 'You don't want to take her into hospital for further investigation?'

'I have twenty years' experience in caring for children, Mr Harper. When your wife spoke to me on the telephone, I feared the worst, but let me reassure you, this is nothing like the sickness these other children died of.'

Ben nodded and the tension went out of him. 'Forgive me if I seemed rude, sir – but I've had some hard experience of medical care and I was protecting my daughter.'

'Understandable, sir, but this mixture will settle her tummy and if Mrs Harper cools her down by taking off one of her blankets and letting her kick her legs in the air, I'm sure you will soon see an improvement.'

'Thank you, doctor.' Sally's eyes were brimming with tears, which she just managed to hold until he'd left and then they just burst out of her. Ben's sudden anger had shocked and upset her, making her fear even worse. She sat down in a chair, shoulders shaking as the emotion poured out of her. Ben came to stand at her shoulder, placing a hand on her. She didn't look up, because he'd hurt her – blamed her when he thought their baby was in danger.

'I'm sorry, Sally,' Ben said. 'I shouldn't have snapped at you. I was worried and it has been a difficult day – but I know it doesn't excuse the way I spoke to you. It's just I couldn't bear the thought of losing her. I don't want to go through that again…'

Sally saw the grief in his eyes and forgave him instantly. It was the first time since they'd become lovers and married that Ben had raised his voice to her and she hadn't liked it, it made her feel guilty and selfish because she'd left her precious baby to others instead of being with her. 'Are you angry with me because I found a nanny and returned to work so soon?' she asked. 'I only leave her for a few hours a day and they both spoil her...'

Ben raised her up and turned her to look at him. He stroked the side of her face and she saw regret in his eyes. 'I love you, Sally, and everything you do is perfect – but to lose you or our little one would break me. I spoke harshly and without thinking, forgive me, please. I know that I can be harsh at times and perhaps I don't deserve you and Jenny...'

'Don't be silly,' Sally said and leaned in to kiss him. He smelled of cedar wood and his own musk and she felt a rush of love, clinging to him as he nuzzled her neck. 'I don't want to quarrel – and if you wanted me to stay home...'

'Of course, I don't,' Ben said and now his eyes were teasing her. 'My sister would kill me if I even suggested it – and she's on her way remember. She has picked out some more stuff she thinks we shall need and I understand there is a huge crate of special tinned fruits, salmon and preserved fruits coming our way. Why on earth she thinks we need all that, I don't know, but she's afraid if the Germans start sinking our ships, we'll starve, so she's stocking us up before it begins.'

'Oh, that's just like Jenni,' Sally said and giggled, her former unease forgotten as she shared the jest with Ben.

Yet as she watched her baby settle down, sleeping peacefully now that the doctor's medicine was taking effect, Sally felt the ice at the back of her neck again. Jenni was American and it was an American general who had told Ben that he thought the Germans were stronger than the British believed. Did they know something that the British government didn't – or were they just not telling the people?

Lingering, Sally thought of something and went to her

bedroom, hunting through her jewel box until she found a little silver cross she'd tied onto a ribbon. She took it back to her baby's cot and looped it onto the wood structure.

'Watch over her, Mum,' she whispered and crossed herself. Sally's mother had given her to the nuns and at times she'd hated her for it, especially when they were unkind and cold to her – but her mother had given the cross to them for Sally and a little part of her wondered if perhaps it was all she'd had to give. The nuns had allowed her to think she'd simply been abandoned – but what if her mother believed it was all she could do for her child? What if the cross had been meant to tell her that she loved her? Somehow the cross hanging there, comforted Sally, even though it made no sense.

Sally didn't know whether her mother was alive or dead, but she'd always felt her mother must have been dying to give her to the nuns – why would anyone condemn a child to those cold-hearted women unless they were forced? Surely there must have been a good reason she'd been abandoned; the nuns just hadn't told her all the truth. Now that she was a mother, Sally refused to believe that any mother could willingly give up her baby.

Smiling at her child, Sally kissed her and then softly pulled the door almost to. Jenny was sleeping now, but they would hear if she cried again.

Satisfied she'd done all she could, Sally followed Ben into the living room and picked up the plans for their extension. It was surprising how much space that small shop had given them once all the walls were taken away and it was opened out. It would make Harpers even more impressive.

'These are good,' she told Ben as she handed them back to him. 'Did they tell you when you could expect the work to finish?'

'Before Christmas, we hope,' he told her and frowned. 'It's funny, but I was so keen to get this done and now...' He broke off and sighed.

'I know, Ben,' she said and went to put her arms about him. 'But other things have intruded and life is more important than material things – but remember, you promised those men their jobs back, which means we'll need bigger premises or we'll have to sack the staff we take on to replace them...' She hesitated, frowning. 'Do we know how many men will leave?'

'Not yet – but most of the younger ones for sure.'

'We'll have to advertise for women to take their place.'

'I dare say a lot of women may take a temporary job during the conflict,' Ben said. 'Some will be glad to go back to normal afterwards but some won't...'

'I doubt if many will,' Sally said. 'Once they've had a taste of earning their own money, they will want to continue, you wait and see.'

30

Rachel's actual wedding was a quiet affair in a tiny church, but Maggie, Minnie, Sally, Beth and Hazel were at the church to see her dressed in her gown of pearl grey silk with a hat made of gauze, feathers and silk flowers that suited her beautifully. They stood misty-eyed to watch her walk down the aisle to greet her groom on Mr Stockbridge's arm, together with a few of William's family and friends, most of whom were polite, smiling but distant. At the evening reception, Jack joined them after work, as did Ben, Fred, and several others from Harpers, including Marion, Becky and Miss Hart, who no one had expected to accept the invitation, but who turned up looking much happier than when they'd last seen her. It was a relaxed but subdued affair because William had to report back to his unit on Monday afternoon and so their honeymoon had been reduced to a night in a prestigious hotel with the promise of a wonderful holiday in Scotland as soon as he had leave. However, the happiness of the bride and the pride of the groom shone through, lighting up their smiles and their eyes.

Tim arrived at the reception just in time to toast the bride and groom and eat a large slice of fruit cake. Maggie poked his spare frame and told him he had hollow legs, but he just laughed and collared a couple of sausage rolls from a passing tray.

'I'm a growing lad,' he told her. 'I thought we might have a nice meal out after we leave here...?'

'I'm not sure I could eat much after this,' Maggie said. 'I've had loads, but I'll watch while you eat a bag of chips.'

'Fair enough,' Tim said. 'Shall we buy them from that place near the river? We can sit on the bench and tuck in – I'll let you pinch some of my chips, but don't try to touch the fish.'

Maggie laughed and took him off to speak to Miss Hart. She asked how she was and was told that the woman she had feared as a floor walker was living very happily with her relatives and now working for her local church, who did a lot for charity.

'I find it fulfilling and rewarding,' she told Maggie and looked pleased with life. 'The curate and I have a good working relationship and that's why I am back in London for a short time and was able to attend Rachel's wedding – so kind of her to think of me, don't you think?'

'I'm glad you're feeling better, Miss Hart,' Maggie said, surprised to find that she meant it. Everyone had felt so sorry for her when she'd had to leave Harpers due to ill health; it was good to know she'd found a new life.

Passing on to her friends, Maggie talked to them all and ended up hugging and kissing Rachel as she prepared to leave for her honeymoon.

'Be happy, dearest Rachel,' she said and smiled as she saw the sparkle in her friend's eyes. 'We both wish you all the luck and happiness in the world.'

'Thank you, dear Maggie,' Rachel said. 'I shall be happy, I promise.'

After Rachel and William had left, Tim had a word with his

brother and Beth, before suggesting to Maggie it was time for them to leave.

'Much as I love your friends, Maggie, I think I shall do murder if we have to listen to any more social chatter. I want a little time alone with you!'

'Tim!' Maggie remonstrated, but she didn't mind him stealing her away and her heart fluttered as she saw the passion in his eyes.

He was teasing her a lot, pretending to be full of nonsense, but she sensed something was bothering him. She placed her hand on his arm.

'Are you worried about the war?' Germany had invaded Belgium on the fourth of August and on the following day a British destroyer and a light cruiser had sunk a German minelayer some forty miles from the Thames Estuary. It had been a small victory for the British but brought the war closer to home, making the situation suddenly very real.

'No, it's not the war,' Tim whispered back. 'I'll tell you later...'

Maggie didn't say ask again until they were sitting enjoying their chips, which surprisingly she managed to eat several of, perhaps because of the delicious smell and the fresh air. Wiping her fingers afterwards on the large white handkerchief he gave her, she looked at him steadily.

'What's wrong, Tim? I know something is – will you tell me please?'

'I meant to take you somewhere special...' he said uncertainly.

'I'm happy here. You can take me to dinner another night if you wish...'

Suddenly, Tim dropped to his knees on the bit of grass in front of her and produced a small blue leather box from his pocket, offering it to her. As he opened it, Maggie saw a beautiful diamond and sapphire three-stone ring and gasped.

'Tim – what are you doing?' she said, although in her heart she knew and was thrilled.

'I'm asking you to marry me, Maggie,' he said. 'I love you and I have for a long time but I wasn't sure how you felt. I knew there was Ralf and...'

'Ralf hurt me,' Maggie said, putting out a hand to stop him. 'We still like each other, but I don't love him.'

'Do you care for me a little?' Tim asked. 'I'm not much of a catch, Maggie darling. I don't have more than a couple of hundred pounds saved and I can't offer you a home – but I do love you...'

'I think I might love you, too,' Maggie said and smiled. 'Sit beside me, Tim; you'll stain your uniform on the grass...'

'Darling Maggie, you just made me very happy.'

'Get up then,' she said, laughing.

He did as she told him, brushing ruefully at the mark on the knees of his Royal Flying Corps uniform. 'Is it too much to ask you to wear my ring?'

Maggie looked at him seriously. 'I might,' she said slowly, 'but I hadn't thought of getting married yet – the thing is, Tim, I'm going to volunteer to train as a nurse...'

'Really?' Tim looked at her as if she'd just turned into a hummingbird, wonder and delight in his eyes. 'If you do that, they might send you where I'm going.' He grinned at her. 'I can't tell you – except that it's not in England – and we leave at the end of the week. It's why I wanted to take you somewhere special so that I could persuade you to marry me.'

'Oh, Tim, you daft thing' Maggie said and giggled. 'You only had to ask me. Yes, I will marry you, but not just yet. We can be engaged if you want, but I'm not ready to get married. I've been taking those first-aid classes for ages and now I want to help, if they'll let me. Men are being hurt already and I know they will need more nurses – besides, I think we should wait to marry until

I'm at least nineteen, or until I've done my duty as a nursing assistant. You know that I can't serve and be married – and it's something I want to do.'

'Yes, if that's what you want,' he said and leaned closer. 'Can I kiss you, Maggie? I mean a proper kiss...'

Maggie inclined her head. Tim often kissed her cheek or her hand, but he'd never given her a lover's kiss and she'd often wished he would, but she couldn't ask in case he thought her forward or fast. Now, as their lips touched and she felt the sweetness of his kiss deepen into something that stirred her blood and made her tremble with a feeling she'd never experienced before, she almost changed her mind and said she would marry him now, as soon as it could be arranged. Yet she knew that something inside her was telling her she needed to volunteer as a nurse.

'I love you so much, sweet Maggie,' Tim said and smoothed his thumb over her sensitised mouth, tracing her lips. 'I think I knew it right from the start, but we were both with other people – and then you quarrelled with him and she left me, and that was my lucky day.' He grinned happily. 'You said you would go out with me for company and I've never been as content.'

'What will your father say? Will he think we're too young to be engaged?' Maggie looked at him anxiously.

'He told me to get the ring,' Tim said confidently. 'He said I should speak to you, tell you how I feel and not regret it afterwards.'

'I'm so glad you did,' Maggie said and leaned her head against his shoulder. 'I wish you didn't have to go away so soon, but...'

'It's war,' Tim said. 'We both know what that means, Maggie. Yes, it may be over in a few months – but it only takes a bit of bad luck and if your kite goes down, it's probably the end. I knew you weren't ready for marriage yet, but I didn't want to leave without telling you how I felt.'

'It would have broken my heart if you hadn't spoken now,'

Maggie said.

Tim drew her closer, his lips against her hair. 'My dearest love. I shall think of you all the time, imagine what it will be like when we're wed.'

'I do love you, Tim.' Maggie looked into his eyes. 'Put your ring on my finger, Tim. I can't wear it for work, but I'll tie it on a ribbon underneath my uniform so I keep you with me all the time.' She looked up at him. 'I shall give my notice in to Harpers next week. I have an appointment this weekend to see if I'm suitable to train for nursing and, if I'm accepted, I'll have to leave Harpers.'

'Won't you be sad to leave?' he asked, because she'd always said how much she loved her job.

'Yes, in a way, but Mr Harper said any of us could leave and get our job back after the war. I'm not giving up forever and I'll tell Mrs Harper that – I'm sure she will understand. If I tell Mrs Craven... Oh, she's Mrs Bailey now – if I tell Rachel, she will try to talk me out of it, but Sally will understand.'

'From what I've heard, Mrs Harper is a woman who knows what she wants and goes out and gets it,' Tim said. 'Not all women can do that, Maggie, but I'm proud of you for wanting to do it, my love. I've seen some of what Germany has lined up against us from the air and I know it won't be as easy as a lot of folk believe.'

Maggie nodded thoughtfully. 'My father wanted me to be a teacher. I know that now there is going to be a war he would tell me I should use my talents and my mind to do something worthwhile and I'm rather good at first aid. I know I have an awful lot to learn, but I know more than many women who will be volunteering, so perhaps I can really help.'

'You know that a lot of the volunteers will end up scrubbing floors and be given all the dirty jobs?'

'Yes, I know. I've spoken to a nurse and she told me it is always like that at first, but she says if the war goes badly, they will need all the volunteers they can get – especially those that have some extra languages...'

'You can speak other languages?' Tim stared in surprise, because this was the first time, she'd mentioned it.

'I'm reasonable in French and I did a smattering of German,' Maggie said. 'My father thought English literature and languages would be a good career for me as a teacher, so I spent as much time as I could learning them and I still study my French books when I have nothing to do.'

Tim sat back and looked at her in wonder. 'I had no idea, clever girl.'

'No, I'm not clever. I never took my exams, because Dad had that terrible accident, and I didn't get to the next grade, but even a few words can be useful,' Maggie said and smiled at him. 'You must have got a few grades at school to be a pilot?' Her eyes met his. How little they really knew of each other – but they had the rest of their lives to learn.

'Oh, English, Mathematics and French...' He shrugged. 'Jack and I both had a good education, because of Dad being a teacher and making us keep our noses to the grindstone. He wanted me to be an accountant – a good safe career – but I fancied the Royal Flying Corps and it is a great life, Maggie. I think flying is the big thing of the future. One day you'll probably be able to fly to France commercially rather than go over in a ship...'

'I'm not sure I'd dare,' she said and then smiled at him as she held up her hand to admire the ring, he'd given her. 'This looks much too expensive...'

'It was my grandmother's,' Tim said. 'Dad gave it to me because I didn't get a chance to go shopping. It belonged to my mother's mother. Jack had my paternal grandmother's ring...' He looked anxious. 'If you don't like it, I'll buy you a new one as soon as I get the chance...'

'It is lovely,' she said. 'I love it, Tim. Tell Fred thank you from me and I'm very happy to wear it.'

'You're wonderful,' he said. 'Keep the ring and I'll bring you something special home from...' He shook his head and leaned in to kiss her. 'We both know where, but I can't say.'

* * *

Alone in bed that evening, Maggie thought about the romance of Tim's proposal and the sweetness of his kiss. It was because he'd spoken out at last that she'd told him what she was planning to do. Until that moment, Maggie hadn't even been sure she was going to enrol in the volunteers. She'd made the appointment to see the enrolment officer, but she'd still been wondering what to do. Feeling Tim's tension, knowing that he'd proposed to her because he was going overseas and understanding that he might not return, had crystallised her thoughts and purpose. In that moment, she'd realised that her future was in nursing, at least for the duration of the war.

Men would be wounded – perhaps the men that belonged to her friends or Tim himself – and Maggie wanted to help in whatever way they let her. The feeling had grown on her slowly since before the announcement of war and seeing those newspaper reports of injured men. Yet she'd hesitated, waiting for Rachel's wedding, because she didn't want to spoil anything. Minnie was getting married too, but although she was a dear and Maggie liked her, it wouldn't matter if she couldn't be there for it, because Rachel was Minnie's special friend and Becky was like a daughter to her.

Maggie would still move into Beth's spare room and leave her things there; it would be her home, a place to return to when she was given leave. Maggie hoped that Sally would understand why she wanted to leave once she'd spoken to her but knew that she would do it anyway. Maggie felt she was called no less than all the brave men who were signing on to fight all over the country. She could almost see her father smiling at her, encouraging her to do it and she knew he would be proud. Her mother would tell her she was a fool – and she wasn't sure that Beth and Rachel would be pleased when they'd trained her to their high standards and given her a pay rise, but it was what she had to do.

'You want to enrol as a nurse?' Sally looked at her in surprise and then smiled her encouragement. 'Yes, I think that is an excellent idea, Maggie. I always did think you were too clever to be a sales assistant – and they will need intelligent girls like you now. Harpers will miss you, of course, as will your friends, but you're doing the right thing and I'm so proud of you.' She moved forward to embrace her. 'If it weren't for Harpers and my little Jenny, I'd do the same.'

'Thank you so much, Mrs Harper,' Maggie said. 'I'm sorry if it causes you inconvenience – and I do hope I can come back after it is all over.'

'We'll welcome you back with open arms and a medal,' Sally said. She smiled and flicked her hair out of her eyes. 'I think you're so brave, Maggie. I know you understand it won't be all wiping soldiers' brows. It's going to be much harder than selling silk scarves and you'll see some terrible things...'

'Yes, I know,' Maggie said and met her gaze steadily. 'I believe it's what my father would expect and I understand that I'll start out doing all the filthy jobs – but if it helps the trained nurses then it's worthwhile...'

'Yes, of course it is,' Sally agreed. 'Good luck, Maggie Gibbs, and send me news of what you're doing. We're still friends and always will be.'

'Thank you – and thank you for understanding. I did feel awkward about letting you down after you'd been so good to me.'

'Oh no, Maggie. You're not letting me down – you're doing something wonderful and I applaud you for it.'

'But it will be a nuisance for you to train my replacement...'

'Not at all. We're recruiting both juniors and older women to replace the men – two thirds of our male staff are leaving,' Sally told her with a sigh. 'Now that is a bit of a problem, but we shall get through. Mr Stockbridge has allowed his daughter Becky to join us while she works for her secretarial exams and that will help. Did you know that?'

'No...' Maggie was surprised. 'Becky said he was completely against it – but perhaps Minnie has persuaded him to let his daughter work while she studies for her exams.'

'Yes, quite possibly,' Sally said. 'Fortunately, Minnie isn't giving up work immediately. She told me yesterday that she will still come in three times a week to collect her work and take it home with her once she is married. She says she can work quicker and more efficiently at home and we've taken on another woman who is a seamstress but can also work in the dress department. One of our senior girls from the dress department is going upstairs to the men's floor and we've taken on another four women to work on the ground floor; more are being interviewed this week.'

Maggie nodded. 'Do you think they will mind giving up their jobs when the men return?'

'I imagine any woman asked to give up her place might resent it, but nevertheless in many businesses it will happen. Here, we hope that our expansion will take up any excess without having to make the women redundant.'

Maggie smiled and nodded as Sally held out her hand. 'I have to report first thing in the morning.'

'Well, good luck,' Sally said. 'I hope you don't find it too awful.'

'I'm prepared for hard work,' Maggie said. 'Thank you again, Mrs Harper.'

'Oh, sometimes I think it's so silly all this formality,' Sally said. 'I'm Sally and you're Maggie and we're friends.' She moved forward and hugged Maggie impulsively. 'You take care, do you hear? I don't want you getting ill or shot at, so you just come back when it's all over.'

'Yes, I will, I promise,' Maggie said and sniffed hard, because Sally had made her feel emotional and sad to be leaving. 'As soon as this horrid war is over, I'll be back asking for my job.'

Maggie left then because otherwise she might have burst into tears. She realised as she left Sally's office that she hadn't told her about her engagement, but for the moment it was something to keep to herself. After all, she wasn't going to be married for a year or two and there would be plenty of time to tell her friends in the future.

She went back down to the department to finish her day. Beth's husband had fetched all her stuff to his father's house the previous evening and she would be sleeping in the spare room that night. Minnie was sharing with her until her marriage, because she said it wouldn't look right if she moved into Mr Stockbridge's house before her wedding, but after that it would be Maggie's room – somewhere to come back to when she needed it.

Thinking about what Sally had told her concerning Becky Stockbridge, Maggie smiled to herself. Both she and Becky had argued that Becky should be allowed to work in Harpers while she was honing her skills as a secretary, but Mr Stockbridge had steadfastly refused – until Minnie asked him and then it was suddenly all right.

Becky must be over the moon.

31

'I couldn't believe it when Dad said I could work here while I continued my studies. I have to attend my college once a week on a Friday, but Mrs Burrows says she doesn't mind that at all,' Becky confided when she met Maggie at closing time that evening. They were attending first-aid classes together but were going for a sandwich and coffee at a café first.

'So, you will be taking my place in the department then,' Maggie said, looking at her with affection. 'I'm so glad for you, Becky. You will like Mrs Burrows. She is very fair and Marion is lovely. I suppose you will be a junior – we were supposed to have a new junior anyway...'

'Mrs Burrows says that she thinks we shall manage and we are going to borrow a junior from other departments at Christmas.'

'Oh, don't think about that already,' Maggie said, though she knew that plans for it were already under way in the store. Christmas was such a big event, it had to be planned for months in advance.

Becky looked at her curiously. 'What made you think of joining the volunteers as a nurse?'

'I'm not sure, but it's been at the back of my mind for a long time,' Maggie said. 'I think it was because of how ill Dad was – and my mother dying in the infirmary. It made me aware of how helpless I was, couldn't do much for either of them, and that's why I took up the first aid – and then, of course, I knew I wanted to help nurse the wounded.'

Becky looked at her seriously. 'I wish I was brave like you, Maggie, but I'm not. I'm all right at classes, but I don't like blood. I think I should faint if I had to nurse someone with his arm cut to pieces.'

'It's a shame, because you're so good at it,' Maggie replied, slipping an arm about her waist, 'but someone has to stay here and keep things going, Becky. People need shopping and I shan't feel as bad about leaving when I think of you standing behind my counter.'

'It would have been fun learning to be a nurse with you.' Becky was a little regretful.

'But Mr Stockbridge would never agree,' Maggie said. 'I don't think even Miss Minnie could make him agree to let you be a nurse.'

'I'm not so sure about that,' Becky said and giggled. 'I think she could twist him round her little finger if she tried – but instead she is always looking after him and he does like it so much.'

'I expect he was lonely after your mother died. I know he had you and he adores you, but he needed someone his own age to talk to when you were in bed and asleep.'

'Poor Poppa.' Becky said. 'Sometimes I can't believe how much he's changed since Minnie walked in. I saw his face that first Sunday she came to tea and he looked as if he'd been struck by a thunderbolt.'

'I never noticed a thing then,' Maggie said. 'I sort of noticed she blushed a bit when he looked at her or passed her a cup, but I didn't realise...'

'I knew he was smitten immediately,' Becky said, 'and I was so pleased. He was lonely and she has made things easier for me, too. I think he was terrified I might die, but Minnie made him see that though I *was* ill last year, I'm completely better now. She is like the mother I never knew, Maggie. I feel so lucky to have her.'

Maggie nodded, feeling pleased for her friend. She knew that once she started her training, she wouldn't be able to meet Becky as often and the girl would miss going out with her. She didn't have many other friends, though working at Harpers, she would have the chance to meet lots of people.

'You should try making friends with Marion,' she said. 'She comes to the first-aid classes sometimes and you could walk home with her...'

'She doesn't always come, though, does she?' Becky said and pulled a face. 'I am going to miss you, though Minnie says she will take me to the church social and to a meeting of the Women's Movement, if I wish.'

'Did you know that Mrs Pankhurst has promised that the militants will stop causing trouble for the government during the war – she says it would be unpatriotic to continue it while we are caught up in conflict.'

'My father thinks the suffragettes are terrible – at least the ones that go around blowing things up are,' Becky said and then gave a cry of pain as someone barged into her. 'Oh, how rude,' she said as the man walked off without apologising. It was a moment or two before she realised that she had been robbed. 'Maggie! That man took my purse...'

'No! Did he really?' Maggie said, staring after the man who had barged into Becky, but he had disappeared into the evening crowds. 'I'm so sorry, love. Did you have much in it?'

'Only my shilling for the classes and my bus fare home,' Becky replied. 'What a nuisance.'

'Never mind,' Maggie said. 'I've got enough to pay your entrance tonight and the bus fares. He would have got far more if he'd taken mine, because I was paid for my holiday this evening and the money is still in my purse.'

'Thank goodness he only took mine,' Becky said. 'I didn't even think when he knocked into me, but I suppose that is how they do it.'

'Yes, I expect so,' Maggie agreed. 'He deserves to have his hand chopped off…'

'Oh no,' Becky said and smiled as her little fright faded. 'I don't want such drastic retribution; it was only two shillings in my old purse.'

'It's what they do with thieves in some places,' Maggie said. 'Come on, I'll pay for our tea this evening. Try and forget about it now, Becky, and enjoy the evening. It could have been much worse…'

* * *

That evening they were addressed by a young doctor in military uniform. He had been booked to give them a lecture before the declaration of war and had kept his promise, even though he'd joined up in the meantime.

'Good evening, ladies,' he said. 'I am pleased to see so many of you here. I think you understand the importance of what you're doing now that we are at war. Once the casualties begin to come home, we're going to need a lot more volunteers at our hospitals…' He paused to look round at their eager faces. 'Tell me, have any of you joined the volunteers?'

Maggie's hand went straight up. Surprisingly, hers was the

only one. He looked disappointed until his warm brown eyes came to rest on her.

'And your name is?'

'Maggie Gibbs,' she said. 'I had my interview a few days ago and I'm joining a training unit tomorrow, sir.'

'Good, we need all the intelligent young ladies we can get,' he said. 'What made you decide to offer your services, Miss Gibbs?'

'I thought I might be able to help, sir. I know that I'm not a nurse, but if I can do the jobs trained nurses do not have time for, I can serve.'

'Excellent.' His smile deepened as his eyes swept the audience. 'Are there any other young ladies who think they might like to join but are not sure what to do?'

Now, hands went up all over. He spent the next half an hour telling them how necessary their limited skills might prove and how much more they could do if they had the courage to volunteer their services.

'Remember, if your father, mother or brother thinks that nursing is not ladylike, tell them that Captain Stephen Morgan asked you to consider giving up a little of your life to help those that will most definitely need your help.'

A round of applause met his closing remarks and then everyone got up. Tea was served with shortbread biscuits and a demonstration of how to give life-saving mouth-to-mouth resuscitation was given by Captain Morgan. His words and actions were watched avidly and there was an eager queue ready to try out the techniques he advocated. Becky was the second in line and demonstrated her skills.

'I hope you are thinking of joining our little band of brave ladies, miss?'

'Becky Stockbridge,' she said and smiled awkwardly. 'I don't think I should be much good at it, sir – I don't care for blood...'

'Ah, I see.' He nodded understandingly. 'Not everyone does,

Miss Stockbridge. I am sorry you won't be joining us, but I suppose we can't expect all of you lovely ladies to become nurses; there would be no one left to do anything else.' He smiled at her and then turned to Maggie. 'I take it you have no such reserves, Miss Gibbs?'

'I doubt if I'll be asked to do more than scrub floors, sir,' she replied with a smile. 'However, I should be honoured if I was deemed good enough to help tend the wounded.'

'I think you'll do well.' He looked at her thoughtfully. 'Remember one thing, Miss Gibbs – Sister is usually right and Matron is always right...'

'That's two things,' Becky said and gave a nervous little giggle.

'Yes, Miss Stockbridge, you are perfectly right,' he said and looked a little stern. 'But I am sure Miss Gibbs understood what I meant?'

'Oh yes, sir,' Maggie agreed. 'Whoever is in charge is to be obeyed and I'm sure it applies to the doctors too.'

'As a matter of fact, most of us are terrified of Matron,' he said and laughed. 'You'll soon discover that's the truth – even though she pretends to refer to us, we doctors know our place.'

Becky caught sight of the clock and touched Maggie's arm. 'I need to go, Maggie, or I'll miss my last connection.'

'Yes, of course,' Maggie said, looking at Captain Morgan as he touched her arm.

'Yes, sir?'

'I thought we might talk some more...'

'Oh, that would have been nice – but Becky has to catch her bus and her purse was stolen on the way here. A man barged into her and took it without us even seeing and so I have to go with her.'

Captain Morgan frowned and looked angry. 'That is disgusting,' he said. 'If two young women cannot walk through the streets without being robbed...' Glancing at his own watch, he said, 'If you would give me the pleasure, I could run you both home in my car, it would give us a little time to talk...'

'Well...' Maggie looked at Becky. 'What do you think?'

'I don't mind,' Becky said. 'We live about a mile apart. Maggie usually gets off and I just continue on the bus.'

'I can take both of you home,' he said, smiling easily. 'You never know, Miss Stockbridge, I might convince you to volunteer.'

Becky dimpled at him. 'You might convince me, sir – but I doubt you would convince my father.'

32

Beth was explaining their stock system to Becky the next morning when Mr Marco entered the department. He hesitated for a moment and then approached them, smiling easily.

'Mr Marco,' she said, looking at him expectantly. 'What may I do for you? Have you come looking for new items for the window?'

'Not this time,' he said. 'Actually, I had a message for Miss Stockbridge...'

'For Miss Stockbridge?' Beth was surprised.

'I came to tell you that the police have recovered your purse,' he said, looking at Becky. 'It was found thrown down in the street and since it had your staff card for Harpers in it as well as a photo of your father, it was taken into the police station. They rang the manager, who is of course your father and he asked us to bring it here. A constable brought it over earlier. I regret to tell you that any money you had has been taken...'

'It wasn't very much,' Becky said, blushing. 'I went to the first-aid classes last night with Maggie – I mean Miss Gibbs – and a man barged into me. Afterwards, I realised that my purse was missing. I didn't expect I would see it again.'

'Well, some rather more honest person found it and took it in for you,' Mr Marco said. 'I decided I would bring it straight up for you, as it is a nice leather purse and I thought you might miss it...'

'Oh, thank you,' Becky said and blushed. 'It is very kind of you, Mr Marco. I really didn't expect to get it back...'

'It looks undamaged,' he said and handed it to her. 'Forgive me for disturbing your briefing, Mrs Burrows. I wonder if I could have a word?'

'Yes, of course, Mr Marco,' she said and moved aside with him.

Becky heard her say, 'What can I do for you?'

'I was wondering if you might spare Miss Kaye for an hour or so, perhaps a longer lunch hour...' He glanced around the department. 'Is she in this morning?'

'Yes – I sent her for a cup of tea because she had a headache. Why?'

'I have something to ask her – something to her advantage, if she is interested.'

'Well, I might be able to spare her, when she comes back from her tea break – but why?' Mrs Burrows looked concerned.

'I should like to see how well she does with window display. I believe she might consider giving part of her service at Harpers in that department, Mrs Burrows. If I could arrange it with Mrs Harper – you could probably have another junior for a few hours a week...'

'If you really think she could do well at it.' Mrs Burrows frowned. 'Why now?'

'I am leaving to join the army on Saturday afternoon. If I'm going to get her started, it has to be now.' He smiled as Mrs Burrows gasped in shock. 'I do have a small team ready – but I think Marion could be a part of it, if you will permit me to give her a little try?'

'How could I refuse?' she said. 'We shall be sorry to see you leave, Mr Marco. Harpers is going to miss you…'

'That is why I want to set up the best team I can and I think that includes Miss Kaye, even if only part-time.' He smiled at her. 'I shall call in to see everyone when I have leave and I hope to return to Harpers at the end of hostilities, of course.'

'Yes, of course,' Beth said, still a little shocked. 'But aren't you Italian? I mean you don't have to join, do you?'

'My grandmother was Italian,' he said with an odd smile. 'I get my looks from her – but my mother was half-French and my father British. My name is actually Mark Henshaw, but for my profession Mr Marco sounded more artistic, and now I must leave you. Thank you for your cooperation.' He flashed her his brilliant smile and went out with a last little wave.

'Well, good gracious,' Beth said, astounded by his revelation. She'd been so taken aback that she hadn't even wished him good luck. 'I had no idea – did you, Miss Stockbridge?'

'My father said his mother was half-French and his father British,' Becky said. 'I didn't know about his Italian grandmother or that his name was Mark Henshaw…'

'I just never thought he would join the army,' Beth said, shaking her head. 'He didn't seem the sort.' Clearly, she'd known nothing about him. Mr Marco hid his heart behind his charming smile and his little jokes. 'We are going to miss him a great deal. I wonder if Mrs Harper knows.' She shook her head and looked at Becky. 'Go and put your purse away, Miss Stockbridge. I hope you were not hurt last evening?'

'Oh, no, Mrs Burrows. I lost two shillings, but Miss Gibbs paid my shilling for the classes – and someone took us home in his car. He was a doctor and recruiting for volunteers to become nurses. He told us on the way home that they will be needed at the front.

Maggie – I mean, Miss Gibbs – told him she would be willing to go out to a field hospital in Belgium or France...'

Beth stared at her in shock. She would have a word with Maggie when she got home that evening. Surely, she wouldn't be so foolish as to risk her life like that?

She frowned at Becky. 'I hope you are not thinking of volunteering, Miss Stockbridge?'

'No, Mrs Burrows,' Becky said and went off to put her purse away as Marion Kaye returned.

'Are you feeling better, Miss Kaye?' she asked her and Marion nodded.

'I took a headache powder that Mrs Hall from glassware gave me and I'm sure it will ease me. I shall be all right, Mrs Burrows.'

'Good, because I am letting you have an extra half an hour for lunch – but you are to report to Mr Marco in his office; he has something to ask you.' Beth smiled at her encouragingly. 'Now, go to your counter, we have customers waiting.'

Beth was still feeling shocked and wondered what her employers would think of their window dresser joining the army. Mr Marco could not be replaced as easily as a sales assistant.

* * *

Marco was thoughtful as he left the department. He reflected on his time here, particularly that spent with Sally Harper, and thought that if he'd been a different man and wanted what most men wanted, a wife and children, he would have envied Ben Harper his wife. Sally Harper understood him, welcomed him with a smile that was filled with the love for all things that was in her. Most women seeing him in the park with the young man he loved would have walked away, pretending not to see, but Sally had linked arms with them both, protected them from the louts who'd tormented him by her very presence and when

Julien had killed himself, she'd comforted him by her quiet understanding.

Marco had had several affairs since he'd discovered the nature of his sexuality but only once had he fallen deeply in love. Julien was the love of his life, the one he would never forget, and the manner of his death was like a weeping sore inside.

Julien was the main reason Marco had decided to fight. *He* would have joined up immediately, because he was brave and beautiful and a patriot and so Marco would take his place. He wasn't particularly anxious to die, although sometimes his life felt like a barren waste without Julien, but he wanted the one he loved to be proud of him. Sometimes, he felt Julien so close to him, whispering in his ear, apologising for taking his own life.

'I've always been frightened of my father's anger – the names he called me, Marco. I couldn't bear it...'

Marco ached to hold Julien in his arms and comfort him, to take him back from that cold dark place that was death and burial outside the holy ground. Instead, because that was impossible, he would fight, and if he died, then he would be reunited with his lover...

Eyes wet with tears, Marco brushed his arm across them impatiently. He'd been lucky. There were good people here. Fred in the basement had talked to him when he was down after Julien's suicide, more understanding than most.

'I had two lads at my school,' Fred had told him as they'd talked once over a brew of tea. 'James was young, face of an angel, Harry was older and more serious. One hot summer day they went swimming in the river in the nude and in the midst of their fun fell in love. Like all young things, they did what came naturally – but they were seen and James was taken away from school by an irate father. He demanded that I beat Harry and then expel him. I did neither, though he left soon after to join the church and is even now in South America working with the street children and saving lives.'

'Was that the reason you were forced to give up your post as a headmaster?' Marco had asked and Fred had nodded.

'That and a few other things I didn't care for, but don't imagine I'm a martyr, Mr Marco. I love this job, because it brought me a wonderful daughter-in-law and a house filled with friends, love and laughter – and that is worth sixty of being headmaster any day.'

Marco had smiled and agreed. Beth Burrows was like Sally Harper in her way. Both of them were remarkable women and he would miss working here, but it was his duty to fight, because Julien couldn't.

* * *

Beth was not surprised when a message came asking her to have coffee with Sally during her lunch break and she went up to the office, expecting to see shock and distress in her employer's wife's face.

'You've heard that Mr Marco has joined the army?' Sally asked as soon as she entered the office. 'I could hardly believe it when Ben told me last night – but he's known for a few days. He couldn't talk him out of it.'

'It will make things difficult for you, won't it?'

'Yes and no...' Sally frowned. 'He has a junior he's been training and Jean is competent, but she doesn't have his flair. Ben says that I'll have to help her come up with the ideas. Jean can do the physical work and she has a young lad to help her – we've just taken him on and he seems to have a good eye. He got a scholarship in art and will combine his job here with college classes. Philip is sixteen and he looks as if a puff of wind would blow him over and he claims to have flat feet, which should prevent him from becoming a soldier. He says he doesn't want to fight anyway – he is a pacifist apparently – so unless they start conscripting boys, he should be fine, for a while anyway...'

'But why did Mr Marco want to fight?' Beth asked, shaking her head. 'I can hardly believe that he volunteered. I mean, if he'd been forced to go, I'd understand, but he's always seemed such a gentle person, and he isn't a young lad, is he? I mean he must be around forty...'

'I think that smile hides a lot,' Sally said and looked serious. 'I can't tell you any more, Beth, but Mr Marco confided in me once and I believe he may have his reasons for wanting to go to war. Perhaps he isn't quite the calm, amusing man we think he is.'

'Do we ever know anyone?' Beth said and shook her head. 'What with Minnie getting married out of the blue and Maggie going off to be a nurse – she may even volunteer to nurse in a field hospital so I've been told...' She repeated what Becky Stockbridge had told her and Sally shook her head.

'Maggie doesn't surprise me,' she said, making Beth's eyes open wider. 'I always suspected the passions ran deep in her – but you could have knocked me down with a feather when I was told about Minnie. I think there is something in the water...' She laughed and Beth smiled. 'Anyway, let's hope that no one else goes off to join up just yet or you and I will be the only ones left running the store...'

'Ben isn't thinking of joining?'

'No, not yet, thank goodness,' Sally said. 'At the moment he feels that he has too much responsibility for the shop and everyone dependent on it – and with the extension to see to, he couldn't think of leaving me with all that.'

'Surely he wouldn't anyway?' Beth said. 'It is different for Jack – he knew the merchant navy would be after him immediately and so he went straight out and enlisted. He joins his ship this weekend...'

'Oh, Beth,' Sally said and looked at her with sympathy. 'I'm wittering on and you're so brave about it all.'

'I'm not brave at all inside,' Beth told her. 'Every time I think about him leaving, I could weep. It's funny, but when he was on the ships, I never used to worry, I always expected that he would come back to me – now I'm terrified...'

'Well, there's a war now,' Sally said and touched her hand. 'I know it hardly seems to have started yet, but it has and there are already casualties out there on the Belgian front. It's just that we haven't seen much action here yet.' The enemy had invaded neutral Belgium almost immediately and the British regular army would soon be deeply engaged in the hostilities.

Beth nodded, biting her lip. 'Fred always seems to know it all. He's got a map of Belgium and France in his room and he sticks pins in it. I don't go in there except to clean, but I know he follows every move.'

'Maybe we'll both be lucky,' Sally said and Beth nodded.

'I'd better get back to work,' Beth whispered close to tears. 'Sorry, I'm being silly. It's better if I don't think about it.'

'What about the hotel?' Sally asked. 'I mean, I know Ben promised to look in – but is everything all right for now?'

'Jack's partner will be in charge.' Beth frowned. 'I know he didn't run it well before, but Jack has changed things a lot and he does have better staff in place. Perhaps he will manage until Jack comes home...'

'Ben will look in regularly as he promised. He has Jack's authority to do whatever he thinks best.'

Beth nodded, gave Sally a wan smile and left. She had another secret sorrow that she didn't wish to tell anyone. She'd thought for a while that she might be pregnant, but her period had come a week late and been heavier than normal. She'd cried a few tears when she was alone. It seemed so easy for some women to conceive and carry a baby full term, but for Beth it was proving a problem.

* * *

'I was surprised to hear that Mr Marco was leaving,' Beth said to Fred as they travelled home on the bus that evening. 'Sally was shocked too, but Mr Harper knew some days ago.'

'Aye, well, he would have talked it over with him,' Fred said, 'to let him know what he was thinking before he signed up. They're good friends – and Mr Harper helped him out when he had that bit of trouble last year...'

'I didn't know he had any trouble,' Beth said. 'Sally knew but wouldn't tell me, of course, but I feel blind for not noticing.'

'Marco took a couple of weeks off. He was in a bit of a state when he left, but when he came back, he had his emotions under control. He laughs and jokes, but he runs deep that one, comes from having a French mother, I suppose.'

Beth nodded. She realised that Fred knew what had happened to upset Mr Marco, but he wouldn't tell her any more than Sally would; they kept the secrets they were privy to.

When they got to Fred's cottage, the light in the kitchen was on and the smell of cooking met them as they entered. Maggie had the table set and she was frying sausages, tomatoes, bacon and mushrooms. Her smile as she saw them lit up her pretty face.

'I thought I'd treat us all to a nice tea,' she said. 'I'm being sent somewhere first thing in the morning and I may not see you for a few weeks. I've been told the first weeks of training are pretty intensive and they need us quickly.'

'Yes, they would, especially girls that can speak a little French,' Fred told her with a nod of approval. 'There are casualties amongst our friends and it will be our boys next. As soon as you've got the basic training, they will have you on a ship and over there.'

'That is what they told me,' Maggie said. 'They asked for French speakers and volunteers and I...'

'Were foolish enough to stick your hand up,' Beth said sharply. She was upset that her friend was putting herself in danger and still couldn't put it from her mind, even though she understood her reasons. 'Oh, Maggie – supposing something happens to you?'

'I'm not a soldier.' She looked at their faces. 'I know it could happen, I'm not silly – but someone has to be prepared to go. The wounded need immediate treatment and even if I'm only fetching and carrying, taking water to those that need it and handing out cigarettes, it matters.' Her mouth set stubbornly and Beth felt tears in her eyes.

'I know, love, and I shouldn't snap at you – but you're like the sister I never had. I love you, Maggie Gibbs, and I don't want to lose you...'

'Oh, Beth,' Maggie said and rushed to hug her, tears on her cheeks now. 'I love you too and I want to come home and visit when I can – but I feel needed, called, and it might be someone we care for that's injured...'

'Yes, of course,' Beth agreed and swiped a hand across her face. 'I am being stupid and I do know you're right. I don't have the courage to do what you're doing, love, but I admire you for it.'

'We can't all leave Harpers,' Maggie said. 'That wouldn't be fair to Sally. It's her husband's business and she might be the one left running it before too long...'

'Ben Harper isn't joining up – at least not yet,' Beth said. 'He's told Sally he has too much responsibility – and he promised Jack to look in at the hotel whenever he can.'

Maggie nodded. 'He's American and he doesn't have to fight, but I saw him standing outside the recruiting office not far from where I was having my interview and he looked pensive. I'll bet he's thinking about it even if he hasn't done it.'

'He couldn't possibly just go and leave Sally in the lurch,' Beth said firmly. 'I mean, the hotel will survive – and, at the most, we'll lose Jack's investment, which won't ruin us because of what my aunt left us, but Ben Harper has everything invested in that store. He would be mad to desert it just to go and get himself shot at.'

* * *

Maggie was alone in her room, sorting through her clothes. Beth was annoyed with her for joining the nursing service – what would she say if she learned that she'd become engaged to Tim?

Tim had told his father, of course, but for the moment, Maggie wanted to keep it a secret from everyone else. The VADs' organisation would not be pleased if they knew she was engaged, because they disapproved of emotional entanglements. Marriage was forbidden, of course, but the service could not afford to be wasting time and money training nursing assistants who might leave to have a child.

Maggie did feel guilty at keeping her secret from her friends, but just for the moment she wasn't ready to share. Perhaps it was because she was nervous, apprehensive about what the future would bring – and their love was so newly confessed that she wanted to keep it private for a little while yet.

She could only hope that they would forgive her when she told them, though that might not be for years. If the war dragged on longer than everyone hoped, it might be ages before she and Tim could even think of being wed.

For a moment, Maggie felt fear. What if something happened to him? What if he should be killed... or she was injured some- how? It might be that they would never marry...

Pain caught at her heart and she wished they had not wasted

the sunlit days of summer. Why hadn't she told Tim she loved him long ago? Yet she had not really been certain of it until that night when he'd proposed over a bag of chips.

Laughter banished the tears. Poor Tim had wanted romance and a special dinner and she'd insisted on fish and chips on a bench.

Maggie lifted her head. She would face the future when it happened. For now, she must think about what she'd chosen to do – and that was to help the nurses who tended their wounded. She feared that there would be far too many for the regular nurses to treat alone and her heart went out to all those brave regular soldiers who were already fighting, and to the thousands upon thousands who were now beginning to train.

33

Ben swore beneath his breath as the woman in a large black hat with veiling over her face thrust an envelope into his hand. He already knew exactly what was inside the envelope because it wasn't the first he'd received. That had happened when he'd spotted one of his staff in the queue at a recruiting office and stopped to shake his hand and wish him well, asking if he was all right for money. A very rude woman had accused him of being a coward and trying to buy his way out of having to fight. His employee had defended him, telling her roughly that he was an American and had helped his staff to do the right thing, but she'd looked disgusted and given him the white feather just the same.

Perhaps since the Government had released all the Suffragettes in prison and they'd agreed not to make trouble for the duration of the war, they'd decided to take up a new cause – driving men to distraction with their white feathers. He could just imagine the woman who had given him the white feather knocking off a policeman's helmet and being arrested for it!

At first, Ben had been more amused than angry, but as the days passed and it happened again, it had begun to get to him, irking him and pricking at his skin. Damn it! He wasn't a coward and if it weren't for Sally, his new-born daughter and the store, he would have been one of the first to volunteer – but how could he?

Yet he knew that Sally was capable of keeping things going. Jonathan Stockbridge wouldn't fight; he suffered with flat feet and the army wouldn't take him even if he volunteered. Fred wouldn't fight either, because he was too old for active service, and there were quite a few women in senior positions thanks to Sally and her friends – so would he really be missed that much? Perhaps if he made sure the building work was finished, and if things got worse out there...

'Ben Harper, you are ridiculous,' Jenni Harper said, her eyes glinting with anger as he made his announcement that evening at dinner in Ben and Sally's apartment. She was over to visit with them as she cabled weeks before and, once here, made her opinion known. 'You can't possibly be considering volunteering for this war. You owe money to the bank; you have a renovation to finish and a new baby, as well as a wife who loves you...' She looked at Sally hard, her fingers tapping on the table impatiently. 'Say something to this foolish man, Sally. Make him realise that he can't risk it – it's not just his fortune at risk, it's mine...'

'Sally could run Harpers without me, and you can help her,' Ben said and glared at his sister. 'I didn't say I would do it immediately, just that I might find it impossible not to if things go badly for the British troops...'

'Why should they?' Jenni said truculently. 'Besides, you're not British – how can you enlist in their army?'

'I can be assigned to special forces and given an honorary rank – I've checked,' Ben told her with a gleam in his eyes. 'I shan't be the only American living in Britain who wants to join up…'

'Yes, but you should be thinking about your family – and what makes you think they will need your services?'

'Why did you bring that huge container of tinned food with you, if you didn't think it would be needed?' Ben reminded her that she too thought it would be a hard war. 'I'll be needed – and, what's more, I need to help.'

'I thought the food would come in handy…' Jenni looked sheepish.

'It will, of course, and I'm grateful. I've had it delivered to the stores and I'll probably end up selling it with the cakes and chocolate.'

Jenni frowned. 'You should keep it for yourselves; it may be difficult to buy stuff like that once the enemy starts blockading British ports.'

'We couldn't use it all – and the Germans are not your enemy, Jenni. America isn't at war with them…' Ben muttered.

'You're American too…' she countered, furious now. 'So why are they your enemy and not mine?'

'Stop shouting at each other, you'll wake Jenny,' Sally intervened. 'I'm glad you brought that container, Jenni. We can sell it in the shop and to friends if they run out and we'll be glad of some of it ourselves if the war drags on longer than we thought…'

'Surely you don't want Ben to join the British Army?' Jenni demanded, her eyes flashing almost as brightly as the large diamond ring on her finger.

'No, of course I don't,' Sally said, 'but neither do I want him to feel shamed or miserable and I know he's feeling that way…'

Ben reached inside his breast pocket and took out a piece of notepaper. He opened it and placed it beside the coffee cups on the table in front of them. 'Do either of you know what is in here?'

'White feathers,' Sally said instantly. 'Oh, Ben, did it happen again?'

Ben looked grimly at his sister. 'I was talking to one of our former employees. Stanley was queuing at a recruitment centre and I stopped to have a chat and shake hands, and then I walked off. One of the sergeants asked me if I wanted to join and I shook my head. As I walked away, three women thrust those in my hand and called me a coward... Stanley was most indignant and defended me loudly, but the women were not convinced.'

Sally nodded. 'He told Fred about it – and he told me...'

'How dare they?' Jenni was outraged. 'That is ridiculous! You're American and we're not at war – besides, Britain needs someone like you to keep importing goods they need into the country for as long as we can send it without our ships being attacked.'

'Yes, that's the stupid thing... I may be doing them more of a service than anyone realises and not just for profit at the shop...' Ben shook his head as both women stared at him. 'No, I couldn't tell you even if I wanted to, but I know some folk back home, just as Jenni does, and I've been contacted by a British Government official... I'm going into have a chat with him about how I can be most useful.'

'Oh, they'll make use of you,' Jenni said and looked annoyed. 'You don't have to tell me, I can guess. I know useful folk – I'm married to one. Henry even mentioned something before I left home...'

Ben nodded. 'Yes, well, that's officially out of bounds, Jenni, and neither you nor Sally can know anything...'

'Then if you're already doing something to help, why...?' Jenni said and then glared at the white feathers. 'They mean nothing...'

'Not to you perhaps,' Ben said, 'but it stings being called a coward and it will make a difference after the war. People will point the finger and go somewhere else to shop because I just got on with making a profit while their men died for us...'

'Ben, don't,' Sally said pleadingly. 'I know how you feel because we've talked about it – but Jenni has come all this way to see us and you're arguing over nothing. Those feathers are from just spiteful women who don't know any better. They call themselves patriots, but they do more harm than good.'

'Yes, of course they do,' he agreed, 'but I met someone else – a man who wanted to go into business with me and he was wearing a uniform. He asked me how you were and said I should stay home and look after you and the baby...'

'Are you talking about Mick?' Sally asked. 'I didn't think he would consider joining up – he's Irish and he's in business...'

'Exactly,' Ben said. 'Michael O' Sullivan isn't British, he's Irish, and he has businesses too, but he lives here and feels it is his home, so he's joining the army – and he's handed his business interests over to Marlene and a couple of others. He expects to lose money too, but he said he couldn't stand by and watch others die for him...'

'He was trying to make you feel guilty!' Jenni exclaimed.

Sally shook her head and Ben smiled.

'Actually, he wasn't,' Ben said. 'He was quite sincere and told me I should take care of business and my wife and child – and he even said it would suit him if I looked after a few things for him. He said he has made me his executor and apologised for not asking beforehand but he made the will in a hurry...'

Jenni stared at him. 'There you are then – everyone thinks the same: you don't need to fight, you're more useful here.'

'I agree for the moment,' Ben told her. 'The new building won't be finished much before Christmas. I'm hoping to open just in time to catch the last-minute trade – and Sally will be feeling better in a few weeks, stronger and more able to cope with any problems at the store...' He looked at his wife and she held her hand out to him in support.

'You fool!' Jenny glared at him. 'Don't throw your life away, Ben!'

'I have every intention of coming through,' Ben said, 'but, if Sally can bear it, I intend to go sometime next year...'

'Surely it will all be over...'

'If you thought that you wouldn't have brought all that tinned food over,' Ben said and she had the grace to nod. 'I'm grateful, Jenni, and we'll keep some but sell the rest on. I'm sure it will be needed soon enough. The ships that manage to come through any blockade will have more than tinned fruit and salmon to carry...' They all knew that he must mean military equipment but couldn't tell them government secrets.

Jenni looked at her sister-in-law. 'Can't you talk him out of it, Sally? Make him see he doesn't have to prove he isn't a coward?'

'Ben has a mind of his own and if he decides to join up, he will,' Sally said and lifted her head. Inside, she was agreeing with Jenni, but she knew she had to stand by Ben's decision. 'Anyway, he's right. We've talked about it and I won't stand in his way. You and I can run the store – and Stockbridge won't be going, nor will Mr Brown in men's clothing, he's too old. I have my girls; I'm busy recruiting more all the time, and some of the older men can't join up for health reasons. Two of them have been turned down this week – one had flat feet and the other a bad heart that he had no idea about, poor man.'

'What the hell difference do flat feet make?' Jenni demanded, still angry.

'Apparently, they can't march as efficiently,' Sally said and laughed as she saw Jenni's face. 'No, it isn't funny. Poor Mr Ashton went off filled with patriotic fervour to join up and they turned him down. He was very annoyed – and Mr Carson was told he was too old and his heart would not stand the strain so now he's worried about losing his job. I told him we needed him as long as he could manage to get in. They both cheered up a bit when I explained we really needed them, but it didn't quite make up for being turned down – and Mr Ashton got a white feather too. He showed the woman his paper that says he is unfit for service and she apologised, but it still stung – so Ben isn't the only one...'

'I still think he's mad... but then he always was,' Jenni said. 'Only a madman would have taken on this place when my uncle died and left us without a penny backing – but we've done OK, I guess...' the anger was draining out of her. 'Henry didn't want me to come over and he wouldn't let me bring his son for a visit – he said it was too dangerous.' She grinned suddenly. 'We're all mad, but we've done all right with Harpers, haven't we?'

'We had a reasonable year one,' Ben said, 'and year two made a small profit. This year should do quite a bit better...'

'Well, it might if you hadn't borrowed for the extension,' Jenni said. 'It will take another two to three years to see us in profit overall.'

'We'll manage,' Ben said. 'As long as the sales are strong and we have a good turnover, we should still make a decent margin this year.'

Jenni glared at him intently. 'You won't want the money I was going to offer as a standby loan then?'

Ben met her stare for stare. 'I thought you had invested all you had when you bought those shares?'

'I did – but Henry bought them from me, because I told him I needed more money to help if things got sticky over here because of the war. It's all right, you needn't worry. He has left them in my name and I don't have to pay him back until I'm ready. He would have just given me the money, but I'm using them as collateral for a loan of thirty thousand pounds for you; it's sitting in a bank, ready if you need it...'

'I'm not sure the shares are even worth that now, because of the war,' Ben told her. 'Your husband could lose his money if we were bombed or the victim of sabotage, Jenni.'

'So what? He has too much of it,' she said casually, but her eyes flashed with humour. 'I thought you had faith in us to run the show while you were off playing soldiers?'

'It's not your ability, it's the war – in war, things can go wrong,' Ben reminded her. 'Thank you for what you did, Jenni, but that money won't be touched unless the worst happens.'

'Sure, I know,' she drawled. 'It's my business too, remember.'

'If you two have finished arguing, the chocolate soufflé is ready and it really won't wait,' Sally said and smiled at them. They were so alike – passionate, quick to anger, sharp with words, but fiercely loyal. It was just like Jenni to put money at their disposal if they needed it.

'It may be years before I see you again,' Jenni said and her eyes filled with tears. 'Henry didn't want me to come over at all. He said I could cable the money and send you the paperwork. I said to hell with that – he's my brother and I haven't seen my niece yet...'

'You're a wonderful person, Jenni, just remind me not to get on the wrong side of you...' Sally said and went to push her arm through Jenni's, squeezing it affectionally.

Jenni looked at her and then burst out laughing. 'You've no idea how worried I've been for you guys. I hate those damned Germans. Why couldn't they leave things alone?'

'Oh, I suppose they think they're in the right,' Sally said. 'It just seems so awful to me – that poor man and his wife shot to death and now all this... Why must people fight each other? I used to buy lovely bread from a German baker, but his shop is closed now, and I'm sure he didn't want a war...'

'I don't mind a scrap now and then,' Jenni said and threw a look of rueful affection at her brother. 'But this war is wrong, especially if it hurts the people, I love...'

'Yes, I agree,' Sally said and hugged her arm again.

'Can't you make him see sense?' Jenni whispered in her ear as they went into the kitchen to take Sally's soufflé from the oven. It had risen to majestic heights and smelled delicious.

'It's no use arguing, Jenni, he won't listen,' Sally said.

'Couldn't you shed a few tears or something, use your wiles to bind him to you?'

'He would hate me if I used tears,' Sally said honestly. 'We just have to trust to our luck that he'll come back, Jenni – and pray...' She blinked hard to stop the tears falling. 'Believe me, I'm not the only woman in England feeling like this.'

'No, of course you're not,' Jenni said and bit her lip. 'I'm an idiot to lose my temper, but Ben means a lot to me...'

'Yes,' Sally agreed. 'I know – but we have to let go, Jenni. It's the only way.'

34

'I couldn't afford a diamond,' Reggie said as he held out the ring set with turquoise and pearl in a 9-carat gold band. 'I bought this from Uncle's around the corner. It isn't much, but I'll get you a better one when I've saved some money...'

Marion stared at the gipsy band of turquoises and pearls and tears came to her eyes. To some people it might look insignificant, but to her it was beautiful beyond compare. She'd never owned even a cheap string of glass beads and this was exactly right. Reggie slipped it on the third finger of her right hand and she stared at it transfixed, feeling as if she'd been given the earth.

'It's not an engagement ring, because yer ma would kick up and we ain't about ter get married for a few years,' he said, smiling at her shocked look. 'Go on, say somethin'...'

'It is so beautiful,' Marion said, overcome. 'I never thought I'd ever have anything this lovely, Reggie. Thank you so much...' She smiled at him tremulously. 'I'd wear it on my wedding finger if I could...'

'It would cause too much bother fer yer,' Reggie said and took her hand, kissing the palm. 'Yer know yer mine now, Marion, but

we don't need ter announce it ter the world, not yet. I've got ter go
in the mornin' and neither of us knows when I'll be back. The
regular army is engaged in heavy fighting over there in Belgium
now and they'll need us lads once we're trained.'

'I don't know what we'll do without you...' she said, a catch in
her throat. 'Oh Reggie, I wish—'

'I know – and I wish we could be married too, but it ain't
possible, love, not yet. I know what yer father's like, Marion, and
he might start hittin' yer if he thought we was plannin' ter get
married and leave yer family in the lurch. We ain't goin' ter do
that and we'll work it out when we're ready – but this is just
between you and me...'

'You spoil me,' Marion said and clung to his hand as he took
hers. His fingers were big and strong and the way they curled
about hers made her feel wanted and loved, something she'd
never really felt before. She smiled at him shyly, loving him for
understanding that she was too young to be his wife but wanting
her just the same and prepared to wait, because she was worth it.

'Shall I see you in the mornin'?' she asked as they lingered
outside the back door.

'No, I'll be off to catch the early train and you'll be too busy
gettin' them lads off ter work,' Reggie said. 'I'll send yer a postcard
sometimes – just ter let yer know I'm OK and keep in touch.'

'Can I write to you?'

'I'll let Ma know if there's an address,' Reggie promised. 'We'll
keep the way we feel to ourselves fer a bit, Marion love, though I
reckon my mother has guessed how I feel and mebbe your
Robbie thinks he knows...'

Maggie nodded, holding back her tears as he kissed her softly
on the mouth. He was very gentle with her and she knew he was
holding back, but he was looking after her.

'Some of the lads are risking the lives of the girls they love,'
Reggie told her. 'They don't think past what's inside their pants,

but it won't be them left holding the baby when they're over in France and they won't be the ones gettin' the bad looks and trouble from their folks. I want yer, Marion, but I'm goin' ter wait until me weddin' day...' He stroked the side of her face gently and then kissed her so sweetly that Marion was sure she would have done anything he asked in the magic of that moment.

She let go of his hands at last and he walked away from her. He didn't look back and Marion went quickly inside the kitchen. Her brother Robbie was making some cocoa in a saucepan.

'Ma asked for a drink,' he said. 'I'll take it up if yer like – give yer a minute to get over it...'

'Thanks, Robbie,' Marion said.

He'd made enough for her, himself, Ma and Dickon. Kathy was already in bed and had hers earlier. Marion was sipping the last of her cocoa when her brother returned.

'Ma said fer yer to go in afore yer go to bed.' Robbie picked up his mug. 'Off to bed then, Dickon.'

'I want ter hear...'

'Off ter bed or I shan't ask fer yer.'

Dickon threw him a dirty look but took his mug and went. Marion put her empty mug in the sink and looked at him.

'What was all that about then?'

'Dickon is fourteen next month and he wants ter leave school and start on down the docks. I told him I'd have a word with gaffer...'

Marion nodded. 'I'd hoped he would stay at school for a bit longer...'

'Dickon is like me; he can add up and write what he needs to and he'll work with his hands. He'll make a good carpenter, but they'll have him sweeping up fer a bit. He knows that, but he still wants to start work next month.'

'Ma might not like it, but she won't interfere and Dad won't care,' Marion said. She kept looking at him as he fiddled with the handle of his mug. 'What else, Robbie? I know that isn't everything.'

'I'm goin' ter sign on,' Robbie said and raised his hand as he heard her indrawn breath. 'I know I ain't quite seventeen, but they'll take me in the cadets, 'cos I asked... I shan't be fightin' fer a while, but I can help wiv a lot of stuff – digging trenches and shoring them up wiv wood and stuff. I know how to do all that and it's easier for someone like me to tunnel...'

'Robbie, no!' Marion burst out before he went any further. 'You're too young, love – and how shall I manage if you go too?'

'Dickon knows he's got to help and he's prepared to take over my chores in return for gettin' what he wants, and he'll be earnin' a few bob. Not much fer a start, but he'll give yer half and yer earnin' more now...'

'Yes, I know...' Marion shook his head. 'Don't you realise that you could be killed? You're my brother and I care about you.'

'Yeah, I know – and that's why I've told yer instead of just clearin' orf and leavin' yer ter find out,' Robbie said, his grey eyes meeting hers steadily. Robbie was the most like her, the one she relied on for so much, and it made Marion feel hollow inside to realise that he'd grown up. Her little brother was a man and she couldn't stop him doing what he wanted. Yes, she could go down the recruiting office and make a fuss about him being too young, but if she did that, he would just go somewhere else and sign on again.

She wiped away the tears. 'Keep your silly head down then,' she said and dashed her hand over her eyes. 'I want my brother to come back and not a dead hero in a box...'

'They won't let me fight yet,' Robbie said. 'The recruitin' officer said I was a brave lad and he wished he'd got another thousand like me. He says they can use my talents and I'll be as safe as if I were tucked up in me bed at 'ome.' He grinned at her.

'You daft idiot,' Marion said and smiled through the tears.

His smile was tearing her heart open, even more than Reggie had earlier. Reggie was a man and although she didn't want to lose him before she'd even had a chance to know and love him; her brother was like a part of her. She felt as if she'd had a limb torn away.

'I shan't stop you; I know I couldn't, but remember I love you, dope.'

'I love you too, snub nose,' he said affectionately and Marion's emotion nearly choked her. Robbie often teased her about her nose, which was a little shorter than she'd like, even though Reggie said it was beautiful – but he thought everything about her was beautiful...

'When will you go?' she asked.

'I'll sign on tomorrow,' Robbie said, 'and they'll take me in a couple of weeks – that's what he said. I'll be sent orf down the coast somewhere and they'll teach me things, and then I'll come back fer a visit.'

Marion nodded. 'All right, love. If it's what you want...'

Robbie came around the table and gave her a brotherly hug. 'Thanks, Marion. Yer the best. I knew yer would understand. Some of the lads said their mothers and sisters screeched like barn owls and started howling, some of me mates couldn't face them at all until they'd signed up...'

Marion gave a laugh that might have been a sob. 'Thank goodness Dickon isn't old enough to go...'

'He's already been down and got himself kicked out,' Robbie said and grinned at her. 'I gave him a clip round the ear and told him when he's strong enough to put me down he can sign on and not before – that's when he said if he couldn't sign up, he wanted to start work.'

'I might have known,' Marion sighed. Robbie had always kept Dickon in line and she wouldn't find it as easy without him. True, it meant less washing, but she would have rather he'd stayed home for a bit longer. However, she knew when she was beaten.

Robbie looked at her uncomfortably. 'I've asked fer some of me pay ter be sent ter to you. Yer me next of kin – the name I put down – and if they need to contact anyone it will be you...'

Marion felt chilled, but she just nodded. 'Keep most of it for yourself, love. I can manage...'

'Why should yer have to put all your money in?' Robbie said and looked grim. 'Yer courtin' now, Marion, and yer will need to save fer when yer get married – and ter send Reggie a few fags and sweets wherever he is.'

'So that's why I love you,' Marion said and smiled. 'I'm going up now – see you tomorrow.'

'Reggie will come back and so shall I,' Robbie said and grinned in the way that was so infectious. 'I'll make yer proud, sis...'

'Of course, you will, you always have.'

* * *

'You look a bit worried,' Becky said to Marion when they had a few moments to spare mid-morning the next day. 'Is something wrong at home?'

'My brother Robbie is signing up today – and my youngest brother has decided to leave school and start work next month. I'd hoped he might stay on and pass a few exams like I did, but Robbie says it isn't right for him – Dickon, that is...'

'Dickon is older than Kathy, isn't he?'

'Yes, nearly fourteen. Kathy is thirteen, and Milly is six – she had a birthday last week. I bought her a little wooden doll and made some extra clothes for it. She was so excited, you wouldn't believe. Robbie got her sweets and a paint box, Dickon bought her some sweets, and Dan sent her a picture book and a lovely card from Southampton.'

'What did your mother buy her?'

Marion shook her head. 'Ma forgot it was her birthday, but I got her a card and a bar of chocolate and said it was from her. I think Milly knew, but she didn't say – anyway, she was lucky. Mrs Jackson next door gave her a dolly's pram that had belonged to her daughters. Reggie painted it and made it look like new for her.'

'That was lovely of him,' Becky said and smiled. 'Is he your boyfriend?'

'Yes...' Marion took a ribbon from inside her dress and showed Becky the ring Reggie had given her. 'We're not engaged, but it's a friendship ring – until he comes home and we can think about getting married...'

'It's very pretty,' Becky said. She looked a bit wistful. 'I don't have a boyfriend yet. My father wouldn't let me even think about it, because he said I was too delicate, but Minnie told him I'm perfectly strong and healthy and if I meet someone nice, he might let me go to tea with him if he asks...'

Marion smiled and nodded. 'I think a lot of young people are rushing into marriage before the men go away, but I'm too young and I have to look after my family...' They both looked serious because the British Army was retreating from Mons, fighting every step of the way before the overwhelming might of an efficient German force.

'Oh, I don't want to get married for ages,' Becky agreed, 'but it might be nice to have a boyfriend to take me out to tea...'

'Look, we've got customers,' Marion said, nudging her as three women walked in. 'I think we're going to be busy now.'

35

Marion noticed the lights were on in her house when she got to the end of her street that evening. It wasn't really dark yet and it was unusual for Robbie to light the gas, and even more so for him to be home before her. She didn't think he'd given in his notice at the docks yet, because he planned to keep working until he got his orders.

As she went into the kitchen, Marion caught the smell she associated with her father – beer and pipe tobacco – and her heart sank. She could hear raised voices from above stairs and knew that her parents were having a row again. Should she go up and try to remonstrate with her father – or would that just make things worse for Ma? She hesitated with her foot on the bottom stair and then shook her head. Pa would only lose his temper if she interfered.

Deciding to keep clear for fear of making things worse, Marion filled the kettle and put it on the stove. She was just about to peel the potatoes for their supper when the kitchen door opened and Robbie entered, together with their older brother Dan. Marion gave a cry of pleasure and ran to embrace him.

'It's lovely to see you,' she said and hugged him. His strong arms held her for a moment and then he let her go as they all heard a terrible scream from upstairs. 'Dan...' she tried to grab his arm as he started towards the stairs. 'Be careful. Don't let him hurt her, but watch out...'

'It's time that bugger was taught a proper lesson,' Dan muttered and pulled open the door that hid the staircase from view. Now the screams and cries were louder, becoming more and more desperate, and Dan's feet pounded up the uncarpeted stairs. Robbie and Marion looked at each other and she moved towards the stairs, but he grabbed her arm and held her.

'No, Marion,' he said. 'You can't do anything. Leave it to Dan. He went orf the last time they quarrelled rather than kill him, but he's not goin' ter let 'im get away wiv it...' His mouth set grimly. 'I can't stop 'im, but Dan will...'

Just then they heard another scream from their mother, followed by a shout from their father, some grunting, and furniture being overturned as a fight took place, and then silence.

'Do you think...?' Marion ventured and then a few moments later Dan came back down, his face bearing a few red marks and a cut lip. 'Dan... what happened?'

'Ma is hurt bad,' Dan said. 'She needs to go to the hospital immediately. Robbie, go down the road and ask Mr Brandon if he will run us to the infirmary in his van. I'm goin' ter carry her downstairs and I'll go with her.'

'Dad?' Marion asked and Dan looked at her hard.

'He was drunk and I put him out for a few hours. He'll have a sore head, but he'll live. When he comes to, I'm going to tell him – he goes and he doesn't come back or next time we meet I'll kill him for sure...'

'We should get the police...'

'They won't interfere,' Dan said bitterly. 'I tried that years ago and was told they don't intervene in domestic quarrels.'

Marion ran up the stairs in her elder brother's wake. Her mother was lying still on the bed with her eyes closed, her face covered in blood and bruises all over her body. Her father was stretched out on the ground. His face showed evidence that he'd been hit a few times, blood on his mouth and his head lying at an angle. She bent over him, fearing for a moment that Dan had killed him already, but a faint groan told her that he was still living but out for a while, just as her brother had said. She felt a surge of regret, wishing she'd tried to stop her father when she first got home, but she knew from experience that he would just go on hitting them both if she'd said a word.

'Get me a blanket to put round her,' Dan ordered and Marion ran to do as she was told, tucking it round her mother's limp form as he held her to his chest and then carried her from the room and down the stairs. When they returned to the kitchen, Robbie showed him the keys to their neighbour's van.

'Bob Brandon says fer yer ter take the van,' Robbie said. 'He's got a job his missus needs him to do, but he says yer a good driver and he trusts yer.'

'Thanks,' Dan said, 'put them in me pocket – and get the door open. I'll need yer to help me take her to the infirmary, Robbie. Are you all right, Marion? If that bugger comes to and starts on at yer, hit him wiv the rollin' pin and run next door, taking Milly and the others wiv yer.'

'He looks as if he'll be out for a while,' Marion said grimly. 'Go on, look after Ma – I can manage here.' Her father usually behaved reasonably around her; it was just his wife that brought out the monster in him.

Dickon came in a few seconds later and asked what was going on.

'Ma is bad, so Dan has taken her to the infirmary,' Marion said and Dickon glared at her. 'Yes, it was Pa – Dan hit him and he's out for the count. Come and sit down and I'll get you a sandwich. There's no point in cooking tea if no one is here.'

'Will Ma be all right?' Dickon asked as he sat at the table and watched Marion make a cheese and pickle sandwich.

'I don't know, love,' Marion said and caught back the sob she'd been holding inside since she'd heard the row upstairs on her return. 'He's hit her so many times and she's survived – but one of these days...'

'Robbie says he'll go too far and then he'll clear off or the police will arrest him and he'll hang for murder.'

'Would you care?'

Dickon thought for a moment and then shook his head. 'I hate him. I wish he was dead...'

Marion nodded, seeing the strain and distress in his young face. 'Sometimes I do too,' she said. 'When he's sober, he's more like Dan and then I like him all right, but as soon as he has too much to drink, he's like a wild beast.'

'Yeah, I know,' Dickon said and she thought he looked as if he might cry. 'I hate him then, but he's still Pa...'

They heard the sound of someone moving about upstairs and then heavy steps on the stairs. Marion had expected her father to be unconscious longer and she sprang back, seizing the heavy iron poker from its stand, ready to defend herself and her brother from the beast that was her father when in drink.

As Pa came into the kitchen, he was wiping his mouth and grimacing as if he could taste the blood. His bleary eyes looked at Marion and he spat blood on the floor.

'Where is the bitch?'

'Don't speak about Ma like that!' Marion cried.

'I'll do as I like in me own 'ouse and don't yer forget it!'

'Dan took her to the hospital,' Marion said, keeping a tight hold of her weapon. 'You hurt her bad...'

'Bloody bugger that one,' Pa said and spat again. 'You needn't look like that, girl. I ain't goin' ter hit yer – it weren't yer that ruined me flamin' life, it were that bitch.'

Marion stared at him in disgust. She wanted to throw his wicked deeds at him and yell defiance, but there was no one here to defend her or the others and if she dared to argue, he might decide to punish her or Milly, or Dickon.

'Well, I'm orf,' Pa said and picked up his kit. He slapped down a couple of pound notes and some silver on the kitchen table. 'I only come ter give yer that, it's all I've got left of me wages for the past few months. I don't reckon as I'll be back fer a year or more this time, what wiv the bloody Germans an' all – that's if I ever get back. Yer still me kids, yer and Dickon and Kathy and the little one, Robbie maybe. She was seein' him again, the bugger what ruined her, around the time Robbie came along; that's why I started beltin' her. I let her get away wiv it once, but no bugger makes a fool of me twice. The other sod ain't mine fer sure – and if yer don't believe me, ask that bitch...'

'What do yer mean?' Marion demanded. 'Why isn't Dan yours?'

'Don't 'ave ter spell it out, do I?' he muttered. 'She cheated me – tricked me into marryin' her when she was havin' another bloke's kid. He'd gorn orf and left her in the lurch, so she let me do it to her when I was half drunk. I knew what she'd done, but I loved her, so I married her when she told me she was havin' that bugger, but then she went to her fancy man again, after you come along, and if she thinks I'll forget and forgive, she's kiddin' her bloody self.'

Marion didn't answer, she couldn't. Instead she just stood watching until he walked out and slammed the door after him. Her hands were still trembling as she replaced the heavy iron poker in its stand.

'He's a liar!' Dickon burst out. 'Ma wouldn't do that... would she?' He looked distressed and anxious.

'I don't know,' Marion said. She felt sick and faint. All of a sudden, her father's rages and resentment made sense. Yet if he'd been cheated, why hadn't he walked out and left his wife for good – why did he keep returning just to punish her? Or was that it – he just couldn't forgive and so he had to go on making her pay for what she'd done?

He had no right to inflict physical torture on her even if she'd made a mistake years ago. Marion could understand he might feel cheated and angry, but that didn't give him the right to beat his wife. He should have forgiven her or walked out and left her years ago.

A sound from the stairs made her investigate. Kathy was standing there shivering in her nightgown, tears on her cheeks. 'I heard...' she whispered.

'Come and sit down,' Marion said. 'Stop crying, Kathy. Pa has gone and he won't be back for a while.'

'I heard her screaming,' Kathy said, looking at Marion, the fear still in her eyes. 'Dan took her away...'

'To the infirmary,' Marion told her. She looked at her brother and then Kathy. 'You are neither of you to tell either Dan or Robbie what he said, do you hear me?'

'Yeah, I hear,' Dickon said and looked at Kathy. 'We don't breathe a word of this, right – Dan is our brother and Robbie. They don't like Pa, but they needn't be made bastards, right? It's a secret we all keep.'

A bastard was a dirty word round here and Marion thought there were still laws that meant they couldn't inherit stuff – not that Pa had anything to leave, but it was a stigma. It would label Ma a whore too and Marion would never say anything to anyone outside this room that made her mother a whore. Everyone felt sorry for her, but if they knew why Pa beat her so remorselessly, most of the men, and actually some of the women, too, would say she deserved it. Marion might have felt impatient with her mother sometimes for just taking the punishment and not fighting back, but she loved her and it was breaking her heart. Pa's accusations had been genuine; she knew that he believed his wife had cheated on him before and after their marriage and it had turned him sour, turned him from the generous father she could just remember from her childhood into the bitter drunk he'd become.

'He's a liar,' Kathy said fiercely. 'Ma told him he forced himself on her before they were wed and Dan was his... I heard her say it when he was beating her. He just said all that to stop you telling the cops.'

'Yeah, that's right,' Dickon agreed, but the look in his eyes told Marion that he didn't believe it. He'd been in the room and seen Pa's bitterness and Marion believed her father too. She didn't know it all, but there was some truth in his story and perhaps one day her mother would tell her what had really happened – and who the man was that she was supposed to have had an affair with before her marriage.

* * *

It was gone twelve when Robbie and Dan got back that night. Marion had lain on her bed fully dressed waiting for them to return and she got up and went straight down to the kitchen.

'How is she?' she asked, but as she saw the look in their faces, she felt cold all over. 'No... she isn't...' The word wouldn't leave her mouth because it was too awful to speak or even to think. 'Dan, tell me, she'll be all right...'

'She's dead,' he said in a cold flat voice. 'The doctors did what they could for her, but it was too late. At least he'll never do that to her again...' He sounded so angry, so bitter, that he could have been Pa, and in that moment, she saw her father in him and knew that whatever had happened before their marriage, Dan was his father's son. Pa just couldn't believe it because of what his wife had done.

Marion felt the sob rise in her throat, but she couldn't speak, just staring at her brother for what seemed like hours. 'He killed her... he's a murderer...'

'I've told the police everything,' her brother said. 'They've told me they will look for him and he'll be arrested – but I doubt he'll hang around to be thrown in prison. He'll be on a ship and away...'

'Will they go to the ports and search for him?'

'We know he's on the merchant ships,' Dickon said. 'Surely the police can stop them sailing and drag him back...'

'If the bloody cops don't get him this time, I shall,' Dan said bitterly. 'I swear to you, Marion, if they don't hang him, I'll swing for him. If he ever gets near enough to me, I'll stick a knife in his guts and watch him die in agony the way she did...'

'Oh, Dan...' Marion's tears were released. 'I'm so sorry. I know how much you loved her...'

'She was a lovely caring mother when I was Milly's age,' Dan said. 'He was all right too then. Didn't make much fuss of me, but he adored you, and he was all right with Ma most of the time. I don't know what happened, but just after Robbie was born, she started to change, little by little I saw the life go out of her until she was just goin' through the motions. I was fifteen before I realised what he did to her – the filthy bastard. I had a go at him the first time I saw her injuries after he'd raped and beaten her; he knocked me flying, told me if I tried it again, he would kill me...' Dan rolled up his sleeve and showed them an old scar of a burn. 'He did that when I was sixteen. I tried arguing with him rather than trying to hit him and he did that with Ma's flat iron. He threatened to put it on her face if I interfered again. The last time I hit him before I left, he stayed down for a few minutes.

This time, I told him that if he touched her again, I would kill him and he knows I meant it...'

'That's why he went after he came to himself,' Marion said. 'He didn't try to touch us, Dan, he just went... I don't think he'll be back for a while, perhaps never...'

'He's a dead man if we meet,' Dan said and she knew that he meant it. 'What will you do now, Marion?'

'I'm not sure – it will be difficult with Milly...'

'Someone round here will look after her,' Robbie said. 'Mrs Jackson thinks the world of her. She'll have her if you ask, Marion – 'specially wiv you and Reggie being friends...'

'That's the first I've heard of it?' Dan looked at her and frowned. 'You're not serious are yer?'

'We're good friends,' Marion said. She wasn't ready to talk about marriage to her family yet. 'I think Mrs Jackson would help out by having Milly until I get home.'

'If Mrs Jackson will have her and give her some tea for a couple of bob a week, I'll pay. I'll have the house put in my name so I pay the rent and you and the others can live here. I've saved a bit for you, Marion. It will keep you goin' if anythin' happens to me in this war...'

'No, Dan, no...' she said, her throat tight with the effort not to cry. 'You're my brother; you've got to survive...'

'I'll do my best...' Dan grinned at her suddenly. 'I've got a girl-friend, Marion. I was goin' ter bring her round fer tea before I leave, but not this time... not with Ma in the morgue.' For a moment the anger was replaced by tears, but he dashed them away. 'I've put me ring on her finger and we'll be married when I get a longer leave. Her name is Sarah and I want yer to be nice to her when she comes.'

'Of course, I shall.' Marion threw her arms around him. 'I love you, Dan. I wish I could make things better for you, but I can't. And tell your Sarah to come round any time.'

'I'll tell her, but she's a bit shy,' he said and his cheeks were pink. 'I love her, Marion. I want my family to welcome her...'

'Why shouldn't we?' Marion asked.

'She comes from a better class than us,' Dan said and frowned. 'Her father owns a bookshop and she works behind the counter, but she went to senior school and passed a lot of exams, could have been a teacher if there had been the money for it. Mr Hardwick is a scholar and a gentleman but not very good at business.' He gave her a lopsided grin. 'So, don't let the lads round here tease her about bein' stuck up – 'cos she ain't.'

'If she isn't, they won't,' Marion told her. 'If she's your girl, she's welcome here, Dan, and you know it.'

'I wish I could have told Ma,' he said and grimaced. 'She was always on to me about gettin' wed and I laughed and said it was a sailor's life fer me – girl in every port – but when I saw Sarah, I only wanted her.'

'You didn't tell us...'

'I wasn't sure she would have me,' Dan said and his eyes lit up from inside. 'She's far above me, Marion, but I swear I'll never treat her the way he did Ma – I'll never lay one finger on her in anger...'

'If you do, I'll take the poker to you myself,' Marion said and then shook her head. 'Only teasing, Dan. I know how gentle you were with Ma when she was ill. Your Sarah is a lucky girl.'

'I hope she will be,' he said and the light left his eyes. 'This war is goin' to be a bastard, Marion. I've had a few close calls at sea, but I know the Germans are only waiting for the right moment to strike. At the moment they're concentrating on the fight for Belgium and France, but their navy is strong. You just wait until they start on us...'

Marion reached across and squeezed his arm. Her boyfriend and two of her brothers were all ready to fight and the thought of it made her blood run cold. She was more afraid of losing one of them to the war than she had ever been of Pa's rages.

'Will you be here for Ma's funeral?' she asked and Dan shook his head.

'I'll arrange it all for you,' he said, 'but I'll have to go. I used up some of my leave with Sarah. I wish I could stay, but if I ask for compassionate leave, the ship will sail without me and I can't do that now. I need to be wiv me mates or I'll get transferred.'

'Yes, I understand,' Marion said. 'I'll leave the funeral arrangements to you but come back as soon as you can please...'

'Only death will keep me away,' he vowed, 'and when I do come, I'll bring my Sarah, and she'll be my wife. She'll be living with her father until we marry and get our own place, but I'll always look out for you, Marion. You have my word...'

* * *

The police visited the next day. They talked to Dan and Marion and took witness statements from both of them but made no comment, except to say that Mr Kaye would be arrested if he returned to the area.

'Useless buggers,' Dan said after the constable had left. 'I'll have ter go after me dinner, Marion – but I'll write and send money.' He hesitated, then, 'You know what ter do about the funeral and the police will let yer have it next week – so when will yer go back to work?'

'Tomorrow, but I'll have time off to take care of the arrangements,' Marion said. 'Mrs Jackson is going to keep Milly off school until after the funeral and then she should settle down a bit. It's lucky she often goes there for her tea...' She caught back a sob. 'I can't believe we're talkin' like this, Dan. I keep thinkin' Ma's still upstairs...'

'I know, love,' he said. He frowned at her. 'I should have done fer 'im while I had the chance...'

'No, don't think that,' Marion said. 'If you had, you would be on trial for murder. I care about you, Dan, and I don't want you to hang – let the police do their work. I hope they catch him or that he never comes back...' Emotion caught at her throat. 'I hate him now, Dan, and I wish I'd done something, but there was nothing I could do to stop him...'

'I should have been the one,' her brother told her firmly. 'She's better off out of it, Marion. That brute never gave her any peace. One day he'll pay – either at the rope's end or I'll kill him.'

Marion nodded. She was still numb with shock and grief, but she knew she didn't want her brother to kill the man she believed was his father, no matter what her father said about her mother cheating on him before their marriage. She wanted him to live and marry this girl he'd found and she wanted the police to arrest her father – or perhaps she wanted him to disappear and never come back. It was all too painful to think about and she couldn't wait for the funeral to be over so that she could return to Harpers fulltime and to the work she loved. Especially now that Mr Marco had recommended her to help with the window dressing. He'd asked her to make a display of hats and scarves and been so pleased, he'd talked to Mrs Harper – and the upshot was that Marion would be trained, going one afternoon a week to art school for a window-dressing course and learn with Mr Marco's other apprentice.

'You will make a good team,' he'd told her. 'Work closely with Mrs Harper and you'll both be fine.'

It was exciting and there had been a hint of more pay, but for the moment all Marion could think of was the wicked waste of her mother's life – just because of a mistake when she was young. It was tragic and painful and she knew that the whole family would struggle to put their mother's death behind them.

However, Marion had things to look forward to and Dan would learn to live with his bitterness and perhaps put it aside when he married.

For the moment, they had to live with the shadow of their mother's murder and hope that with the funeral their lives could begin to recover.

36

'You look lovely, Minnie,' Rachel said as her friend tried on her wedding dress for her benefit. 'It is such a beautiful gown – as I expected, because you made it yourself...'

'The headdress and veil were my mother's,' Minnie said. 'My father gave it to me when I agreed to marry Jonathan the first time and I've kept it in tissue and lavender. I never expected to use it, but I'm so glad I looked after it and didn't throw it away. Mildred thought it would just remind me, but I kept it in my things...'

'And now you're going to marry the man you love,' Rachel said and smiled at her lovingly. 'I'm so happy for you, Minnie. It's wonderful that you've found each other again.'

'Yes.' There was a faint colour in Minnie's cheeks. 'I feel so lucky, Rachel – and it's all because of you...'

Rachel looked stunned. 'No, how could it be?'

'You took me to live with you and you gave me the courage to take on that job at Harpers. If it hadn't been for that, I should never have met Jonathan again...'

'No, I suppose you wouldn't,' Rachel acknowledged. 'I wanted to make you safe, Minnie – and I suppose I've done that and more.' She smiled. 'It's funny how these things happen. I never expected to marry again and then William walked into my life. I almost shut him out because of a misunderstanding, but fortunately we sorted that out and now I'm so glad that I married him, even though he isn't around at the moment...'

'You must miss him terribly,' Minnie said, looking at her in sympathy. 'All you had was one night in a hotel.'

'Yes, but I'm going to make up for it this weekend. William is getting a weekend pass and so I hope that we shall have at least a few hours to be together before he is off again.'

'This awful war,' Minnie said, looking concerned. 'It isn't fair that you should be separated from your husband so soon after being married.'

'No, it isn't fair,' Rachel said, 'but it's the same for every woman with a husband in the army. Now, I've pinned the waist as you asked so you can finish the dress.'

'Yes, thank you,' Minnie smiled at her. 'I was going to ask if you would like to have tea with us on Sunday, but if William is home...'

'We would love to come for tea,' Rachel said. 'I'll bake a lemon drizzle cake. I know you like them, so I'll bring it along.'

* * *

'I almost wish you hadn't told Minnie that we'd go to tea,' William said as he kissed Rachel that Saturday evening. 'I've got forty-eight hours and I'd like to spend them all in bed with you...'

'William...' Rachel blushed, still a little unused to his passion. Paul had never been as open about wanting her and would just reach for her in bed without speaking. William's lovemaking was sweet and tender and had brought tears to her eyes the first time. 'I can always send her a telegram...'

'No, of course you won't,' William said and looked at her with love in his eyes. 'I want you, my darling, so much you may never know just how much – but I'm not greedy. Your friends are expecting us, so we shall go, but we'll spend the whole of the morning in bed...'

Rachel laughed and clung to him, responding to her husband's tender loving with pleasure and excitement. William had opened life out for her again and she was so grateful to him for coming into her life, showing her just how lonely and sterile it had been.

* * *

Tea with Jonathan Stockbridge and Minnie was pleasant. Minnie had prepared dainty sandwiches, cakes, home-made biscuits and some fruit tartlets that made Rachel's mouth water. She complimented Minnie on her cooking and saw her blush.

'Mildred and I were both taught, but she never liked it – I was always partial to those fruit tarts and I never forgot what Mama taught me before she died. She was a wonderful cook but fragile and Papa was never the same after he lost her.'

'Well, I shall steal the recipe from you if I may,' Rachel said and smiled. 'I have enjoyed my visit so much and I shall hope to visit often when you're Mrs Stockbridge, Minnie.'

'Thank you, dearest. Jonathan knows how much we owe you – and he has a small gift for you...'

Mr Stockbridge handed her a black leather box. Rachel opened it to reveal a lovely oval cameo brooch surrounded by gold.

'This belonged to my mother,' he told her. 'I never gave it to my first wife and both Minnie and I want you to have it.'

'That is lovely,' Rachel cried, her eyes moist. 'Thank you so much, both of you.' She took the lovely brooch from its box and pinned it to her dress. 'I love it, thank you again.'

After helping Minnie to clear her table and embracing her, Rachel and William took their leave. They travelled back to their apartment building in his car and he smiled at her as they went up to the second floor in the elevator.

'She is a lovely lady, Rachel. I'm not surprised you're fond of her – and he's not a bad old stick. He has a passion for roses, which I happen to share, as you know – got some lovely old roses in his garden. When we have time, I'll show you the garden at my home in the country.'

'I shall look forward to it,' Rachel said. 'Does your aunt or sister live there?'

'No, I made certain of that, though they often descend and treat the house as if they own it,' William said ruefully. 'I couldn't gift the house to you, Rachel, because it is entailed and if I die without issue, it will pass to a cousin. However, all I have personally will be yours if—'

Rachel stopped him with a kiss. 'Don't! I forbid you to say it,' she whispered against his mouth. 'I love you and I can't bear to lose you, so never say it to me or even think it, William. You will come back to me, you have to.'

'Then I shall,' he promised and drew her into his arms. 'I have about ten hours left, my darling, and I want to spend them all making love to my beautiful wife.'

* * *

Rachel held back her tears as William left her. She let him go with a smile, because he would need to carry that memory with him. Their precious hours had gone all too soon, but neither of them would ever forget the happiness and joy they had known in that short time. They were only just beginning their life together, to know and to appreciate each other's qualities, their likes and dislikes.

William had avowed his love so many times that she smiled just at the memory. Rachel prayed with all her heart that he would come back to her, but she also knew that even if she lost him and suffered the pain of widowhood again, it would have been worth it just for the love she'd experienced in his arms. Life could hold no greater joy for her – unless they were ever to have a child and welcome it in the world together.

Sighing, she dressed for work that morning. The coming weeks and months would be lonely and she would need her job at Harpers and all the friends she had made there until William returned.

37

Maggie looked ruefully at her red hands. It was a Saturday and Minnie was marrying Mr Stockbridge that afternoon, and she'd expressly asked Maggie to be there, because she was one of her few friends.

> *I don't have any family and only a few friends, so I am really hoping that you will be given leave for my wedding, Maggie dear. We all miss seeing you every day and we hope you can come to the wedding.*

Maggie had asked her supervisor for leave immediately, shown her the invitation and been given permission to take the weekend off, something that had surprised her a little. Mrs Pamela James was in charge of the detachment Maggie had been assigned to and she was a bit of a dragon. Most of the girls were terrified of her, because once you signed up for the service it was like being in an army for women. The uniform they all had to wear was ugly and made Maggie feel like something out of the workhouse, but it was the same for all the young girls. As at

Harpers emporium, no jewellery or make-up was allowed in the hospital, and certainly no perfume. She was addressed as Miss Gibbs by the nurses and looked down on as little more than a skivvy, which was exactly what she was for the moment. Her training at the first-aid classes was scorned and dismissed as irrelevant and, so far, all she'd been permitted to do was scrub the floors of the ward she'd been assigned to or, even worse, scour the bedpans after emptying them of their unpleasant contents.

A deep sigh left Maggie's lips as she rubbed a little cream into her sore hands. She'd always kept her skin soft and smooth so that she could safely handle the expensive scarves she showed her customers. Now she wouldn't stand a chance of being picked for such delicate work – and yet she wasn't sorry that she'd signed up to the service. A lot of the young women who had joined were constantly in tears, some wished they'd never joined and a couple had already left, dismissed for various reasons: lateness or talking in corridors when they should be working, or simply not fit enough to do the hard work required. One girl had fainted in front of Matron when being sent to discard bloody cloths and been sent home to find work more suited to her delicate health.

'You volunteered to be nursing assistants,' Mrs James had boomed at them when she harangued them after two girls had been summarily discharged. 'That means long hours, dirty, hard work and – if you're sent to the Front – danger. Only the strongest and fittest of you will survive this training course. It is hard because it needs to be. If you do not wish to continue, come to my office and I will give you a discharge or see you transferred to another branch of the service.'

'Cor blimey, she's a tough old trout, ain't she?' a young girl had whispered in Maggie's ear. 'I worked down the bloody cannin' factory and we'd spit most of this lot out fer breakfast.'

Maggie couldn't help but laugh, which she'd instantly

regretted because Mrs James glared at her. 'Did you find what I said funny, Miss Gibbs?'

'No, Mrs James, of course not,' Maggie had said at once. 'I needed to cough that's all.'

Mrs James had looked daggers at her but decided to ignore her lapse. Maggie had known it meant a black mark against her, but she'd kept her expression unmoving, innocent even, when the girl dug her in the ribs and whispered in her ear again.

'Sorry, love,' she'd said. 'I'll talk ter yer after.' The girl had caught her arm as they left that lecture and given it a squeeze. 'I reckon yer will make it,' she'd said and grinned at Maggie. 'I'm Sadie Birch and I've seen yer a couple of times, but I'm on the kids' ward – yer on the old men's ain't yer?'

'Yes,' Maggie had replied. 'Not that I've done anything yet but scrub floors and bedpans. I did fetch a glass of water for one elderly man, but Sister Hendry tore me off a strip. I'm not allowed to give patients anything unless instructed by her or a nurse...'

'That's right, love, in case it upsets 'em,' Sadie replied. 'What's yer name then?'

'Maggie Gibbs,' Maggie offered her hand and they'd shaken hands, laughing. 'She thinks she's so tough – but we had a floor walker when I started work at Harpers Emporium in Oxford Street that would have made her look like a kitten.'

Sadie had grinned and hugged her arm. 'You're one of them Harpers girls then?' She'd looked envious as Maggie nodded. 'Why did yer give a job like that up ter come to this place?'

'For the same reason as you,' Maggie had replied and a little shiver went down her spine. 'Did you see the pictures in the newspapers – all those poor men after the defeat at Mons...?' Tears had sprung to her eyes. 'Everyone thought it would be over quickly. All those young men killed... Do you think they knew what it would be like?'

'Nah,' Sadie had shaken her head. 'Poor little buggers thought it would be a lark, rushed orf ter take the King's shillin' like idiots. Nah look what's happened to them...'

Throughout the whole of September and the beginning of October, the French, Belgian and British had been in action together in a bitter struggle. Some seventy thousand men had crossed the Channel in secret, but despite the skill of the regular British Army, the enemy had proved too strong at Mons. The ordinary people of the town were caught in the conflict and suffered many casualties, as did the British troops. Fierce and terrible battles had been fought along a shifting line from Belgium to Alsace and the Lorraine where the bulk of the French forces were stationed. In September, the action had shifted to the Marne, north-east of Paris. On land, the British were suffering huge casualties, over half a million men killed or wounded, though at sea the navy was showing its muscle and three German cruisers had been sunk. However, they had retaliated and three British ships were torpedoed, with the loss of over fourteen hundred men. Submarines were a new and deadly threat in war!

The reports in the newspapers told the sorry news that it looked as if the allies were being remorselessly forced back towards the Somme, the last barrier before Paris. And from posters all over the country, Lord Kitchener pointed his finger and told men, 'Your country needs you!'.

As the weeks of her training intensified, Maggie and all the other volunteers scoured the newspapers for any scrap of information about the way the conflict was progressing and fretted because it took so long for them to become useful. Each and every one of them longed to be out there helping with the wounded as the reports of hospitals overflowing mounted daily.

Maggie put all her thoughts of war and the terrible injuries that some men must have received from her mind. Today, she could forget her training and the lectures she needed to attend, because she was going to a wedding and she would be seeing her friends again.

* * *

Maggie wore little white lace gloves with her pretty blue and white dress and the long jacket that came down to just above her knees. It matched the blue of the forget-me-nots in her dress and her straw hat was white with a contrasting and darker blue rose at the front. Her outfit wasn't new; she'd worn it several times to go out with Tim, but she hadn't had time or the money to buy herself new clothes and she knew it suited her because it was Tim's favourite.

She saw Rachel and Sally as soon as she got to the church and went to sit with them. 'Is Beth coming?' she asked as she sat next to her friends.

'No,' Sally replied. 'I offered to stand in for her, but she said she would come to the reception after Harpers closed. We've put an extra member of staff on to take Rachel's place for the afternoon and a junior in your old department, but Beth says they've been quieter the last few days, so I'm sure she will manage.'

'No one feels like buying treats at the moment,' Maggie said. 'I just wore my best dress.'

'You look lovely,' Sally said and smiled at her. 'Rachel was just telling me that Minnie wondered if she ought to call the wedding off because of what happened.'

'Why should she have her plans ruined because of what is happening over there?' Maggie asked. 'It wouldn't bring back those men that were killed and I think it will happen a lot more before it is over...'

'Yes, everyone is upset though,' Sally said, looking worried. 'Even the older men are saying they ought to volunteer now, but when they do, they get sent back with a flea in their ear. At the moment, it is just the regular army that is fighting. I doubt if any of the young men who rushed off to volunteer are ready to be sent out there yet.'

'It's the same for us,' Maggie said. 'All the volunteers do is clean and attend lectures. They don't let us near the patients and I haven't seen a wounded soldier yet.'

'Is it all right?' Sally asked, looking at her anxiously. 'I've heard it is hard work and not very well paid.'

'Nowhere near what you paid me,' Maggie said ruefully. 'But I don't have to pay for my lodgings or my food, so I can manage. I don't mind anyway. I just want to help... even more now after what happened at Mons...'

'Yes, of course. I think we all do,' Sally said. 'I've been asking various government departments what I can do, as a person and as Harpers. So far, they've let us contribute some tinned food for the soldiers. I've been asked if I will organise some fundraising events and that seems to be about all I'm good for.'

The music started just then and the bride appeared, with Becky in attendance just behind her. Minnie was wearing an ivory dress of shimmering silk that she'd made herself. It had cost a fraction of its price from a bridal store, but it looked wonderful on her. Behind her, Becky was wearing a dress of damask pink and a little crown of roses on her head, her hair swept up in a soft roll. Minnie's veil was shimmering lace worn with a faux pearl tiara and looked expensive even though it wasn't. Maggie knew it had belonged to Minnie's mother, because Becky had told her so in a recent letter.

'Oh, look at her,' Maggie whispered. 'She is so happy.'

'Yes, she is,' Rachel agreed. 'They both are.'

Everyone hushed as the service began and then the vicar was blessing the bride and her veil was back. She lifted her face for her husband to kiss her and that was when they could all see how happy and beautiful, she looked.

'She is so lovely,' Rachel whispered. 'All those years without hope and now look at her, she deserves to be happy.'

'She owes it to you,' Maggie said. 'If you hadn't made her come and live with us and got her that job at Harpers, they would never have met again. Becky says her father has never been as happy. You should be proud of what you did.'

Rachel wiped a tear from her eye. 'I was so fond of her and I just wanted her to be secure and safe,' she said. 'I didn't have any idea that she would meet the love of her life, I didn't even know she knew Mr Stockbridge. She never said a word about it even after she started working in the alterations department, and now she's married to the man she always loved. It's a perfect story...'

'I don't think she expected to find love again,' Maggie said. 'Becky said that at first she was very shy with him, very formal – but when she had tea with them and he took her to see his roses, the years seemed to fall away and they knew they still cared. They both felt so many years had been wasted that they didn't want to wait any longer.'

'Yes, which is why she decided to go ahead, even though she felt it was wrong with so many men being killed and injured.'

'I'm glad you made her see that she couldn't change anything,' Maggie said. 'It would be so sad if she'd wasted more time after all those years of remembering and loving him.'

Maggie and the others watched Minnie's triumphal march down the aisle on her husband's arm and out into the sunshine. It was still warm, even though it was now autumn, and the scent of flowers was in the air as the happy couple paused to have a photograph taken and the church bells rang out. Confetti was thrown and a lucky horseshoe presented with several other small tokens.

Although there were only a handful of guests, it was a happy group that went off to a nearby pub that had a pleasant restaurant at the rear. It overlooked a garden with lawns and rose beds and the three long tables were set tastefully with flowers, laundered linen napkins and gleaming silver plate knives and forks. The glasses were sparkling cut glass and the wine was a light fruity white that all the ladies enjoyed.

A meal of grapefruit cocktail, followed by tongue and ham with warm new potatoes, salad and dressing, was eaten and then a strawberry trifle and cream was offered to those who had room for it. Afterwards, the cake was cut, toasts drunk and the bride and groom showered with rice and rose petals as they left in a hired car for their train. They were going to Clacton-on-Sea for a few days' honeymoon and both looked slightly bewildered, as if they'd been swept up in a high wind and didn't quite know what had happened to them.

'Bewildered but happy,' Maggie whispered to Sally as they waved the happy couple off. 'Do you think they were really in love all those years?'

'Yes, I believe so,' Sally said. 'I asked Rachel if she thought Minnie just wanted a husband and a home and she said she was sure it was real love.'

'Good.' Maggie looked at her and made up her mind to share her own secret. 'I didn't tell you – but I wanted to – I've promised to marry Tim Burrows. We said we'd wait until the war was over, but he gave me a ring... Fred knows, but no one else...'

'Why aren't you wearing it?'

'I'm not allowed at the hospital, and I thought you and Rachel and Beth might think I was jumping in too fast again. I thought I wanted to marry Ralf and then he let me down...' She sighed. 'He apologised and asked me to give him another chance, but I said we'd just be friends. I wasn't sure then whether Tim saw me as more than a friend – but it all happened so quickly and I knew you would all think I didn't know my own mind again...'

'And now – do you know?' Sally asked, looking at her curiously. 'Are you sure he's the one, Maggie? You were very young the first time, but you're eighteen now.'

'Yes, I am and I do know what I want,' Maggie said. 'I realised when Tim told me he was leaving and wouldn't be seeing me for a while – and I miss him terribly. He sent me an address I can post to; it isn't where he is, of course, they send the letters we write on and I'm not sure they're always delivered. I've written twice, but I haven't had a reply yet...'

'Maybe he can't because he's too busy,' Sally said and touched her hand. 'Don't worry too much yet, Maggie love. I'm sure Tim will be in touch as soon as he can.'

'If he can...' Maggie said and bit her lip. 'Those men that were killed were in the army, Sally, but I'm sure there will be deaths in the air – and in the sea...' She blinked hard. 'A lot of women will lose their loved ones before this is over.'

'Yes, I know,' Sally said and the sadness was in her eyes. 'All of Harpers' girls – they all have someone serving. Marion Kaye has two brothers that have volunteered and her boyfriend, and her father works on the merchant ships too, but you may have read about it in the paper?' Maggie nodded. 'Her mother died from a brutal beating by her husband and Mr Kaye disappeared. Marion thinks he probably got away on his ship, because the police haven't been able to trace him.'

'That is awful! Poor Marion. It must be so upsetting for her.' Maggie could understand some of what Marion was going through, because her mother had deserted her father as he lay dying – but murder was so vile. 'Has she had the funeral yet?'

'Yes, the police let them go ahead, because they said it was an open-and-shut case – Mr Kaye is guilty and if they get him, he will hang...'

'To have all that – and her brothers in the army too – it's a lot for anyone to bear, Sally.'

'Yes. She was having a few tears at work after she read something in the paper the other day. Beth asked her what was wrong and she told her that her brothers and her friend had signed up – and Beth said she was sure the friend was more than just a neighbour, though Marion hasn't told anyone. What with that and her mother... I told Marion to take a few days off as soon as I heard. She was back to work the day after the funeral, said she'd rather be with her friends.'

'Yes, I felt the same when my mother died,' Maggie said. 'It's no good sitting at home brooding.' She hesitated, then, 'Give her my love when you see her please...'

'You should send her a card,' Sally said. 'You were friends in the department, why not keep it up, even if it's just a card every now and then...'

'I don't know her home address.'

'Send the card to me and I'll deliver it to her – if she writes back, she can give you her address herself.'

Maggie nodded and smiled. 'I should've asked before I left, but it was all a bit of a rush.' She leaned in to kiss Sally's cheek impulsively. After all, today they were just friends and not employer and employee. 'I ought to catch my train. I need to be back at work by tomorrow morning.'

Sally smiled and gave her a quick hug. 'Of course. It was lovely to see you. We all miss you, Maggie, but we know what you're doing is important. Take care of yourself.'

'And you, Sally. Is everything all right with you – and Jenny?'

Sally nodded and hesitated, then, 'Ben is getting restless. He feels he needs to look after Harpers and keep an eye on Jack's hotel – and yet he wants to join the army. He has been given six white feathers – six! Imagine how that makes him feel...'

'Oh, those stupid women,' Maggie said, shaking her head in disbelief that Ben Harper should be thought a coward. 'What do they think that achieves? It just sends men rushing off to join up whether they're suited or not – and a lot of them will die for no good reason. They should make their own minds up and not be pushed into it if they don't wish to, at least until the Government calls them...'

'The trouble is, Ben does want to fight,' Sally said and sighed. 'I know he will go, Maggie, the only question is when...'

38

'Alone at last, my dearest,' Jonathan Stockbridge said and took his wife's hand as they stood in the hotel bedroom, turning it to kiss the palm. 'I do love our friends and they've all been so kind, but I've been looking forward to this moment for a long time...'

Outside, they could hear the sound of seagulls calling and the autumn winds were driving the waves hard against the promenade, the sound of it pleasant when one was inside in the warm and safe from a biting wind. The summer seemed to have disappeared, but neither of them minded a brisk walk along the front and on the pier. Now, though, they were alone in the pleasant room they'd been given, the excitement of the wedding and the train journey behind them.

Minnie felt the blush start at the base of her neck and spread upwards. She did love him so very much and always had, but she was no longer the lovely young girl that had caught his imagination all those years ago and she knew her body had aged. She was a size 38-inch hips, instead of the svelte size 34 she'd been when eighteen, and gently rounded, though, as Rachel had told her, in all the right places.

Jonathan's gaze became intent as he noticed that she was nervous and trying to hide it. 'What is wrong, my love?' he asked softly. 'You're not sorry you married me?'

'Oh no, never!' she declared passionately. 'I've dreamed of this for years, Jonathan dearest...' She cast her eyes down. 'It's just that you fell in love with me when I was eighteen and quite pretty, and now, I'm in my forties and...' Minnie faltered and then saw the smile in his eyes.

'Don't you know that you're still beautiful to me?' he asked softly. 'I adore you, Minnie Stockbridge – and don't forget that I'm not the dashing young hero who proposed to you over the damask roses.' He reached out to touch her cheek with reverent fingers. 'I've kept a picture of that young girl in my mind ever since you sent me away, but the woman I see now is every bit as beautiful and her soul is as lovely as ever.'

Tears stung Minnie's eyes as he took her gently into his arms and kissed her in a way that set her senses tingling. 'I do love you so much – and you will always be my hero...'

'Minnie, I know you've never been touched by a man and I know you must be a little nervous, but I promise I'll never hurt you, my love. If there's anything you don't understand or can't bear...'

'No,' Minnie said and suddenly her fear had gone. 'I asked Rachel the things my mother should have told me years ago had she not died too young – and I'm not afraid. I'm yours, Jonathan. Teach me to be a good wife...'

'Minnie, my sweet angel,' Jonathan said, bending down to sweep her up in his arms and stumble towards the bed. The effort it cost him had them both laughing as they collapsed in a jumble of arms and legs together on the bed and then, somehow, nature took over and what happened next was the most natural thing in the world.

Kisses, laughter and touches so sweet that they made Minnie's heart sing and showed her what she'd been cheated of for so many years and she thrilled to her lover's touch, smiling up into the eyes of the young knight she'd fallen in love with by a bed of sweet pink roses. In that moment, Minnie fell in love all over again with the true loving man who was a little bit stouter than he should be and slightly thinning at the temple but would be forever young and handsome to her eyes...

* * *

'I can't stop thinking about those poor young men over there,' Minnie said as, well wrapped up against the cool sea air, they strolled along the sea front at Clacton on the following Monday. In Belgium, the fighting had begun in earnest and once or twice, they had thought they could hear the boom of gunfire. There was a show on at the pier theatre and Jonathan had already bought tickets for later in the week and he was taking her to a dinner dance at a hotel that evening. Yet even in the throes of pure happiness, they could neither of them dismiss the thought of what was happening at the Front. 'Do you think that rumbling sound we heard at breakfast this morning was thunder or gunfire?'

'I think it might have been guns,' Jonathan said. 'I spoke to old Major Fawcet when you went upstairs to get your jacket. He told me he thought we should hear the guns when the wind is in the right direction.'

'It is dreadful to think that our young men are being shot at...' Minnie gave a little shudder. 'Mr Burrows told me that he'd had a postcard from Stanley – the young man who worked with him in the basement – he says they're training hard.' A smile touched her mouth. 'Stanley says they don't have guns yet and one of the recruits brought his dog to the parade ground on a leash and it marched up and down with him.'

'The sergeant major will soon put a stop to that,' Jonathan said. 'I suppose for the moment they will train with any weapon they can get their hands on. I'm sure the government didn't prepare for war as soon as they ought, so there is likely to be a shortage in all kinds of things.' He looked over his shoulder. 'This is in confidence, Minnie, but I know I can trust you – Mr Harper told me that he is buying military equipment for our boys from America and his sister is already having it shipped over. It's to make up for a shortfall in our own supplies...'

Minnie nodded. 'Mrs Harper told me that her husband wants to fight, but surely he is already doing his bit?'

'He will do all he can from the supply situation,' Jonathan agreed, 'but no man likes to be called a coward. I was given a white feather myself the other day...'

'Oh, how foolish those women are,' Minnie said and looked alarmed. 'You won't feel the need to join, will you, dearest?'

'If I was ten years younger, I should already have signed up,' he told her, 'but at my age, I'd only slow them down, and then there's my flat feet. Besides, some of us have to stay here and look after the country, Minnie. I'll join the civil defence when we get back, my love, and that will have to be my contribution to the war.'

Minnie smiled at him and squeezed his arm. 'Good. I'll be joining one of the fundraising groups. Our troops are going to need lots of stuff to keep them going over there. I shall knit bala-clavas and socks and raise money to send them cigarettes and sweets...'

Jonathan nodded and looked down at her lovingly. 'Then we'll both do our bit in our own way – and for now we can enjoy ourselves. They are still doing inshore boat trips at the moment, so if you'd like, we can go on one of them this afternoon...'

'Oh yes, I do love the sea,' Minnie said. 'I thought they would have stopped the boats trips?'

'Apparently, the fishermen who run them in their spare time are useful as spies. If they spot an enemy boat, they signal the shore immediately – but, don't worry, the navy is patrolling the channel so it isn't likely the enemy will attack a pleasure boat.'

'I suppose the fishermen have to go out anyway,' Minnie said. 'We need the fish to feed the nation.'

Jonathan nodded. 'Yes, they fish early mornings and do the pleasure trips afternoons.' He smiled down at her. 'I've been to the sea with Becky most years and I like to talk to them, that's how I know.'

She nodded, her hand closing on his arm. 'Your dear Becky – such a sweet loving girl. She has been so lovely to me, Jonathan.'

'Of course, she has, Minnie. No one could help loving Becky – and no one could help loving you. I am a very lucky man.'

'We are all lucky,' Minnie said. 'Becky is happy working on the counters at Harpers, but I shall encourage her to keep on with her shorthand. I find it quite fun to decipher those squiggles and I think she will learn quicker with a willing partner.'

Jonathan's smiled deepened. 'I knew you would make all our lives better,' he said. 'It will give Becky a proper home life, Minnie. I want her to make more friends and to go out with girls of her age – but I never had the time to do the things a mother ought to do with her daughter, though I tried...'

'Becky has me now and I shall see she has all the opportunities she needs, Jonathan. We want her to be happy and one day she will fall in love and want to marry.'

'Yes, I suppose she will,' he acknowledged. 'I still see her as a little girl, but of course she isn't.'

'No,' Minnie said. 'She will be happy staying with Rachel while we're away, but when we get back, I'm going to make sure she does all the things she needs to do – and one of them is to learn to dance so that when she goes courting she will know what to do.'

39

'There is a fundraising social at the Southwark church hall this evening,' Rachel said to Becky that morning as they had breakfast before catching their bus to work. 'I've been helping to organise it and I've bought six tickets. I shall be going and I've offered one to Beth and, of course, you'll come with me – so I have three to give away.' She looked at Becky as she raised her cup, pausing for a moment. 'Is there anyone you would like to offer them to? Any friends you'd like to come with us?'

Becky shook her head. 'Maggie is working away, as you know. I don't think Marion would be able to come, because she has to get home every night to look after her sisters and her brother...'

'Yes, I did offer one to Marion, but she turned it down. If there's no one you particularly want to ask, I'll give two to the girls in the dress department – Debbie and Carol – and to Sarah in the cosmetic department. They are all about your age, Becky, and it might help you to make friends.'

Becky looked at her shyly. 'Thank you, Mrs Bailey. You're very kind to me, having me here while Minnie and Papa are away.'

'I was happy to do it,' Rachel assured her. 'I get lonely when

William is away for long periods. He comes home whenever he can and that is every other weekend at the moment – but I would be happy to help you whenever you wish. Minnie is my friend and you are a lovely girl.'

A blush swept up, turning Becky's delicate colouring a dark pink. She was a pretty girl, her hair dark brown and inclined to curl at the ends, her eyes a soft melting brown. 'Thank you.' She looked happy as she said, 'I do love Minnie so much. She is just as I imagined my mother might be. She says she is going to make me lots of pretty dresses, not just special ones like Papa had made for my birthday but dresses that I can wear every day.'

'Yes.' Rachel mentally agreed the girl's clothes were a little plain and serviceable. No doubt her father asked for advice and was given sensible clothes to purchase for his daughter, but Becky needed softer colours and prettiness in her life. 'Minnie is a wonderful seamstress and she cooks well too.'

'We have a cleaner who also cooks for us, but she doesn't cook as well as Minnie. Papa says he's going to keep her coming, because Minnie has her own work, but I think Minnie will cook us nice things.'

'It will be much better for you,' Rachel said. 'I'll take you to the social this week, but when Minnie gets back, she will take you lots of places – is there anything you need to learn or anything you would like to do that you didn't want to ask your father?'

'I'd like to learn ballroom dancing,' Becky said. 'I like to draw and Minnie is teaching me to sew and to cook – but I'd like to help out with fundraising for our men. I couldn't be a nurse, as Maggie is, because I don't like to see blood – but I do want to help.'

'Then I'll enrol you in some of my schemes. You and Minnie can come along together. We'll be making gloves, scarves, blankets, anything the men might need, and we'll be making things to sell – running tombola evenings and all kinds of things to raise money.'

Becky jumped up and rushed round to hug her. 'Thank you so much, Aunt Rachel – may I call you that when I'm not at work please? You've been so kind and I was feeling lonely now that Maggie has gone off to be a nurse...'

'Of course, you may,' Rachel said and felt delighted. 'Now, what shall you wear for the social this evening?'

'I'll wear the new dress that Minnie made me,' Becky said. 'I know it is very fancy, but everything else is a little plain, a bit schoolgirlish...'

'Yes, wear your best dress,' Rachel said. 'It is just a church social, but it is a fundraiser and there will be dancing...' She smiled as she saw Becky's face fall. 'They will be barn dances and you'll soon pick the steps up.'

'If anyone asks me,' Becky said.

'Oh, I don't think you need worry about that,' Rachel said and laughed. 'I think the men will be queuing up to dance with you.'

* * *

'Lucky you,' Marion said when Becky told her about the church social they were going to that evening. 'I would have liked to come with you, Becky, but Mrs Jackson has Milly until I get home, so I can't just go off and leave her to do it all.'

'It doesn't seem fair you can't have any fun,' Becky said, feeling sorry for her, but Marion shook her head.

'I have to be careful, because otherwise the welfare people might poke their noses in and decide to put Milly in care. Dan put the house in his name and said to tell the council he is responsible for us and paying the bills – but I don't want to risk it. Besides, I'd rather not go without Reggie. It would seem as if I didn't care that he may be in danger.'

'He hasn't been sent over there yet, has he?'

'No, I don't think many of the volunteers have yet,' Marion told her. 'I know Reggie is still in this country. He was home on a thirty-six-hour pass at the weekend. They can't tell you where they're training, because it is secret, but he says they are working hard all the time. Reggie has blisters on his hands from digging trenches. He says they feel like bloomin' navvies...'

Becky laughed. 'Has he got a gun yet?'

'He hasn't got half his kit yet,' Marion told her with a grimace. 'He got his trousers, boots and cap last week, but he's still waiting for his blouson; they hadn't got one big enough, so they're ordering it for him.'

'You'd have thought the army would have all sizes,' Becky said and shook her head.

'Reggie thinks they never expected to get so many volunteers so quickly and they can't keep up...' She smiled. 'I never thought Reggie would be one for letters, but he's written to me twice – lovely long letters, too.'

'He sounds lovely, but it's a shame about his uniform.' Becky shook her head in wonder. 'They need Mrs Harper down the war office,' she said. 'She'd soon have the forces running like clockwork.'

'Yes,' Marion nodded her agreement. 'You don't see Mrs Harper letting us run out of things.' So far, Harpers' shelves and rails were filled with stock and their trade was steady.

'Now then, you two,' Mrs Burrows came bustling up to them. 'Chatting is all very well, but we have work to do. In another five minutes, the store will be open to customers – get the hats uncovered, Miss Kaye, and Miss Stockbridge make sure you have all those scarves that came in yesterday written up...'

'I did them last night,' Becky said, 'but I'll just check, Mrs Burrows.'

The new junior was brought into the department by Mrs

Bailey then. Rachel smiled at them, but the new girl looked frightened to death. She was introduced to them as Shirley Jones, a shy girl with mousey brown hair and light grey eyes, a little plain but with a nice smile. Becky grinned at her to make her feel at ease and offered to show her how to keep the sales and stock books.

'Thank you, Miss Stockbridge,' Mrs Burrows said. 'We'll all help Miss Jones to learn for a few days, but she has passed several exams and should pick the system up quickly.' She smiled at the new girl. 'Miss Stockbridge hasn't been here long, so I'll let you all make friends.'

The day had flown and Becky was pleased they had a new girl to help make up for losing Maggie. She had picked up the system easily herself and Shirley soon showed that it wouldn't bother her either. Mrs Burrows had let them go together at break time and they had a cup of coffee and a bun across the road in Bessie's café.

'If I'd known you were starting, you could have had one of Mrs Bailey's tickets for the social this evening,' she told Shirley and the girl smiled shyly.

'That's so kind of you,' she said. 'I'd like to come another time please. My father has joined the army – or re-joined, because he was a sergeant major before he left to start his own business. My mother died last year and Papa has handed the business over to his brother for the duration. I'm his only child and he wanted me to go to college and become a secretary, but I couldn't stand being at home all day alone, so I decided to take a job and continue my training at night school...'

'That's exactly what I'm doing,' Becky replied. 'My college is in Southwark, where's yours?'

'In Spitalfields,' Shirley said. 'I suppose I could change – if they'd take me on. What year are you?'

'I'm through my typing course but getting a bit stuck with my shorthand.'

'Oh, I'm quite good at that,' Shirley told her. 'Perhaps if we work together, we could both improve...?'

'Yes, that would be good,' Becky looked at her speculatively. She liked Shirley but didn't know her well. From what she said, she lived next door to her aunt and uncle in Spitalfields and her uncle managed the wood yard he owned with her father. She'd decided she didn't want to move in with her aunt and yet was fed up with living on her own. It might be nice if Shirley came to stay with her sometimes. They could share a room and go to technical college together in the evenings...

* * *

After she'd dressed in her best gown that evening, Becky went down the hall to join Rachel in the living room. Rachel was wearing a dark blue dress that moulded to her shapely figure and suited her well. She turned and looked at Becky, smiling as she saw her.

'Oh, you do look lovely, Becky. That colour gold suits you so well – the tawny shade highlights your eyes.'

Becky blushed and looked down at her leather slippers, which were a deep gold colour to tone with the dress. 'Thank you, Aunt Rachel. Do you mind if I ask your advice?'

'No, of course not.' Rachel looked a little surprised.

'It is about Shirley Jones from work,' Becky said. 'I think we shall be good friends – and she's taking classes in typing and shorthand. We thought she might change to my college so that we could attend together, do you think Minnie would mind if I asked her to stay the night sometimes?'

'Ah...' Rachel nodded and looked relieved. 'I am sure Minnie will say that you must invite whoever you like to stay, Becky – but you should get to know her a little better first, though her school gave her excellent references.'

Becky nodded. 'I knew she must have good references because Mrs Burrows said she was a good scholar. She is living alone since her father joined up, though her uncle and aunt live next door. I think she doesn't have too many friends... a bit like me...' She sighed. 'Especially since Maggie left.'

'Yes, we all miss her. I must write to her soon.'

'So, should I make friends with Shirley – I think she is a nice girl, the sort Minnie will like...'

'Then she sounds ideal for you, dear,' Rachel agreed. 'Now, are you ready to leave? We have quite a busy evening ahead.'

* * *

Becky tumbled into bed that evening feeling a little bemused but very happy. *He'd* been there at the social and he'd asked her to dance twice and spent half an hour with her, just talking, laughing and treating her to drinks of iced lemonade and a throw of the hoops. He'd actually won a small china fairing, which he'd presented to her with a flourish that made her laugh.

Captain Morgan, the charming doctor Becky had met at the first-aid classes with Maggie. He'd insisted on taking them both home in his car that night, because Becky's purse had been stolen. She'd wondered if he might try to see her again, but he hadn't – but he'd recognised her at once when he walked in and saw her talking to one of the girls from Harpers dress department.

'Miss Stockbridge,' he'd said, bowing his head to her. 'What a delightful surprise. I hope you will forgive me for not visiting you at home before this, but I was called away. I've been very busy training nurses for the Front and I'm afraid it slipped my mind...'

'I'm not sure I should forgive you for forgetting me,' Becky had replied, giving him a flirtatious look.

'Oh, I never forgot you for a moment,' he'd said, 'but I forgot to write to your father for his permission to call...' His eyes had danced with merriment and Becky's heart did a little flip of excitement. She did like Captain Morgan so much, even though she'd tried hard not to think of him.

'Have I converted you into joining the nursing corps?' he'd asked.

'No, but I'm going to be knitting for the troops, rolling bandages and raising money,' she'd said, lifting her chin at him. 'Will that do instead?'

'In your case, I believe it will,' he'd said. He'd glanced around the room. 'Is your father here this evening, Miss Stockbridge?'

'Papa is on honeymoon with his lovely new wife,' Becky had replied. 'I am staying with Aunt Rachel while they're away, and she brought me this evening so I could have some fun...'

Captain Morgan had clicked his heels and inclined his head. 'In that case, may I have the honour of this next dance?'

'I should warn you that I've never danced...'

'Then I shall teach you,' he'd said. 'This is just a two-step, Miss Stockbridge, and I don't think either of us can go far wrong.'

In the event, she'd felt as if she was floating on air as he guided her expertly around the floor. After their dances, she'd introduced him to Rachel and he'd promised to call on Saturday afternoon to take her to tea after work.

'At four outside Harpers,' he'd promised before he left. 'I shall look forward to it – and I hope you will put in a good word for me with Mr Stockbridge, Mrs Bailey...'

Becky gave a sigh of content as she curled up in bed. Aunt Rachel liked Captain Morgan. Now that Papa was married, it looked as if Becky's life was suddenly going to be far more inter-esting. She was making new friends, Aunt Rachel and Minnie had both promised to take her out, she had a wonderful job she enjoyed and now she'd met Captain Morgan again, life couldn't be better.

Becky decided to write a letter to Maggie and tell her what had happened. She liked her new friend Shirley. They got on well together and she thought they could spend more time together in future – but she did miss Maggie so much. Her thoughts were with the girl who had befriended her when she needed it so much and she wondered how Maggie was getting on at her new place of work. It would be so different to the job she'd done at Harpers and Maggie was so brave to leave everything she loved. Becky would write and tell her so and remind her that she always had friends to come to if she needed them. She did so hope they wouldn't lose touch because of this horrid war.

Becky had so much to look forward to, but she did worry about Maggie, because she knew her friend would volunteer for overseas nursing when the time came and she just couldn't bear it if anything happened to Maggie...

40

Sally knew the moment Ben entered their office that morning. There was something in his step, a firm confidence that had been subdued of late. She'd been afraid it was coming after the news the previous day. It was now November; a German raid on the seaside resort of Yarmouth had taken place and Britain had annexed Cyprus, declaring war on the Ottoman Empire. At sea, the losses were high on both sides – which had Beth looking permanently worried – and, on land, the troops were bogged down in the trenches as the bloody conflict continued, with no hope of an end for the foreseeable future.

In September, it had seemed as if the Allies had the upper hand. Paris had been saved by fierce battles that put the Germans into reverse and had them retreating. General Joseph Joffre had been reinforced with fresh men and, together with other French troops, had managed to push the enemy back. The British had suffered massive casualties during the offensive, but it had been a huge and terrible battle and Kitchener had praised the bravery of the troops while calling for half a million new volunteers to boost depleted forces.

It was after the panic a German plane had caused in Paris by dropping bombs in the crowded Champs Élysées that Sally understood that Ben had reached his decision. If they could do that to the citizens of Paris, they could do it here in London and that meant he had no choice but to offer his services to the British forces in whatever way they wished to use him.

Looking at him now, she saw the relief in his eyes; his pride was back and she blinked hard to stop herself crying. Ben had done the right thing and she wouldn't risk his peace of mind by letting him see how distressed she was over his decision.

'Is it the Army or the Royal Flying Corps?' she asked as he poured them both a glass of wine.

'The Army,' Ben said. 'I considered the Royal Flying Corps, but I was told that I'll be starting off in logistics – and of more use to the army. I'll need training first, so I won't be over there immediately.' He smiled at her and sipped his wine. 'I may never actually see any fighting, Sally – but I shall be doing something useful.' And he would be in uniform and safe from more white feathers!

'What about Harpers and Jack's hotel?'

'I shall be away for three weeks training,' Ben said with a grin. 'They are making me an officer immediately, but, after that, I'll be in charge of an office here in London and sometimes on the south coast for the time being so I can keep an eye on things here. Besides, you and Stockbridge and the others can look after Harpers, and I'll ask Stockbridge to look in on the hotel now and then if I'm not around. Jack will be home between the Atlantic runs. It's one of the most dangerous sea lanes, but we have to pray his ship makes it back...' He looked thoughtful, his smile gone as he considered the risks Beth's husband was taking, and then nodded. 'Jack's new manager seems a decent sort – has a weak lung apparently so he can't fight, but he's fit enough to work at a desk. Jack was lucky to find him just like that, because I don't like his business partner much. In fact, I shall advise him to sell out if he gets a chance. I'd invest his money in something better for him after the war.'

'I doubt he'll get a chance,' Sally said. 'The war has made it inadvisable for anyone to start a new business...'

'I'm not sure – Jim Barclay might take it off his hands,' Ben said. 'That's the young chap that manages it for Jack now.'

'Does he have the money?' Sally was doubtful. Jack had been keen on owning a hotel but might feel differently when he returned from the war. Things changed when men had to fight for their lives every day.

Ben shook his head. 'I doubt it – but Jack might find a way of loaning it to him.' He grinned at her again as his enthusiasm returned. 'That's up to Beth and Jack, of course. They've got a few dollars between them, I imagine... and I may be busy...'

Sally nodded. Ben looked far too pleased at the idea that he would eventually be drawn into the conflict, even if only in the background. 'At least we're nearly ready to open the new premises...'

'Next week, I hope,' Ben said. 'I should be here for that, Sally. I've been told I've got a couple of weeks to sort out any business that is urgent and to complete a little transaction with someone back home who can help us out with a few bits and pieces and then I'm off for my crash course in officer training. They seem to think that as a businessman I know how to organise and lead.' He grinned at her, as happy as a sparrow. 'I told them I'm a crack shot so that just leaves bomb making and statistics.'

'Don't tell me anything more, Ben. I'm sure it's secret...'

'Yes, it is,' he agreed, still on a high. 'I don't think you're going to tell the enemy anything, Sally...' He moved towards her, taking her in his arms to kiss her softly and look into her eyes. 'You do understand why, my love? You don't think I'm deserting you and Jenny?'

Right on cue, they heard a little cry from the cot Sally had had installed in the office so that she could bring Jenny with her sometimes. As Jenny grew and slept less in the day, Sally had found herself unable to tear herself away from her baby and so brought her in several mornings a week. She bent over the cot and lifted the sweet-smelling baby in her arms.

'You know I'd never do anything to endanger you or Jenny?'

'Of course, I know...' Ben's concern almost broke her, but she fought the wave of emotion that swept her. 'You have to do what you feel is right and I'd be selfish and needy if I begged you to stay.'

'I want nothing more than to be with you and Jenny,' Ben said as he touched the tip of her nose. 'I love you so much, my darling, but I have to do my bit, to fight if need be, because I love you – which is why every man in this country is going to want to fight eventually, for their loved ones. We shall do it to keep the Germans from dropping bombs on you and sweeping in here to make you all suffer the humiliation of defeat.'

'Yes, I know,' Sally said and she did. Every woman in Britain was feeling the same way. They understood why their men needed to fight and they were going to support them any way they could. It was a time for women to stand up and be counted, to stand as sisters and friends to keep the country going through the rainy days ahead. 'You're not to worry about the store, Ben. Jenni and I will do whatever is necessary – and we're in a good position because of the standing loan she made us...'

'Yes, it might have been worse had she not done that,' Ben said. 'I've spread myself a bit thin financially. Maybe I shouldn't have taken the extra premises on at a time like this...'

'If you hadn't, we should've lost it,' Sally said. 'We'll manage, Ben. You've done all the hard work – getting the plans through and selecting the builders, electricians, keeping them at it until it was done. I know that isn't easy...'

Leaving the office together, Sally carrying Jenny in her arms, Ben led the way to his car and drove them home to the flat, where Sally put her baby into her cot and smiled. Jenny had fallen asleep on the way home and was still sleeping peacefully.

In the sitting room, they returned to the conversation they'd had in the office.

'As I was saying, you've done all the hard work at Harpers, Ben. I could never have sorted all that out as well as you did...'

'It's easier here than in America. Back home, we often have to bribe them to get them on site – but here it was straightforward once the contracts were signed with my present builder. And that was thanks to Mick. If he hadn't put me right, we might never have got started. Still, it's worse back home. You're more civilised here, fewer gangsters, I think.'

'Oh don't,' Sally said with a shiver. 'That's the last thing we need...'

'You have them, hidden in the shadows, but I was lucky. Mick put me on to a good bloke and we've had no trouble or threats to walk off and so we'll be finished in time.'

'Wonderful.' Sally put her arms about his neck, looking up at him.

'You're wonderful,' he murmured and kissed the end of her nose. 'I know I'm lucky, but I'm glad you have good friends, Sally. If anything happened...'

'No,' she said at once. 'It won't – don't say it, don't think it...'

'It has to be said,' Ben told her. 'My shares, this place, all of it is yours –and Jenni has her shares, so she'll always support you. I know you'll do whatever you have to... and it is what I would want. I don't plan on not coming back, but if it happens, you should know...'

'I want you not the rest of it,' she said, not wanting to listen.

'I know,' he murmured against her ear. 'What do you say we have an early night?'

Sally lit up as she gave herself up to him, feeling the surge of wanting and need. 'I thought you would never ask,' she murmured as he swept her up in his arms and carried her through to their bedroom. She loved her work at Harpers and all her friends, but when he was away she would miss this, miss the togetherness and the lovemaking that gave her so much pleasure.

* * *

'How do you think Jack would feel about selling the hotel to his manager if he had the chance? He could reinvest his money in something else after the war – something with Ben,' Sally asked Beth when they had coffee together in her office a week or two after Ben had gone to his training camp. They had fallen into the habit of meeting twice a week so that they could talk and exchange news without impinging on their busy lives. For Sally at least the friendship had become ever stronger, especially now that Ben wasn't there when she got home at night. The apartment seemed empty without him, even though she had their darling daughter to care for.

'I'm not sure,' Beth said. 'I'll speak to him when he comes home on leave. I think it may be soon now.'

'How do you manage without him all that time?' Sally asked sympathetically. I find it hard and Ben has only been away two weeks. He phones me most evenings and he'll be back at the end of the week – after that he will be based in London for a while, though he has to travel all over the country sometimes.'

'You should be pleased that Ben is in logistics for the moment,' Beth said. 'At least it will stop him getting white feathers. Those stupid women will leave him alone once he's in uniform.'

'Do you think they have any idea of the harm they cause?' Sally frowned. 'Fred had one the other day – at his age!'

'I know and it is ridiculous, but they think they're doing their bit to rally the men into making the sacrifice the country needs.' Beth laughed. 'Fred thought it was funny and told her he was very flattered but his country didn't need old men like him cluttering up the army.'

Sally gurgled with laughter. 'Yes, that's what he said to me,' she said. 'He showed me a postcard from Mr Marco. Apparently, he's enjoying his training and somewhere on the south coast. Fred says it must be bracing, to say the least...' It was well into October now and cold at night.

Beth nodded and shivered. 'I love the coast when it's warm, but the wind can be bitter this time of the year. It's still autumn, but it feels like winter...' A frown touched her brow. 'Have you heard anything from Maggie? It's ages since I had a letter. Marion Kaye says she had a card three weeks ago. Maggie said she was working hard but might get leave shortly – but since then no one has heard anything...'

'You don't think she has been sent overseas?'

'Normally they get leave first,' Beth said. 'I know Maggie is stronger than you'd think – but I worry about her. Rachel says she is tougher than we know, but I still remember her the day we first met, so shy and unsure...'

'Yes, she was,' Sally agreed, 'but she isn't any more, Beth. I'm sure you'll get a card or a call soon to say she's coming home on a visit.'

'Yes, I expect so,' Beth agreed. 'I know I'm no relation, but she feels like my little sister.'

'Yes, I know,' Sally said, 'but we have to let go, Beth love. Maggie chose her own path and we can only hope it leads her back here one day.'

* * *

Maggie was feeling desperately tired when she came off duty that day, walking from the hospital in the drizzling rain to the nurses' home. She'd been scrubbing floors until her hands were sore and her back ached enough to make her feel as if she could weep. So far, she'd done nothing remotely helpful to the wounded men and she felt miserable. Why on earth had she given up her lovely job at Harpers for this life?

Shaking the raindrops off once inside the gloomy hall, she sighed and looked at the letter rack above the table. Everyone's post was placed here for them and nothing was in her rack. Her heart sank and she felt lonely and abandoned. Wearily climbing the stairs to the small room she shared with Sadie, Maggie had never felt more miserable. It seemed that her friends from Harpers had forgotten her...

When she suddenly saw three letters waiting for her on the bed in her room, Maggie's eyes stung with sudden tears. She hadn't been forgotten after all!

The first she picked up and tore open was from Beth, wishing her luck and telling her how much she missed her. She devoured it hungrily and went on to the second, which was from Becky and much the same, only it was filled with Becky's news and her longing to share it all with Maggie. She ended it with a tender message from her heart:

You are my dearest friend and always will be. You're one of Harpers girls even though you've left us. I miss you so much, Maggie dearest, and I want you to come home to us safe.

Rachel is writing soon and sends her love. I think she's a bit worried about William. She hasn't had a letter from him for weeks. I do hope nothing awful has happened. No, I'm sure it hasn't; it's just the post is so poor from over there. I'm making friends with the new junior at Harpers. I like her a lot – but I love you, Maggie. I do wish you were still here...

Maggie's tears flowed now and she could hardly see to read her third letter, which was from Sally Harper.

Dearest Maggie,

I thought I would just tell you how much everyone at Harpers misses you. Your friends do, naturally, but everyone else is thinking of you too, asking if we've heard how you're getting on. Here, we've lost a lot of our young men to the war, but we're taking on more young women who are eager and willing to serve. We all have a sense of purpose and of belonging, because we know we're needed to keep the home fires burning for our men to come back to. I truly believe that Harpers' girls will see us through this terrible period.

Never forget, Maggie, dearest, you are one of Harpers' girls. You belong here and will always be one of us. We couldn't do without you and we all love you. Write to us soon and let us know your news. And come back to us safe!

Your true friend, Sally Harper.

Maggie stared at the letter and suddenly she no longer felt the sting of her hands or the pain in her back. She was smiling as she thought of the store she loved and all the people there and knew they were all pulling together to get them through this awful time. Maggie couldn't be with them, because she'd chosen to help the wounded men – and some of those men would be Harpers' men, or men just like them. She was doing her bit to keep Harpers and all her friends safe and now she felt proud. Even if she was just a skivvy for the moment, she was playing her part – just as all the girls were who were keeping Harpers going while the men fought.

Maggie smiled as Sadie entered the room and grinned at her.

'Yer got your letters then,' she said. 'I brought them up for you because letters from home are so important – especially when yer down.' She chuckled. 'It's been a rough day, ain't it?'

She glanced out of the window. 'Bugger never seems to stop raining!'

'Yes, it has been a rough day and, no, it never seems to stop raining recently,' Maggie said and then started to giggle. 'But we're tough – we can take it.'

'Yeah,' Sadie agreed. 'We East End gals can take anything.' She laughed and flung herself down on the bed. 'The dragon sister has been breathing fire down my neck all day, but I don't care – I've got you for my friend and that's why I'll be all right... If we stand together, they can't break us...'

Maggie smiled inwardly as her friend popped a mint humbug in her mouth and offered her the tin. She accepted one and sucked happily. It was true for the young women learning to be nurses that the hard times and rainy days could not break them if they stood united, and it was true for Harpers' girls, too. They would all do their bit and see it through to the end of the war, however long and however hard...

MORE FROM ROSIE CLARKE

We hope you enjoyed reading *Rainy Days for the Harpers' Girls*. If you did, please leave a review.

If you'd like to gift a copy, this book is also available as an ebook, digital audio download and audiobook CD.

Sign up to Rosie Clarke's mailing list for news, competitions and updates on future books.

http://bit.ly/RosieClarkeNewsletter

If you haven't already, explore the rest of the *Welcome to Harpers Emporium* series now!

ABOUT THE AUTHOR

Rosie Clarke is a #1 bestselling saga writer whose most recent books include *The Mulberry Lane* series. She has written over 100 novels under different pseudonyms and is a RNA Award winner. She lives in Cambridgeshire.

Visit Rosie Clarke's website: http://www.rosieclarke.co.uk

Follow Rosie on social media:

 twitter.com/AnneHerries

 bookbub.com/authors/rosie-clarke

 facebook.com/Rosie-clarke-119457351778432

Lightning Source UK Ltd.
Milton Keynes UK
UKHW021849150522
403019UK00005B/683